MW00471230

THINGS I OVERSHARED

KELSEY HUMPHREYS

© 2022 Kelsey Humphreys
Things I Overshared
First edition, December 2022

Magnamour Press
magnamour.com
kelseyhumphreys.com

Editing: Shayla Raquel, shaylaraquel.com
Cover Illustration: Shana Yasmin

Things I Overshared is under copyright protection. No part of this book may be used or reproduced in any manner whatsoever without written permission except in the case of brief quotations embodied in critical articles and reviews. Printed in the United States of America. All rights reserved.

This is a work of fiction. Names, characters, businesses, places, events, locales, and incidents are either the products of the author's imagination or used in a fictitious manner. Any resemblance to actual persons, living or dead, or actual events is purely coincidental.

ISBN: 978-1-959428-02-2

To everyone who's ever been told they're too much.

And to my favorite extrovert, my mom Lynette, who is, a lot of the time, entirely too much.

AUTHOR'S NOTE

Introvert: one whose internal battery is recharged by being alone

Extrovert: one whose internal battery is recharged by being around others

These two groups are not monoliths, and most people fall somewhere on a sliding scale between the two extremes. There are introverts with no social anxiety whatsoever, and extroverts who are quiet and do not overuse exclamation points. Still, tragedy and comedy are found in the extremes.

Enjoy!

CHAPTER 1

Uh-oh.

Let me think, let me think, let me think.

Why would Skye be calling me?

She never, never, never calls.

My introverted older sister could be bleeding out in a dirty ditch surrounded by axe murderers in clown masks, and she'd still text instead of call, and probably only "911" and her location.

Still, fun to get an unexpected call . . . unless it's Dad? Or one of Susan's kids? *Dear Lord, who's died?!*

"Skye? What's wrong?" I gasp at my desk, almost spilling my coffee as I answer.

"Hey, Sam, are you sitting down?"

"Crap, yes! No, I was. Now I'm not. Is it Dad? Grandpa? Oh, it's Grandpa, isn't it?"

I hear my sister through the speaker, cackling like I imagine a gleeful female Voldemort would laugh. I sigh and feel my cardiac rhythm begin to slow from arrest levels, but just barely. "Skye? This is not funny! I just lost a decade of my life! An entire decade!"

"Oh, the drama. Man, I am so glad I happened to hear about this first so I could be the one to tell you."

"Tell me what, you horrible wench of a sister? What?!" I yell way too loudly and then clench my fists, mad at myself for getting

away from, well, myself, so quickly. And in my office with my door open. Just adding to the jokes and nicknames I already inspire. *Fantastic.*

"Okay, okay, I'm sorry." She chuckles. "So, you know you've been getting Darrin ready for the big Europe trip in two weeks?"

"Obviously, yes, it's my whole life right now."

"Well, turns out Nina is super knocked up and didn't know it, already in the second trimester," she says slowly.

"Aw! A little baby Darrin! So cuuuuuute!" I chime in, unable to help myself. My boss is such a fun, lovable guy, and his wife even more so. He's about 5'5", and she's even shorter, both so sweet . . . the thought of them in miniature squishy baby form? Ovary explosion!

"Yes. Adorable. Anyway. Focus. He's not comfortable leaving her for over a month, so that means his second-in-command needs to go in his place."

Oh no, all my weeks of meticulous planning! Are they canceling the . . . wait, she said . . .

"His . . . second . . . ?"

Brain.

Malfunction.

He's the VP of sales.

I am his senior director of sales, his right-hand man, er, woman.

Me. I am his second.

"That's me!" I inhale the words.

"Aaaaand there it is! Yes, you. You're going to London, Sam!" Skye exclaims happily, very unlike herself.

"WHAT!" It's all finally hitting me, and I've yelled again with my door open. *Dang it! But also! I'm. Going. To. London. And. Paris!* "Yep, you get to go on the big 'shake hands, kiss babies tour' of Europe, the London convention, Paris, the gala!"

"*Ohmygoshohmygoshohmygosh!*" I can't believe it.

"Listen, I know it's been a hard year, and I know you hate that I'm moving out soon, and I've been staying at Matthew's—you've been alone a lot—so I'm so happy for you. We all are, we're all so glad you get to do this, Bob." The nickname makes me smile. "You deserve it. You've earned it."

"I can't. I don't. I mean!" My mind is reeling.

I have planned all the minutia of this trip so Darrin could meet with our biggest overseas contacts. I found the absolute best wining, dining, touring, and schmoozing opportunities. I was so wrecked with FOMO looking at the gorgeous scenes and settings, I almost started canceling cool events and excursions because planning was making me sad. Doesn't help that Europe is so freaking romantic and well, the romance in my life . . . *anyway!* Now, instead of Darrin and Emerson, it'll be me and Emerson.

Wait.

Wait, wait, wait.

No. Nooooooo.

"Wait, Skye. Darrin was going on the trip with *Emerson Clark.*" I can hear her wince. "Yeaaahhhh."

I get up and close my door as I whisper-yell "Iceman Emerson. Mr. Freeze. Chief Frigid Officer! Frosty McClark!"

"Ha, I hadn't heard that one," she cuts in.

"He hates me, Skye."

"No one hates you. That'd be like hating sunshine," she says, but I'm too terrorized to appreciate a genuine compliment from the queen of snark.

"People do! People do hate sunshine—you know where they live? They live in London! Which, you'll remember, is where E-Robot is from!"

"E-Robot, nice, did you just make that one up?"

"Skye! Listen! The man cannot stand me. I can't go. It'll be torture."

"It'll be fiiiine." She's half laughing.

"No, you don't understand. He avoids me, says nothing in meetings other than the absolute least number of words he can, or he's asking me to be quiet without asking." I do my best Emerson impression: "'Yes, we quite understand, Miss Canton.'"

"Terrible impression."

"Ugh! The point is, this is going to be awful! My dream trip, and I have to take it with a snowy cyborg who cannot stand me."

"Sam, I'm sure he just can't stand anyone. And if you guys never talk, then he doesn't really know you enough to hate you."

I think about this. He does seem to hate everyone, but he also seems to hate me, especially.

And I get it—I'm a lot.

I've been told I'm too much my whole life. Too talkative, too happy, too loud, too optimistic—I've heard it all. I wear bright colors and greet strangers and pet every dog. I get excited about, well, almost anything.

I am not forcing it or faking, even though mean girls have insisted so, in whispers behind my back, since grade school. Big reactions are just my natural reactions. I love loving things. I love feeling big feels. And I've worked to get to the point where most days I love me, as I am.

I also realize that that makes me grating to some people. People who are shy or serious. Emerson Clark is exactly that: shy and serious. At least I think he's shy—either that, or he really is the world's biggest jerkoff. He's the CFO, a numbers genius, and known in Manhattan, not just our industry, for being ahead of his time, ruthlessly logical, totally unfeeling, and exact.

So where I am too much, Emerson Clark is . . . he's a freaking void, that's what he is. If I'm sunshine, he's not a cloud.

He's a black hole.

Plus, while he's the CFO of the billion-dollar Canton Cards, I'm an actual Canton. One of the boss's daughters. It's a weird dynamic. Maybe he resents me? Even though he really does run this office, outranks me in every way, and is about ten years older? Could be.

But!

Skye is right in that he doesn't know me, and I don't know him, not really. We have never once hung out or chatted at a happy hour or at one of the million business events we've attended over the years. So maybe I just need to get to know him? Maybe he isn't a cold, sucking, swirl of nothingness?

"Bobbinator? You've been quiet for like twenty whole seconds. Are you dead?"

"You're right. He doesn't know me."

"Yeah, so just stick to work, have your meetings, and then run off to explore the sights separately."

"You mean explore Europe *alone*?!"

"Oh, Sam, you're never alone. On day two, you'll be best friends with the concierge and the bartender and whoever else you lay eyes on."

"Hmm," I say, my Emerson Clark wheels still turning.

"And hey, since you've sworn off men after . . . everything, you'll have a built-in non-date. A cold, wet buffer blanket between you and all of Europe's eligible bachelors! It's perfect!" she teases. "I'm walking into the studio now. I'll talk to you later, okay?"

"Okay."

We hang up, and I continue staring out my window, contemplating her words. I shake off a shiver that crept up when she mentioned "everything." The fact is, Emerson and I just don't know each other. Maybe he's the introvert of all introverts, even more so than Skye, clenched shut, in need of someone patient enough to see him unfurl and show himself. In need of someone who will go the extra mile to become his friend.

If I can encourage him to get to know me, if I can win him over, we can be friends. Not a bestie like Nicole, not laugh-a-minute coworkers like Darrin and me, not confidants or anything crazy. Friends. And then we can get through this trip, maybe even enjoy it.

I create a new note on my iPhone.

Operation Thaw
Days Until Trip: 15
Temp: -1,000°

FRIDAY 4:52 P.M.

Sally: Congrats on the trip, Sam!

Susan: Yes, you deserve it!

Me: Thanks, boss.

Skye: You guys should've heard her freak out when I called. *priceless*

You are *THE WORST* Skye.

Sadie: So happy for you!

Skye: Just sorry you have to go with the Clarksicle.

Susan: LOL He's not that bad.

I have a plan for that.

Sadie: Oh, do tell.

Sally: Who?

Skye: Emerson, our lifeless CFO.

Sally: Oh yeah! [Snowman emoji]

I'm going to become his friend!

Skye: Yikes. Good luck with that.

Susan: Oh, give the guy a break, he's not good with people.

Me: Or eye contact. Or the English language.

Susan: He talks fine in meetings.

Maybe on Zoom with you and Dad, CFO to COO to CEO.

Normal human beings?

Day-to-day here at the office?

Not so much.

Sadie: He's a Sooner, he can't be a total loss.

Sally: I thought he was British?

He is. He went to OU with Adam though.

Skye: Suze, how is your husband friends with him?!

Good point, Skye.

I should ask our dear brother-in-law for some tips!

Cuz Emerson Clark is NOT ruining my Europe trip!

Sadie: At least he's easy on the eyes.

Sadie: More than easy [Fire emoji]

Sally: Isn't he like 50 years old?!

Susan: SUNNY! HE'S MY AGE! YOU'RE GROUNDED.

Sally: I'm in college now, sis, you can't do that anymore.

Skye: 36ish, I'm guessing? And totally gorgeous.

Doesn't matter.

His looks are hidden behind his frigid personality.

So! Starting Monday, I have two weeks for Operation Thaw!

Susan: Operation what now?

Two weeks to make Frosty become my friend!

Sadie: OMG "Operation Thaw"?! Stealing that!

Skye: Seriously, Sadie, we write your novels for you, I want a check.

Sally: Same $

Same! $$$$$$

Susan: Go easy on him, he tries.

I will not, and he does not.
Skye: Oh boy. Susan, you better add this to your prayer list.
You think she needs to pray for me?
Skye: No, she needs to pray for Emerson!
Susan: [Prayer emoji]
Sally: LOL 100% Poor guy won't know what hit him.
Sadie: [Prayer emoji] [Prayer emoji] [Prayer emoji]
I hate all of you.

"This is *so* amazing!" Nicole gushes before taking a sip of her margarita and leaning back in her high stool. We're at our favorite cocktail spot near the office, and it's packed. The lights are low, the space is small, everyone is young and flirty, and we fit right in.

"Right? The only thing standing between me and the most fun month of my life is *Mr. Clark.*" I spit his name.

"But you said you had a plan?"

"Yes. Become his friend"—Nicole makes a concerned face at me—"with help from my *best* friend." I smile wildly.

"I'm not his assistant, Sam, I just help Margaret sometimes. If you want insider info, you'll have to cozy up to her."

"One does not 'cozy up' to Marge In Charge. She's almost as frosty as her boss."

Nicole chuckles. "They are quite the pair."

"The first step is obvious." Nicole asks me what I mean with her eyebrows. "Socials. Let's see what we're working with."

I pull up my phone, and a pang of anxiety—or maybe grief, and maybe shame?—*pangs of many feelings* strike me. I open Instagram first and type in his name.

"Not on Instagram, it looks like." I show her the search results.

"Well, not a huge shocker." She cocks her head to one side.

"Right." I pull up Facebook. "Private profile. Not going to request him now after four years. So. That leaves us with the one he's sure to be on: LinkedIn." I make sure I'm signed out and search for his name. "Yep, there he— What? Dang! Icy has accepted over *five hundred* connections!"

"I'm not too surprised."

"I-I'm in legitimate shock." I move on to actually read his profile. "Still, not much to work with. After OU, he went home to England for his master's degree, worked there for a few years, then came to New York and started with us. Wow, almost ten years ago."

"I can work with his headshot, that's for sure," she mumbles out of the side of her mouth. I laugh too loudly, not expecting her comment.

"Same." I sigh. "Looks like he's peering through the camera into my soul. And no smile—why is it so hot that he's not smiling?"

"I don't know, but it is." She sucks on her cocktail straw without looking away from the screen.

"Too bad his personality is that of a frozen porta potty."

She smacks my arm. "Ouch! If you keep that up, I'm going to start calling you Skye. He's just quiet and professional, probably shy and misunderstood."

"Okay, okay, I'll try to ease up." I zoom in on his headshot and talk to my phone screen. "Prepare to be understood, Mr. CFO."

A waiter appears at our table with two margaritas as I'm putting down my phone. She looks at me with a wink. "This is from the gentleman at the bar, and another for your friend." I trace the gesture over her shoulder to a hot guy across the bar area smiling our way. He gives a nod, and I give a small wave. He's sitting but looks to be a bit on the shorter side, and as if maybe he logs extra hours lifting weights to compensate. He'd probably be a lot of fun, if I were up for fun right now.

"Nice, what'd you do this time?" Nicole whispers to me, her gorgeous dark curls falling in front of her face a bit as she eyes our patron.

"What? Nothing!"

"You didn't eye him walking by or something, Flirts'R'us?"

"When? I've been sitting here with you!"

She sighs. "I bet your crazy donkey laugh alerted him to your gorgeous presence."

"Excuse me, my laugh is delightful."

"Uh-huh. I'm sure that's what he's thinking about and not the girls you've got propped up on the table."

I laugh too loudly again, then cover my mouth.

I do have my chest smashed up against the table, but I can't help my laugh or my curves. I'm grateful that curvy is a desirable adjective these days, but I still get flashes of self-consciousness. I was on the far side of "thick" as a child, and even now with a trim waist, my body is the type that will retain pounds if I so much as look at a donut. Shoot, if I even *walk by* a donut shop. I'm not one who can just ignore calories or neglect exercise. "You going to go talk to him?" Nicole breaks through my thoughts.

"Wha— No. You know I—"

"Right, right, sorry." She sighs again. "All your mojo gone to waste." Something crosses over my face. "Sorry, Sam. Not waste. I bet it gets stored up—all your magnetism—and when you're ready to date again, watch out, New York!"

I laugh it off. "You know it!"

———

When I get home to Gus, who barely greets me because he is 1,000 percent my introvert sister's cat, I pull out my phone again. I text Susan that I'm logging into her Facebook and laugh that she's sur-

prised we all know her password of the last sixteen years, Sooner-
Suze1234. *Real secure, Ms. COO.*

She's friends with Emerson because of my brother-in-law, so
I pull up his profile. I'm not surprised his Facebook is lacking in
juicy details as well. The only nugget of interest for me to chew
on is a few profile photos with a stunning redhead thirteen years
back. Gosh, Facebook is so old and lame. But hey, how else would
I stalk my friend-to-be? The woman, Chelsea Wittington, is with
him a few times, for about two years, then he updated his profile
to a solo pic . . . right around the time he came back to the States.

Wait.

Did Emerson Clark cross the pond over a breakup?! Is that
why he's so cold? Do we have a classic *hurt people hurt people*
situation going on here? I text Nicole.

> **Me: How have we not discussed Mr. Clark's love life?!**
> **Does he have a girlfriend?**
> Nicole: You can't be serious.
> **NO!**
> **Not like that!**
> **I found an ex of his on FB.**
> Oh okay. Yes, I think he might. She's never come to the office,
> but when he actually goes to events and takes a date, he al-
> ways has the same plus-one. Miranda-something.
> **Roger.**

I find a Miranda Pinell in Emerson's friends list. She has a
public profile, and no wonder. Legs for days, thin arms, flat abs.
She's also English. So basically, Hailey Bieber with a sexy accent
and white-blond hair. *Damn. Well done, Emerson!* I copy her profile
over to Nicole.

Me: This her?

[Facebook link]

Nicole: Yep

She's got to be a model.

Yep

Well, with a supermodel girlfriend, I imagine Emerson has recovered from his broken heart. Which means I'm back to the question of the day: Is this man cold and rude or quiet and shy? Can one be both? On Monday, I plan to find out.

CHAPTER 2

MONDAY 6:55 A.M.

Sadie: I'm dying to know if you're ready for Operation Thaw.

Susan: Poor Emerson

Me: He goes by Mr. Clark at the office.

Susan: Does he really?!

Really.

Anyway, I am locked and loaded.

Look what I found over the weekend:

[Link: How to Befriend Introverts]

[Link: How to Become Friends with Your Boss]

Susan: He's not technically your boss.

He's the boss of the NYC office, I assure you!

Skye: OMG LOLOLOL

Sally: You guys woke me up [Angry emoji]

Skye: Sam, I'm reading that first article, you're doomed. You literally do ALL of those things it says not to do. I'm dying. DEAD.

[Middle finger emoji]

I have my mantras

I am wearing neutrals and quiet shoes

Skye: Neutrals! The horror!

I have Sooner Football stats

> **I have quarterly sales numbers**
> Sadie: If you want him to be your friend, maybe also be yourself?
> Skye: Yourself . . . but like watered down. "Samantha Lite" LOL
> Sally: Skye, this is on Sam's behalf: [Middle finger emoji]
> Susan: I repeat: Poor Emerson
> **I have Nicole, my secret weapon.**
> **And on top of aaaallll that, I have baked goods!**
> **I'm unstoppable!**

"Stop!" Marge commands, almost yells, as I head toward Emerson's office after giving her an easy-breezy "Good morning" rather than my usual chat about her weekend. I'm on a time crunch to make a friend here, and that friend isn't her. It's so early I'm pretty sure she, myself, and The Cold One are the only people in the office. Nicole isn't even perched at the front desk yet.

"Oh, I just wanted to chat with Emerson really quick."

"Sorry, Miss Canton, but you'll have to make an appointment."

"Oh, is he on a call already?" I smile and give the lashes a flutter, seriously doubting he's doing anything important before 8:00 A.M. Marge shoots me a look. She's what Dad would call *an' ole battle-ax*. She's in her early sixties, and warm in a northern way, which is unlike the motherly warmth of an auntie from the South. That's to say, she can be friendly, but when it comes to her job, she's as firm as the skyscraper she sits in. And while she looks more like a poodle with her slim figure and coiffed hair, she is all pit bull when it comes to protecting Emerson's privacy, preferences, and schedule.

"Mr. Clark is unavailable right now. Looks like he is free at ten forty-five?"

I fail at suppressing a scoff. "He doesn't have a five-minute break in the next two hours and forty-five minutes?"

She is unmoved.

"I'm afraid not." She shoots my sweet smile right back at me.

Score one for Marge.

"All right." I sigh. "Well, I brought an assortment of beignets, chocolate croissants, and crepes to get him excited for all the amazing French food in two weeks. Maybe you can slip them to him before they get cold." I set the box on her desk.

"Oh, Mr. Clark doesn't eat sweet breakfasts."

I blink for a couple seconds. "Um, what?"

"He rarely eats sugar at all, but I'm sure he'll appreciate the thought."

Doesn't eat sugar? Freaking robot!

I breathe through my shock, frustration, and cutting disappointment. Cutting, not because of the severity but the timing. My plan has been in motion for maybe five minutes, and it's already veering off its tracks.

"Well, bummer! I guess you and Nicole and anyone else can enjoy them, and I'll see him at ten forty-five! Thanks Mar— Ms. Wayne!" Whew, glad I didn't slip and call her Marge out loud. The pit bull does not like nicknames, or even first names, just like her icy master.

Do I give Emerson's large corner office a blazing side-eye as I turn from Marge's desk? Yes, yes, I do. But I can't see details, only the fuzzy outline of his large silhouette at his desk.

And *poof*, I'm even more annoyed.

Just knowing he's in there silent, at his, I assume, perfect and uncluttered desk with his perfect hair in his perfect three-piece suit. *Grrrrrr.* My sisters weren't wrong about the ease at which my eyes—anyone *with* eyes—have taken in my quasi-boss. He's unfairly gorgeous. So much so, I get nervous speaking around him in meetings . . . me, get nervous talking? Ugh. If he's going to act like an ogre, why couldn't he look like one too?

I slump a bit as I take the few steps past Darrin's office to my own small space. The other offices and conference spaces remain dark, as I suspected. These offices aren't grand, especially by Manhattan standards, but man, I love them.

Our sprawling Canton headquarters in Tulsa is impressive, with multiple buildings, green spaces—complete with bikes and scooters, like a flyover-state, family-owned version of Google HQ—plus studio spaces for marketing and our warehouses containing hundreds of thousands of units of cards and gifts. It's awesome. But it's not New York City.

I sip my coffee in defeat, looking out my window onto building after building after building, all teeming with energy and excitement. A thrill fills me, as usual, thinking of all the people surrounding me beyond the glass and concrete. So many conversations, plans, hopes, dreams, impromptu meet-cutes, coincidental accidents. I wonder if right now someone is walking right by their soulmate or bumping into their future husband at a coffee shop. *Ugh, there you go again, Nimrod! Get a grip!*

I open a message to Nicole.

Me: Why didn't you tell me Frozone doesn't eat sweets? I showed up early with beignets and chocolate croissants. FAIL!
Nicole: Oh crap! Margaret is a stickler about having plain bagel and toast options on hand. I should've thought of that. Sorry! I will step up my insider game!

I groan a bit thinking about how hard this whole idea might turn out to be. *Doesn't. Eat. Sugar.* I mean, I track my diet like a tween watches TikTok—never two big carbs or desserts in one day—but nothing? Hello, um, brownies? Cheesecake? Effing chocolate croissants?! Ugh.

I've been racking my brain to think of the last time he said words to me, actual sounds from his mouth to mine. A few weeks back, at the end of a meeting with myself and Darrin, he'd said "Miss Canton" as a goodbye, with a slight nod. I've had nods in elevators and earned sighs or dismissive grunts on conference calls. And that's it.

I give my own dismissive grunt a spin as I stare out. It helps. Normally, I would head out to meetings with distributors, but today, as with most days the last few weeks, I focus on the upcoming trip. The purpose of the trip is to foster relationships with our retailers, manufacturers, buyers, and consultants in Europe, primarily London and Paris. And by foster relationships, I mean we're setting out on a month-long schmoozapalooza.

I don't actually like the term *schmooze*, though, because it implies the interest and affection is disingenuous. I am genuine with everyone. Do I like everyone? No. (See His Freezing Highness two doors down.) But I'm interested. I like people in general. And people like to be liked.

If we want to maintain our current sales with Whosits & Whatsits Gift Shops, the Gage brothers need to like our products, sure, but they need to like *us.* Same with the buyer for Sainsbury's locations all over the UK. So, in addition to detailing our dinners and cocktail hours, I've also made a master binder containing the people we'll be meeting with, their families, hobbies, likes, dislikes, and of course, their sales records, and which of our product lines they prefer. I sit down at my desk and dig back into said binder.

Time flies until an alert pops up on my computer, thanks to Marge's devotion to digital scheduling down to the millisecond. I ready myself. If there's one thing I'm a natural at, it's making friends. In the few steps from my door to his, I remind myself: *Grin and hold it in, Samantha: Easy-breezy conversation, to the point, without all the unnecessary details and detours and exclamations. I got this.* I steal a glance at Marge at 10:45 on the dot, and she nods.

I knock twice as I push on the door, and at the same time, a deep voice answers, "Come in."

Crapitty crap crap crap on a cracker.

He is just so intimidating. Like a mash-up of beefy Henry Cavill and beautiful Jude Law, he sits there in a charcoal-gray suit and vest with a light-blue tie almost as vivid as his eyes. I was right about his desk—immaculate—and his hair, with every wavy light-brown strand perfectly combed to the side. He looks like one of my very first imaginary boyfriends, my hand-me-down Ken doll that was Susan's in the '90s.

"GOOD MORNING!" I basically shout, causing him to startle in his chair. *Damn it!*

He inhales. "Miss Canton," he responds in a quiet, pinched way. Even grumpy, his accent is so sexy, it's cruel. He briefly glances at me . . . me wearing a white shirt tucked into a beige pencil skirt with nude heels, all of which is just begging for a bright orange scarf or magenta earrings or some sign of life, which I denied myself in order to be more palatable to the beautiful beast sitting before me.

It's just a moment before he snaps his gaze up to my eyes, but in that moment, a flash of something crosses his face—distaste, maybe? Disapproval? Annoyance? He doesn't say good morning or ask why I'm standing there. The awkward pause twists my nerves into a bundle and shoves them straight out of my mouth.

"So, I don't know if Margaret told you, but I brought some beignets and chocolate croissants and other French breakfast foods to get you inspired for our Paris trip, because you know I'm going with you now instead of Darrin, right? Oh, wait, did you

know that? Of course you did. Anyway, I'm sorry I didn't bring
like toast or crumpets or whatever Brits eat. Um . . . sidebar, what
exactly is a crumpet?! Ha! But then that wouldn't be very fun for
you, anyway, would it? I will look and see if there are sugar-free
French breakfast options, especially before we leave, which is in
just two weeks! Isn't it so exciting?"*I'm* super excited, anyway,
since I planned the whole thing. It's basically my dream trip, you
know? So I'm so excited we get to go together. I mean, *not* together,
obviously, but that I get to go with you. Or that I get to go. Period,
end of sentence. Full stop! As you say! Ha! Because I won't be with
you all the time, obviously, you will want your space and to, like,
get your introvert on! Right?! And some time to go see your family
in London, obviously, of course.

"So, anyway, how 'bout them Sooners, am I right? Dad says it's
gonna be one heck of a season!"

What.

The hell.

Just happened.

That's what I'm asking my mouth.

That's what Emerson Clark is clearly asking himself.

He's staring at me, blinking, like his brain could only keep up
with maybe a third of what I just projectiled out so fast, as if speed
talking is an Olympic sport and I'm going for gold. I also felt myself
get louder and louder as Iceman leaned farther and farther back
in his chair, begging it to swallow him whole and deposit him out
onto the pavement below by way of a magical escape chute.

I did not grin and hold it in. Nope, I sure did not.

Now I just stand, unsure that I can open my mouth again without further exploding syllables all over the room.

"Yes, they do look promising this season." He finally leans the
tiniest bit forward from the Emerson indentation in the leather
chair. "And thank you, for the pastries. Is there something specific

you wanted to discuss?"

"Um, well, no, I—"

"All right, then I really should—"

"No, wait! Yes! I wanted to ask you if you had any specific requests for the trip. I had really planned the whole thing with Darrin, and he was the one giving me feedback, but I'm thinking you might—"

"I'm sure whatever you have planned will be perfectly suitable, Miss Canton." He stands, cutting me off, looking irritated. Actually, he looks beyond irritated. He looks pained, constipated even, as if talking to me upsets his bowels. *I upset no one's bowels, asshole! I'm a flippin' ray of dadgum light!*

"Of course, Mr. Clark." I force a smile, concentrating on keeping a light tone. I am frozen in a cloud of confusion and rage. This freaking man. He's standing there blinking without even a hint of a reciprocal polite grin.

"Then I really must get to my next appointment." He gives a small nod and walks around me, giving me the berth of a rabid leper, and leaves his office.

He—

He just left his own office to flee from me.

I turn and stare at the closed door, my bottom lip hanging down to brush the carpet fibers.

Operation Thaw
Days Until Trip: 12
Temp: -10,000,000,000°

CHAPTER 3

MONDAY 6:43 P.M.

From: Samantha@CantonIntl.com

To: MWayne@CantonIntl.com

Tomorrow

Thanks for scheduling that meeting with Emerson today!
Could you please get me another fifteen-minute appointment at his earliest convenience?

Have a great day,

Samantha Canton

Senior Director of East Sales

Canton Cards International

Re: Tomorrow

Miss Canton,

Of course, that will be Wednesday. And what is this meeting regarding?

Best,

Margaret Waynes
Executive Assistant to Emerson Clark, CFO
Canton Cards International

Re: Re: Tomorrow
Europe sales figures and targets.

Thanks, you're the best!!!!!
Samantha Canton
Senior Director of East Sales
Canton Cards International

I wince at myself after I've already hit send. Apparently, my anxious determination flew through my fingers and landed in Marge's email box as exclamation marks. Five there at the end, and just when I thought I was getting better at that. *Lovely.*

> MONDAY 6:43 P.M.
> Skye: So? Sam? How was Operation Thaw Day One? Is he your bestie yet?
> Sadie: Yes, do tell.
> Sally: Also, please send a selfie of your subdued outfit.
> **Me: [Selfie]**
> Sadie: Gorg as always!
> Skye: OMG YOU'RE SUSAN!
> Sally: lol that's what I was going to say.
> Susan: No surprise then that I think you look fantastic!

MONDAY 7:20 P.M.

Skye: ???? You didn't answer how it went.

Me: Bad.

MONDAY 7:52 P.M.

Sally: OMG you just texted us one text at a time, and it was only one word.

Sadie: Skye, maybe you should swing by and check on her.

Susan: I am genuinely concerned. What happened??

Skye: Spill it!

Me: Ugh fine.

He doesn't eat sugar.

And I went full SamStorm on him.

So bad that he LEFT HIS OWN OFFICE to get away from me.

Sally: hahahahaha!

Sadie: Yikes!

Susan: [Nervous emoji]

Skye: [Animated GIF of woman falling down]

I would be mad at you, Skye, but that GIF is painfully accurate.

Still, I have 12 more days.

And I'm not about to give up.

I'm a Canton for shit's sake!

Skye: Ya you are.

Susan: Language.

Sally: [100% emoji]

Sadie: [Flex emoji]

Susan: [Prayer emoji]

WEDNESDAY 7:55 A.M.

Me: I have another meeting with him today. Haaalp!

C'mon, you do so much planning with Marge In Charge.

Nicole: Is that why you're dressed like her today?

Can you think of a list of things he loves/hates?

Topics to avoid?

I already told you there's not much. He hates being late, if meetings run late or start late, etc.

He hates video conferencing, ice in his drink, the subway.

The man is a vault.

Does he actually LIKE anything?

He seems to like rain. And snow.

OF COURSE HE LIKES RAIN AND SNOW.

I hate my life.

Babe, maybe you should skip this trip.

What?! It's Europe!

Yes, but it's Europe *for work*

Plan this trip, but for fun instead.

And go without the Snow King.

And admit defeat?

Never!

I'm going on this trip.

And I'm going with my soon-to-be friend.

I ready myself for round two when Margaret's calendar no-tification pops up on my screen. I can do this. *Slow it and stow it, Sam. I will speak calmly and at a normal person's volume, and I will shove down all the extraneous commentary.* I take a deep breath as I connect eyes with a nodding Marge and push into his office.

"Hey!" I say on my exhale. I try my best not to greet him by name because calling him Mr. Clark adds a brick to the wall of formality I'm trying to bust down. Friends call each other by their first names.

"Miss Canton." Again, he briefly looks me over, and then his eyes dart away. He has the same disgusted expression for half a moment, but I force myself not to reveal that I notice or care.

Just because he doesn't like my physical appearance doesn't mean we can't be friends. In fact, that probably helps, since straight men and women sometimes struggle in platonic friendships. He continues: "It says we're to discuss Europe sales figures and targets?"

I step to his desk, blank and sleek, like his entire office, save the few family photos along the windowsill behind him. I move to hand him the printouts.

"Right, I brought—"

"If there are to be changes, they really should be discussed with Darrin, not me," he cuts me off.

"Oh, well, I just thought—"

"Whatever he has approved, I approve." He shifts in his seat after he cuts me off yet again. He is clearly about to dismiss me. I take a deep breath, inhaling my bitter defeat. I turn to exit but whip back around quickly, nerves taking over. My brain shoots an arrow to my mouth, the memory of an article I read that said Brits love to discuss the weather.

"Brutally hot today, isn't it? Gosh, I just wish it would rain, don't you? Like just pour good ole cats and dogs down on us so you could get out your ole brolly and take a stroll?" I can feel myself blushing. But my mouth carries on without my permission. "Brolly is the British term for umbrella, Google told me, but of course you know that. But there's just nothing quite like it, is there? I just love it, being wet. I mean, getting wet! I mean, in the rain! I mean, walking! Out in the rain!"

Aaaaand he has started coughing.

Now I'm the one wishing for his chair to suck him into its plush fabric.

"Quite right," he finally says, his face almost as purple as my own. "If you'll just . . ." The words are so painfully stuck, he has to clear his throat. "Just close the door on the way out, please."

"SURE!" I yell as I turn on a dime and run for my life.

Lord God Almighty! I guess you haven't been hearing Susan's prayers? Help me!

———

My face has not returned to its normal color palette by the time we gather in the conference room for the Senior All Hands. For these meetings, most of the New York office attends, joining the team in a large Tulsa conference room via video chat. Sometimes Dad or Susan or the other C-level executives conference in separately if they're traveling, but it's encouraged everyone be in the room together.

This means that despite his objection to these types of calls, Emerson is going to head to the conference room. I decide to follow after him so I can sit by him during the meeting. I love meetings—phone, video, or otherwise. Maybe seeing me in my element will help him open up to the idea of, well, not even a friendship at this point. Right now, I need him to open up to the idea of me, just in general, as a human.

Three minutes before the scheduled start, he exits his lair and I wait a beat to follow behind. He takes one of the last few available seats, joined by Nicole on his far side, and I sit beside him on the other. I flash my friend a smile. Double-teaming him, I like it! I turn to him with that smile, willing my face to remain calm.

"Any idea what this All Hands is about?" I ask him.

"The invitation said social media training," he answers flatly.

"Oh, right! It did! Probably your least favorite thing in the world, am I right?" I jab at his elbow with my own.

He doesn't respond because the ping of the meeting software draws all our attention to the giant screen at the far end of the table. Jenn, our CMO, waves in greeting, and everyone chimes in with a hello or a wave. Everyone except the statue to my left. Instead, he exhales as if he's truly exasperated, even though the meeting has gone on all of fifteen seconds.

As she launches into the agenda for the meeting, Emerson gets up and leaves the conference room. I watch him leave, curious and confused. Can he just bail on meetings like that? Surely not. If he was invited to a high-level meeting, Dad must have wanted him present.

I forget about him as I listen to Jenn and her team talk about new social media trends and corporate guidelines. I crack a few jokes and ask a few relevant questions, as always. I just don't see the point in holding back something that may be helpful to the group, including a well-timed joke at my expense or Dad's or any other Canton in the meeting. It's fun. I like to add some fun. I'm feeling pleased with myself and wishing Emerson had stayed to witness my legendary meeting skills.

Until Jenn addresses Emerson in the back of the room.

He's in the back of the room? He's in the back of the room.

He wordlessly nods at whatever Jenn said, leaning against the wall. He left the seat next to me at the table, came back, and instead of returning to the available seat by me, chose to stand in the back.

A lesser (or maybe sane?) person would wave their white flag at this point. But I can't. At least, not yet. Because this thick tension with him cannot be carried onto the plane and across the sea with us. It simply cannot. I have *got* to find a way to cut it.

Time for reinforcements.

WEDNESDAY 6:40 P.M.
From: Samantha@CantonIntl.com
To: Adam@BellConst.com

Your Stupid Friend
Dear favorite brother-in-law,
Your wife may have explained I am trying to befriend your silent arctic ogre of a friend Emerson Clark. I am getting nowhere fast. Please advise ASAP!

Have a great day,
Samantha Canton
Senior Director of East Sales
Canton Cards International

Re: Your Stupid Friend
Ha, I am still your only brother-in-law. Emerson is a guy. A quiet, private guy, but overall a nice dude. One of the best, actually. Get some beers in him and just be chill and talk. Ask him about his work, and he'll nerd out and babble on. Or tease him about England. Just don't try to force it.

Sincerely,
Adam Bell
Bell Construction

I cringe. Don't try to force it. That was spelled out on the *Don't List* in one of the articles I read. At this point, I'm thinking of changing my legal name to Samantha Forcing It Canton. Still, I am on a timeline. My brother-in-law doesn't understand. I can't just sit back and wait for a friendship to naturally happen when we never see or talk to one another. Being chill is not my strong suit, but beers . . . now beers I can do. I shoot an email asking Marge for an end-of-day appointment for tomorrow.

I reply to Adam for a beer recommendation and start to brainstorm questions about work and England. I can feel the sinking feeling in my gut—the spark of hope about this—starting to flicker out. I shake my head a bit. Rome wasn't built in a day. Buzz and Woody didn't become pals overnight. *Patience, Samantha. Patience!*

WEDNESDAY 9:00 P.M.

Sadie: Update?

Me: Welp, today he got up and left the conference room

So he wouldn't have to sit next to me

Sally: F this guy. You don't need him as a friend.

Susan: Oh please, I'm sure he just had to pee!

I'm sure that even if he did, he didn't come back to his seat

Like a normal person

And instead sneaked in the other door to STAND the whole

meeting

Skye: Maybe you need to switch deodorants!

Sadie: Admitting defeat?

Not yet.

Trying beers tomorrow.

Sally: I say abort.

Sadie: I say do it because I think you'll grow on him.

Skye: I say do it because I want to hear how badly it goes!

Susan: I say I don't want to know any details, esp if you're drinking at the office!

Skye, [Middle finger]

Susan, sister first, COO second!

And all y'all: pray harder!

CHAPTER 4

It's 6:55 P.M., and I've got my ammunition.

I am wearing a new fitted gray dress, which is bordering on too tight to be considered professional. For the Beautiful Android, I'll basically blend in with his office walls, but for myself, I've paired it with my black power stilettos. They always put a little confidence in my step.

Do I normally need my power heels for a happy hour? No. But something about this man's aversion to me is getting under my skin. My skin, which is donning a little less makeup, under my thick blond hair that is down but tucked behind my ears. I went with twisting it up first, but then I really did look a bit too much like Marge.

I have a variety of freezing-cold lagers, which is apparently the favored type of beer in the UK. I have our itinerary, printed, with my questions written and some ideas highlighted. He's from over there, so surely he wants to weigh in on some of the plans for wowing our partners. I'm a tiny bit embarrassed I didn't think to ask him before.

But that just shows how little we have thought of one another or interacted until this point. Any financial meetings with Emerson regarding sales were run by Darrin, and if I was even present, I mostly listened, as Darrin tended to say what I was thinking. Office meetings and company events were a whirlwind of conversations for me, and, I'm assuming, a series of hiding alone in dark corners for Mr. Clark.

I tap my custom painting from Skye on the wall on the way out the door like a good luck charm, as I do before high-pressure meetings and presentations. I realize as I make my way down the hall how insane it is that I'm viewing beers with a coworker, even if he's a superior, as such.

But I'm nervous. That's just the straight-up truth. I say my life mantra to myself as I walk straight to his office and knock. I don't let myself in since Marge is gone for the day. It takes a second before he commands "Come in" in his stupid sexy stupid deep stupid British voice. I steel myself.

"Hello," I say with cheer, but not too loudly.

"Miss Canton," he says stiffly. He has also braced himself, it appears, his back as stiff as the monitor he's glaring at. But I march in and set the beers on his desk and take a seat without it being offered, my notes at the ready. He has yet to look at me. He clicks on something. "You wanted to go over our itinerary?"

"I did! Thought we could make a happy hour out of it."

He glances at the beers starting to sweat on his spotless glass desk, then up at me. That same unhappy expression repeats across his features as he quickly glances over my body. The pressure bubbles over under his gaze.

"Okay," I blurt. "What, you don't like my dress? It's new, I just got it."

He gives a small dismissive shake of his head. "Wha— No, it's fine."

"Fine? It cost a fortune and it's gray, which I would bet *one million dollars* is your favorite color."

He sighs and closes his eyes, once again pained to be talking to me.

"C'mon, what? I can read a room, Mr. Clark, and I know you do not like something about my appearance, in an almost disturbing, visceral way, so really, I'm a big girl, you can go ahead and just—"

"It doesn't suit you," he cuts in quickly, as if to get me to shut up.

He succeeds.

I am, in fact, shut up.

Shut up and fed the hell up. *Inside voice, Sam, inside voice.*

"All right, you know what?"

"Miss—"

"No, forget it. We are about to travel together *for over a month*, Emerson. Excuse me," I spit in a British accent before I can stop myself, "*Mr. Hoity-Toity Pants.* And I know, I'm 'So Much Sam,' as everyone around here says, among other nicknames I know all about, by the way. And you're on Forbes lists and *The Financial Times* man of the year, and you know what? I don't freaking care. You don't scare me. I was *trying* to be your *frriieend.* I was trying to make the next six weeks of our life bearable or *maybe*, can you imagine, *fun?!* My mistake! You want to be enemies, Bucko? Well, fine! You got it!"

I storm out.

Then I turn back and go and grab the beers, which were not cheap and he does not deserve.

"Miss Clark—"

"Nope! Bye!" I cut him off for a change, willing myself not to cuss or call him an asshole, because I am not totally confident he wouldn't report me to HR, after which Susan and my father would absolutely lose their minds. And their shit. Without ever uttering the word *shit*, of course. Canton Cards is a family brand, after all.

For a genius, already a global CFO at just thirty-five, he sure didn't think this through. His entire itinerary for the next month is in the hands of the most extroverted of extroverts. I start to dream up all the nonstop peopling, parties, happy hours, small talk, loud bars, and strobing dance clubs I can add to our trip.

I storm out of our offices, having swung by to grab my purse and walking shoes, and going the long way to avoid the Snow King. As I do, I smile wide thinking of the brightest, happiest, most obnoxious outfits I have. I will be packing all of them.

All. Of. Them.

You did not think this through, Emerson Clark.

THURSDAY 7:33 P.M.

Me: Operation Thaw is scrapped

Now I'm on Operation Rue

BECAUSE HE WILL RUE THIS DAY

Skye: Oh, dear God in heaven, help him

Sally: Yes! Love this energy!

Sally: You don't need him!

Susan: What happened??

Sadie: Beers didn't work?

Didn't even crack one open

He clearly was pained to just talk to me, again

And he gave me this disgusted look, again

So I just straight up asked him

I said, you don't like my dress, just tell me

And that asshole said, "It doesn't suit you"

I'M SORRY WHAT

Sadie: What an idiot

Susan: [Facepalm emoji] [Facepalm emoji]

Skye: What dress?

Sally: I hate this guy.

Sadie: What did you say back?

I said you wanna be enemies?

YOU GOT IT

And stormed out.

Skye: SamStorm OUT! Love it.

Sally: Oh man, this guy is doomed

Sadie: And what does being enemies entail?

Susan: Should you all switch to a thread without me?

Suze, so help me, if you do not take off your COO hat right now . . .

And enemies means I cram all his worst introvert nightmares into our trip

I'm going to have the time of my life and he is going to SUFFER

Skye: I just got nauseated

Sadie: Are we sure that's not extreme?

Susan: Sorry. #TeamSam

No, not extreme.

If he can't have a conversation with me about our itinerary He can deal with the consequences.

Sally: #TeamSam

Sadie: #TeamSam

Skye: #TeamSam

Skye: [Animated GIF Jimmy Fallon "Oh It's On"]

———

THURSDAY 9:53 P.M.

To: Samantha@CantonIntl.com
From: EClark@CantonIntl.com

Our Itinerary
Miss Canton,

I believe it is best to keep work relationships professional, and I overstepped this evening. I absolutely do not wish to be your enemy, so I hope you will excuse me. I sincerely apologize for my candor.

If you would like my feedback on the itinerary, feel free to email it to me. I'm happy to review it, though I am positive you've chosen ideal activities.

I look forward to them.

Warm Regards,
Emerson Clark
Chief Financial Officer
Canton Cards International

"No, Mr. Clark, I do not want your feedback on the itinerary! That ship has effin' sailed, Sir Frozen Tundra!" I snark at my phone as I reread his message.

"Not your strongest nickname," Skye says next to me on the couch.

I sigh. "I know, I felt it when it came out. Thanks again for coming to hang out here for a change."

"Of course."

"You needed a break from the sausage fest at your *fiancé's* place?"

"Sure did. Cannot wait until we move into our new apartment. But! I also felt like your all-caps messages were a cry for help." I laugh as she takes a scoop out of my pint of ice cream, and I take a scoop of hers. "You really do have your work cut out for you. Remember what he said to me last year after I made him suffer through *one* dance with me, just to make Matthew jealous?"

We say together in unison, with an accident, "Miss Canton, I believe I have fulfilled my obligation."

We crack up. Skye nudges me. "So, what are you going to reply?"

"I'm not."

"You're not?" She jerks her head in my direction, surprised.

"No. What am I gonna say? 'Well, you are my enemy, I don't excuse you, I don't want your feedback, and you shouldn't be looking forward to the activities because they are going to torture you'?" She makes a face that shows she sees my point. "No, I will reply at the office, loudly."

"What does that mean?"

"What it means is, I'm gonna need you to tell me aaaallll your worst introvert office nightmares so I can bring them to life for *Mr. Clark.*"

Skye's eyes become slits. "I gotta say I love this dark, scary side of you, sis."

"Pff. You would, Stormy. You would."

FRIDAY 7:40 A.M.

Me: Operation Rue Day 1

I've scheduled two all-office meetings to go over coworker conduct

Where I am going to have them zero in on commenting on people's appearances

Susan: I really don't want to know this

Sadie: OMG this is next level

I've also set up our office-wide speakers we've never used

Which will now be playing pop music

All.

Day.

Long.

Susan: Please move this to another text thread

Sally: Epic.

Skye: I'm so proud

———

"By three, he looked sick." Nicole stretches next to me on the studio's fake wood floor. We've grabbed our usual spot at the front of the class, near the wall-to-wall mirrors for the people in other classes who actually know how to dance.

"Really?" I say with glee.

"Yeah, he didn't even have his suit jacket on, because he was sweating."

I try not to think about the image of him with his jacket off. "He can't even hear the music in his office with the door closed, can he?"

"I bet he still can a little bit. You had it cranked so much, Margaret left at lunchtime."

I snicker as I switch from stretching over my left-wide leg to my right. "Did you see his face during the HR meeting? It was like he was gray and ashy but also blushing purple at the same time." I chuckle. "It was a little disturbing, if I'm being honest."

Nicole sighs.

"What?" I ask her, urgent because our Zumba instructor looks like she's about to start our class.

She hesitates with her words. "Just feel kinda bad for the guy."

"Um, what? You feel bad for Chief Bosshole? C'mon, you're my best friend! You have to be on Team Sam here!"

"I am, you're right. You're right. I just . . . think a little goes a long way with him, is all, and I love you, but we both know your personality is anything but little."

I roll my eyes as we get up on our feet. I do feel a pang of guilt for a second. If she thought today was bad, my bestie definitely won't approve of what I have planned for tomorrow.

"Who's ready to dance off some calories!" our peppy little teacher yells.

"I am!" I yell back.

———

MONDAY 7:56 A.M.

Me: Operation Rue Day 2

Today I will be using Darrin's office while he is out

It shares a wall with The King of the North

Did you know I like to blast rock music while I work? ;)

Susan: Poor Emerson

Sadie: Is this with the pop music still going in the hall?

Yep

Skye: Brutal. It's perfect.

I also may drop things and slam some binders shut

Who knows, I can be klutzy sometimes

Sally: This is my new favorite way to be woken up for class.

Susan: I am thinking of changing my number.

TUESDAY 7:29 A.M.

Me: Last night I took every healthy snack out of the break room

And replaced it with something composed of 99% sugar

Sadie: Maybe Susan should change her number, after all.

Skye: Tell them the other part!

Tomorrow there will be a team-building exercise

Sally: Oh no

Whole office.

There will be trust falls.

Skye: I'm in hives right now with secondhand discomfort.

Susan: Um, totally as your sister, how are you scheduling this mandatory stuff? Margaret hasn't said anything? That is not at all within the scope of your position!

MY LAST NAME IS CANTON

WHO IS GOING TO SAY NO TO ME

DUH

Sally: Badass

Sadie: Oh my

Susan: Okay, I am officially muting this thread until Sadie calls me with the all-clear.

Susan: Love you all.

CHAPTER 5

"All right, who's excited for a day of fun!" Hannah calls to the room. She's the epitome of a professional meeting facilitator: bubbly, sincere, articulate, funny . . . *maybe I should change careers?* She's wearing corporate attire, but her hair is wild and free, giving her the feel of a hippie in disguise.

I look across the room, which no longer has a long conference table in the center, to see Mr. Clark looking a bit green already. I stifle a victorious smile. This was definitely the best idea I've ever had.

After some enthusiastic responses and muffled almost-moans, Hannah continues. "We'll ease into this with something simple as everyone's coffee and donuts kick in." There were bran muffins and egg bites on Nicole's initial breakfast order, which I promptly changed. This office is now all sugar all the time!

"First, we're simply going to go around the room, and you'll introduce yourself to me, then tell the group what you actually do all day. Not your title, which everyone knows, but in a few sentences, what do you really do here? Then add a tidbit that no one at the office knows. It can be simple, like a favorite vacation spot or your pet's name or something small, but something not even your work wife or boss or assistant knows."

The room grows quiet with everyone thinking. She has us go

around in a circle, and I enjoy everyone's answers. I didn't realize what an average day entailed for some of my coworkers. Darrin is next to me, and he explains how he does a lot of sales planning and number crunching, in addition to meetings with our large accounts, set up by yours truly.

I'm not Darrin's assistant, but I often function as one, as the sales associates do for me, and he mentions that he couldn't do his job without me. He's told me this regularly, but it feels good to hear him say it in front of Old Man Winter across from me. For some reason, I think he, and others in the office, probably assume I just goof off all day, simply because I like to have fun while I work. Or maybe they assume I eat bonbons and go shopping while on the clock, taking advantage of my last name.

Next to me is Nicole, and I wonder what she can possibly come up with that I don't already know about her. I watch with pride as she says her piece.

"Hi, I'm Nicole. I am the office manager, and my day entails a lot of email correspondence and phone calls to coordinate a million things at once. I work with Margaret and Jake closely, and they let me know whatever our mighty CFO and CTO need, but there are also the needs of every department, so maybe I'm making an order for supplies, handling the scheduling of every conference room, all of that. And um . . ." She thinks for a second. "I desperately want to go to Disney World someday. I've never been."

What?!

I am shocked I didn't know this. Also, I'm surprised she never told me. I could've made that happen in a flash. Although people think I'm some kind of trust-fund kid, Dad actually cut all of us off financially after college graduation. He also forced each of us to go through all the things by Dave Ramsey. Cash is king . . . yada yada yada.

Still, I'm dripping with advantages, I know this. I had no col-

lege debt and had saved my generous allowance up throughout
high school and college. I split rent with Skye, but she buys the
groceries because I'm often out, so the only thing I really spend
money on is my wardrobe, makeup, and accessories. I have a
pretty good-size savings account with a whole digital "envelope"
earmarked just for fun. What's more fun than whisking your best
friend away to Disney?!

I realize Hannah is staring at me.

"Oh, yes. Hi, Hannah! My name is Samantha, and I am the
senior director of sales. My average day is actually a lot of mem-
orization and then answering questions. I do coordinate a lot for
Darrin, but most of the time, I'm going on sales calls all over the
boroughs, every day. Then at all those meetings, I have to be ready
to answer a million random questions about our products.

"So I memorize during my commutes—what's selling best in
the RainyDaze collection this year, for example, suggested retail
price, average profit margins of other sellers, where they place
them in their displays, how many cards per unit, and so on. I also
memorize facts about the people I'm meeting with—do they have
kids I can ask about, which sports teams are their favorite, which
leads me into another rabbit hole of that team and their best play-
ers and their record and—" I realize, as Emerson stares at me with
an almost-grin, that I have said more than anyone else with my
answer, by a long shot. SamStorm strikes again. *Dadgummit!*

"Sorry. You all get the idea. And um, let's see, you guys probably don't know when I was little, I had a pet bird named Fivel."
There is a murmur of various ways to say "We knew that" and
scoffs throughout the room of about forty people.

Hannah says, "Ooops, what else you got?"

"Oh. Right. Ummm. Oh! One of the things I miss most from
home is Earl's Famous—"

"Barbecue," half the office finishes in unison. I start to turn a brighter coral than the blouse I have tucked into my red pencil skirt.

Nicole laughs next to me as Hannah starts to say, "It's all right, we can just—"

"Okay," I interrupt too loudly and then blurt, "up until college, my life plan was to become a pediatrician." There. No one knows about *that*, that's for freaking sure. Everyone shuts up in surprise, except Nicole, who makes a gulping-laugh type of noise. I guess I shocked her like she shocked me. I can almost hear the collection of thoughts around the table: *Silly Sam a doctor? Ha! No way!*

I focus on everyone else and their answers, breathing through my embarrassment. I guess I am a chronic oversharer. At twenty-six, I feel like I should have a better handle on myself and my giant mouth. But then I wonder, is being an open book all that bad? If my contents are genuine and spilling them puts others at ease, helps them to open up too, what's the harm? After what feels like an eternity, it's Emerson's turn and my thoughts quickly quiet.

"Right," he starts, looking at Hannah for a moment. "Emerson Clark, CFO. I spend my day in spreadsheets, emails, and calls. And . . ." He pauses.

"Wait, wait, wait, that's not a few sentences. C'mon, Mr. Clark," I interject.

Hannah glances at me and then back at him with a half nod.

He sighs, as he has to start talking again. I kind of love how pained he looks. "I work on projections for the future—what will we make next quarter, what will our expenses be, what can we adjust. I meet with department heads, the CEO, the COO, the CTO. But mostly, the spreadsheets. And . . ." He finally looks at me for just a second. "My favorite color is canary yellow."

I squint at him. *Liar!* And cheater. There's no way that's his favorite color and there's no way Margaret doesn't know his favorite color already. There's also no way anyone is going to pipe up about that, since I already interjected once. There's also no way I am wearing anything yellow on my trip. Guess I need to do some repacking when I get home.

It's clear as the day goes on that Emerson Clark hates team-building exercises as I expected, and his glares convince me he hates me for making him spend his day this way. I avoid his angry eyes through the straw-house-building exercise and the minefield exercise, where I laughed so hard and died a thousand pretend deaths.

I did watch him during his turn in the minefield game, since he was blindfolded. Unlike me, getting excited and chatting and overcorrecting, he listened intently to the directions of everyone yelling at him and successfully made it through the room without touching one plastic disk on the floor. My only comfort was that he looked miserable as he did it flawlessly.

"All right, last exercise, and everyone's favorite at all my workshops. This is called Inbox, and for you introverts in here, you'll be happy to know we're done with all the group chatting—it's all done via text message."

Everyone chuckles as she explains, "Each of you go to the link on the screen and you'll see a form, with a field for each person in this room. Go through, and next to each person's name, type in something you appreciate about them and their work here at Canton Cards. When everyone is done, I'll hit Export, and each of you will get one email containing all your notes. The person will only know the message is from you if you sign your name, and it's totally fine to keep your note anonymous if this sort of thing makes you uncomfortable, or if maybe you don't know the person all that well so you're grasping at straws.

"I have to add, however, just a required disclaimer due to past experience: the messages can be tracked through the system, so this is not a suggestion box and any bullying or nasty messages will be grounds for probation or termination. Though I'm sure no one here at this company would even think of such a thing." She tilts her chin down as she finishes her warning.

I smile at this exercise. I know everyone in the office and easily have something nice to say about all of them, even people I never work with, like Dina in the IT department. I rarely talk to her, but her shoe collection is amazing, which I know because Skye is a sneaker head too. Telling her that her taste in sneaks is to die for will make her day.

But. There it is. The name I've saved for last.

Screw it. I tap next to Emerson's name and type what I want to say. Let them reprimand me if they want.

I appreciate your candor, so I know you'll appreciate mine: I am going to make our trip a living hell for you! Bon voyage! Sincerely, Samantha Canton

After a good half hour, Hannah excitedly exports our emails, which she wants us to pull up and read right now, all at the same time.

Aaaaaand I'm crying.

Two seconds in. I'm not even embarrassed about it, since other people are clearly moved too.

Nicole tells me I'm the best bestie ever, Darrin says I single-handedly make this the easiest executive sales job he's ever had. More than one person anonymously writes that I make meetings bearable. A couple people say thanks for always making them laugh. Someone has put that they love my fashion sense (*I'm on to you, Dina!*). Someone says I'm nice to a fault, which feels like code for "I don't like you, but it's fine because everyone else does." I guess that one is from Emerson.

Then there's one message that takes my breath away. "You are a human bulb, lighting up this whole office just by being you!!" I copy and paste it to Nicole immediately.

> **Me: That isn't from you, is it?**
> Nicole: No, mine said you are the best bestie.
> **Oh, right, duh.**
> **It's just so nice, I can't imagine who it's from, if not you or Darrin.**
> I know exactly who it's from.
> **?????**
> Chase
> **The accounting guy?**
> Yes, he is always staring at you.
> He's cute! You should ask him out!
> **[Thinking emoji]**

Hannah tells us great job, and I make my way over to her to say thanks and help pack up her gear. I make sure not to look anywhere near Emerson's direction. I'm sure he is unaffected by my message. I almost think I should've gone with something meaner. *It doesn't suit you . . .* My blood boils anew remembering.

After walking Hannah out, I linger at Nicole's desk.

"Hey," I whisper.

"Why are you whispering?" she asks, not looking up from her screen where she's typing something with comic-book superhero speed.

"I don't think that was sent by a guy." I lean in closer but raise my voice slightly. "There were two exclamation marks. What guy do you know who would do that? Definitely not an IT guy."

She pauses typing to consider what I've said. "Yeah, I bet you're right, but just in case, you should still ask Chase out."

"I'm off men. I've told you this."

"But think about it: he knows you already, works within the company, and you'd be approaching him, not the other way around."

"Hmmmm, I will think about it." I stare off for a moment, then look down at my dear friend. "How about you? I bet your email was glowing with praise, right?"

"They were all really nice, and then there was Emerson's message: 'You are extremely efficient and proficient.'"

I chuckle. "Yeah, mine said, 'You are nice to a fault.' Which definitely feels like an insult."

She laughs too. "I'll call you later." I give a small wave as I head back to my office the long way. I don't want to look at the man in the corner office's stupid, handsome, cruel face ever again.

CHAPTER 6

THURSDAY 6:02 A.M.
Meeting Invitation From: Margaret Wayne
8:45 A.M. Emerson Clark and Samantha Canton
Re: Trip Itinerary

"Ohhhh it is on like Donkey Kong!" I mutter out loud as I click Accept at the bottom of the email. *He's* inviting *me* to meet?! I practically jump out of bed, immediately done scrolling through Instagram dog accounts. Each one tugs at my heart, begging me to choose their breed and buy a puppy as soon as humanly possible. I remind myself that after Europe, I'll find a new roommate, a new apartment that allows dogs, and a new furry best friend.

I flip through my tiny, overstuffed closet to find the perfect soft, silky, tailored battle armor for my meeting. I hurry through my shower, eager to get to the office. I have enjoyed torturing my enemy and can't wait to see what he has to say, but my urgency is more than that. I want to get to the office because I really hate living alone.

Since Skye found Matt, she's stayed here less and less, which

I understand. But multiple nights in a row on the couch with only Netflix for company have left me physically drained. I've added an extra weekly Zumba class, and I have Pilates, and I have my standing happy hour with Nicole. But it just doesn't seem to be enough. And it bothers me that being alone bothers me so much.

I shake off the thought as I pile my hair into an obscenely high, bouncy ponytail. No point in fighting the way I'm wired. God made me with a battery that runs on peopling. I didn't choose it, I popped out that way. I just have to learn to adjust for a while until I find a new roommate. And a dog. I start to think through different breeds as I go through my routine of packing my lunch, gathering my office shoes and my oversize work purse, and head out the door.

I arrive at the office just in time, noticing the pop music is turned down so low I can barely hear it. I don't go to change it or give Marge the side-eye. I want to see how this trip itinerary meeting goes before I make my next move.

Margaret gives me a glare that could kill as I approach Emerson's door, but she nods, since it's exactly 8:45. I knock, and I can barely hear the quiet "Come in" from inside. As I push the door in, the air from his office fills me with nerves. Because there he is, looking a little tired, a little disheveled, and still freaking handsome as ever.

Today, he looks like coffee ice cream, good enough to lick, in a crisp white shirt and cream tie under a tan suit, which I'm sad to notice doesn't include a vest. *Wait, ice cream? A vest? Focus, Sam!*

I tamper down a smile that wants to erupt at the contrast of the two of us.

Because I am wearing a neon—yes, neon—pink shift dress with dark blue heels, oversize matching blue dangle earrings, and a big blue silk scrunchie around my fun ponytail. I'm glad our feud landed during the summer, or else I wouldn't be tanned enough to pull off this look, which I am sure Emerson finds offensive to his precious eyes.

"You wanted to see me?" I say flatly.

He waits a beat before looking up from his clasped hands on his desk. This time as he looks at me, there is a tight flash of some emotion across his face, but it doesn't read as obvious disgust. He must've practiced.

"Please, take a seat." The words are slow and cold as he glances at the chairs in front of his desk.

"I'd rather not," I slowly say right back.

"Bloody hell," he mutters under his breath so soft, I almost miss it. "Miss Canton, I would like to call a truce." He looks me in the eyes.

And he doesn't look away.

And I am on fire.

His ice-blue eyes never hold mine, hold anyone's, this long. It feels like a secret or a privilege. I guess maybe that's why in that moment, it feels like it's one of the sexiest things to ever happen to me. And, I mean, I go on a lot of dates. A lot.

"A what?" is all I manage to get out. *Speechless? Who am I?! C'mon!*

"A truce, Miss Canton. I would like to officially change my position," he says, and I feel my eyebrows pinch together. "On workplace relationships," he adds, as if I should have caught on to what he means by now. I decide to make him say the words, and force myself not to start smiling. He clears his throat. "I think you're right . . . that it'd be good for us to be . . . friends."

I let my smile take over my face. "You want to be my friend?"

He can only nod, as if speaking the last few sentences was as much work as a triathlon.

I cross my arms and shake my head a bit, and I feel words bubbling up and out before I can *slow 'em and stow 'em.* "Pff, I'm not sure you know how to be a friend, *Mr. Clark*. I kinda don't think you'll be any good at it, to be honest. And you know what? I am really freaking good at it. I am a great friend. I am fun and loyal and dependable, and I mean, you really missed out, didn't you? But I guess we are going on the trip together and I don't particularly want to travel with an archenemy nemesis quasi-boss, so . . . I'll think about it."

"You will?" His eyebrows shoot up.

"Yeah, maybe I can be friendly enough for the both of us," I spit out. To my absolute shock, the corners of his mouth flinch, almost raising to a shadow of a grin. Almost.

"Maybe so," he replies in a soft, low tone that fills my chest with frenzied butterflies.

"Do you actually want to go over the itinerary?" I ask in a threatening tone.

"No."

"Because I slaved over it for a month, and if you think you can waltz in and change things two days before we leave, you've got another—" I realize he's already said no. "Oh. Okay, good." He gives a tight nod, with his lips in a polite, straight line. I switch gears. "So. We're meeting at the airport Saturday. I guess I should at least get your phone number."

"You have my number," he says.

"What?" I have no idea what he's talking about.

"You took my phone, added yourself, and replied to yourself, at your welcome party."

"I did?"

"As you know, I tend to err on the side of brutal honesty, Miss Canton."

I roll my eyes at that, then think for a second. "Well," I chuckle, "that does sound like me." I shrug. "Okay, see you Saturday afternoon."

He barely dips his head.

I turn back. "This is not to say we are friends."

He nods.

"And if we are, you're going to have to quit calling me Miss Canton."

Another nod.

"And you may have to use actual words instead of just nodding."

He closes his eyes and sighs, as if I've officially dragged the conversation on too long.

"See you Saturday," I say quickly, letting him off the hook and rushing out of his office.

In my office, I close the door and breathe for a second. The man just makes me so stinkin' nervous! And I've been nerves-free around plenty of hot, well-dressed men, so what gives? I quickly step around my desk and grab my phone. I search in my messages.

Sure enough, there it is. I sit down involuntarily, my heart racing for absolutely no logical reason. I see our thread from the week I arrived in New York, when I'd graduated from intern to an official job as sales associate.

> **Me: This is Sam!!!!!**
> **Nice to remeet you!**
> Emerson: Welcome to New York!!!!!

Okay, I had clearly grabbed his phone and typed that to myself, as Emerson would never in a million years a) text me or b) use five exclamation marks. Ugh, Skye was right: I do have an exclamation point problem.

But there was one more message.

> Emerson: Happy Birthday, Miss Canton

He had texted me on my birthday months later, my first birthday here in the city. But I'd never replied? That's not like me. I sat and thought, drumming my thumb on the side of my phone as I stared at the screen. Between Facebook, Instagram, and texts, I get tons of messages on my birthday. That's the only explanation. He must've gotten lost in the shuffle. Huh. Feeling badly about never replying, I start tapping.

Me: You were right, I do have your number!

Immediately, the three dots pop up, surprising me.

Emerson: As any friend of mine should.

I get a weird tightness in my chest, knowing he's sitting two doors down, looking at his phone at his desk just like I am. But then I imagine him in his subdued, stoic perfection and catch a glimpse of my neon-rainbow bracelet on my wrist. *It doesn't suit you . . .*

Yeah.

Not my friend, Evil Iceman.

Not even close.

———

Friday is a blur of finalizing things at the office in the morning and packing like crazy in the afternoon. After work, Nicole joins me at my apartment with sustenance.

"Where are you going, fashion week?!" She gasps, entering the disaster zone that is my bedroom. I'm not much of a decorator, but I have a nice bedroom set and a few bright girl-boss prints on the wall. Though none of that is even noticeable with the rainbow of clothes strewn everywhere.

"You know how I am. I like to have options."

She points to the corner of my bed. "What's this pile?"

"Unpacked after I found out he likes yellow."

She starts to scold me. "Sam. I thought you said he asked for a truce?"

"Correct, and it is no longer my life's mission to make him miserable, but I'm not going out of my way to bring him any joy, either." She grunts at me, but I don't understand why. "What?"

"You will, though. You'll find yourself being nice and doing things he likes, taking care of him and making him laugh—it's just your nature."

My head rears back. "Huh. A lot of good it's done me so far. The man cannot stand me. I literally haven't seen so much as a grin."

"True. And you can't stand *him.* So . . ." Nicole rubs her hands together, plotting. "Let's forget him and talk about Chase."

I squint at my friend. "You mean when I get back? Because I'm leaving tomorrow, and I'm not going out tonight, if that's where you're going with this."

"Where I'm going is that you guys could text while you're away, get to know each other as friends first, with no physical stuff or dating on the table. Might be the perfect scenario for you right now, after . . . everything."

I tense up at the thought of all she's not saying out loud. I try to shake it out of my shoulders. "Eh, I'm out of the game."

"These don't look like the undies of someone who is out of the game." She raises her eyebrows along with one of my matching thong and bra sets.

I snatch them from her hands. "Those are my power under-wear sets for meetings! I'm on the sidelines of the dating scene, officially. I think it'd be better to take these few weeks to be on my own than to be calling home and penpal-ing the whole trip."

I wonder for a second if Emerson will be calling and texting with Miranda the Fashion Model. I remind myself I don't care. But . . . what if Emerson thinks I care?

"Wait." I drop the panty set, my heart spasming. "You don't think that Emerson thinks that this whole friend thing has been a ploy to get in his pants, do you?!"

Nicole laughs. "Doubtful. Anyone who's been around you longer than five minutes knows you are flirty with everyone."

"I am not f—" I cut myself off. "Yeah. You're right. I am!" I shrug, and we laugh together as I move all my clothes from the bed to the suitcases.

CHAPTER 7

"Holy crap balls, that's heavy!" Skye pants as she grabs my backpack from behind the passenger's seat of Matthew's Tesla.

"I feel like you packed a little light, Sam," my future brother-in-law says with his cheeky smile as he surveys my two massive check-on bags, large carry-on, and backpack the size of a small bus.

"It's over a month! Lay off me, Runny Monkey!" His expression flattens at the use of his college nickname, a play on Chunky Monkey, the disruptive smoothie he had right before going running across the University of Texas campus. Skye told me the hilarious story in disgusting detail.

"I still cannot believe you told her." He growls at my sister, who is avoiding eye contact with him.

"I tortured it out of her with threats of large crowds and long conversations," I tell him. "And I promise, again, not to tell anyone . . . probably."

"She does not get to be a bridesmaid, Tiger, I forbid it." He sighs with a smile, calling my sister his sweet nickname for her. Skye sighs. I sigh at them both, happy for them and deeply jealous too. I'm not above admitting it. I want what they have.

I want what my parents had. The fact that my logical mother had such a whirlwind romance still floors me. Maybe I want the dramatic love without the drama. Eh, who am I kidding. I want the drama too. I want the longing, the words, the romance, the happy ending.

Someday.

Years from now.

After I've recovered from the last year.

And the years before that, if I'm being truthful.

Skye brings my thoughts back to the present.

She takes me by the shoulders. "This is your dream trip, Bob. The work stuff is in the bag. I'm not even going to pep talk you about that. It's Europe! You enjoy every second of it, no matter what Mr. Clarksicle does or says or thinks, okay?"

"Okay," I breathe. I'm stupidly nervous.

"No men. No flings. No hookups. No dating, whatsoever."

"Absolutely. You don't have to remind me this time."

"You're about to be surrounded by men with sexy accents, I do need to remind you." She has a fierce tone that sounds angry but actually says *I love you* underneath, if you know her.

"*Okaaay*, no men whatsoever."

"Sadie and Nicole will be there for convention, so they'll make sure you're still on the straight and narrow."

"Psh, Nicole wants me to start a love-letter romance with Chase from accounting."

"What! Nicole is a dead woman. Seriously, it's time for you to focus on you. Take care *of you*. Have fun for yourself, k?"

I nod.

"No crap?" The question always makes me smile.

"No crap," I say before I hug each of them again. I use all my strength to wheel the luggage cart inside to the counter. I see my grumpy travel partner waiting outside the line.

He looks stunning.

And I'm mad about it.

Again, if a man is an absolute butthole, he needs to at least look like a massive turd, and Emerson never, ever does. We're about to be on a seven-hour overnight flight—why is he wearing a crisp white dress shirt rolled at the sleeves with charcoal-gray dress slacks? He couldn't just wear jeans? Now I'm going to be distracted by his thick, exposed forearms until my sleeping meds kick in! *No, I'm not! He is a terrible human . . . with a girlfriend!*

I'm glad I went with one of my cuter traveling outfits as he looks up and spots me. He looks away quickly, another strange expression on his face. I think about my outfit, which is my best black leggings and a black-and-white T-shirt with a huge Stories of Loya graphic, a gift from Skye. She has given me many franchise tees: Harry Potter, Star Wars, OU, I Heart NY, T-Swift, and of course some of Sadie's movie merch too—anything that may spark conversation with strangers who are also fans of my favorite things.

On top of my shirt, a glaring bright pink sweater is hanging open. The sweater matches the pink in my Adidas sneakers perfectly, and my hair is up in an unoffensive topknot. I can't see why Mr. Stuffy would be offended by this outfit—the pink is only an accent. But I'm a little too anxious to think more about it as the time for takeoff draws near.

"Miss Canton," he says as a way of greeting. I start to scold him for not using my name but then notice his bags, or lack thereof.

"Where are your bags?"

"These are my bags." He motions to his one normal-size suitcase and the small messenger briefcase bag on his arm. The messenger bag hardly counts.

"One bag for the whole trip!" I almost yell. He winces, and I give him an apologetic look as I switch to a loud whisper. "Seriously, you fit everything for over a month in there?"

He looks at my bags. "And good for our plane that I did, by the looks of it."

I glare at him, unsure if he's teasing, trying to joke around, or scolding. I guess that it's the latter and squint at him.

He takes my cart without asking, pushing it with ease, and goes to the counter. He gives the gate agent both of our names and stretches out a hand for my passport. He's . . . such an adult. I mean, I am too, obviously. But other than Dad, I've never seen a man swoop in and just take charge. I hand him my passport without a word. *Maybe this won't be totally terrible.*

Wrong.

Because as we get up to the conveyor belts inside airport security, I notice a mother traveling along with three small children ahead of us. Everyone notices them, really. One baby is crying, and the two older toddlers, twins, are not listening to their mother at all, whining about the process like all of us adults secretly wish we could do. The poor mom is trying to wrangle her stroller, diaper bag, luggage. It's a disaster. I cut the line, rush to her side, and help with her bags.

"Oh, thank you." She is almost crying. Which makes me almost cry because *what the hell is wrong with people?* How am I the only decent human who has offered to help?

"Hey, look, guys! We get to go through a magic door! Wow, can you believe it?" I say to the twins, my voice too loud and my facial expressions completely crazy.

I look back to Emerson to help the situation, as there are more bags to load and he simply stands there, frozen. I can't tell if he's angry or irritated, but he's definitely clenching his jaw. I just motion at my bags, which he will have to take care of, if he's not going to help me.

"No, no, don't touch anything, or the magic in the door won't work," I call to the twins, who are reaching with their hands. I know that look in their eyes—they're about to go into destructo mode on the fabric straps that make a temporary partition.

"Wassit do?" the boy twin asks me. He's adorable.

"It fills you up with fairy dust to help the plane fly!" I say with awe in my voice.

"Wow. Fairies," the girl twin whispers.

"I know, right?" I whisper back, enjoying seeing the world from her little eyes for a moment. Crazy as my tactics may be, both of them finally still in the line and start to focus on the scanner ahead.

I help the mother again on the other side, and she hugs me like I'm a fairy myself. I am actually grateful for the distraction, since I'm starting to feel the panic build in my bones. By the time we've got her kids loaded up and bags ready to roll away, I'm a bit sad to see them go, especially as Sir Grumps A Lot catches up to me.

"Thanks for all the help, Mr. Clark," I sneer. He barely looks at me as he hands me my bags. I huff at him and stalk off, not concerned if he's following behind me or not.

We get to our gate and onto the plane with absolutely zero conversation. My hands shake as I get my backpack pushed under the seat in front of me. I flex my fingers as I look out the window. I can hear my breathing growing louder and more erratic.

Emerson leans toward me slightly in his chair to my right. He's still within his own bubble of personal space, though, since we are in first-class. "Miss Canton?"

"Huh?" I turn to see a very concerned-looking pair of striking eyes trained on me.

He clears his throat. "Afraid of flying?" he asks me softly.

"Not flying, specifically, no." He stares, so I continue. "Um, I just have a thing about freak accidents." Realization and understanding smooth out his furrowed brow. I give a slight nod. "The odds of being hit by a car if you're out walking are one in forty-three thousand. Did you know that? Probably not, nobody knows that, but I do. And like, that accounts for walking cities like New York, right?

So, when you think of the odds of being hit by a drunk driver while you're out for an early morning jog in Tulsa, Oklahoma, those are some really slim odds," I say, tightening my grip on my armrests.

"I'm sorry . . . about your mother," he says softly.

I nod and carry on. "I know it's irrational, but I think about it when I cross the street. My sisters do too, every time, I know they do. And on the subway, the odds of dying are one in five hundred thousand, and, like, in New York, that is kind of a small number, isn't it? The odds of dying in a plane crash are way better, one in eleven million, but uh, I kinda feel like that exact *one* might have the last name Canton." I let out a crazy-sounding chuckle. "Sorry, everyone, sucks for you that you're on this flight with me!"

Emerson's beautiful eyes go wide, and I realize I've ventured past the socially acceptable volume level for plane conversation. "Sorry!" I whisper, and I can't stop. "Listen, I realize this is like your worst nightmare to be next to me on a flight, but I took two Benadryl and I'm going to have a glass of wine, and then I will be *out*. No chatting at all. But until that happens, maybe we could talk so I can take my mind off things? That would probably be good, that'd probably help."

"Talk." The word comes out slowly, as if he's never heard of the concept.

I snicker. "Your favorite pastime, right?" He huffs at me. I think he's going to flash a grin, but, unsurprisingly, he doesn't. Ever the statue.

I sigh. "I'll make it really easy for you. One-word answers—it'll be fun." I see him tense in his chair. "Mr. Clark, do you want to be my *friend* and help me get over my fear of dying an odds-defying fluke death or not?"

He glares at me as if to say he hasn't said no, which he hasn't. I think of where to start.

"Are you excited about this trip?" I say with a little too much cheer. I realize it's not like he can say no, since I planned the whole thing.

"Yes."

"Are you looking forward to seeing your family?"

He thinks about it. "Yes."

"Wellllll, that pause was so long, I almost nodded off. You don't get along with your family?" He cocks his head to the side with a shrug, as if to say it's complicated. I sigh. "Okay, don't want to talk about your family. Got it."

Just then, the flight attendant comes by and takes our drink orders.

"So," I restart, "I know you've been to London, obviously. Have you been to Paris before?"

"Yes."

"Even all the sightseeing stuff?"

"Yes."

"Well, crap! This is all old news to you then. Not me. Thank the good Lord Darrin knocked up his little wife, because after all the crap upon crap since we were outed months ago, I needed this trip like I've never needed anything in my life, Mr. Clark, *in my life!*"

He looks confused, which I take as a cue to explain further. "Outed in the press. You know? Skye and Sally and I weren't in any official Canton family photos or articles—it was just Grandpa, Dad, Susan, and Sadie. But then someone leaked that photo and our names and personal information to the *Tulsa World*, and then it was tweeted everywhere? Surely you know about all this?"

"Not fully," he says slowly.

"Well, for a while, it was paparazzipalooza, following me around, and Skye sometimes, being hounded by journalists like we're the freaking Kardashians. We're not billionaires, and we're Okies, for crap's sake. None of us expected the reaction, but Sadie thinks maybe because we were hidden and under the radar for so long, it made us a bigger deal than we really are? More intrigue, maybe?" A large thumping sound in the plane's underbelly causes me to jump.

"And why did you?"

I look over at him, shocked that he just asked me a question. "Hide?" He nods. "For Skye, it was about proving herself without the family name. For Sally, she's still in college, so Dad wanted to shield her in our Oklahoma bubble as long as he could—we all did. For me, well, it's because of exactly what ended up happening! I mean, the photographers were not that bad compared to—" I shudder, starting to relive it all. " . . . anyway! It was nuts."

He studies me for a second. "You don't enjoy the attention?"

"Oh, I did. I did. I'm not gonna lie. I loved it at first. Shocker, I know. But then it got—" I am cut off by the arrival of my wine and Emerson's beer. "So, you *do* like ale," I say with a smirk.

"I do." We both take a drink, mine more of a gulp since I'm eager to die to the world and wake up in London. "It got . . . ?" he asks, not without effort. It takes me a second to realize he's urging me to go on. I am so surprised, I get goose bumps.

"Um, ugly. Things got pretty ugly. Not just the hate messages and dick pics and stalker stuff either." His face changes for a second. The phrase "dick pic" must be too much for Stuffy McStufferson. *Ha, you don't even know!*

"As much as I like people, it turns out they don't really like me, or, I mean, men don't like me. Well, not the men that I thought liked me. Or the men that I wanted to like me. Instead, they liked my name. Or the attention. Or money. That's why I'm off men. Completely. This is a no-men trip for me, absolutely zero, zilcho, noneski. No dates, no drinks, I'm not even going to flirt." He locks eyes with me for a second. "I know, I know, salespeople flirt, but I'm serious about this! Clearly, I don't just pick losers—my picker is flat-out broken. Hashtag *facts*. Because how dumb am I that I

didn't see it coming? I mean, twice I was
. . . well, I'm sure you know, I'm sure the whole C-suite saw me in
all my glory."

Emerson starts choking on his beer, and I realize I've gotten
much too loud again. Too loud and too open, spilling way too many
deeply personal beans with my coworker. *Did I just say "me in all
my glory"?! Idiot!*

As Emerson collects himself, the plane begins to take off.

All the odds and stats and fears barrel into my mind as fast
as the plane thundering down the concrete. I see flashes of my
mother's accident, gory photos I've tried to unsee over the years.
Blood on pavement. One bloody running shoe in the grass. I see
snapshots of the funeral, my dad's eyes watering, my older sisters
stoic. Rose petals blowing away in the strong Oklahoma wind. My
breath fails again.

Without meaning to, I reach out and grab, clutching the hard,
warm forearm next to me. For half a second, I feel a charge in my
fingers and a comfort in my chest. Until Emerson stiffens and
flinches, as if he's been burned.

I pull my hand away and feel my face flush with embarrassment. Swift anger rises in my cheeks that I'm so embarrassed over
touching this ice sculpture of a man. This man, who is still clearly
repulsed by me and my too-big, too-loud, too-much personality. I
suck down the last of my wine.

"I know, I know. Overshared, too loud, too much, and to top it
off, too touchy, apparently." I gesture at his arm that I just violat-
ed. "Sorry. I think we can just agree to ignore each other until we
land." I start to dig in my bag, blocking out whatever facial expression he's throwing at me. I'm guessing one of relief.

"As you wish," he mumbles.

"As you wish? *As you wish?!* No." I laugh angrily. "*No.* You are
not Wesley in this scenario. I don't care if you have the accent and

the hot, quiet pirate thing going, you . . . you are freaking Scar is who you are, buddy."

"The murderous uncle?" He sounds genuinely offended.

"Okay, maybe not a murderer, but Hans. Definitely Prince Hans."

"Hans?"

"From *Frozen*?" His face is still twisted in confusion. "You've never seen *Frozen*?!" I say, loudly enough that he raises his eyebrows and pinches the bridge of his nose. "Oh, give me a break—anyone in this cabin who heard me is also shocked you haven't seen it. It was Disney's revival into animated musicals and won like one billion awards. The music is awesome, and Kristen Bell is a dream in that movie, a dream, Emerson Clark, and you are most definitely evil Prince Hans." He takes a deep breath and lets out an even deeper sigh. "Now, you'll be happy to know I am done talking to you for this flight—hell, probably this whole trip. So. Good night!"

I can feel him watching as I pull out my eye mask, pillow, blanket, and ear plugs, setting them all on the side of my seat. I yank slippers from my backpack and put them on my feet, not caring if he thinks my exposed socked feet are inappropriate for the plane. He can tell that to my perfectly comfortable toes while his feet swell like sausages in his stupid dress shoes.

I know he's still watching as I fluff out my blanket over my legs and put my eye mask on my forehead, not yet over my eyes. I open the plastic baggy of fresh earplugs and put them in, avoiding looking in his direction. Finally, it's time to blow up my inflatable pillow.

I feel it then.

The purple coming to my cheeks—on top of the existing plethora of pinks—confirming that I am, in fact, the most high-maintenance of high-maintenance fliers. And that it's hard to make a dramatic post-argument exit when you don't actually exit.

My ears get hot as crimson spreads outward from my cheeks, because I have to blow and blow into the pillow. The *whooooooosh whooooooosh* sound is getting louder by the second. I see Emerson cock his head out of the corner of my eye, but I will not look at him. I will not. *Good luck with your free paper-thin blanket and jankity little neck pillow, Frosty!*

After one hundred long years, the deceivingly large travel pillow is inflated. I shove it over to the wall, slam down my window shutter, and push the recline button on my seat. The seat mocks me with a long, slow squeak. After another century, my seat is flat and I am curled onto my side facing away from my travel partner. Sweating and fifty shades of dark pinks and purples, I pull my eye mask over my eyes and let my sedatives take over.

CHAPTER 8

I wake up grateful to see there's only an hour left in the flight. My body cooperated, and I slept hard—only stirred for one quick trip to the restroom a few hours in. Iceman was asleep, but barely reclined, the weirdo. Good thing, though, because I really had to go, and my bladder may have interpreted climbing over his seat as a direct challenge.

I had only let myself stare at sleeping Emerson for a few seconds, max. He looked the tiniest bit softer when he slept. Thawed just a smidge. Younger too. I looked away when I found myself feeling the urge to straddle him on the wide seat and both slap him across the face and also maybe take a big, deep neck-sniff of his manly scent.

But I managed to look away, peel off my sweater, and sit for five minutes, wondering if I was having a seizure. *I don't even like the man! I'm off men! He has a girlfriend!* Clearly, it was just my body's reaction to a physical need. A need I hadn't taken care of in a while. Not to mention, there would be no sniffing or kissing or need-meeting with anyone for this entire trip. Yikes. This was going to be a long six weeks.

I blink hard a few times to wake myself and forget my mid-flight mental lapse. I brace myself for what I'll find to my right, as I can feel myself looking oily and disheveled, and am positive

Bossman will look stellar, as usual. I am mostly right but also glad to find a hint of fatigue around those sharp, light blue eyes.

He wordlessly hands me the boxed meal from his tray. My face must show my confusion.

"Breakfast," he explains plainly. I think I feel my lips part. "Your blood sugar," he adds with a look that says "duh, obviously." Now my mouth is definitely hanging open.

"H-How do you know about my low blood sugar?"

He runs his bottom lip through his teeth in irritation before responding. "I believe you've mentioned it in every meeting over the last four years."

"I have not!"

"Along with a lengthy description of whatever snack you'd brought into said meeting."

I start to argue and falter fast. I am too stunned to comment on the absurd "every meeting" and "lengthy description" parts of what he just said. Because he is not far off, if maybe exaggerating a little.

Everyone in the office probably knows this fact about me. I don't know if I should continue to be embarrassed about my oversharing habit. I do know, quite abruptly, that I am annoyingly famished. He goes back to focusing on his iPad, and I have to pull my eyes away from him.

"Thanks," I finally offer. He doesn't respond.

I pack up my airplane sleep accoutrements and scarf down the meal, which is pretty bad, with the exception of the two mini cinnamon rolls. I focus on the views outside the window and breathe through the descent, forcing myself not to blurt my thoughts at the creature to my right. (*Nearly half of all airplane accidents happen during the descent or landing!*) I clutch my chair in lieu of his arm as we land safely back on the ground.

When it's time to stand and ready for our exit, I can't get my gigantic bag to pull free from under the seat in front of me. I feel the pressure of people behind us, and my hands sweat. No one wants to be *that* idiot who slows the whole process, as if there weren't fifty warnings it was almost time to disembark. With a rather unattractive grunt, I give my bag another forceful tug and hear a small ripping sound.

"Let me," Emerson offers, looking appalled. I move out of his way, and with irritating grace and patience, he gets the bag free and lifts it up. "Bloody hell, woman!" The words slip out of him in a loud whisper as he lobs my backpack onto the seat.

The shock and exasperation on his face forces me to giggle. "I know." I wince slightly as I reach out to take the strap from him.

"Go!" He motions with his hand toward the aisle because it's our turn to leave. He puts my backpack on over his small messenger bag.

I can hear him muttering very British-sounding curses behind me.

It brings me great joy, because I am mature.

When we get out of the gate area and into the breezeway, I finally look back at him.

"I can take my bag now, thank you."

"No." He seems annoyed, as if I asked him to carry my bag, which I most definitely did not. He doesn't look down from the information screens as he says it.

"Uh, *no*? Seriously, it's fine, I can carry it," I say, my irritation growing.

"Miss Canton." He sighs. "I am too tired to make sure you do not fall over backward trying to lug this monstrosity all the way to our car. Please, let's just go."

He gestures in the direction of the customs desks, according to the overhead sign, and I start walking, but I turn my eyes into little slits. "Are you going to be this grumpy the whole month?"

He only sighs in response.

I realize, as we start walking, that I. Am. In. London! Mom convinced Dad to splurge on a family Europe trip when I was a child, our only overseas adventure, which I don't remember. So I do not offer any excuse or apology to Old Man Clark when I skip and squeal a little bit as we get closer to customs. And at my awkward screechy sound, he winces, or maybe he has a facial tick. I don't care.

At the customs counter, he takes charge again, as if we're traveling together. I mean, we are traveling together, but not together, obviously. I don't hate his whole take-control thing, though, especially since this is all familiar to him and totally foreign to me.

At baggage claim, he sloughs my bag at my feet with a dismayed shake of his head and says, "I'll go get us a trolly."

"A what?" I say as he walks away. When he comes back with a luggage cart, I can't help but smile. "Ohhh, a trolly is a cart! Man, this is going to be so fun. Will you please call everything by its British name? Really lean into your accent too. Ooo is your family cockney? Is that how you say it? Will your accent get worse like mine does if I spend a week at home? The 'y'alls just fly outta me."

He sighs and walks to the carousel. His sigh seemed less irritated this time. I realize sighs are probably an entire facet of his oral communication skills, and decide I will need to study them closely.

I push my bag with my feet closer to the carousel, watching his large frame from behind. The guy is built. I bet he works out to relieve stress, but is he a runner? Tennis, maybe? His broad, thick shoulders imply swimming or maybe rowing. I can't see him as a gym rat, but his butt . . . that's some kind of StairMaster butt right there. Mmhmm.

I blush and realize what I'm doing and where I'm staring. *Exhaustion! Must get coffee!*

Emerson grabs my giant bags from the conveyor belt effort-lessly and without my asking. He turns back to me with the cart—trolly!—and scoops to pick up my backpack. But I need to shake off these romantic knight-in-luggage-carrying-armor vibes he's giving me.

"No, I got it." I put out my arm to stop him. Then as he starts to grumble, I quickly throw the straps over my shoulders. "Really, I *got it!*" But I sling the bag too hard and it's too heavy. "Oh, shit," I mutter under my breath, feeling myself tipping straight back like a freaking felled tree.

His arms are locked around me in an instant, one around my waist, one catching the strap of my backpack at my shoulder. My mind can't sort it all; how fast he's all around me, encompassing me, the intensity in his eyes, the sweet musk of his cologne, the feel of his hard chest against the thin cotton covering my soft curves.

As he rights us, he closes his eyes and takes a giant, exasper-ated inhale, jaw clenched. I am keenly aware of his aversion to me as he flattens his lips into a straight line. When he opens his eyes, all he has to do is cock his head to say, *I told you so.* I roll my eyes with a huff as he pulls on the bag, and I adjust to release it off my shoulders. I am too embarrassed and irked to admit he was right or thank him for catching me. Instead, I make a mad dash toward the line of cute little uniformed men with signs. I find the one that reads CANTON.

"Hi! I'm Samantha Canton!" I extend my hand.

"Charles, ma'am."

"Chaaalz!" I say in my best British accent. "Can I call you Char-lie? Or Chuck? What's your last name?"

He falters for a second, and Emerson steps up next to me. "Em-erson Clark, Canton Cards."

"Yes, sir." Charles smiles nervously as he takes over command of our luggage trolly.

"You're our driver for the whole stay, right, Charlie?"

"Yes, ma'am," he answers, but the way he says *ma'am* sounds like *mom* and makes me think of Hugh Grant for no real reason other than that I love Hugh Grant.

"Please, call me Sam. Even if Sir Stick in the Mud here calls me Miss Canton, he's the only one."

We climb into one of many waiting Mercedes town cars in a row. It's so big and new, it feels like a limousine. I can't contain my excitement as I slip into the plush leather seat. "I want the full tourist treatment, Charlie. I'm a first-timer. I mean, we came when I was a kid, but I don't remember any of it, so really, any weird facts and tidbits as we drive, you got 'em, I want to hear 'em!" I ignore how Emerson puts one hand up to his forehead against his window and instead focus on the smile Charles flashes in his rear view mirror.

I keep babbling because I'm too pumped not to. "Can I connect my phone to your sound system?"

"Of course, mi— of course." He says from up front, "It's—"

"Oh! Is it MB1833?" I find it before he has to carry on with his instructions. "Perfect! I have a whole London playlist." Horns from Lily Allen's "LDN" burst out, and I squeal. I cannot help it.

"The Rosewood, please!" Emerson almost shouts over my tunes, eyes shut.

I laugh and look over at him. He looks like he has both a migraine and a stomach bug attacking him simultaneously. "I know you have noise-canceling headphones on you, boss. Just go ahead and bust 'em out. We don't mind, do we, Charlie?"

Charles nervously eyes back and forth between the two of us, and I laugh again. Emerson shakes his head slowly and gives a sigh that I think means "I give up." I don't push him. I even turn my music down a bit. No one is dragging me off cloud nine right now, not as my music plays and London's outskirts start unfolding outside my window.

During the hour-long drive, I ask one million questions and Charles offers one million happy answers. I learn that he has been a driver for ten years, after retiring from a logistics manager position for Argo's, one of England's big-box stores. Of course, this launches a fun conversation about our company and the purpose of our trip. Charles keeps up with genuine interest and interesting tidbits.

"*Wait!* I see the Ferris wheel!" I exclaim involuntarily as I spot it off in the distance. "That means Big Ben is right over there! I can't see it, but it's right there, right?" I look over to Emerson. He gives a nod, but Charlie responds.

"Quite right. Westminster is just there, and we're about to pass the Buckingham Palace exit. You won't be able to see it all, but a good deal will be off outside your window just there." He points with a sparkle in his eye. You don't become a professional driver if you don't love two things: people and your city. Well, and I guess driving. I think Charles and I are going to be best friends in no time.

I hop again in my seat. "I'm just so happy to be here! I wasn't supposed to even come on this trip, even though I planned every amazing little detail—can you believe that? But then whatdyaknow, my boss got his wife pregnant and now it's me and Grumps here. Basically, my arch nemesis."

Emerson's head snaps to glare at me. I am pretty sure his eyes are commanding me to quit babbling our dirty laundry to our driver. I glare right back. *Too bad!* "You can call him Grumps too if you want, Charlie. He loooves that. And in case you're worried, he's not actually my boss. I mean, technically he's like a super genius and third-in-command of Dad's whole empire, and I think both Grandpa and Dad would give him their left nut if he asked."

Emerson mumbles something under his breath, and Charles's eyes go as wide as saucers. I laugh again. "Buuuut I'm the one with the last name Canton, right? So, really, I'm in charge here, is what I'm saying."

Charles says softly, "I have no doubt, ma'am, no doubt."

CHAPTER 9

SUNDAY 11:30 A.M.

Me: Look at this hotel

CAN YOU EVEN?!

[Photo]

Susan: I can't! I can't even!

Susan: How was the flight? How're things with Emerson?

Wow, I can't believe you're up

Good flight, slept almost the whole way.

Still Icy. No thawing in sight.

I don't care though bc

I AM IN LONDON BITCHESSSSSS

The Rosewood hotel is everything Google Maps, Instagram hashtags, and Yelp reviews said it would be. The Edwardian graystone building boasts pillars, cornices, balustrades, and an overall Old England vibe that I am ecstatic about.

Emerson takes charge again, thanking Charles, coordinating with the bellhops, and checking us in at the front desk. I would admire his leadership and thank him, but I'm too enthralled with the grand foyer we're standing in. The arches, the wood paneling, the mirrored ceiling, the huge paintings, the marble black-and-white floors . . . *I can't believe I get to stay here!*

I am pulled back to reality by Lydia, who insists on escorting Emerson personally to his suite. Not sure she even realizes I'm here. I get it, he's a tall drink of water, albeit a frozen one. A frozen one who, I'm sorry, did he just flash her an actual smile?! Really? Lydia didn't book this hotel for you, Mr. Clark. Lydia doesn't have to put up with your surly sighing all day long. *But* she *gets a smile?*

We are shown into our suite, and Lydia rattles off the amenities and details I already know by heart. As soon as she leaves, the mood in the room stretches tight like the pull-cord on the fancy lamp next to me. Emerson turns to me with a glare that could wilt a flower—a whole field of them.

Okay.

Did I splurge on a house suite, a luxurious two-bedroom penthouse with a living area, dining room, and kitchen? Yes, yes, I did. But does it warrant the death daggers my CFO is throwing at me? No, no, it does not.

"I don't know why you're looking at me like that—this was approved."

"By *whom*!?" he asks.

"You! And Susan! This will be our home base for weeks, plus we will take meetings here. It needed to be nice."

"It's a bit more than nice, I'd say." He pulls at the back of his thick neck with his left hand.

"Will you relax? Didn't you wonder why we didn't have our own fancy sleeping pods on the plane? I didn't splurge on everything, just a few important things."

"I'll try to remember that when we have to forego everyone's bonuses at the end of the year," he spits at me.

My turn to sigh. I am no stranger to the burden he carries. Dad and Susan have almost aged a decade each year as the rise of tech has replaced printed paper goods and physical retail shopping. "I-I was given a budget and I stuck to it. If you want to try to find us a different hotel now, be my guest." He deflates with a sigh that sounds a lot like "I'm sorry." I deflate too. "The master is supposed to be off that way from the living room, and over there after the kitchen is the other bedroom." He starts walking toward the kitchen. "I don't mind taking the—" He holds up a hand to cut me off as he walks away.

I rush through the gorgeous living room, complete with a lounge area around the seventy-five-inch TV—like, four sizes bigger than the one in my apartment—plus a separate reading nook with a fancy gold-and-glass bookshelf already stocked with books. I step into a bright, overstuffed master bedroom that doesn't disappoint.

It's classy and modern but still a bit stuffy, like I'd want a British room to be. The only thing more exciting than the dreamy king bed in layer upon layer of white linens, with its own sitting area by the window, is the sprawling marble bathroom and its massive soaking tub. *Come to mama!* I do more than one small jig as I move around my little slice of England for the next three weeks.

I look at my phone. Noon. That's 5:00 A.M. to my body. I planned a nothing day today so we could recover from our jet lag. If I can stay awake until, say, 7:00 P.M., I'll flip my body clock on the first night.

After a quick shower, I realize I'm going to need an injection of caffeine, and fast. I think about the fancy coffee maker in the suite's kitchen, but if I'm going to stay awake all afternoon, I need to get moving. I throw on a pair of running shorts and a loose sweatshirt over a sports bra, ready to hit the streets. June in London is what I'd consider spring weather, at best, but it's actually sunny out and I plan to get my heart rate up.

I walk out into the living room and pause. I expect Emerson to hole up in his room, alone, as often as possible. I wonder if I should tell him where I'm going? Or invite him along? Or ignore him altogether when we're not working?

I walk into the kitchen and dining area enough to see that his door is shut. Knocking would probably wake him up from a just-started nap, which is, everyone agrees, the stuff of nightmares. Cut-off-nap nightmares.

I decide to send him a text and head out.

> SUNDAY 12:22 P.M.
> **Me: Headed out to get coffee somewhere!**

I make it to the lobby before my phone chimes.

> Emerson: Wait, I'll join you.

It bugs me that he doesn't ask if he can join me—he just announces his plans. And why would he want to join me? Shouldn't he be introverting? I reply.

> **Me: Okay**
> **I'm in the lobby**
> Emerson: Be down just now.

I flash him a polite toothless smile when I see him approach. He's got on a similar outfit as before—slacks and a white shirt rolled up—but it's clear he's showered. He doesn't return my smile. In fact, I'm pretty sure he just frowned at my legs.

"You know, you really don't need to come with me," I say, even though what I want to do is pester him about his latest thoughts on my outfit choices.

"I do, actually."

"What?"

"We didn't arrange security here, Miss Canton. You shouldn't be flitting around London on your own."

"Yes, I should. No one here knows me. I'm totally safe."

"I'm not going to risk it."

"You're not my freaking bodyguard, *Emerson*."

"No, but I'm not about to let you get nicked on this trip."

"Nicked?"

"Stolen."

I sigh so hard, it's more of a groan. "You would rather be alone, I would rather go do this thing people like to do called *have fun*. Not sure you've ever heard of it. So, how about I just share my location with you? Then you can watch me on your phone alone in your room like a creepster, and I can actually enjoy myself. Perfect compromise."

His jaw flexes as he studies me. "Fine." He finally grunts, looking relieved.

"Fine!" I storm toward the gorgeous front doors that lead into the hotel's front courtyard complete with wrought iron gates.

"Wait, your—"

"I'll send it to you!" I yell over my shoulder.

As soon as I get out onto the sidewalk, I spot a bright red double-decker bus. I let out a shocked laugh. I pull up the maps app on my phone to see my coffee options. A text from Emerson comes through that reads "No location yet?" I resist the urge to send him a middle finger emoji and instead share my location with him. I find a café nearby with amazing food photos and start walking. Focusing on my exciting surroundings, I push my fear of pedestrian accidents out of my mind.

At first, the streets are pretty similar to New York, except where I'm walking, there aren't any skyscrapers. But then I start to see just how old and beautiful some of the buildings are. There are parts of Manhattan that I thought seemed old. Um, false. These cobblestone streets are *old* old. And it's funny how many of the buildings remind me of the flat iron building, but everywhere instead of just the one.

Also, of course, the cars are on the wrong side of the street. It's so weird!

Even in my excitement, I feel a twinge of disappointment. I think if I'm honest, I would have rather had Emerson with me. Why? As I've practiced many times, I stop and ask myself an important question: Do I want *his* company, or do I want *any* company? The latter. Definitely. I shake it off. I can have fun alone. *I can, dammit!*

After a snack, giant coffee in hand, I decide to walk to Big Ben, a thirty-minute trek. I steel myself for all the crosswalks, more nervous because I'm not in my home city. Still, London is a walking city like New York. *I'll be fine,* I tell myself again and again.

I put one headphone in, jamming to my London playlist, and leave my other ear open to all the city sounds. On the way, I can't help but imagine the joy of dragging Emerson along with me. I smile thinking of the sighs. Yes, I took a photo of a policeman on horseback with a funny hat. (Sigh.) Yep, took a multitude of selfies in the first red telephone booth I found. (Sigh.) Sure did go down into the underground just to see it, even though I'm not taking the train anywhere. And I most definitely squealed when the overhead voice said, "Mind the gap!" (Double sigh.)

SUNDAY 1:20 P.M.

Me: The National Gallery Selfie!

(From The Davinci Code!)

[Photo]

Trafalgar Square (Skyfall!)

[Photo]

Sadie: So gorgeous, where's your jet lag?!

Wiped away by my triple espresso!

Sally: Are you exploring London *by yourself*?!?!

Yep.

I have mixed feelings about it.

lol

Skye: Atta girl! Selfie game strong!

Susan: Is that safe?

Frosty has my location shared to his phone

Susan: Good

Sadie: How many strangers have you chatted with so far

Only three

Sally: lol

Skye: London's not ready for a SamStorm!

[Lightning emoji] [Lightning emoji]

Sadie: Three new besties already

Susan: Just stay safe!

CHAPTER 10

This is so crazy.

I'm pinching myself, standing just feet away from Big Ben. I take approximately one million photos on my way up to the famous clock tower. Then I take a few ridiculous selfies and ask a nice, normal-looking woman to take a photo for me. I pull out my phone to send the best couple shots to my sisters, but there's a notification.

Emerson: So, is Big Ben all you hoped he'd be?

Yes, he is, Stalker McGee

Be glad you stayed there

You would've had to take 103,039,290 photos for me already

The horror.

But at least then I'd be awake.

There's a fancy coffee machine in the kitchen

And I imagine tea, kettle, milk

And other tea things

Tea things?

I don't know, British tea fixings?

I drink coffee!

Fixings?

You gotta read it without the g.

Fixin's.

You know, accessories, trappings.

I found the coffee and tea. Thanks.

But did you find the fixin's???

I chuckle at the exchange. Look at Emerson, texting like a normal, warm-blooded human being. Though I'm not surprised he stops replying. That was probably a long exchange for him. He probably needs a little nap after that much conversation, even via text.

I also have a little skip in my step knowing he's keeping tabs on me. At the same time, my body feels like it's been hit by a truck. It's only after two o'clock, though, so I need to hang in at least five more hours. I decide to take the long way back, stopping for selfies at Buckingham Palace, Piccadilly Circus, and the British Museum.

I can feel I'm moving slowly, but I have another stop near-by the museum, it looks like from my notes. It's just a few more blocks, and it's on my list of London's most Instagrammable spots. Not that I have a public Instagram anymore—sad trombone—but I want the vibes.

I put the St. Pancras Renaissance Hotel in my phone and keep walking, listening to music in my headphones and people watching as my lids grow heavier and heavier. But wow.

The Pancras has vibes on vibes.

I feel like I'm inside *The Crown*, *Harry Potter*, and *Bridgerton* all at once. The huge winding staircases have paisley carpets, fleur-de-lis wallpapers, pointed archways, gold light fixtures, stained glass windows, the works. I actually get a little dizzy.

Thank goodness for hotel bars. I make it to the swanky bar off the lobby as my vertigo subsides. I sit and get a water and a 7 Up, which somehow costs me over ten US dollars, but I don't care. I gulp both. I quickly realize it . . .

Sitting down was a terrible mistake.

How will I ever get back up?

I try to rally, standing on sore feet, my legs screaming that they should be in bed. I manage to get moving again, off the chair and out through the lobby. *Must get back to the hotel. Just keep moving.* But at the crosswalk outside of the hotel, groggy, I step out without looking and almost get hit by one of those old-timey-car-but-modern taxis.

As I leap backward in a rush, I stumble and sidestep into a metal trash can, killing my shin. I stand and try to breathe. I can't believe what just almost happened. I can't find oxygen. I'm so tired, I almost lived out one of my greatest fears. That taxi almost crushed me. I also realize how close I'd come to pulling a Skye, as we call it in my family, and falling face-first into the concrete. I get out my phone with shaking hands. I have a twenty-five-minute walk to the hotel with a throbbing leg. *Crap!*

Me: Hey so
I need Charlie's number
Mistakes were made.
Legs were injured.
Emerson: Are you hurt??
I'm not bleeding.
You're at The Pancras?
Yeah
And it really is very Instagrammable
Also, can jet lag make you high?
Asking for a friend.
Just stay there.

I sit for fifteen minutes, texting my sisters and calming my pulse with deep breaths. At the start, it felt like a real panic attack might settle in, and flashes of the taxi and images of my mother's accident kept pressing into my thoughts. But the throb in my leg and the pings on my phone help me relax. I look up for Charlie's Mercedes every few minutes.

"Miss Canton," I hear. Emerson is getting out of a taxi and heading toward me.

"Where's Charlie?"

"Can you walk?"

"Yeah, yeah, I can." He looks beyond worried as he watches me take a few steps. "What are you doing here?"

"The taxi was closer than Charlie." He gestures back toward the car with one hand.

"Okay, but I'm fine, really. You didn't need to come."

He sighs again.

"Right. Not getting nicked." I climb into the back of a car identical to the one that almost smushed me like a bug.

"You're shaking," Emerson observes. I'm not sure if he's asking for more information, because the words sound like a command. I explain anyway.

"I wasn't looking at that corner. I-I st-stepped out in front of a taxi." He starts to say something, but I cut him off. "I just kicked a trash can, though. I jumped back kinda crazy and lost my balance and fell into the metal trash can." He is still glaring at me and gives one of his frustrated exhales. "You didn't need to come get me. I was just exhausted and not paying attention."

He inhales an exaggerated breath before responding to me. "You do realize you didn't need to see the whole of London on your first day?"

I scrunch up my face and imitate him. "The whooole of Lundun on ya fehst day."

"Your accent is rubbish."

I can see he's about to crack, so I push.

"It's *fantastic*."

"Utter garbage."

"It's the best British accent you've ever heard in your life! You love it! You can't get enough. Your absolute *bloody* favor— AHH! Ah ha ha ha!" I can't help but cry out. "I saw it! You smiled!"

He did.

He smiled.

At me.

I can't believe I saw his full smile of perfect, straight white teeth. Now I know the full extent of it, how his skin crinkles around his unbelievable eyes. His face brightens and softens all at once. It's like a hit of oxygen when I didn't even know I was suffocating. The triumph I feel now, the swelling under my sternum, is so powerful I actually put a hand to my chest.

"You've gone loony." He looks out the window, but he's still smiling. It's smaller now but still there. I, meanwhile, am beaming.

"Let's see, today's Sunday . . . sixteen. Took sixteen days to crack Emerson Clark!" I squeal. He looks back at me with confusion. I point at his now-scowling face. "That's the first time I've seen you smile."

"Absolutely false."

"Okay, second time. You did smile at Lydia."

"At who?"

"Lydia at the front desk. You know, the blonde who, uh, wanted to *show you to your room*, if you know what I mean." I waggle my eyebrows. I'm being ridiculously goofy, and I can't help it. I'm so tired, and this whole smile-showing-teeth incident has made me downright giddy.

His scowl deepens. "Are you drunk?"

"On the taste of sweet victory, yes." He shakes his head some more, which just encourages me. "I can't wait to tell Skye I saw your actual teeth. She won't believe it."

"You're cut off," he says as he grabs my phone out of my hand.

"All I had was some weird-tasting 7 Up! Cut off from what?!"

"From functioning. Just sit there." He's still almost smiling. "Quietly, if possible."

"You're really just going to take my phone like I'm not going to freak out and try to—"

"Have you eaten?" His deep, smooth voice cuts me off as he shrugs his hands out of reach.

"I had a snack hours ago, but, uh, wow. Now I don't know which is worse: the hunger or the tired . . . tiredness. Tiredness? Fatigue."

"Right." He hands me back my phone with the hotel room service menu pulled up. I'm so tired I forgot he'd had my phone hostage for a minute. Instead, I'm thinking about how he already pulled up a menu and is once again taking charge of our situation.

"Wait, we had the whole afternoon free—shouldn't you be with your family?"

He just shakes his head.

"Ooookay. Let's see." I scroll through the menu. "Oh, man. I've let myself get too hungry. Now I'm in the Everything Zone where all the choices sound amazing and I can't choose. I should proba-bly make myself get a salad, but there are three delicious-sounding options." I catch Emerson moving his hand up to pinch the bridge of his nose. "Sorry," I loud whisper at him. "What are you getting?"

"The salmon," he says as he releases his brow.

"That comes with veggies. Bummer, I was hoping it came with fries, and then I could steal some. If I order some fries, will you split them with me?"

"No."

"Jeez. No sugar and no fries. What a sad, sad life. All right, I guess I'll get the chicken Caesar salad and—" I cut myself off when

his hand resumes another exasperated position, holding his forehead. I must give Snowy a constant migraine. My turn to sigh. This
is going to be such a long trip.

I add my food to the app and realize he's already put in his
order. Again, I'm impressed. I've had men order food for me before, at a restaurant, in a presumptuous sort of way, which I didn't
mind. But I don't think I can remember a guy ever pulling up a
menu on my phone and taking care of ordering. It's always been
more of a "Will you order us some food, babe?" type of situation.
I keep my mouth shut for the sake of Emerson's head the last ten
minutes of the drive.

Back at the hotel, I head to the bathroom to splash my face and
use the facilities, and then the suite doorbell chimes with our food.

"Yaaaaasssss!" I call out as I head for the door. "Thank you!"
I tell the attendant as I gesture for him to come in. He wheels the
cart to our dining room table and transfers the covered dishes. As
he moves the cart back to the door, I realize I don't have any cash
on me. "Oh, I haven't found an exchange yet—"

"Cheers." Emerson appears behind me, quickly handing the
guy a few pounds. I give them both a big, relieved smile as he
leaves and Emerson shuts the door.

"It smells so good, I think I'm gonna die." I skip back over to
the table. I start to open up the dishes to see what's what. "Oh
man, these look like good fries. You never know if fries— Chips?
Crisps? Whatever. You never know if they're going to be soggy
duds, ya know? But these look perfect. I won't tell anyone if you
have some." I smile at him, but he doesn't look up. He gathers his
dish and cutlery and starts to head toward his room.

"See you in the morning, Miss Canton," he says softly.

I feel a fresh sting of disappointment, even though just hours
ago I told myself Emerson would spend all his time introverting in
his room, and that that would be fine with me. I take a breath and

pull out my phone, eager to look through the day's photos. And I'll text my sisters, who will keep my company.

Wait. No.

I don't need company to enjoy my meal. I need to get used to this. This will be my reality for the next few weeks. My eyes start to burn, but I tell myself it's just the fatigue. A few meals alone in this gorgeous hotel room won't kill me. And he'd be terrible dinner company anyway.

After I finish eating and recover my plates, I head to bed. I can't fight the fatigue anymore, even if it's only just after 5:00 P.M. I put in a valiant effort. After my sacred six-step nighttime facial routine, I hit the sheets. I plug in my phone and decide to double-check with The Cold One.

Me: Tomorrow is our retail locations
Starting at 10
Leave here at 9:30
Emerson: Right.
Sorry if I woke you
I was trying to make it to 7
But I can't carry on
It's all right
Shoot, I did wake you?
Why didn't you put on DND, you weirdo!
My bad!
I will let you go back to sleep!
Good night!

No reply. *Ughhhhhh.* Suddenly I fear that tomorrow is going to suck.

CHAPTER 11

I wake up and stretch with a smile. I feel like I've slept for an eternity—had to have been ten hours.

Nine hours! Yes!

Oh.

It's 2:00 A.M. here.

I close my eyes and will myself back to sleep, but my body is buzzing with enough energy to power a small town. It's only ten at home.

Me: Well, I'm up for the day!

. . . At 2 AM.

=(

Nicole: Oh nooooo

How was yesterday, other than your gorgeous selfies?

Pretty good!

Jack Frost here went to great lengths to make sure I didn't get "nicked" Taken style

But then he bolted to his room

So I sat and ate dinner alone at our dining table.

Womp womp.

Forget Emerson and message Chase already!

Ehhhh I don't know

Think of the transatlantic sexting
[Link to Instagram profile]

I smile at Chase's profile. He's got the hot-nerd thing going on, complete with bowties. And even suspenders. Suspenders could be hot. If I'm remembering right from the office, he's about my height with my heels on, which is not ideal but not a deal-breaker. He has a nice average build, but mostly I'm drawn into his smile. He smiles wide for every photo, like he's not holding them back, like some *other* numbers nerd I know. Also, he posts pretty regularly, out at bars, out with friends, at work.

Me: You might be on to something.
Great smile, right?
Nicole: Right, and that bow tie is working for him.
Ask Emerson about him. He's his boss, after all.
Right!
But I have a feeling he'll say he's efficient and proficient
LOL
Lol. I'm going to bed now. Night!
I should try to go back to sleep too.
Night! <3

I try.

I fail.

I get back on Instagram. I check out Chase again, and almost follow him from my new private account but stop myself, shame and grief washing over me before I can tap the button. *No men, Sam!* Without thinking about it, I go to Miranda the Model's Instagram account. I scroll for a bit past artsy photos of her and her other giraffe-esque model friends and find myself getting grumpy. She is super skinny, like unattainable skinny. But not gross skinny.

She still has some boobs somehow. *Cough, they're probably fake, cough.*

I almost abandon her profile, and then I find one: a photo of her and Emerson at an event. The man knows how to wear a tux, that is undeniable. And they do look gorgeous together, like they stepped out of an ad for expensive vodka with her bleached hair and his icy eyes. But he's not smiling a real smile. No teeth, no crinkles. And that makes me glad, even though it shouldn't. I shake my head at myself and put my phone back on the nightstand. Next to my phone, I find my master binder and decide to flip through and do some review to pass the time.

I manage to get in a few more hours of sleep sometime between two and seven, but at seven, I can't stay in bed anymore. I throw on a bra under my tee and sleep shorts and grab my binder to head out in search of coffee. As I near the kitchen, I catch Emerson as he turns his back to me and heads into his room.

In a robe.

Emerson in a soft, white robe.

He shuts the door, never noticing me, and my brain is fully scrambled.

To see him in a state of undress, wet hair, coffee in hand. Was he wearing slippers? Barefoot? I'm so befuddled I actually imagine that he's probably wearing a suit under that robe, and he just threw it on for warmth. Because I can't comprehend that under there, just feet from me, maybe he was just in his underwear? Or . . . naked?

My pulse is racing. *Calm the heck right on down, Samantha!*

I take a deep breath and get my coffee and rummage through the breakfast options, making noise so he'll know I'm also up. In the back of my mind, I hope he'll appear again in his fluffy, cozy not-suit. Then, as I eat a few microwaved egg bites and flip through my binder at the table not far from his door, I find myself hoping he'll pop out—fully dressed, half-dressed, I don't care.

But he doesn't.

I go to my room and get ready for our day out at one of three Canton Cards shops across London. I'm excited. Walking into a Canton store has always felt like home to me, ever since I was a child. I decide on a bright coral sundress with a black suit jacket and black wedges that will be the least offensive to my feet, which still haven't recovered from yesterday.

I walk out into the hotel suite to see Mr. Clark in all his suited glory. There at the table, eyeing my binder, he stands with one hand in his pocket. He's wearing a black suit, black vest, shiny, large black shoes—I should not be noticing how large his shoes are—and a yellow tie. A yellow tie? I feel like I'm being punk'd. Where are the cameras? I've never seen him sport a bright color in his life. I let out a snorty scoff sound, causing him to look up at me.

"Nice tie." It's an accusation. He looks confused. "C'mon, Mr. Brutal Honesty, fess up. It's just us here. There is no way yellow is your favorite color. In fact, I don't even buy that that's your tie. Did you steal that tie from a man on the street? A happy man who likes happy things? Oh, no, did you take that off a dying man? A home-less man?"

"This, a homeless man's tie?" He holds it out, so I walk closer to him. I want to reach out and touch the fabric. It's irrational and honestly a bit scary how badly I want to touch that glowing yellow silk. But my dinner alone, his brow that is already itching to be pinched, his shudder when I grabbed him on the plane—they stop me. I lean over and take a close look instead. *Crap! Now I'm in his manly scent cloud!*

I hop back. "Okay. You didn't steal it from a homeless man. A dying rich man, then." He sighs. "And there it is! My first sigh of the day!" I turn and start to head toward the door at the same time he does. "Think I'll reach twenty today? Fifty?" He says nothing as we head down the hall. "One hundred? Boy. Ambitious goal, but I'll do my best." He pushes the button on the elevator and turns to me and sighs with passion.

I smile and raise my eyebrows. "Man! I am off to a great start!" I laugh as we get onto the elevator. Emerson, on the other hand, looks miserable. I decide to stop talking to spare the poor man. I decide inwardly to see if I can actually keep his exasperation to fewer than ten sighs today.

"Hold it, would you please!" a gruff, accented voice calls from the hall. Emerson holds the door for a family to join us. The man is a giant, his wife is not petite, and two teen boys, in uniforms of some sort, are about the size of two small houses. They also have a good-size toddler boy in tow. Emerson and I shift back into the corner to give them room. The toddler stares at me, so I make goofy faces the entire ride. Eventually, he starts giggling and making my crazy faces right back.

But I barely register what my face is actually doing. Because the entire side of my right arm is touching the left side of Emerson. My arm starts to warm, even though I tell it not to. Even though I remind my brain that the man next to me is rude and grumpy and cannot stand me. I tell that thump in my chest that he is too old, too stiff, too vanilla, and too frigid for any of my parts to be melting around him.

None of me listens.

———

"Bernard!" I say as I bound into the Canton Cards shop on the east side of the city. I'm ecstatic our first few days are with our home team of franchisees. Bernie, as I call him in my mind, is the owner and manager of this location, and he's approaching the front door as we step in. His face, which looks like a young Santa Claus, is sporting a wide welcoming smile.

"Miss Canton, welcome, welcome." He beams as he reaches us and extends a hand.

"Samantha, please." I smile. "And this of course is Emerson Clark. Emerson, as you know, this is Bernard Johns."

Emerson gives him a polite grin and says "Pleasure" as Bernie moves from shaking my hand to his. I take in the store. I am not at all distracted by that word coming out of Iceman's mouth. *Not at all!*

"It looks great in here!" I say, turning to survey the aisles, and it mostly does. The space is cozy but bright. The signs and displays in signature Canton purple pop against the wooden shelves and tables. Every inch is covered in cards, paper goods, and cute little gifts. There are areas of the store that clearly need work, but I never open with anything even close to negative when I audit our shops.

"Oh, thank you. I'm sure you'll have lots of tips for us to spruce up the ole gal." He gestures his arms around the shop, showing his nerves a bit.

"We're here to help, yes." I spin back around. "I thought I'd work my way around the shop while you two dig into your numbers, and then we can break for a late lunch."

"Lovely, right," Bernie says.

"Will Stacy be joining us for lunch?" I ask him.

"Oh, she'd be gobsmacked, I think. Are you sure?"

"Yes, please, we'd love to meet her! We're a family company, you know that!"

"Quite right. Big boss's daughter here and all, yes, she'll love that."

"Perfect. I'll just put my purse behind the counter and dive in."

"Shall we go to the office then?" Bernie looks up at Emerson.

"After you." Emerson opens up his arms. I force myself to

look away from the man who truly stands out like a Greek statue, handsome and chiseled and towering over me and Bernie and all the displays.

I move to the front display windows with my pen and note-book, waiting for my excitement to kick in. I am not one of the merchandising geniuses Dad has back in Tulsa who comes up with the creative in-store displays, but I know how they're meant to look. I know when something is off, or how a small adjustment of product can make a display pop.

I make small notes of what I notice, but the rush of giddiness I used to find in our stores doesn't greet me, like it hasn't for at least a year. I was hoping that seeing our brand in Europe would rekindle my fire for this work, but now that the excitement of trip planning has worn off, I'm wishing I was just out sightseeing.

Still, I lose myself in the tasks that need to be done. There are so many small tweaks to be made that will really help Bernie's numbers. I move shelving units and adjust shelves. I carry various items back and forth across the store as I rework a few of the displays. I take off my jacket and put my hair up, and at one point without realizing it, I take off my shoes. Susan would absolutely die, but the store is carpeted and I'm steering clear of any customers.

I bend over to pull some tea towels off a bottom corner shelf when I hear a throat clearing behind me. I snap up and turn to see Emerson, whose eyebrows are up high above those light blue la-dy-killers that dash down my sweating, jacket-less figure and land at my bare feet. I'm about to mutter some almost-apology about my impropriety, but he turns to leave.

"Lunch," he says flatly.

"Lunch," I mimic him softly, sticking out my tongue. No one hears or sees it, but it makes me feel a bit better. I find my shoes and jacket and purse, and we head out to a nearby pub. Bernie and his wife Stacy are delightfully laid-back, laughing at my jokes and sharing funny stories about their kids. I gush over their family photos and share stories of my nephews. Emerson says almost nothing the whole meal, but the rest of us don't seem to notice or mind. After about an hour, Stacy excuses herself and I start to go through my notes with Bernie. It's then that I'm attacked by a case of the yawns.

As I launch into my second page of ideas, coffees appear at the table and Emerson thanks the server. I look over at him for the first time in maybe the whole meal and realize he looks nearly dead. I wonder what I must look like.

"Well, between the two of you, we'll be right sorted for next quarter." Bernie grins as I take a couple sips of coffee.

"Oh yeah?" I look between him and Emerson.

"He really is a wizard, this one." Bernie gestures at Emerson, who is a stark contrast sitting still and ramrod straight. "Must be that English upbringing." Bernie winks.

"I prefer robot over wizard myself, but yes, numbers seem to be his primary language, don't they?" This gets me a hearty laugh from the young Santa and an irritated grin from the Android himself. No sigh, though—*win!* "Let's head back, and I can show you a few more things before we call it a day."

Emerson holes up in the office while Bernie, two employees, and I go over a few of the example displays I changed for them. They ask great questions and show genuine excitement for the changes. Excitement I used to feel.

Hope springs up in Bernie's eyes, and it makes my chest tight. I know it's been a hard year for him, for all the retailers. I also know when we come back in a couple weeks, the interior of the store will go from good to absolute amazeballs. I hope Emerson is working similar—no, much bigger, better—magic in the back. I may not love my job like I used to, but I know thousands are depending on us, so I put on a smile to match Bernie's.

———

"Oh man, I'm glad I went with the burger this time. Again, you should take a couple fries." I pad out into the dining room in joggers and a sweatshirt. Emerson has lost his jacket, but otherwise, the man is unchanged. He doesn't even look famished. The nerve. He starts to grab his plate, but we'd been silent zombies in the car. Refreshed by my shower, I stop him.

"Wait, can I just ask you a few questions, and then you can go back to your lair?"

He sighs.

"Hey! That's only number three!" I smile at him. He squints at me, unbelieving. "Now, hey, if you sigh when I'm not around, those do not count. I cannot bear the burden of all your sighs on my dainty shoulders, Mr. Clark. Look at me—I can shrug, but I'm no Atlas."

He rolls his eyes and sits down and mumbles, "So dramatic."

"So? How bad is it for Bernie?" I ask, taking a bite of my burger.

"Not ideal." He grimaces and then takes a bite of his chicken.

"Uhhh, not ideal like he's closing next month, or not ideal like all retail sucks right now and he'll be fine?" I study him.

"Close to the latter."

"Do you think he'll actually do everything you told him to do?"

He looks down at the table. "Reluctantly."

I nod and wince a bit. "My advice is much more fun than yours. Way easier to move price tag stickers from the front of a product to the bottom than to, oh, you know, fire a beloved employee."

He nods again. I am still energized from the day, so I carry on.

"Well, at least we left him with hope in his eyes and a list of boxes to check. Everyone likes a clear list, right? He's not wondering what to do or how to fix things—now he just has to follow through." Emerson gives me a half nod. "That lunch place was fun, even if it was, as you'd say"—I throw out my most obnoxious cockney accent—"'a real bit dodgy.'"

That earned me a choking cough and an eye roll.

"I read online they had amazing fish and chips, and Bernie said it was the best he'd had *in ages*, so score one for me and the binder!" He eyes my binder on the table but doesn't say anything, which irks me. He could flip through there and find any contact of ours and prepare himself for an amazing meeting. That binder is a dadgum work of art *and* science, and he has yet to comment. "Anyway, tomorrow should be better. We'll hit both central and west side, and neither of them are as bad off as Bernie. So. Should be fun!"

He gives me a slow nod that says "if you say so." I ramble on a bit more about the stores and owners we'll meet tomorrow, and some of the changes I'm imagining. I talk about London, the trip, and my texts with my sisters. By the time he's done eating, I've recapped my entire day and plan for tomorrow. He stands, covers his dish, and gives me a slight bow like it's the freaking 1800s.

"Good night," I say. He doesn't respond and goes to his room. I imagine him on the other side, leaning against the door, eyes closed, breathing in sweet relief to be rid of me.

My turn to sigh again.

CHAPTER 12

I was right that the next two stores were much easier. Emerson and I split off right at the start to work our respective magic. I didn't see much of him, but I heard his rave reviews again over lunch. Maybe, inexplicably, talking about numbers gives him a much more human bedside manner?

Somehow his number crunching puts our owner operators at ease and gives them hope. The response was obvious on Otis's face as we wrapped up lunch after going through his store in central London. Then I saw it in Farrah's smile after our afternoon with her on the west side.

"Are you all up for some dinner?" I ask.

"Absolutely!" Farrah says in unison with her daughter Trina, who I'd guess is a little older than Sally, and very hip and London-y.

"Wait, can we grab a photo for the gram?" Trina says as we head out onto the sidewalk.

"Yes, good idea, Trina. We've got an actual Canton here, after all. And the bigwig CFO home from 'cross the pond!"

"Oh, okay, sure!" I say. "Maybe just under the awning?" I throw my arms up as if presenting the store.

"Yes, lovely!" Farrah coos. "And you too, Mr. Clark, c'mon."

Emerson walks over as fast as a slug and stands next to me

like a lamppost.

"C'mon, Mr. Clark, I won't tell Miranda." I smash into him, loop my arm through his, and throw up my back foot. He remains frozen. Trina bursts out laughing at whatever is on the screen.

"What?" I ask her.

"Maybe, uh, give it another go." Farrah giggles.

I squeeze Emerson's arm.

"Dammit, just smile for five seconds, Icy!" I say through gritted teeth.

"Got it!" Trina says, and I dart away from Emerson before he actually vomits on me. "You want to post these on your Insta?"

"Oh, I don't have social accounts anymore, actually." I hear how sad I sound and feel equally pathetic. "But! Send me all of them, and I'll make sure they get posted to all our main corporate accounts on all the platforms!" I pat myself on the back for recovering so well. When the photos arrive on my phone, I see what she's laughing at.

Oh, wow.

It is perfection.

It's the first shot she took, and I am cheesing hard at the camera while Jack Frost looks down at me with utter shock. I don't know that I've ever seen someone look more uncomfortable. I start laughing, hard and loud, letting the fatigue, embarrassment, and irritation take over my vocal cords.

"Bloody hilarious, isn't it?" Trina asks.

"Holy crap, it's our entire relationship, and this trip, caught in a rectangle. I can't look away!" I walk with her down the street, Farrah hovering as well. Emerson is ahead of us, well on his way to the restaurant already.

Over dinner, the girls and I talk and talk and talk, and Emerson listens, nods, and listens. Farrah tries to ask him about his family, but he shuts her down. He's not rude, but he's also not subtle. I recover for him with questions about London and Farrah's sisters and gaggle of nieces and nephews.

Trina insists I let her and her cousins take me out on the town one of the nights we're here. I promise to try to make it happen, and I mean it. It sounds like everything I need, just on a different night, after I've adjusted to the time change. We happily exchange hugs and cell phone numbers before I climb into Charlie's car behind Emerson.

"Well, I thought today was *smashing*, Mr. Clark, don't you agree?" He's holding his head with his eyes closed. "Well, Charlie, lemme tell you, it was. It was smashing. Much better than yesterday. The stores are in better shape, our franchisees loved us, including Mr. Clark and his spreadsheets, I was actually awake the whole time, and I think Trina is pretty awesome. That's our franchisee's daughter—she said she'd take me out on the town. Isn't that great!"

"Very good, Miss Samantha," Charlie's voice is soft as he peers out from under his chauffeur hat.

"I know. It'll be so great to have a friend for this trip. I mean, other than you, Charlie, of course."

"And Mr. Clark." Charlie eyes us sheepishly, and his full cheeks turn pink.

I look over at the potential friend in question. "Um, are you all right? Headache?"

He nods.

I whisper loudly to Charlie, "Kill the music for our *friend*." Charlie nods. The rest of the drive, I stay mostly quiet, only talking softly to Charlie here and there.

At the hotel, Emerson and I practically stumble our way up to the suite, jet lag catching up with our limbs. He waves his hand wordlessly on his way to his room.

"Wait!" I say.

His body seems to crumple in response.

"No talking, I promise," I say softly. "I just wanted to tell you peppermint or lavender tea helps with headaches. We have both." His brows raise. "I can make some—it'll take two seconds."

"I can—"

"Don't talk. You're looking very vampire-turns-zombie. Just sit down."

He obeys.

I start the tea kettle and find the packets. I hold up the two options in front of him. He chooses peppermint.

"Good choice, who wants to drink lavender? That'd be like sipping potpourri or perfume or something. Blech, no thank you," I say, then realize I'm talking. "Sorry," I whisper. I dig around for cookies and pull out a box, then remember he doesn't eat sugar. The kettle clicks, so I pour the water in the bag and hand him the cup and saucer. He nods slowly, gets up, and goes to his room.

No thank-you.

No grin.

No tap on the side of my arm to acknowledge me.

Well, o-freaking-kay then, see if I ever help you again, Ice Hole!

> **Me: How it's going, you ask?**
> **Like this:**
> **[Photo]**
> Skye: Bahahahahaha
> Susan: OMG What is happening? Explain!
> Sadie: This isn't staged? You didn't tell him to look at you like
> . . .
> Sally: Like he hates you
> Susan: Like he's confused
> Sadie: I'm going with befuddled

Skye: Like he needs to take a fat dump and also cry

Simple, I touched him.

Note my arms are wrapped around his arm.

That's all it takes, ladies.

I've officially lost all my mojo

Susan: You didn't say something?

Skye: Good call, Suze. What were you blabbing immediately before and after this was taken?

I said I wouldn't tell Miranda, his gf

Is that a big deal?

I was joking because he didn't want to take the pic

Skye: We need truckloads of context to advise

Susan: Sounds harmless to me

Sadie: I'm with Skye, paint us a picture

Sally: OMG if you're going to write a novella, please type it all out in one text and not 10,000 short texts.

Skye: What Sally said.

There is no context, that's it.

"C'mon, Mr. Clark, I won't tell Miranda."

Then THAT face.

Skye: Maybe he has a thing about physical touch

You know what, maybe.

He caught me falling at the airport

And looked disgusted then too.

Skye: I'm sorry, he what now?

Sadie: What kind of fall! Details!

It was nothing

I fell backward, and he caught me before I went all the way down Skye style.

Skye: [Middle finger emoji]

Sally: lol

Sadie: Well, that was chivalrous of him.

I guess, but the facial expression ruined it.

Susan: Maybe no more touching Emerson.

No problem, boss lady.

———

I am excited for our plans today, and still not adjusted to the time, so it's before six when I make my way to the coffee pot.

And there in the kitchen is Emerson.

Without a shirt on.

Sweaty and panting.

I am now panting too.

I am also staring.

I tell myself to look away. I beg my eyes to stop, but they can't. I knew he was built, but I mean . . . *Shit balls motherfffff—*

I was right. A six-pack, defined pecs, huge arms—I was not expecting such huge arms!—and that V thing leading into his gym shorts, the distinct muscle that you only see in underwear commercials.

"Pardon?" he asks.

Oh! I said shit balls mother out loud.

And my mouth is still making an F sound.

"No, uh, I didn't see anything!" I blurt like a moron, standing there, seeing everything. "I mean, okay, yes, I, um, see everything, but it's not like you're naked and you're the one in the common area. This, this is the common area." My arm starts gesticulating without my consent. "You're the one out here glistening shirtless and like how? Why? How? Personal trainer. Has to be. For eight hours a day or something. How do you ever get any work done, Emerson? How? And you know what, I just gotta say, damn it, well done, Miranda." My hands are now clapping of their own volition.

I'm clapping. His eyebrows raise. "Yeah, I said it—go, Miranda. I'm woman enough to admit it. That freaking beanpole model girl-friend of yours is one lucky little bitch."

He throws his head back and laughs.

Emerson Clark laughs. Hard.

And the jolt of it, well, somewhere a zip code with a broken transformer box just got their power restored, I am sure of it. His torso shakes with the throaty sound. His eyes crinkle. His sweaty hair falls back from his face. It is entirely, utterly too much.

"Now you're laughing?! Are you kidding me? With the teeth!? Get out, go, get out of here. Go to your room." I hold up my hand to block my view of him. "Seriously, get your water and get out of *the common area*!"

I realize I sound hysterical. I also realize that it has been a long time since I've been around a man, or on a date, or seen a man shirtless. Months. This is not a crush forming on the Ice King. This is the by-product of loneliness, shame, dashed dreams, broken ex-pectations, everything the last few months have been. This is just a stage of grief—that's got to be what this is.

After he leaves, I get my coffee and a banana and go back to my room to get ready. I will not be coming back out into the com-mon area until the absolute last second before we depart. I will also strive to stop calling it "the common area" like a nervous tick.

I finally build my courage to face him again, popping out of my door, just as, I'm positive, he was about to call out that it was time to go. He's there in a three-piece navy suit, which is now a whole separate thing, because I know what's underneath that sucker. I can feel my face flushing as I look up at him, but he's not looking my way.

It's not until we're next to one another in the elevator, his eyes straight ahead, that I even register he's wearing a pink tie. A pink tie? What the actual hell? I am dying to comment, to demand to know who bought these new ties and when. Come to think of it, yesterday's tie was a deep purple. So dark I didn't think of it, but his tie was purple. There is no way he had these ties before this trip. Is he mocking me? Trying to match me? Trying to meet me in the middle?

I think these questions and one million more, but I keep my mouth shut. He is his normal chilly self, as if this morning's world-changing laugh never happened. He doesn't engage with me or Charlie, doesn't make eye contact. I am relieved but also annoyed. I thought a bit of nudity, and my utter ridiculousness in response to said nudity, was just what we needed to find the beginnings of a real friendship. I guess I was wrong.

I shake off my thoughts when we get close to the Sainsbury's corporate office. Sainsbury's is like Walmart back home, which means huge orders from us each year. We're meeting with Julie Nymes, their cards and party buyer. As the car slows, I say my mantra to myself under my breath.

"Hmm?" Emerson turns to me, suddenly noticing he is not alone in the vehicle.

I shake my head. "Nothing. Let's do this."

I wonder if Emerson is nervous at all. This is the biggest meeting I've ever been to in my life, by far, but it's really his show. I can talk small numbers and product specifics, but today, he and Julie will talk huge orders, margins, and projections. I will take notes and try to keep up.

After pleasantries are exchanged and beverages are poured, Julie jumps right in. It's then that I see Emerson Clark's bedside manner in all its glory. Adam told me to get him talking about numbers—now I see why.

First, he listens, and not absently or even actively. He listens deeply. As if he's trying to hear words behind words, meanings underneath meanings. Julie has explained something she noticed with sales of our products last quarter, and I can see Emerson's mind working for a beat before he responds.

"Brilliant, yes, I agree, that's exactly what these number show," he says with . . . enthusiasm. I'm shook. Julie gives a small grin, happy to be on Team Genius. Emerson wakes up his iPad. "Now, look what next year will look like if we exchange the quantity of these two orders and increase this margin here by just three percent."

"Wait, three percent? That's it?" Julie sits back.

Emerson grins, and I am pretty sure I blush at the sight. "Just three, yes."

Julie is smiling and shaking her head. "That's negligible. No one will balk at that."

"Precisely." Emerson pulls up a new spreadsheet. "We can do that in a few places in your last order, again negligible, and change things dramatically. Here, let's see what you think about this one." He turns his body toward Julie with his iPad.

Julie is lighting up like a Christmas tree before my very eyes, and I get it. While he is the clear genius, and could've come in with rigid step-by-step instructions, he has already complimented her, let her figure out his methods, and asked for her to weigh in. He could almost be a teacher. Except for the whole people-in-a-classroom part. But now my mind is picturing him in an elbow-patch sweater at the desk of my hot history teacher Mr. Brandt, and I'm blushing again.

I get back to writing my notes, which I have completely forgotten about while watching the Emerson Show the last ten minutes. I can feel my heart racing and my temperature climbing. This is not good. I cannot crush on the Clarksicle! I cannot! I write NO on the top of my notes, underline it, and circle it fifteen times for good measure.

Just get through this meeting, and it's my turn to do the wowing! Focus!

CHAPTER 13

After the meeting at the Sainsbury offices, it's time for the fun part of our day. We climb into a limo together and head to our lunch destination. Julie's personal Instagram is littered with plant porn like a bona fide hashtag plant lady. So we're headed to the amazing Sky Garden, an indoor sanctuary at the top of a skyscraper overlooking the city.

"Have you been to Sky Garden before?" I ask Julie on our way.

"Yes, once when it first opened—2015, I think it was?"

"That's where we're headed for lunch, I hope that's okay."

"Okay? That place is gorgeous! I always tell myself I need to go, but you know how it is. Never go sightsee in your own city, right?"

"Totally. New York is the same." I turn to Emerson. "Have you been?"

"I've not, no."

"Oh, you'll love it, it's absolutely stunning." Julie gushes.

I knew there was a chance she'd been, or even that she went regularly, but I also knew she'd never experienced what I set up for us. The garden has a restaurant and bar, but I paid an obscene amount—*remember, biggest European account, Mr. CFO, calm your balls*—to have a dining table set up in a corner of the garden itself. Not only will we be at a private table surrounded by indoor jungle, but we'll be floating in a far corner of the glass building, with noth-

119

ing but windowpane between us and the sweeping view. I'm giddy as we pull up to the building.

As we bundle into the small elevator, I look over at Emerson, hoping to see some signs of pride or approval at my amazing plan. He looks grumpier than usual. As we step out into the garden, my breath leaves me. It's incredible. Glass, light, and green green green everywhere. It's a plant mom's dream. Julie and I are beaming, and Emerson looks a bit sick.

"Canton," I say to a hostess at a podium by the restaurant.

"Oh, yes, we've been waiting! Wicked setup. Can't believe we haven't done it before." She is squealing in delight. "Right this way!" Julie looks intrigued, and I am about to burst at the seams. Emerson is turning a shade of green that rivals the bright, almost neon leaves of a plant by the hostess stand.

As we make our way slowly through the garden paths to the corner, Julie oohs and aahs, commenting on new plants and wondering how they manage to keep some of the peskier varieties alive. Our special corner comes into view, and Julie gasps. I break into a huge smile and make some involuntary squeak noise. I look back to Emerson, who's taking his precious time joining us, and notice he is sweating badly. Like make-everyone-around-you-uncomfortable levels of sweat.

"Go ahead. Emerson and I just need to talk to the staff real quick!" I say to Julie and turn quickly to pull Emerson aside before Julie sees the full scope of whatever exactly is happening on his face.

I whisper-yell, "What's going on! Headache? Do you need to run to the little boy's room? Because now is not the best time to go full Hulk—the color, not the muscles . . . well, actually the muscles too. I guess I can indeed verify that! Again, I'm going with personal trainer— I mean, wait! Focus! This is our biggest account, you know that!" I tug him over toward an exterior wall out of the walkway.

"Damn it," he grumbles as he reaches the window, then he turns in my direction and all two hundred–something pounds of beautiful, stacked hard muscle starts to fall over.

Onto me.

"Huuuffff! Emerson! I can't!" I grunt out, trying to catch him, wobbling on my stilettos. He shifts up and steadies himself with one hand on each of my shoulders. I look at his face and then back at the window behind him. "Holy crap balls, it's heights. You're afraid of heights?!"

"Just a tad," he grunts out, still using me as a support. "It's nothing."

"Emerson Clark," I grit through my teeth as I move one foot back to steady us. "You are as green as that palm right there! I can't believe this! This! This is why I asked you multiple times to check our itinerary! I wouldn't have planned a lunch floating in the sky if I'd known! Uggghhhh!"

"But a bloody smart idea—you said she loves plants," he slurs.

"Shh! You can't go to the table like that. Go back to the hotel, and I'll tell her you're ill."

"No, I can—"

"You can't, you really, *really* can't. I'm getting ill just looking at you looking ill. We're about to have that swapping dry-heave-sounds-back-and-forth situation any second. Go." I push him away from the wall and back toward the walkway.

"I'm sorry," he rasps as he steps away. I roll my eyes. *This is why we write out detailed itineraries! Idiot!*

I make my way back to Julie and explain Emerson's illness that's so sudden it must be food poisoning, because what else could it be, right? She's so giddy she barely registers his absence. We then have an award-winning lunch with an award-winning view and with what I dare say was some award-winning plant-based conversation.

I asked a few questions here and there with my basic knowledge of pretty succulents and trendy fiddle-leaf figs, and the woman babbled on for ages. Somewhere in the back of my mind, I registered that this must be what Skye feels like when she asks me a simple question and then doesn't get a word in with me for twenty minutes. It feels very weird to be on the other side of this kind of conversation. I don't hate it. And I love that Julie is positively glowing. By the time we're finished with our late lunch, dessert, and cocktails, it's early evening. We hug, and she thanks me for a lovely day, then I make my way to Charlie at the curb.

When I enter the hotel suite, feeling triumphant, a deflated CFO is waiting for me on the couch. He stands and joins me in the entry area. He's still in his amazing suit, but his vest is open and his tie is pulled loose. His hair is mussed above his exhausted yet still-almost-perfect face.

"Miss Canton, I'm so sorry." He looks so distraught, I feel the need to reach out and touch him, to push his tendril of hair off his forehead, but I refrain, hearing Susan's voice in my head.

"It's fine. In fact, today was more than fine, don't you think?" I cross to the kitchen, and he follows. "I mean, I get it now. You really are great with your spreadsheets—even I was getting excited about column adjustments and three percent changes, whew! And then with me and the garden lunch and the plant talk bringing it home? *Fuhgeddaboudit!*" I grab a water from the fridge.

"Still, you're right, about the itinerary. I should've said." He reluctantly accepts a water bottle from my hand.

"Abso-freakin-lutely I'm right. Also, what the hell? You work in a skyscraper."

He swallows a big gulp from his bottle. "I close the east shades. It's the vast, sweeping views that affect me."

"Dang. Well, anything else I should know? Fear of water?

Arachnophobia?"

His eyes snap from his bottle back to mine. "Do you have grand plans involving spiders?"

"Um, don't ask me, ask the itinerary, dude." He almost smiles, which makes me smile wide and free like a little kid. "Did you see her face at all, before you got all vomit-y?"

"I did, yes." He commits to the grin and looks me in the eye. "Surprisingly, we make a good team."

Aaaaand I'm swooning. The eyes, the grin, the positive words coming out of his full lips above that chiseled jawline. Chiseled. Now I'm picturing him in his sweaty state from this morning. And I'm blushing, again.

"Chase!" I say so loudly and randomly, it could be argued I have some sort of disorder.

"What?"

"Chase, in your department—what do you know about him?"

"The young kid with the bow tie?"

"I think he's my age. So, I mean, not geriatric like you, but it's not like he's an intern or something, jeez. But yes, him. Is he a good guy?"

"A . . . good guy?" Emerson asks as if I'm speaking a foreign language.

"Yes, you know, like a nice, normal, trustworthy, date-able guy?"

"Date-able."

I look around the room. "Is there an echo in here? Am I stuttering? He's in your department, c'mon, give me the inside scoop." He still looks confused. "If you say 'inside scoop' like a question right now, with God as my witness, I will take off one of my shoes and throw it at you." I expect a smile, but I don't get one. *Ixnay on the iolencevay, Sam!*

"Didn't you say you were off men?" It doesn't sound like a

question as the flat words leave his mouth. My nervous explosion of words during our flight comes back to me.

"Eh, I also say I'm off carbs, and as you know, I've been pounding bread and french fries like it's in my job description, soooo . . ." I shrug.

He shakes his head no. "I was just about to order dinner. What'll you have?"

"Uh, excuse me, no? Just like that? What are you, my dad? The dating police? C'mon, I thought we were friends now. Help a girl out!"

"Do you often call your friends Icy?" he asks, his eyes staring straight into mine, his expression as cold as the word.

I feel the blood drain from my face. I rack my brain—when did I say that? How could I have let that slip?! The photo. *Shit!*

I clear my throat. "I know you know your secret nicknames, just like I know mine, and let's not pretend you care about my opinion anyway." He grunts. "So? Chase?"

He thinks, then shakes his head with unusual vigor. "Pff, you would . . . eat him alive."

I feel my mouth drop open. Why? Why do I keep asking this beast questions when clearly I don't want to hear his answers? Surprise, surprise, Mr. Clark thinks I'd be too much for a quiet numbers guy.

I spit out, "Just because I am too much for *you* to handle, Mr. Clark, doesn't mean I am too much for everyone." I stalk to my room, feeling the burn behind my eyes. I am not going to let him see that his comments affect me.

Forget the truce. Forget the war. This is a work trip, and from now on, I'll be like Emerson: cold, detached, to the point. After I throw myself face-first onto my bed, my phone dings.

Emerson: Dinner?

Me: [Animated GIF Hard Pass]

[Animated GIF I'm An Asshole]

[Animated GIF That's Correct]

I'm sorry again, Miss Canton.

No need to apologize.

Shall I order what you had last time? Extra fries?

No thanks.

I pat myself on the back for my restraint. Because I want to *go off* on this jerkwad. But coworkers do not go off. They remain professional.

I text my new pal Trina to see if she can do dinner, but she can't. I debate going exploring again, but my feet are killing me and my body is still unsure of the time. A bit sad, I decide I need some comfort food. I change into comfy joggers and an old Dunder Mifflin T-shirt and head out into the common area. I spot a speaker in the living room, which I grab on my way to the kitchen.

Emerson is in his room, I assume, as I try not to care. I connect my phone to the Bluetooth speaker, launch the next song on my London playlist, and head to the fridge, finding the groceries I ordered. I pull out the ingredients for my grandma's garlic butter chicken. I get out a pan, and I'm not gentle about it. I'm going about my business, but it'd be a fun bonus if my business happened to irritate Jack Frost on the other side of the wall.

Emerson emerges sans vest, tie, and jacket. If I hadn't seen him in nothing but exercise shorts this morning—*no! Block it out!*—I'd guess he sleeps, works out, even swims in a dress shirt and slacks.

"Are you . . . cooking?"

"They don't call you a genius for nothing, huh?" I snort, not looking in his direction. He stands there, aghast. "It's one of the few things I'm good at," I say with a laugh. It stings, my comment about myself. Doesn't mean it's not true, though. Emerson is still standing, staring, his mind clearly blown. Is it that hard to believe that Silly Sam cooks? Jeez.

"People," he finally says.

"What?"

He takes a half step forward. "You're good at people . . . you're amazing. With people."

"Pff, not all of them," I say, gesturing at him.

He nods. "Quite."

No argument, no laugh, no insistence that we're friends. Nope, he just turns and goes back into his room, which is where he stays for the evening aside from the brief break to get his room service order and tip the attendant.

Coworkers. That's all we are. I remind myself as I eat my delicious, comforting meal, as I sit and watch *Love Is Blind* on Netflix, and as I crawl into bed. Even as I fall asleep, I tell myself it doesn't matter, that it's just a few weeks with a cold, quiet boss. I have plenty of friends back home, plenty of exciting things to look forward to on this trip.

So why am I so sad?

CHAPTER 14

The next two days are an almost carbon copy of our day with Julie, minus Emerson's episode. And without the early morning sweaty nudity, fortunately and unfortunately. I hear him return from the gym in the mornings, though, knowing he's out there glistening, and force myself to wait for coffee until I've heard his bedroom door shut. Since I'm awake and . . . inspired . . . I have been doing my Zumba workouts on YouTube at the same time.

We spend the days wowing our buyers with our respective talents. Emerson is downright mesmerizing. It's not just his mind at work—it's his quiet confidence, the ease with which he works. And talks. He talks with ease about his work. And damn if I'm not a bit jealous of numbers and clients and spreadsheets. Why can't he talk to me like that? I am the easiest person to talk to ever.

We end the days with fancy dinners at two of the most exclusive restaurants in London. I delight with questions about children, spouses, and hobbies. Emerson orders wines that I'm sure cost as much as a used car, a talent that seems to make up for his overall silence throughout the social portions of our days. He also quietly takes care of everything, as if, while the rest of us are chatting, he's anticipating our needs: the next round of drinks, a huge sampler of desserts, the bill already paid for, the cars already waiting at the curb.

For both days, even while I notice him more and more, I try harder and harder not to show it. I focus my attention and conversation on anyone and everyone except Emerson himself.

I give Charlie detailed recaps of our triumphant meetings, not speaking to the man in the seat next to me on the drive home. Ignoring him is getting harder, though, not only because he is brilliant and unbelievably gorgeous, but because he's becoming increasingly mysterious. Why the bright ties, which have continued the last two days? Why hasn't he gone to see his family in the six days we've been here? He could've met them for dinner or dessert multiple times. What does he do holed up in his room? Is he texting Miranda?

Last night we got in late, so I retreated to my room, where Netflix was waiting. Tonight, though, I need to brush up on Thomas and Timothy, the brothers we're meeting with tomorrow. I set up with my binder and a snack at the table, playlist engaged at the speaker.

"All right." Emerson bursts out of his room. "This supposed 'London playlist' is pitiful. Where are the Beatles? The Stones?"

It's the most expressive I think I've ever seen him.

"'Here Comes the Sun' is on there. I just haven't gotten to it yet, I guess."

"That's it?"

"I don't know, there are like a hundred songs. I'm sure there's more Beatles on there. Do you mind? I'm studying here."

"You cannot possibly study with that on."

"Literally just said that's what I'm doing."

He picks up my phone and pauses the music.

"Hey!"

He's scrolling on my phone, looking disturbed, as usual.

"No 'Blackbird,' 'Yesterday,' 'Let It Be' . . . do you only listen to upbeat songs?"

"I like happy songs," I say with a shrug.

"This is a travesty."

"I disagree. Now, I can put in headphones, but either way, I'm clearly busy." I motion to the binder.

He sets down my phone.

"May I?"

"Psh, uh, what? Was that you asking? Because you never ask before manhandling my phone, my bags, or my passport. I think I'm in shock."

He grabs the binder before I finish talking and slumps down in the seat. He flips through, scanning, saying nothing.

Toward the back, he finds an insert I forgot about. The top of the page says a name with his headshot, like all the others. Below that are my handwritten notes.

EMERSON CLARK, CFO

Likes rain, snow, gray, silence, suits, punctuality.
Hates sugar, happiness, fun, color, meetings, tardiness,
human beings.
Sooners?
Soccer?
Runner or rower?
Family?
Actual heartbeat?

He glares at me. There is no way out, so I own it.

"What, like it's not accurate?"

"No."

"Well, by all means, feel free to fill in the gaps for me."

He sighs, and his shoulders slump a bit.

"You know what? Forget it, we don't need to fill it in. I made this page when I was trying to be your friend, but we don't need to be friends, right? We're coworkers. And that's fine. We're good. Forget about it."

He gives me a tight nod, then stands and mutters, "See you in the morning."

"Wait," I blurt, seizing a small window of opportunity, despite my internal pep talk not to interrogate him. "Why haven't you seen your family yet? We've been here six days. You could have—we've had breaks."

He tilts his head as he considers. "We're not all Cantons."

"What's that supposed to mean?" I straighten, ready to be pissed at him for whatever he's about to say.

"Born into a Norman Rockwell painting," he says cautiously.

"Norman Rockwell? You think my family is perfect?"

"Are your sisters not your best friends? All working together? Are you not close with your father and grandparents?"

"Yeah, I guess so." I chuckle thinking about it. "I mean, my sisters have probably hurt my feelings deeper and more often than anyone, but that's family, right? But yes, we are all pretty close."

Emerson says *my point exactly* with his eyebrows.

I can't stop myself. "Do you even have siblings? Are your parents alive? Do they live here? Are you going to see them?"

"Yes, two younger brothers. And yes, we'll be having a family dinner while I'm here." He turns, done with the conversation. "Good night."

"Good night," I say softly.

He turns back at his door. "It's impressive," he says on a tense exhale. I just stare, unsure of what he is talking about—my family, I guess? "Your binder," he adds.

"Oh." I literally bite my cheek to keep from smiling.

"Your work . . . is impressive. You are impressive, Miss Canton."

He closes the door.

What?!

I bite harder on my cheek, tasting metal. I will not audibly exclaim about the fact that the Winter King just gave me a real-life compliment. It's a strange feeling, like it's beyond a compliment. For a man who says only a handful of words a day, for him to use one, more than one, to offer me praise, it's heady. I'm high. And I can see how if I'm not very careful, I could easily become an addict.

———

Me: Mayday! Mayday!
The Gage brothers are HOTT
With two Ts
Nicole: Didn't you stalk their photos?
They were old and from far away
One was hiking
One was in a street in like Italy or something
Tim is married, but Thomas
Hellooooo, Thomas!
Nicole: Send pics!
LOL I'll try to sneak a few.
Tell me not to throw myself at this Bearded British Beefcake
Nicole: Um, what?
He's like a hot lumberjack in a suit jacket with sexy vowels.
I'm dying.
Nicole: Go for it! I'm sure he's into you too!
Well, I just met them, and when we shook hands, I said
"Hi, I'm Canton Cards Samantha."
Nicole: LOLOLOL
But I recovered.

Nicole: What are you wearing today?

It's a more casual day, so I've got on that hot-pink deep-V shirt with slacks

Nicole: Oh man, then the girls are poppin!

Nicole: Go get him!

You're supposed to tell me I'm off men!

Nicole: If you wanted to hear that, you would've texted Skye.

Nicole: Go on a date, get kissed, ditch Emerson, and have some actual FUN.

Twist my arm ;)

I finish up in the restroom and head back to the office, where Emerson is starting the meeting. I'm surprised to hear laughter coming from the room as I reach the door.

"Can't believe it, almost twenty years!" Tim chuckles. He sees my confusion. "We went to prep school with ole Clarky here."

"Really?" I shoot Emerson a look that could kill.

Emerson nods with a tight grin. "I didn't put two and two together."

"Ah, mate, you don't remember us. That's all right. We were a couple years younger," Thomas says with a wave of one hand.

"Plus, I'm going to go out on a limb and guess he wasn't the most, uh, social student," I joke, and the twin hotties give a little laugh again.

"No, mute as a mouse, but a bloody good polo player," Tim says.

"Rugby too," Thomas adds. "Don't reckon he had any trouble being social, if you know what I mean."

"You're kidding! You were a jock?" I ask Emerson, who is maybe . . . is he blushing a little bit?

"Hardly," he scoffs.

"Now a big-shot CFO! Can't say I'm surprised," Tim says.

There's a lull for a second, so I shake myself out of my shock.

"That he is. I'll let him work his magic, and then we can head to the main event," I say with a smile.

The brothers own twenty gift shops across the UK, and their orders from us are relatively small. If we can get them to change the lines of cards and gifts that they order, order bigger quantities, and adjust their pricing just a bit, they could be making a lot more off our goods. This will be a big win for us since they have so many locations.

Emerson shows them the big picture with his usual surprising and genuine enthusiasm, then turns to me for details about each product line. I gush about the quality of not only our cards and calendars but also our coffee mugs, candles, coasters, tea towels, and hand-painted gifts. I pull up a few of the best sellers on my iPad, and I get emotional about my favorite cards each time. I can't help it—some of them are so touching, or sad, or funny in a sweet way. It just gets to me.

The three men seem to pick up a nice rapport. I am feeling fairly confident the Emerson school connection is a bonus and not a drawback. But as we head for the entertainment portion of the day, I grow concerned.

We're taking them to the Bermondsey Beer Mile, an unofficial pub crawl of over fifteen pubs. We won't hit all fifteen, of course. The brothers have probably been, but we're about to do it up right with all the flight samples, fancy appetizers, and special cocktails. I've prearranged for shot-glass-size samples and special menus with heavier food, since this is a *working* happy hour, after all.

At the start, the twin stud muffins are beside themselves at the idea of a professional pub crawl.

"What, don't get out much now with the wife and baby, Tim?" I say on our second set of tiny samples.

"Oh, hardly ever. Haven't been down Bermondsey in a decade!

The little lad's worth it though!" he says.

I light up. "Have any pictures?"

"'Course." He nods as he gets out his phone.

"Oh, now you've done it." Thomas smiles.

"You're telling me you don't have your own album of your nephew on your phone?" I snipe at the single brother who's looking sexier by the second.

He laughs. "Busted."

I ramble on and on about Junior, who is two, and add in a few stories of my own nephews. I show them my own munchkins album on my phone. I am *that* aunt who takes a thousand photos every time I see them. Even Emerson joins in to look at the photos and give them a nod.

"It's the best, though, being the aunt or uncle, don't you think? Then you can just get them all riled up and call it a night. 'Right-o, it's been swell, I'm off to my clean, silent apartment!'" Thomas makes the perfect symbol with both hands. He's funny, and I'm pretty sure he's giving me sexy eyes.

"Totally. Get to squeeze the cuties and then go back to the single life." I realize Flirt Mode has been engaged.

"Right, next stop," Emerson commands suddenly. We've finished our samples and a basket of fries, I realize.

"Emerson, the cruise director," I say up to him, surprised he's engaging but also not surprised that he's again taking charge. "I don't hate it!"

I don't. There's a comfort there, like I can let go because he has my back and wouldn't let anything happen to me. Although, I realize sadly, he probably sees himself as the chaperone and me as his little charge. As a "kid," like he said about Chase the other night.

Irritated, at the next bar, after our new set of samples arrive, I work harder to ignore Emerson completely and to keep a handle on myself. I eat first, drink second, and find easy, hilarious conversation about having siblings. The twins confirm that they do have weird ESP, and I explain how close my sisters and I are, even though we're all so different.

"Emerson, you must know a bit about it. Your younger brothers are twins, yeah? Year behind us, I think they were? Maybe two?"

I turn to Mr. Freeze in shock. He nods. "They describe it as you do."

"Twin brothers, huh? Man, you're just a wealth of information. I bet you have nieces and nephews too?"

"A niece," he admits casually, as if we weren't all sharing with each other just an hour ago, gushing and bonding, while he stayed aloof. What the hell is wrong with him? It feels like a betrayal somehow, like he stood there and lied.

Because God forbid he get closer to us, to me, to being friends.

We head to the next spot, and I'm fully pissed inside my head. Tim asks Emerson some financial question about the stock market, which prompts me to turn my body away from their conversation and toward Hot Thomas.

"So, what about you? Girlfriend? Boyfriend? Engaged? Married with no ring? Not everyone wears a ring, you know. My brother-in-law Adam doesn't wear his because he works in construction, so I get it." Oh boy. Flirt Mode doubles as Speed Talk Mode, apparently. I decide to suck down the sample in front of me to shut myself up.

"None of the above." He gives me a slow grin as he says it. He doesn't clarify the girlfriend part, but with how many times he's glanced at my chest, I wasn't ever really unsure.

"Same." I try to stay casual. "And do you guys live in London?"

"Tim's in Richmond, but I do—not far from here, actually." He juts his chin toward the pub windows. My insides jump up and down. Not that I want to go home with him, just that he clearly is open to the idea, by the way he said it. I reach down to my beer and see it's been replaced with water. I am thoroughly annoyed with my babysitter, even if it's not a bad call, since I already feel a bit loopy.

I enjoy going out and getting buzzed, but I don't get drunk often. My mouth gets me into enough trouble when it's fully sober. And as I've learned recently, my judgment is impaired all on its own, no assistance required. Still, I'm itching to flip my chaperone the metaphorical bird.

"Is pool called pool here, or is it billiards?" I ask, eyeing the table by the back wall.

"Just pool. D'you play?"

"I do. *Fancy a game, ole chap?*" I say in my terrible accent, gaining me a bright, full laugh from Thomas as he agrees and turns to lead the way. I feel a thrill as we reach the table. Not only am I a good player, thanks to Skye and her ex-boyfriend who had a table in his douchey dudebro apartment, but I know I'm about to put on a full bend-down, bend-over lady show. *Grab your popcorn, boys!* After Thomas sets up the table, he hands me a pole, holding his grip for a second.

"Need any pointers?" he asks.

"She doesn't," Emerson says suddenly from across the table where he and Tim plan to watch. "Bit of a pool shark, in fact." I glare at him. One, he's completely stolen my thunder, and two, he's robbed me of the *Pose My Arms From Behind Like You're About To Ravage Me Tutoring Session* I was so looking forward to. Wait . . . and three, how does he even know that?

I glare at him for a moment, meeting his rigid, cloaked stare. I cannot read him, at all. So, angry and filled with more questions than ever, I stop trying. I go right back to forgetting he exists, focusing instead on Thomas, who is open like a book. I know my shirt gaps a bit when I shoot, nothing risqué but not unexciting— to human males who are not robot statues, anyway. I know my cigarette pant–style slacks hug my butt to perfection too.

I also know Thomas has no trouble taking in the view, and revealing he likes what he sees. He bites his lip. He grips his pole. I laugh at his jokes harder than I need to. I compliment his shots. He does the same, asking questions about my college life, my life in New York, how I got so good at the game. Thomas smiles wide and free, holding my gaze in a way that's easy, fun.

The exact opposite of the way that Emerson appears at my elbow after our game. He gestures to Tim as he pulls me away. He's on his phone, which he shows them as we walk. I'm confused and exasperated by the time we turn the corner to the hall that leads to the bathroom.

"We're leaving," he barks at me.

Oh, the hell we are.

CHAPTER 15

"Um, what?" I ask in a loud whisper, hoping they don't hear us in the small hallway not far from where Tim and Tom sit.

Emerson glares at me. "Charlie is on his way."

"I thought this was some work emergency?" I say, gesturing at his phone.

"I was listening to a voicemail."

"Um, well, that was actually kind of genius. I'll have to tell Skye about that little introvert trick." I shake my head, trying to push the fuzziness away from the edges of my brain. "But um, no, I am not leaving. If you want to go home and go to bed, old man, have at it. It's only eight thirty!"

He lowers his chin. "We have an early morning."

"Oh, look who finally studied their itinerary," I say, snarky.

"I thought you might need the restroom before we leave. It's a half-hour drive back to the hotel."

My mouth hangs open for a minute.

"Listen, *Dad*, I don't need a chaperone or a sitter, and for a friend, you absolutely *suck* as a wingman, so *you* can leave and I'll see you later."

"Apparently you do, or do you think it's a good idea to shag a buyer? Never mind your pledge to stay off men—do you think that idea is wise? Professional? Is that the kind of *Canton quality assurance* Thomas Gage can expect?"

My face burns with embarrassment.

He didn't call me a whore, but that's exactly what those words sounded like when they met my ears. *Slutty Samantha.* He's not anywhere near the first to treat me this way, just because of some innocent flirting. My eyes start to sting, and anger boils over inside me. "Fuck you, Emerson."

He doesn't seem as surprised as I am at the words I let slip out. Instead, he sighs, shakes his head, and carries on. "Charlie will be here in five minutes. I will tell them we've been called off to see to some arrangements for tomorrow."

I rush into the bathroom, suddenly in a violent storm of emotion so rough, I'm swaying and feeling seasick. Maybe he's not wrong. Maybe I flirted too much for a professional setting. Maybe this low-cut shirt crosses a bunch of lines.

One place he hit the nail on the head was my pledge, which was on its way out the proverbial window. I clearly haven't learned my lesson and can't keep promises to myself. Weak, silly, stupid, same old Sam. *Damn it!*

I decide to go into a stall and hurry up, angry he was right that I'd need to go and eager to distract the tears that threaten. I am not going to cry about this in front of him or the Gages. I am not.

I wash my hands and blink hard at the mirror, telling myself that I can do this. I can make it to my hotel room without crying. I repeat my steadfast mantra to myself. *No effing crap, Samantha!* I shake off my hands and put a firm, toothless smile on my face.

I rush out to Tim and Thomas and offer smiley handshakes. "So sorry to have to run on you!"

"Feel free to carry on. Just use the Canton name in any of the pubs, and you're already set." Emerson's voice is gruff.

"No worries, we'll see you at convention, yeah?" Thomas says to me with a grin.

I can't tell if he knows what happened, but I give him a wide smile and a nod.

"Absolutely."

Emerson's hand lands on my elbow as soon as I say it. Before I can hardly blink, I'm in the back of the car that's already pulling away. Charlie gives us an awkward greeting, feeling the tension fill the cab of his car like a visible cloud.

I am vibrating with rage. Who does he think he is? It was harmless flirting, but he's acting as if I stripped naked and danced with a pool cue on top of the felt table. I'm shaking my head and muttering under my breath, my head spinning from the shame and the beer. Emerson sighs that sigh. That's the last one I can take.

"Charlie, does this car have a partition thingy that goes up?"

"It doesn't, I'm afraid."

"Might want to invest," Emerson mutters so softly I barely catch it. I glare at him before turning back to Charlie.

"Well, sorry for this. Actually, no, you know what? It's fine. Emerson here has nothing to hide, right, boss?"

"Miss—" Emerson tries to calm me.

"No! Don't even. We're doing this. It's one thing to be treated like a child, when I am twenty-six damn years old and, I don't know, um, have planned this entire trip from top to bottom? Uh, know what we're doing here back and forward in my sleep? You know damn well you could give me a pop quiz on the whole freaking Canton empire right now, and I'd have all the answers. So don't treat me like you are Mr. High-and-Mighty, deigning to play babysitter, *Mr. Clark.*"

"I—"

"Not even close to finished, Frosty. Not even close."

"Frosty," he echoes softly.

"I mean, without me on this trip, we would be *sunk*! Canton

Cards could just go ahead and close its doors." I turn to Charlie. "Seriously, can you imagine being wined and dined by this guy? We'd lose every account!"

I turn back to Emerson, who is holding his head in his hand.

"What you saw back there was harmless flirting, and you know it. You're completely overreacting. Why, I don't know. Maybe because of my name, because you're Adam's friend and you have a big-brother complex going on? Doesn't matter—you have no right to scold me or to freaking cock block me, if I'm being honest."

Charlie breaks into a fit of coughs.

"We should—"

"Seriously." I stop him from stopping me again. "Even if I wanted to ride Thomas like the dadgum Underground, that is none of your business, Emerson. None. People hook up at work events all the time—it's not a big deal. And again, that's *if* I even wanted that, which is not what it means when a woman simply flirts with someone. Maybe no one flirts with you, so you don't know. I get that."

I let out a growl of frustration. "Ughhrrrr! Of course women don't flirt with you! You're so freaking intimidating. It's infuriating! I get so nervous with you, and I never get nervous! Never! You're just another person!

"I guess I thought it was really hot for a long time—your eyes, when you stare at people, the whole pensive thing, I did, but now I realize quiet and brooding doesn't always mean introverted and misunderstood. Sometimes broody guys who seem like assholes are just—wait for it, *you guessed it, everybody*—big ole assholes."

Charlie has turned the music up in the front of the car, and Emerson's jaw is so tight, I wonder if a man can break his own jaw from biting and grinding like he does. And if they can? Serves him right, I think, but my mouth is already way past my brain. And its volume is set to maximum.

"And you know what else? If you're going to be a big ole anus on the inside, why can't you look like steaming crap on the outside? Why do you have to be all beautiful and muscular like that? It's unsettling, honestly. Are you a vampire? Pretty and mysterious to draw women in, then kill them with some bloodsucking comment?" I go into imitation mode suddenly, half surprising myself. "'It doesn't suit you. You'd eat him alive. You gonna give him that Canton quality assurance?'" I gasp, feeling myself starting to shake again remembering our last conversation. "And that's really it. Beyond all of that, how dare you call me a whore? For some innocent flirting? Or even if I did want to get it on with a colleague? Where do you get off, Emerson? Ha! I guess you *get off* with Miranda, who must be as cold and as cruel as you. Congratulations to the two of you. But as for me, you can go ahead, admit it, you think I'm some kind of slut."

"I—"

"Don't! Don't deny it. Just don't say anything to me again ever. I tried to be your friend. I did. I'm done. If we're not working, leave me the hell alone."

He doesn't respond. Tears fall down my face as I stay turned toward the window, but I at least hold in any sniffs or sobs. I'm sure they both know I'm crying, but silent tears are fine as long as they don't devolve into snotting and wailing.

It's a long, frigid walk from the car to our suite. Emerson stares at me, but I don't look to read his facial expression. In the elevator, he makes the start of some sound, but I hold up my hand and shake my head. It takes all my strength to keep it together. When we get through the door, I can feel Emerson walk behind me for a step, ready to try to say something again, but I almost run to my room.

I shut the door, go to the closet, flip the light, shut the closet door behind me, and let it rain. I shake with sobs. *Shit shit shit!* I overshared so much tonight. It's washing over me now, the vulner-ability hangover. I grab my head in my hands and sob.

People have called me a whore before. Men have said I was a slut; women have called me a bimbo. Even if reality is almost the opposite, people just assume. Once a flirt, always a hoebag. It's so unfair. Still, why do I care if Emerson joins their ranks? What is wrong with me right now? When have I been so overtaken by what someone thinks, when he's not even right?

Other people's opinions of me are not my concern. His thoughts about me are out of my control. He still doesn't even really know me. Enough. Enough of this. Emerson is my coworker, who thinks lowly of me. Okay. Fine. Let him think what he wants.

As soon as I've gathered my resolve and stepped out of my closet, I hear my phone.

> Emerson: Can we talk?
> Please let me explain   •

I throw my phone on my bed and get in the shower. I put on my songs, take my time, do a deep-conditioning rinse on my hair, and do a sugar scrub on my joints. I take care of me and my battered self for a while, and it feels nice. By the time I'm in my pajamas on my bed with a granola bar I found in the bottom of my bag, thank the Lord, I feel somewhat refreshed. I pick my phone back up, surprised at what I see.

> Emerson: I need to apologize
> Please
> How can I convince you?
> What if I keep texting?
> And send you your very own
> SamStorm?

My heart flips over.

> **Me: How do you know what a SamStorm is?!**
> Emerson: You've talked about it at the office, with Nicole.
> Many texts in succession
> And you
> Break up sentences
> Am I
> Doing it right?
> **Was LEAVE ME ALONE not clear enough?**
> You have to
> Break up the sentences
> You're not doing it right
> At all.

I want to be irritated that he's telling me how to be me, but it's actually so . . . I don't know, cute? Sweet? That he's out-me-ing me. *But it's only sweet because it's such a contrast from his usual cold brutality, Sam, get a grip!*

> **Me: Leave.**
> **Me.**
> **Alone.**
> Emerson: Let me come talk to you
> Please
> **No.**
> I'm sorry.
> **So you keep saying.**
> It's unusual for me
> **Apologizing?**

I'm shocked.
Behaving in an apology-worthy way so often.
Let me guess
I push all your buttons
I drive you insane
You can't stand me, unlike any other
You're not the first, King of the North
[Meme Winter Is Coming]
[Meme You Know Nothing, John Snow]
Miss Canton, that's not what I meant earlier.
I don't think of you that way.
What way?
You were right
About the flirting.
It's fine, forget it.
It is absolutely not fine.
Please let me explain.

I notice that my heart is pounding, and as exciting as texting with him is—*why? Why am I so excited?*—I'm emotionally exhausted too. I can't bear the thought of talking it out with him. There's no way it will be quick or painless, and we do have an early morning tomorrow. I can't find the energy to continue this fight-not-fight. So, I let him off the hook.

Me: No, you're forgiven.
It was the beer.
It's fine. We're friends.
I'm going to sleep.

CHAPTER 16

I stall the next morning to the point of making us show up at exactly on time, which, in our world, is late. Paper people are punctual people, I guess. All those planners. And planner stickers. *Man, I love me some planner stickers.*

As I took my precious time and hid in my room, Emerson seemed to camp out in the common area waiting for me. I didn't even get to sneak out for coffee and a bite of breakfast. Instead, I ran from my room directly to the coffee yelling "I know, I know" and grabbing a banana. My plan worked, as there was no time for chatting.

I was supremely nervous. Not about the meeting. About the fact that last night, in a tipsy rage of embarrassment, I managed to mention, to Emerson himself, that I find him brooding hot, that he makes me nervous, that I think he's intimidating, and gorgeous, and I like when he stares. I like when he stares? Lord help me. Facepalm of facepalms.

Oh, and I take the elevator ride down to turn purple as I remember what Frozone offered to me in response: I drive him insane and cause him to act like a jerk. *Actually, Lord, you could just take out this elevator right now. Just smash it down to the basement. That'd be fine. Yes, and Amen.*

Emerson is his usual self, in his coffee-ice-cream attire, good enough to bite and as cool as ever. The only difference I notice is that he keeps looking my way, as if he wants us to have a conversation we have absolutely no time for.

We climb into the car, and I greet Charlie and then get busy chugging my coffee. I also take a couple bites of banana, making sure to break it into pieces instead of inhaling the thing porn-star style. Don't want to add to my already glowing image.

After five whole minutes, I'm sure, Emerson is staring at me. I look over at him, and he looks down with a half grin, then out the window. But he's back at it minutes later.

I don't look at him when I speak up. "Don't do that."

"Pardon?"

"You're staring."

"What?"

"You're staring because yesterday I blacked out and said something about your stare, and now you're using it against me, which is a real class-A dick move, don't you agree, Charlie?"

"Uhh . . ." Charlie turns maroon and starts fiddling with the air vents.

"He agrees with me," I say to Emerson. He opens his mouth to say something and then closes it again. "And remember everything nice I said about you was past tense. So . . ." I shrug. *So? Wow. That'll show him, Samantha, really slick.*

Our meeting today is with one of our big suppliers. It's not as fun or as high stakes since they're technically trying to sell to us. However, we want them to give us better deals on our massive orders that we know support a huge chunk, if not the majority, of their operation.

As usual, the beginning conversation is all numbers and reports, most of which Emerson leads. I pipe in a lot more, however, talking about specific needs for specific lines, why we order the way we do, etc. Emerson doesn't know the drill-down specifics of our products like I do.

By the time we break for lunch, I'm feeling like a bit of a rock star. If I hadn't been there to catch a few things this morning, Emerson probably could've been pressured into orders that look better in a spreadsheet but would've been worse on the retail floor.

At lunch, the wine flows and the laughs roll, more so than usual, since even though we're footing the bill, it feels like we're the ones being wooed. Again, I talk to both Paul and Rhonda about their families and hobbies, anything to get us off shop talk for a while. Both of them gush about their children and, in Paul's case, grandchildren as well.

"Goodness me, you really have a gem here, don't you?" Rhonda gushes to Emerson suddenly, gesturing at me.

"I'll say!" Paul chimes in. "You know, it's not just the lovely face or the last name either. Wasn't sure what to expect when a Canton sister herself was coming to call, but I've never met anyone who can spout off details like you, Miss Samantha, dear."

"Yes, she is impressive." Emerson looks at me just for a second. "Canton Cards is very lucky Samantha happens to be a Canton." He looks back to Rhonda. I wasn't smiling or blushing before, but now I most definitely am.

"Th-Thank you," I manage to say.

"You're clearly born for it, definitely found your calling, I'd say," Rhonda says.

"Definitely," Paul adds.

Then Emerson decides to stare at me, the jerk. I chug some water.

Thankfully, the conversation moves on. Not because I mind being the center of attention, I clearly don't, and I don't have a huge problem accepting compliments. If people work up the courage or the kindness to say something complimentary, the least I can do is graciously accept, not hem and haw and make them feel awkward.

I want them to feel energized so they walk around the rest of their day throwing around more and more little compliments like confetti.

It's not compliments. It's *that* compliment. I was born for this? For . . . sales? For saving the family business three cents per unit on a ceramics order? I try to shake it off. This line of thought never leads me anywhere sunny, and honestly, I'm in a bit of a dark place already with the year I've had and this trip so far. But the comment nags at me all day.

On the drive home, the same thoughts, about my purpose and my job and my so-called skills, bounce around my brain like pin-balls. At some point, I realize Charlie has asked how the day went, and Emerson, to Charlie's shock, answered that it went very well.

But I'm watching the city pass by. I'm romanticizing again, I know, but I can't help but think of it. All the people the car passes, headed home from work, off to happy hour, meeting for a date. So many hopes and dreams, and disappointments too, on the faces.

We pass a crowd of people as we drive and then in the lobby of our hotel. How many of them are doing what they were *born to do*? How many are painters or engineers or teachers, doing something big, building something larger than themselves? Canton Cards is much larger than me and my family, of course, but it used to feel like it expanded across the universe. It doesn't feel that way anymore. I can't remember the last time it did.

"Okay. I can't take it," Emerson blurts as we get into our room. I'm surprised, like I almost forgot he was there, except I could smell him. I may have inhaled his scent on the elevator. And I may have known in every cell of my arm that his hand was only about four inches from mine.

"What?"

"Where's the recap?"

"What?" I almost laugh the question, because the Emerson

standing before me is more than just depleted—he's . . . bothered.

"The recap. Every day, you're so energized after our activities, you're practically bursting, so you recount each moment, and then you blast your music, or blare your show, or make noise in the kitchen."

"I'm sorry, I didn't really realize, I guess."

"Well?"

"Well, what, Em— Mr. Clark?" I say, still unsure what has happened to my stoic travel companion. I'm tempted to glance around for a spaceship and the floating remnants of a human-replacement-tractor-beam.

"Well, I've gotten accustomed to it. To you."

I let out a laugh. "I've *My Fair Lady*'d you?"

"Apparently, because the silence the whole entire drive has put me on edge. Is this punishment? The silent treatment? Because, listen, about yesterday—"

"No! No, I really do *not* want to talk about yesterday, okay? I just had . . . an off day, I guess."

"Come." He grabs my wrist. It's not an intimate gesture, but I feel the touch of his hand throughout my whole body. He pulls me to the table and lets go of my wrist to head to the kitchen. "Sit." I want to say no, mostly because I desperately want to pull off my bra and put up my hair. But his behavior is so odd, I can't help but obey.

I sit and watch him rummage through the kitchen, enjoying the view. *StairMaster. Got to be.* He places an unopened bar of Cadbury's royal dark chocolate on the table in front of me, with a water. I look up at him, confused, and find he's doing his stare again. My insides, still tingly from the heat lingering on my wrist, tighten under my skin.

"Something has upset you. From today. What was it?"

Okay, what kind of Jedi mind-trick voodoo magic is this? I feel my mouth drop open, but that's all that happens in response to his question. I am still sitting frozen, staring.

He sits down and settles in his chair like he's bracing himself. Then he levels me with a weaponized stare—no, smolder—that makes my pulse pound in my head. The look on his face makes me wonder if he really wants to sit and listen to me babble. He couldn't possibly. But his face also says we're not getting up until he gets what he wants.

It's brutally hot.

"You're *sure* you want to start me chatting? Because you know once the Sam Train leaves the station, it quickly goes off the rails, deep into the mountains, on and on and—"

"Please," he pushes, even though his face is still unconvincing.

I open the chocolate. "Well . . . oh, wait. I'll talk, but you have to eat a bite of this." I hand him a small rectangle. "Prove you're not a robot, Emerson Clark."

He rolls his eyes and takes the chocolate and actually eats it.

"Okay! So, flesh and blood. Doesn't rule out the vampire thing, but it's progress." He sighs. "I mean, when was the last time you had chocolate? Isn't this the best dark chocolate you've ever had in your life? Ugh, it's almost better than—" His eyes pop up to mine from the table, and I manage to stop myself before saying *better than sex* out loud. "Um, yeah. Okay. So today. Well, it's just my job . . . even saying that is odd. It didn't used to be *a job.* I loved it at first. But to be told this is what I was born for? *This?*" I motion toward the binder.

"You don't enjoy your work?" he asks cautiously.

"I do enjoy a lot of it. I love peopling, as you know—the conversations, and even the thrill of the sale is fun, but I mean . . . where's my opus, you know?"

"Hmm." His brow scrunches.

"Have you seen *Mr. Holland's Opus?* The movie? Susan made

me watch it when we were kids. And, like, all the nineties movies. But anyway, it's pretty good." I shake my head, realizing I'm
getting distracted again. "So, like my sisters. Skye, she's this
amazing artist, with big dreams and goals. Opus. Obviously, Sadie
has written, what, forty novels now? She found her big opus, to
write. Susan was always going to head the company—she always
wanted to—and it happens to fit how she's wired perfectly. When
Dad retires, no one will be surprised to see her at the helm, right?"
He nods. "And Sally is on her track to be a surgeon just like Mom
was, healing people and changing lives. A big, grand, meaningful
life. Aaaaand then there's me. Shallow Sam." I wince as the words
come out. It's maybe the most painful of my nicknames.

"You're not shallow." His voice is firm and low.

"Aren't I? I mean, sales? That's my big calling?" I scoff and
shove a large piece of chocolate in my mouth.

"So, go back to school. Become a pediatrician, after all." He
watches me as I shake my head and smile that he remembers my
answer from that silly team-building day.

"I don't want to start over and do that much school. Not to
mention, after my mom, hospitals are . . . not my favorite. Sally is
maybe too young to remember, so she doesn't have the lingering
feelings I have, I'm guessing. The hospital was a fun place—we'd
go visit Mom at work—and then, it wasn't. I don't think I could do
it."

He reaches over and breaks off another tiny piece of chocolate. Satisfaction crosses my face with a wide smile, but I don't let
myself comment.

"It is good. I'd forgotten." He lifts the piece before putting it in
his mouth. He begins to chew, holding eye contact with me. Now
my pulse starts to pound not everywhere in my body, but rather in
one specific place. I look away first.

"What about you? Are financials your calling? Did you dream

of being a big CFO someday?"

He considers before he answers, as I'm learning he always does. I almost think he won't answer, unwilling to share with me even though I'm constantly turning myself inside out around him. I sigh and start to give him an out, but he clears his throat.

"I was very young when my affinity for numbers became obvious." He takes his time with each word, and I force myself to be patient. "Then it was as if I simply followed them."

"The numbers?" I ask, and he shrugs, almost embarrassed. The vulnerability makes my chest tight. "That's kind of poetic." He gives me a look of confusion or maybe disgust? He is the hardest person to read on the entire planet. "I never had that—any poetry. Even when I thought I'd go into medicine, it wasn't like I was great at science. You always hope some great passion or talent will reveal itself, some eureka moment where the clouds part and angels sing. But it never came. Just an internship at the company that became a sales job that . . . continued."

"And what if you simply can't see it?" His voice is soft, and he's staring once again.

"What?"

"The clouds part, Miss Canton. Angels do sing. I just don't think you can hear them." He stands up immediately after the words tumble out. My mouth falls open, allowing me to start panting. Those may be the sweetest words anyone has ever said to me. And they came from the most surprising, gorgeous, quiet mouth.

It feels as if we've crossed a line and taken down many layers of the wall between us. He must sense it too, because he quickly mumbles good night and escapes to his room. I sit at the table, stunned.

Stunned isn't the right word. I am completely ruined. There's no coming back from tonight, from what's building down deep in my soul, from these feelings.

Big, warm feelings for icy Emerson Clark.

CHAPTER 17

I am giddy today. And nervous for many reasons. One of which is our meeting this morning. Graham Roberts is the buyer for one of the UK's biggest grocery chains. They're about to expand their stores to include an in-house pharmacy, which will include a gifts, cards, and party section. It's a huge opportunity for us. We need to wow them in the morning meeting.

Another reason I'm all fluttery is that after said meeting, we are setting off on a true adventure. Thanks to a wealth of insider information from his assistant, June, Mr. Roberts is in for a treat.

He doesn't know the big surprise, just that he and a few members of his staff were invited for a "casual adventure." Since Emerson and I are still the only Canton employees in London, I've invited Trina to come along as an unofficial third. It's a tiny risk since I don't know her that well, but I got such a great vibe from her. Plus, I was to be the only woman on the adventure, and I wanted a gal pal to break up all the testosterone.

The last reason I'm all twitchy is looking down at his phone as I approach him in the living room. I told myself last night, over and over, this cannot happen. Nothing will happen. The man can barely stand me. He is grumpy and standoffish. Cold and unfeeling. Blunt to the point of cruelty. And he has a posh English supermodel girlfriend.

Plus, I promised myself I wasn't doing this again. Romanticizing, dreaming, painting a rosy picture of a future in my head, as I always do. A picture that is always quickly trashed by rejection after rejection, or as I'd learned this year, even worse.

There is nothing to be all fluttery about, I reminded myself.

Then he looked up at me from his phone with a tight, barely there grin and my hopeful-to-a-fault self flipped me the bird and proceeded to jump somersaults in my chest. Today he is wearing a light linen shirt untucked—untucked!—over khaki slacks and loafer-style boat shoes. The thin fabric pulls as he grabs his messenger bag from the entry table, pushing detailed images into my mind of the firm ridges that lie underneath. Cue additional somersaults.

As we make our way toward Mr. Robert's office, the flips and skips in my heart go ahead and sit down in defeat. Emerson doesn't look my way, doesn't chat, doesn't even grunt or scoff at my morning ramblings with Charlie. Had I imagined it all last night? The held eye contact? The sincerity in his encouragement? The gentle clutch of my wrist? I must have. That's what I do, after all.

I focus on the meeting instead of those nagging questions. I use the drive to review stats and figures in my head, as well as reciting names of the men we're meeting with, along with their wives and children, hobbies, and so on. I even went through some key terms and tidbits I'd picked up about soccer.

The meeting goes very well. It couldn't have gone much better, actually, unless Emerson had maybe shown a bit more enthusiasm. He seemed more tense than usual, more reserved. He didn't make any eye contact with me or engage with me in any way, other than our usual volleying in our meetings, so I had no idea what was going on with him. One guess was irritation with Mr. Roberts's second, Damian Weiss.

The guy was attractive, energetic, and funny. He made eye

contact, said our names often, even knew tidbits about us. He was like a male version of me . . . kind of. The problem was, he dominated the conversation, talking over others, laughing too loud to the point of seeming fake. Honestly, he was one of those sales guys I wish wasn't in sales because he makes all of us look bad.

Am I like that? I am too loud sometimes, maybe, too excitable. But I never talk over other people intentionally, and I would never dole out big fake laughs. But what if this was how I come across? I could see Emerson's distaste for Damian grow throughout the meeting. Does he see me the same way? Damn. I hope not.

"All right then!" Mr. Roberts stands and essentially ends our meeting. He's a tall man with a serious face, nice-looking but starting to gray and to bald. He doesn't have the frat-boy vibe of his salesmen, but it seems like they make a good team. "I'm very interested to see what this afternoon excursion is all about. June made quite a fuss—I hope she didn't oversell whatever this is." He gives us a sheepish eye, as if he's prepared to be annoyed.

"Miss Canton never disappoints." Emerson stares him down for a beat, then moves toward the door to lead everyone out. My heart drops down into my shoes for a second at his vote of confidence. So, maybe I didn't imagine his walls crumbling the tiniest bit? But he avoids my gaze, which keeps finding him, as we walk and then load into a limo and head to our destination.

Mr. Roberts's face lights up when we pull into the marina twenty minutes later. "Well, we're off to a promising start!"

We unload out of the limo and join Trina, who's waiting for us at the eighty-foot catamaran sailboat. Well, yacht is more accurate than sailboat. I do ramble through freak yacht death stats in my head. But I have a job to do, so I focus on my tasks.

"All right, Mr. Roberts, I know you're a sailor, so I thought you'd enjoy taking us out for an afternoon on the water," I say with excitement.

"In *that?*" His voice almost squeaks.

"Yes, I know it's a bit bigger than *Believe It or Knot*, but she's fully staffed with a crew and a backup captain, not that you'll need him." I am beaming at his obvious glee. *Way to go, Sam!*

Mr. Roberts lets out a huge laugh and turns to Emerson. "Well, you were quite right, after all. I am surprised to say I am *not* disappointed!" I look to Emerson too, but he nods without looking my way. I introduce Trina to everyone as one of our London team members, and the men are so excited about sailing, lunch, and beer that they couldn't care less who she is or what she does.

Captain Freddie and the crew show Mr. Roberts the ropes, literally, and get us underway. Beachy music plays through the boat's sound system, and champagne is passed out by one of the crew. A lunch display is ready when we board, so everyone starts on the mini sandwiches while the crew and Mr. Roberts find a rhythm.

Soon we're cruising quickly with one sail up and much ado about turning the engines off and switching to wind power. Mercifully, the sun makes a rare appearance, bumping the whole experience from nice to exceptional.

"Thanks so much for inviting me. This is gorgeous!" Trina gushes quietly.

"Thanks for coming!" I whisper back. I turn to the group. "We're going to go enjoy the sun for a bit and leave you men to talk soccer."

"You mean football." Damian gives me a wink.

"You all keep telling yourselves that." I wink back and shrug off my suit jacket onto the built-in lounge chair. I'm glad I chose this thin spaghetti-strap dress as the sun warms my shoulders. I give Emerson one last glance as Trina and I head toward what I learn is called the foredeck of the center of ship. But of course, he's not looking at me. He is loosening up, though, literally, unbuttoning the top few buttons of his shirt. My mouth waters, so I force myself to look away.

Damian has abandoned his shirt entirely, as has one of Mr. Roberts's other team members, but it doesn't seem inappropriate. Damian, specifically, has every reason to be comfortable shirtless. He's no Emerson, not even close, but he's got a nice build and he's tanned beyond what London's sun can offer. He catches me looking and smiles. I can feel his stare on my back, admiring the view as Trina and I walk away along the side gunnel.

"So, what's the story with you and Emerson, then?" Trina asks as we get settled on the sundeck with our backs to the ledge, legs outstretched in the sun.

"Story? No story." My pulse quickens. Am I so obvious?

"Really? The two of you so gorgeous and such a good team, I thought I felt some chemistry."

"You did?" I ask, trying to play dumb.

"Okay, not some, loads. Loads of chemistry. You're telling me there's nothing? C'mon, I'm your London gal pal, you can tell me." She smiles and leans into me.

I huff and shove back into her. "No. No chemistry. Not that I wouldn't— I mean, you've seen him."

"Wouldn't mind seeing a lot more of him, if you know what I mean!" She giggles and jabs me with her elbow.

I laugh too. "Same, girlfriend, same. But he can barely tolerate me. And he's known me since I was, like, fifteen, so I've got that whole best friend's annoying little sister thing going on."

"I don't think he looks at you like you're his sister, love."

"You're imagining it. Trust me." I suck down the last of my champagne before I can start babbling about how much I wish she was wrong. "More champagne?" I ask her.

"Of course," she says with a wicked grin.

"I knew inviting you was a good idea!"

"Bloody *great* idea."

I laugh at her comment and stand, hearing some commotion and cranking noises, but hearing them too late. Next thing I know, I am smashed in the ribs by a hard metal pole.

"Fuck! Samantha!"

I hear, and then there's a splash.

A second splash.

Because the first one was me.

Because I'm overboard.

In the ocean.

I struggle to move my arms and not panic, but the impact knocked the wind out of my lungs. I can't breathe. *Shit, I can't breathe!*

"Samantha! Samantha, are you all right?" Emerson is suddenly there, holding me with one hand and pushing my hair off my face with the other. Relief crosses his features as his bright blue eyes meet mine. "Shit, I was afraid you'd hit your head." He's holding my face in one hand now and panting, in the water, fully clothed.

He jumped in after me?

He jumped in. For me.

I cough, still struggling to catch my breath. "I— My—"

"Shh, it's fine." He's talking softly now, calm and intense. "I've got you. Just breathe, try to calm down, okay? Shh." I try to nod. He grabs on to something, and I feel a pull around us in the water. I close my eyes and cling to him for dear life, feeling myself shake. My teeth start to chatter, and I can't tell if it's from the frigid water or the shock.

"Shit," Emerson whispers. "Towels!" he yells as I'm suddenly hauled out of the water by two of the ship's crew. I'm on my feet but wobbling for a split second before Emerson's arms are around me, holding me steady and also crushing my head into his chest.

"She should sit," I hear someone say.

"I'll get some water," Trina calls out.

"I'm-I'm all right," I manage to get out as Emerson wraps a towel around me and then scoops me up into his arms like I weigh nothing. He takes a couple steps and sets me down on the bench seat next to the built-in table.

"Are you all right, dear?" Mr. Roberts asks.

"I'm so sorry," a crew member mumbles.

I nod firmly and try to smile. "I'm-I'm all right. I should've been paying attention, really."

"Drink this." Emerson takes the water bottle from Trina and hands it to me. I take it from him with unbelievably shaky hands. I close my eyes and try to calm my body down. This is ridiculous—it was just a hit to the lung and a bit of cold water. I'm fine.

"I'm so sorry, sir, we should've called out louder before adjusting the boom," I hear Captain Freddie say to Emerson. He has a towel around him now as well, but I can still see his shirt clinging to his firm chest and every defined bump of his six-pack. He turns and walks toward the small cabin that I would assume is called the bridge. The other men follow, mumbling about finding a spare shirt and a jacket.

"You sure you're all right?" Trina's face is earnest as she squats down in front of me.

"Yeah." I nod. "I am."

She moves to sit next to me on the leather seat.

"Still shaking." She rubs a hand up and down my back.

I try to make my voice steady. "My body is freaking out more than I am."

She scoots closer and says near my ear, "No chemistry, my big flabby ass!"

"What?"

"That man looked like he was going to die. I've never seen such intense fear on someone's face before."

My eyebrows raise, and I think about the look on Emerson's

face. He had called me Samantha. He called my name, over and over. And he cussed, which was so very human of him. "And then after he got you out, did you see the look he gave them? I wouldn't be surprised if he kills both the fake captain and the real one—what's his name? Freddie?"

"Yeah . . ." I look toward the bridge.

Trina gives me a squeeze as she jokes. "Well, bye-bye, Freddie, hope you had a good life."

I shake my head, not wanting to let her words go from my ears to my heart. "That's just Emerson. He's intense."

"No, no. This was not just being broody, girl, this was rage. He was shaking."

"It's cold," I say.

"Samantha. Quit being a daft twat and listen to me! I don't care how he normally is—he was fucking terrified. Over you. And then he was pissed as all bloody h—" She cuts herself off as Emerson walks back to us. He has on a crew shirt that's a smidge small, making his biceps bulge out from below the sleeve. Trina wasn't exaggerating. He looks like he wants to snap some necks.

He hands me a big crew wind jacket and another dry towel.

"Thanks," I say, looking into his eyes. He quickly looks away.

His voice is gritty. "We're headed back to take you to a hospital."

"What!" I stand to my feet, but I'm wobbly. "I don't need to go to the hospital. I'm fine! Today is important—we can't just leave."

He looks at me, with all the rage Trina mentioned. "We can. You could be concussed."

"This is ridiculous, Emerson." I realize what I've done and try to recover. "Uh, I mean Mr. Clark. I didn't hit my head. It was my side, I'm fine, Mr. Clark." I sound like maybe I have hit my head now. He levels a glare at me and then reaches a hand in suddenly, under my towel and just barely touches my ribs. "*Ah!*" I wince and instinctively put my hand over his.

"Your ribs could be broken. We're going to the hospital," he says through clinched teeth as he pulls his hand away and stalks off again. My hand stays where his was, not because of the pain but because of the fireworks that have erupted on my skin under his firm touch.

"*Not* like a sister," Trina whispers in my ear.

"He's probably just irritated because he thinks he's responsible for me—like the family will get mad if anything happens to me under his watch or something."

"Oh, he's irritated, all right, but I'd bet a million pounds: either that man is in love with you, or I'm the fucking Dalai Lama."

"I don't think the Dalai Lama says the F-word," I say.

"Pre-fucking-cisely!" she cries out as she bursts out laughing. I laugh too and then wince in pain.

"Ooooo. Okay, no more joking."

"You all right, gorgeous? That was quite a spill." Damian studies me as he takes a seat across from us.

"I'm fine, thank you. It's nothing, really. We don't need to turn back early for me." I blush a bit at his tone, caring and flirty. I look for Emerson and see he's chatting with Mr. Roberts, probably making up for my big flop—literally.

"Better safe than sorry, though," Damian says.

"Yeah, I guess so."

"This really was a great idea to wow Roberts. How'd you know?" he asks with a sparkle in his eye. For the rest of the cruise back, we chat about June's insider information, along with my other tricks for planning our Europe trip. He is genuinely impressed.

Trina joins in the conversation, and we talk about her experience running one of our retail stores with her mom. It's an easy conversation with plenty of laughs, even if they hurt my side. I notice Emerson glance our way a few times, but he stays engaged with Mr. Roberts.

As the boat pulls into the docks, Damian texts both myself and Trina so that we'll have his number, and I wonder if maybe I misjudged him as a sleazy sales guy, especially when he gives me a lingering hug goodbye and gushes in my ear about how he's glad I'm okay. When I pull away from his hug, Emerson grabs my elbow and clears his throat. It's awkward, and for a split second, I wonder if he's jealous, or at the least, feeling possessive of me.

I exchange a quick glance with Trina, who is smiling wide. Just before I turn toward the car, I catch her mouth: "Not. Like. A. Sister!"

CHAPTER 18

Me: Four bruised ribs on the inside,
One purple Sam on the outside.
[Photo]
Susan: OMG!!!! Are you sure you're all right?
Skye: So you weren't exaggerating
Sally: Holy crap
Sadie: We need more details. So you fell off and what? They threw you a rope?
Skye: Here we go. Prepare to star in her next novel, Sam
If I tell you, do I get book royalties?
Sadie: It must be pretty interesting if you think it's book-worthy
. . .
Susan: Yes, what exactly happened?
Skye: I'm intrigued. Commence SamStorm
Sally: I'm still not over how big that bruise is. I want to see the X-rays!
Well, I got whacked, then I was freezing.
Realized I was in the water and couldn't catch my breath
Then Emerson jumped in after me.

My phone is silent for a beat, and I can imagine every single one of my sisters, holding their phones, each reacting in their own way, rereading the text a couple times. Messages incoming in three, two, one—

Skye: Emerson CLARK????

Sally: You're joking

Susan: He jumped . . . in the ocean????

Sadie: Even *I* can't imagine this. Tell us more!

Me: Yes, Susan, the ocean LOL.

He jumped in and swam to me

He was afraid I'd hit my head and might be knocked out

I was struggling to breathe since my lungs were hit so hard

He held me up and then grabbed on to the life preserver

And they pulled us in

Skye: Again, are you sure this was Emerson CLARK, our CFO?

Susan: See, I told you he's a good guy!

Sadie: Okay, definitely book-worthy. Was it as romantic as it sounds?

Sally: Romantic? With that robot? [Thumbs down emoji]

Skye: This is Sam we're talking about, of course she thought it was romantic

It might've been if I could, you know, BREATHE

Lot of talk about Emerson and romance

Not enough

"OMG Sam you could've died!"

"What would we do without you!"

"Our favorite sister!"

Skye: Are you naming your future children yet?

Susan: NO she is not. She's off men, remember!

Sally: Does he even qualify as a man [Snowman emoji]

Sadie: Oh, he qualifies as a man, all right. A man who jumped in to save her life.

What Susan said.

No future children. No men, snow or otherwise!

Can you all pretend to be concerned about me almost dying now?

Susan: I was concerned! I'm so glad you're okay.

Sadie: What would we do without you!

Skye: OMG Sam you could've died!

Sally: Our favorite sister!

Me: [Middle finger emoji] [Dead Emoji]

I smile and shake my head and go back to straightening my hair, but right after I put my phone down, it pings again.

Trina: Headed your way!

Me: Great, text me when you're in the lobby.

I send Charlie a twenty-minute warning and put the finishing touches on my hair. I flip through my clothes in the closet, settling for a tank top and jeans with heels. I hadn't really brought any clubbing attire, of course, so *casual but also super tight from head-to-toe* would have to suffice.

When I head to the kitchen to grab a bottled water for the ride over, Emerson is locked away in his room. I decide not to say anything. If there's one thing I can still be sure of in this strange situation, it's that Emerson Clark does not want to go clubbing.

The afternoon at the hospital was heavy and tense. Well, Emerson was heavy and tense. I tried to keep things light, but he was extra serious, even for him, and my casual attitude seemed to irritate him more than usual. It was as if he wasn't just angry about what had happened but rather angry *at me*.

I didn't ask him about it, though, because I wasn't in the mood for one of his brutal answers about how I should've been paying attention, or maybe that I'd ruined a very important day for us.

So, we had a strained, quiet doctor visit and ride home. When we entered our suite, Emerson had stalked to his room and I'd called out to stop him.

"Thank you for jumping in after me," I'd said. He had simply nodded and gone into his room. He seemed more exhausted than me, even though I was the one with the bruised ribs. I shrugged it off, trying to give the guy a break. After all, it had been a super-weird day.

I'd showered and ate some leftovers out of the fridge for dinner while Trina ate at her place, since we figured the club wouldn't have good food.

I take my water and head down to the lobby, feeling confident in my decision to leave Emerson alone for a while. I'm excited to let off all the pent-up steam I'm feeling from the day.

And from the feelings I'm trying *not* to feel.

How I savored how his eyes looked above the waves, wide and worried for me. The way my skin tingled along my forehead as his hand pushed my hair from my face. How amazing it felt when he forced open my towel and put his hands on my rib cage with no hesitation. And all this just added onto the new and improved Emerson sound bites I replayed in my mind:

You are impressive, Miss Canton.

Miss Canton never disappoints.

Angels do sing. I just don't think you can hear them.

"Ready to get pissed and dance our asses off?" Trina bursts into the lobby with a wide smile.

"*So* ready!" I say. We squeal and head out to find Charlie.

Trina promised a cool London club, and she delivered. While there are easily a thousand people in here, the low ceilings—complete with disco balls, fog machines, and various colored spotlights—give the club an underground feel.

Trina gets a martini at the bar, and I start a tab, but I ask for an unopened beer, just to be safe. We survey the crazy crowd from the bar while we down our first drink. I find myself worrying about Emerson back at the hotel, if he wonders where I am, if he'll think to check my shared location, if he'll be angry. Maybe I should've stayed and made him a thank-you dinner. I wonder if he's working out, sweaty . . .

Trina pulls out her phone and yells to me, "You care if Damian and his hot buddies join us?"

"Sure!" I say, excited to add more people to the fun. Damian could be a nice distraction from the confusing mix of feelings and thoughts bumping through me to the beat of the music. She fires back a reply to him, and we head to the dance floor. I don't know how many songs have passed, during which we jump, sway, and even grind on each other a tiny bit, before we head to the bar again.

"Hey, gorgeous!" I turn and see Damian and his two friends. Trina was right. They are hot. "This is Will and Zander. Guys, this is Samantha and Trina."

"Hey, you found us!" Trina calls over the music.

"Hi!" I give them a wave.

Damian steps up to buy drinks, unimpressed with my beer order. "I'll watch your drink for you, gorgeous. You can get what you like," he yells over the music.

"Thanks, but I'm good!" I say. I don't know him well enough for that, but I appreciate his offer to look out for me. We suck down our drinks and head to dance once their glasses aren't spilling over. I stick with Trina for the most part, even though Damian moves in behind me a few times. It's sexy, for sure, but I'm not totally comfortable with it. As much as I love going out, dancing for me is usually a girls' night situation. I move around and dance with everyone, keeping things light.

After a few songs, we head back to the bar, but I make a detour for the bathroom. Trina either doesn't hear me or doesn't know wing woman code, because she doesn't follow. I make quick work of finding the restroom, doing my business, and getting back to my friend.

I don't love navigating the club alone. I'm not sure if I'm being more paranoid than usual or reasonably cautious. Probably the latter since I'm in a foreign city with people I barely know. *Yikes.* I probably should've asked Emerson to join us.

I find Damian back at the bar, but no Trina.

"Where's Trina?" I ask him.

He puts his hands on my waist to answer me. "She's dancing with Will. C'mon, what'll you have to drink? A real drink this time!"

"Just another beer, please." I smile, then pull out my phone as a way to get free of his hands on me.

"Psh, bit of a downer, gorgeous, but okay!" He motions to the bartender and puts his other hand back on my waist.

I get my beer, but it's opened already. I frown.

"C'mon, babe, let's go dance." His hand squeezes my hip and moves down closer to my ass as he talks into my ear.

I shake my head with a smile. "I think I'll drink this one here. I need a dance break."

"What! Now, now, we're here to dance, babe, so let's dance." He starts to really grip me, and I pull back, feeling my pulse starting to hammer in my veins. Every warning bell in my brain is sounding off.

I push his hand off mine and shove it toward the dance floor. "You go on ahead. I'll be there in a minute."

"C'mon, gorgeous, you know you want to dance with me." His smile tightens, and his gaze turns predatory as he takes a big step toward me. Then a body is in between us.

"Piss off, Damian, she's with me." Emerson, suddenly rescuing me again, slips a hand around my waist. "Sorry I'm late, Angel," he says loudly to me and plants a kiss on the side of my forehead. My brain melts completely at the feel of his soft lips on my skin.

"Oh, shit, you two are . . . ?"

"We are." Emerson's voice is icy and low as he pulls me into him. In a swift motion, my back is tucked flush into his front, with both of his arms firm around my middle, but leaving his grip loose where my bruise is. I am immediately drenched in desire at the feel of his body all over my back and the possessiveness of his voice.

"Sorry, mate, I didn't realize," Damian offers, but Emerson just stares him down. Damian withers and gives me a small duck of his head, turns around, and walks to the dance floor.

Emerson releases me the second Damian is out of sight, and I feel a small crack inside as it happens. It was as if when he'd said the words, that I was *with* him, the rose-colored hope I hadn't fully let myself admit, of some future *with* Emerson, was cemented into something real; but when he pulled away, it suffered a very real, painful blow.

Another hit lands across my hopes when I turn to face him. His face is twisted up in a million emotions, all negative.

"Thank you," I yell up to him. My eyes search his for something, anything to tell me I'm not imagining everything, yet again. But my search comes up empty.

"Do you want to stay?" he asks, his jaw tight. I shake my head. He looks behind me at the bar. "Tab?" I nod and turn to the bar, but he steps in front of me and gives my name.

I touch Emerson's arm, and he tenses under me. "Let me just

get Trina!" He nods without looking down at me. I find my friend in the horde of bodies and yell in her ear. "Damian got handsy. I'm gonna go." She apologizes, but I tell her it's fine and that she should leave with us. As she starts to explain that she has two more girlfriends on their way to meet us, she looks above my head.

I feel his firm chest behind my back again, and I smell his scent and lean back into him involuntarily. He doesn't touch me, but he doesn't push me off. Trina gives me a smile, and I snap out of what my body is doing to me, then give her a quick hug goodbye.

Emerson turns toward the exit, and I grab on to his forearm again. His warm skin tightens underneath me, but he doesn't shake me off. *Take my hand. Slip my grip down and hold my hand, Emerson!* But he doesn't.

Then I remember as we climb into the car, Emerson can't really play pretend boyfriend to me because he's the real boyfriend to someone else. Another smash to the hope that has turned solid and heavy in my heart. I decide to do what I do best: deflect with words.

"Is that how you treat Miranda? Bit cold and rigid, not your best boyfriend act, I don't think," I tease as we get in the car. He glares over at me. "I mean, thank you for saving me, really, things were going south fast, but I just don't think that was an Oscar-worthy performance." He is still staring at me with a fervor that makes my thighs clench together. "Or, if it was your best, maybe Miranda is not the lucky girl I thought she was." I smile as I say it, clearly trying to rile him.

He sighs, then he grunts out, haltingly as always, "Miranda is just a friend."

I decide to pile on. "Ohhhhh, *that* kind of friend. I see, I see. So no hand-holding, but there's some holding going on." I wag my eyebrows. He shakes his head and looks out the window. I put on

my best Scarlett O'Hara: "I do declare, Mr. Clark, are you blushing
right now? I say, I believe you are!"

I thought I'd get a smile, but I don't. He seems genuinely upset.
By tonight? By the drama earlier today? I can't tell, and I want to
ask, but I won't in front of Charlie. I've put that poor man through
enough.

"Not going to tease me about my accents?"

He barely shakes his head, acknowledging me as little as
possible. My turn to sigh. Why is he so tense? I didn't ask him
to swoop in and save me, either time! I don't need him being all
chivalrous and freaking dashing. Yes, we're in England and he is
downright dashing. That's the perfect word for him. I'm still annoyed, especially that he's annoyed, but I'm also beaming so much,
it's hard to hide.

Because Emerson Clark doesn't have a girlfriend.

CHAPTER 19

Emerson's demeanor gets colder as we get closer to the hotel, through the lobby, up in the elevator, and finally through our door. He starts to make his signature mad dash for his bedroom.

"Are you mad at me?" My voice is loud in the silence.

He stops and turns around. He doesn't answer, but his jaw twitches and his eyes squint the tiniest bit.

"I mean, I didn't mean to fall into the ocean, obviously, and I don't know if I've said thank you enough for that . . . but really, it was very knight-in-soaking-wet-armor of you. Dashing, really. I've never used that word before, but I do think that. That you're dashing, I mean."

I shake my head. "But! I didn't ask you to come along with us tonight because I knew you'd hate it—you didn't want me to invite you, did you? And I didn't ask you to come rescue me tonight, although I'm really, really glad you did. Honestly, after everything, I should just never go out again ever, but the promise of a fun night out with people is like my siren's song, I guess, just calling to me over and over—"

"What happened?" He cuts me off. "Why, why did you delete all your social media, all your apps?"

"Oh." Crap! I do not want to talk about this with anyone, let alone Hottie McSavior over there. *Hottie McSavior? Oh. I am so screwed.* I fumble with the hem of my tank top. "Um, it wasn't a huge thing, really."

"Samantha." He says my name like a command, but a kind one, an order that's soft around the edges. I snap my head up and meet his burning ice-blue eyes.

"W-Why do you want to know?"

"You keep mentioning it."

"Oh, okay." I let out a fake chuckle. "Well, uh, sorry. I'll stop doing that then. I—"

"Damn it, Samantha, what happened to you?" he almost yells, and I jump. I've never seen such raw emotion from him.

"I was blackmailed!" I blurt. I hope maybe I can get away with just that, but his eyes say otherwise. I take a breath before explaining. "You know, textbook: secretly knew who I was, seduced me, told me all the things I wanted to hear." My eyes start to burn. I do not want to be telling the beautiful, meticulously perfect man in front of me about my deepest shame. "But the really bad part was it . . . it happened twice. Two different men, months apart, same MO. And I was too dumb to see it. Stupid Silly Shallow Sam, hopeful and trusting to a fault, and of course my family was so ashamed and livid and just . . . I mean, it was horrific.

"Dad just paid them off, to keep it all out of the press. They tried to hide it from me, but I knew they were disappointed in me. I mean, I almost single-handedly ruined the Canton family name. It's not like I woke up one day and decided, *Hey, today I'm going to star in my very own sex tape,* you know?"

That sends Emerson into a fit of coughs. He gets two waters out of the fridge and hands me one, without looking in my direction, and I'm pretty sure his hands are trembling with anger.

"I know, okay? It's really bad, but I thought I knew them, especially Drake. I mean, I thought he actually loved me. I thought we might get freaking engaged." The tears are falling fast now—I can't help it. "I should've seen, I know. I make people out to be better than they are in my head, Emerson, *I know.* I was bad for the company, bad for Dad, Grandpa. *I know, okay?* And everyone is sure the leak last year is my fault too even though they don't say it, I know they do, and they're probably right! I mean, it's me. I'm the loser in the family, the screwup, the disappointment."

As I let the words and the pain bubble over, things I haven't even admitted out loud before, Emerson makes his way over to me. He wipes the tears from my cheeks with his warm hands that dwarf my features. His fingers are still trembling, so I can't bear to look up at him. I open my mouth to apologize again, for the shame I seem to keep bringing onto the Canton name—a name he's worked so hard to grow, for a decade.

"You are not a disappointment," he says softly yet roughly. I hold back sobs, forcing myself not to break down in front of him.

I can't look up. "You're angry with me, though."

"No. Well, yes." He drops his hands and lets out a heavy sigh. "I wish you'd taken me with you tonight . . . let me . . . protect you."

"From Damian?" I look up at him, my forehead pinched. I don't think I was in any real danger beyond being very uncomfortable or maybe having to make a bit of a scene to break free of him. Not that a scene doesn't hold some danger when you're me. It could've been filmed and posted on social media before I'd even gotten his hands off my hips. I shudder.

"From yourself." Emerson's hands are fists at his sides, and his face looks almost distraught.

I search his eyes. "What do you m—"

"You *are* too trusting. Too optimistic, too good. You let people into your orbit, boys, idiots, twat arseholes who don't deserve to be there." He swallows. "But you're not a screwup."

I shake my head in frustration and wipe my tears. This is so embarrassing. The fact that he just said he has to save me from myself confirms every theory I just confessed.

"Ugh! Just forget it. I have got to quit babbling to you! Telling all my deepest, darkest secrets to Mr. Perfect Genius. It's like you have some superpower to make me open my mouth, and then embarrassing crap falls out. I don't know what's wrong with me!"

He scoffs. "I am not perfect."

"Oh, okay," I mumble, sounding sarcastic and childish.

"I actually *am* the disappointment in my family."

"Please, Emerson. Don't lie to make me feel better. You're taking this from bad to worse."

"It's not a lie. You picked up on the fact I'm not keen on seeing them while I'm here."

"How could they be disappointed in you?" I'm genuinely upset by this idea, especially as I see a flash of my own shame in his beautiful eyes. "I remember everyone freaking out in the office because you weren't even thirty-five and *The Financial Times* put you on the cover and literally crowned you the King of Manhattan!"

He gives a small, sad smile. "Ah, but Manhattan isn't London."

"Seriously? Manhattan isn't good enough? Who the heck are these people, your family?"

He crosses his arms and brings a hand to his chin, looking like a portrait staring back at me. "You really don't know much about me, do you?"

"Emerson. No one knows much about you," I deadpan. He gives a small laugh. "So? Who are they? And where do they live so I can pop on over there and give them a good ole Oklahoma what for, because they're pissing me off." That earns me a real smile— it's not wide, but it reaches his eyes. My chest explodes with bubbles of one million different emotions, bursting all at once.

"A story for another night." He dips his head and uncrosses his arms to turn and go back to his room.

"Wait." I grab his arm, desperate to keep him near me, to keep his mouth talking and his eyes fixed on my own. His arm tenses again, just like on the plane, firm as a rod. "We have a pretty open day tomorrow. I have to get Sadie and Nicole from the airport and swing by the convention center at some point. Do you want to join me?"

"I am seeing my brothers tomorrow, I'm afraid."

"Oh. Okay." I search his face. "Will it be at least a little bit fun?"

He gives a small shrug. "Maybe."

"Well, thank you again, for saving me. Twice."

I don't think—I just do what I need to do. What I have to do. I rush forward and wrap my arms around him. He is hard, tense, strong—everything he was in the water earlier, except dry and warm. He stands frozen, shocked, for what feels like minutes but can only be a couple seconds.

I can't tell if he's disgusted or angry or uncomfortable or what, but instead of letting him off the hook, I squeeze him tighter, close my eyes, and bury my head in between the two bulges of his chest. I may never have the excuse to hold Emerson Clark ever again, and I'm not letting go easily.

When I squeeze, life sparks in his limbs and he finally, tentatively wraps his arms around me in return. His hands barely touch my shoulders at first, like he thinks I might break. Then I feel him inhale, and suddenly he is hugging me.

No, holding me.

He splays his hands and moves his arms as if to touch as much of me as he can, but somehow he remembers the bruise along my side that even I'd forgotten in the moment. He rests his jaw on my head. We stand that way for a few glorious seconds.

"You're welcome," he says softly, and then he pulls away. He turns quickly and goes into his room. Once more, I'm left alone in the kitchen, soaking in the aftermath of an emotional storm that just erupted between us.

I have no idea where I stand with him, but I know it's a lot closer to friendship than it was at the beginning of this trip, and maybe even past friendship into something else. I feel the hope in my gut, for that something else. I close my eyes and take a breath. Because hoping has never gone well for me. Ever.

What if I'm seeing things that aren't there again? Am I making Emerson sweeter, softer, better in my head? I truly don't think so. I think Operation Thaw just took longer than I thought, and finally, blissfully, I have worn down the frozen edges of that CFO façade to reveal a truly stunning man underneath.

CHAPTER 20

> **Me: [Photo]**
> **How happy are you to NOT be hanging out with us today?**

I hope for the three dots but don't get them. I thought surely a selfie in front of London's famous Ferris wheel would warrant a response from Emerson. It doesn't—just like my good morning text about breakfast and a midday check-in text teasing about being with siblings.

It's been radio silence all day. If the song "Hot n Cold" were a person, it'd be Emerson. Actually, that's a classic Sam exaggeration: making things out to be better than they are. The reality is more like "Warm n Freezing."

"Covent Garden?" I ask the girls after we hop off the Ferris wheel.

"Yes! I want to check my two favorite shops there for anything new." Sadie sounds very much the famous, best-selling, world-traveling author that she is. I smile, happy to have her here. You can tell we're sisters, although her hair is a bit darker, her skin is dewier (thanks to a fifteen-step, custom-made skin-care routine), and her curves are tighter, thanks to her personal trainer.

I try not to be jealous of her, I do, but it's hard some days. Not as much today, though, as she pulls her floppy hat farther down on her head, smashing into the oversize sunglasses she can't take off unless she wants to be recognized. I'm also not sure how I'd feel about having a constant bodyguard.

Dean, an older guy who reminds me of a less attractive, more jacked Liam Neeson, is silent and almost invisible, but always there. It seems like it would be suffocating and comforting at the same time.

She's fun, though, my sister. Not as extroverted as me—is anyone?—but not as hard and hermit-y as Skye. She and Skye are a lot alike in their tough love and quick wit, but Sadie has smoothed out her rough edges much more. It's admirable, considering all she's been through, none of which we are allowed to talk about.

"I can't believe you get to come here regularly. Quit being so cool," Nicole jokes as we get out of the car.

"Can't help it," Sadie jokes back. We make our way down the adorable cobblestone street that is giving me serious modern-day Hogsmeade vibes. The road is lined with storefronts, most with little awnings decorated with hanging potted flowers. The center is filled every few paces with a new set of roped-off outdoor seating, complete with folding chairs and individual umbrellas over each table. We pop in and out of shops, laughing, browsing, and sending selfies to my sisters.

"So, Emerson didn't want to shop with us today, huh?" Sadie asks as we make our way to the next crosswalk.

"Can you even imagine?" I chuckle. "I think that would count as a legitimate method of torture for him, walking and talking with us. He's hanging with his brothers today."

"And how's Operation Thaw going? Are you friends yet? Did the big rescue make it weird?"

"Yeah, how in love with him are you on a scale from One to He Saved My Life and Now I Must Have His Babies?" Nicole piles on with a laugh.

"That'd be a zero, thank you very much," I say quickly. My stomach tightens, because it feels like I just lied, which I don't do. But love? I may have the start of a crush. No one is loving anyone else. *Not happening.*

"Good. He's so not your type, Sam," Nicole says.

"My type?" I ask, not sure what she means, especially since now that I know him better, I feel like Emerson is basically everyone's type: hot, brooding, gentlemanly, British . . .

"Yeah, you know, someone more like you. Not so serious." She flips over one hand as she explains. She must catch the glance I give her, because it feels a lot like she just called me Shallow Sam without using the words. "You know, someone fun! Flirty, chatty, adventurous. Someone who can handle you in all your glory." She bumps her hip into mine playfully.

"I don't know, maybe serious is exactly what she needs," Sadie chimes in as she checks out a sale rack on the sidewalk.

"I don't *need* anyone. Absolutely off men, remember? Why are we even talking about this? Sadie, would you like for us to talk about your love life for a change?"

She doesn't look at me. "Point taken."

"And Nicole? When is the last time you even went on a date? It's been like a year."

"I'm picky." Nicole shrugs, causing her gorgeous dark curls to fall away from her shoulders.

"Uh-huh. Both of you can just shut up about . . . Emerson?" He appears before us on the sidewalk, with two lookalikes. The three of them could honestly be triplets.

"Miss Canton . . ." He's surprised. It takes all my concentration to keep my face from falling and my shoulders from slumping. We're back to Miss Canton, then.

"Hey, Emerson." Sadie smiles at him beside me.

"Miss Canton," he repeats, lighter this time. "And Miss Moreno, these are my brothers, Byron and Benedict."

"Ben's fine," the second one says.

"Hi, I'm Nicole." She offers a slight wave.

With a practiced smile, my sister says, "Sadie."

"Hi, I'm Samantha, so nice to meet you both!" I say, a bit too cheery.

"It's our pleasure. Dammit, Emerson, what exactly is in the water at Canton International? Can I get a job?" Byron says, giving us all an obvious once-over. The three of us blush and smile in response.

"May I remind you you're married, Byron." Emerson huffs quietly.

"Well, I'm not," Ben says with a wide smile. Emerson exhales in his signature exasperation, a distinct contrast to his brothers, who are both totally at ease. Charming, even.

"We'll let you ladies get back to your day." Emerson motions for his brothers to walk around us.

"I don't know, looks like they could use a tea break to me," Ben drawls.

"I could use a tea break myself," Byron adds, clearly enjoying making his older brother squirm.

"We just had tea at Bageriet," Emerson mutters.

I decide to save the day. "As much as I want to hear every horrible and embarrassing childhood story you have on Emerson, in excruciating detail"—I shoot him a look that I hope explains he owes me one—"we're on a mission, actually. We want to hit a few shops before we have to get over to the convention center."

"I don't know . . . I think we have time, don't we, Sadie?" Nicole pushes me. She glances around and then pauses to offer Ben a wide, playful smile. Sadie watches the whole situation as if she's on the outside of us, studying us all like puzzle pieces.

Finally, Sadie makes the call. "Samantha is running the show here, so I guess it's a no this time, boys. But nice to meet you." A polite nod of her head explains that the discussion is over. Relief washes over Emerson's blushed face.

"Our loss, then. Lovely to meet you all as well." Byron joins his brother in his efforts to move past us.

"Well, if you find some time while you're in town, do let us know. I'll drag the old man out for some fun." Ben points toward Emerson, who rolls his eyes.

"See you tomorrow," Emerson says to us before turning and almost pushing his brothers down the street. The three of us watch after them for a moment.

Sadie grabs my elbow. "Okay, who are you and what have you done with my sister?"

"Huh?"

"That was the most un-Samantha thing I've ever seen in my life. Saying no to sitting and chatting over tea? Not to mention tea with three hotties, *British hotties*, and pestering them with questions about Emerson? Explain. Immediately." She levels me with a no-nonsense glare.

I shrug and try hard to sell more half lies. "What I said. We have to get ready for convention with a skeleton crew, and I haven't had time to even run by and check on our inventory. We don't even really have time to mess with these shops, honestly."

Sadie squints at me, debating if she believes me, or more likely debating if she's going to call me on my BS or not. Nicole just watches us both tentatively.

"All right, let's head to the convention center then," Sadie says. "Dean, we're heading back to the car!" she calls to her bodyguard, who I didn't realize was just a few steps behind us.

"Aw, man. Goodbye gorgeous Covent Garden." Nicole pouts. "Why isn't Emerson helping with the convention prep?"

"He will tomorrow. This is the first time he's taken to see his family since we've been here."

"Okay." Nicole sighs. I do feel for her, having to rush through her first time in London. Sadie says nothing as we drive along, but I catch her studying me more than once. It's unnerving. Skye does it too: sees things, studies people, notices what most miss. But Sadie seems to go beyond noticing and almost reads people's thoughts. I think it's what makes her such a great writer, her superpower for understanding others, as if she could emphasize with any and all points of view.

As soon as we reach our area inside the convention center, we split ways to check our shipping crates. Once I'm alone, I whip out my phone.

> **Me: Emerson Saves: Three**
> **Samantha Saves: One**
> **You're welcome**
> Emerson: Three?
> **I'm counting Near Death by Heavy Backpack**
> It was dangerously heavy.
> And thank you.
> **Would tea with all of us really have been so bad?**

He doesn't type a response, which I take as a big fat yes. Is his issue the group and the conversing, in general, or tea with me and all my babbling? Is he afraid I'd ask too many personal questions? A legitimate concern, for sure. I'd try to hold myself back, but once I get on a roll, conversations get carried away from me, by me.

I sigh, frustrated with myself. If only I was more like Sadie, even-keeled between two extremes. She enjoys people, in small groups and large settings, but she can also sit and write alone for days. I shudder at that thought as I take my clipboard and head to the next set of boxes.

I fumble into the door of the suite after dinner, totally exhausted. I surprised myself with the desire to skip dinner altogether, which must have everything to do with my aching feet and nothing to do with the silent man who shares my temporary apartment.

I steal a glance at his door, wondering about his day: What did he have for dinner? Is he watching TV in there? Or reading a book? What book? Is he on his bed shirtless and in sweatpants? Does he *own* sweatpants? I swallow, suddenly parched.

I head to the kitchen and—

"*Ah!*" I close my eyes and put a hand to my chest, panting. "You scared me! How do you not make any noise? Are you even breathing?" I reopen my eyes and wish I hadn't. Because there he is—silent, shirtless, and dripping with sweat, water in one hand, phone in the other.

"Sorry." I barely hear his reply because I am lost in the ridges along his torso. So many of them, so defined, each one glistening. I bite my bottom lip and try to look away but instead imagine myself licking the sweat off him. *WHAT! Who thinks that?! Sweat! Gross!*

"Y-You work out at night too?" I whisper. I still haven't managed to look at his face; there are just so many other interesting places for my eyes to find, like the top curve of his bicep, the waistband of his shorts.

"Not normally," he says, and I realize from his voice that he's smiling. I look at his face, which is grinning. Smug, even. And why wouldn't he be? I'm ogling him. Straight-up ogling.

Insert nerves.

"Oh. Yeah, you seem much more like a morning runner. Like at five A.M. sharp or something. Every single day. Same path. Probably like fifteen miles every time, same exact pace, super fast, totally."

"Do I?" He's still smug. It's the most relaxed and what—maybe happy?—that I've ever seen him.

"Mhm." I swallow again. Right! Water! I make my way toward the fridge next to where he's leaning. "Just coming in here for a water. Worked up a sweat at the convention center. I mean, not a real sweat, like you, obviously, or I'd be all wet. I mean! Like, drenched. I mean. You know what I mean.

"It's not a good look on women. Like, you can stand there looking like a warrior, as if you just fought an entire army by yourself. Very Thor, you know? But on women, it's just gross. Like after Zumba, I'm super disgusting. Have you ever tried Zumba?" I finally make it to the fridge, and he doesn't move out of the way. He just absorbs the space of the entire small kitchen with his frame as heat rolls off him in waves. I get a water bottle out of the fridge and close it, and his expression is the same: contained, mild amusement.

"No, of course you haven't tried Zumba! Ha! What am I thinking. It's a dance class, and we all know how you feel about dancing. Not to mention, it's a group activity, so I'm going to guess that's a hard pass for you. Very hard." I choke on the last two words, looking right at his pecs as they tumble out. I chug my water, hoping it will save me from myself. *Deflect, Samantha! Deflect for heaven's sake!*

"So? Was your day a little bit fun, after all?" I ask. He tilts his head back and forth to mean so-so. "C'mon, it was, admit it. I don't even know why you needed saving today. By the way, it was just us girls, who you already know, and your brothers seem like tons of fun." He grunts, but his expression changes, like I've said the wrong thing. I try to go back to our usual teasing. "You never said thank you for my save, either." I raise my eyebrows.

He pushes off from the counter. "Thank you, Miss Canton."
He says it tightly, and then he's through his door. What? What the
heck was that?! One minute he's beaming salty sex rays at me with
his grin, the next he's as cold as a blizzard blowing right out the
door.

I call bull. He liked the way I stared at him. Something about
peopling or his brothers set him off, but he's just being a coward.
That's it. New goal. He's not the only one who can prance around
half naked.

I have my wiles and I know how to use them and I know he's
not immune. He held me in his arms last night, tight and firm. He
called me Samantha, more than once. It was real and it was hot
and dammit, I want more of that. More of my name on his soft lips,
more of his stare boring into me, more of his hands on my skin.

Commence *Operation Melt.*

CHAPTER 21

I hear Emerson rummaging in the kitchen, and I almost sprint through the living room, slowing to a normal pace when I get to the kitchen.

"Morning," I say as I casually walk to the fridge and bend over to grab a water. I can feel his eyes on me, and I force myself not to smile or blush or cough or react in any way. Take those wiles, Emerson Clark.

I am wearing a tight workout tank over yoga leggings, the pair that has a bit of gathering over my butt crack. They're called Ass Leggings online, and for good reason. I don't know if the Adonis next to me—who is in a perfect button-up shirt, open at the top to show a teasing hint of skin, over well-fitted slacks—is a butt man, but in these tights, I'd bet any guy with a heartbeat is a butt man.

I close the fridge, and instead of giving him a normal berth of personal space, I stay within inches of touching him.

"What're you making?" I look at the counter in front of him.

"Toast." The word cracks and barely makes it out of his throat. *Do not smile, do not smile, do not smile.* "Toast." The second time almost sounded normal. He got a good view of my fridge bend and now can see a hint of cleavage from his towering height. It's not a low-cut tank, but the girls are pushed up in the lined sports bra I chose specifically for this moment. I finally look at his face, but his eyes are definitely not meeting mine. *Victory!*

His toast pops up, breaking him out of his trance.

"Sounds good, actually." I reach across him to pull out one piece of toast, which just so happens to cause my right nipple to brush against his left arm. I turn around, feeling his gaze on my backside as I reach for the peanut butter in the cabinet on the top shelf. I stretch up on my toes, but still pushing my butt out a little bit, of course.

I smell him for a second before I'm frozen. Because he's behind me, caging me in effortlessly as he reaches for the jar. The fabric of his pants barely brushes against the thin spandex of my leggings, but the heat of him consumes me whole. Wanting pools in my center with a force that takes my breath away.

I involuntarily lower my hand and the heels of my feet as he sets the peanut butter on the counter. I want him to linger, to push me against the counter, to say something in my ear, or even better, spin me around and kiss me senseless. I'm shocked by how badly and plainly I want that. Want *him.* But he is gone almost as quickly as he was here. I realize he's turned back to his toast but still hasn't taken it out of the toaster.

"Thanks," I say. My turn to croak. *Crap, is that one point for me or for Emerson?*

"Mhmm. Thief." He takes his toast out and sets it on his plate. I turn back to my toast and feel the tension between us as we each doctor our slices. Silent tension gets to me every time.

"Who eats two pieces of toast?!" I blurt. "I'm only carb loading this morning because today is going to be a doozy. There are a million boxes to unpack, displays to assemble and all that. So that's an arm workout right there. Then there will be so much squatting and lifting, so there's my core and glutes. And then walking all over the convention center, surely that will add up to a whole Zumba class, don't you think?"

"No." His voice is soft behind me.

I give an exaggerated sigh. "Well, then maybe I'll just have to *run* around the stupid convention center." I turn and look as I take a bite, but he keeps his back to me, taking approximately one million years to fix his toast. I leave the kitchen with my slice to finish getting ready for the day before we head out. I don't feel his eyes on me as I leave, but I'm still smiling because I have a feeling it's going to be a very long, hot day for my Frosty.

"Okay. Who are they for? Emerson?" My sister corners me with her whisper yelling the second the group splits up to tackle various jobs around our convention display.

"What?"

She takes off her ridiculous sunglasses, since we are indoors, in a grand convention ballroom that's bright with fluorescent lighting, as well as chandeliers. She shoots daggers at me. "Don't *what* me. It's me. Who are the Ass Leggings for?"

"Hey there, Samantha!" We're interrupted before I have to answer her. By the handsome-as-ever Thomas Gage.

"Thomas, hi." I smile, blushing at the look he gives me. I've added a sweatshirt to my outfit, but since he walked up from behind, he's had a little show already. I didn't think about anyone other than Emerson when I put these on, but I guess there are, in fact, other men in the universe. Sadie shoots me a satisfied and obvious smile. "This is my sister, Sadie. Sadie, this is Thomas Gage. He and his brother Tim own Whosits & Whatsits."

"Of course, Sadie Canton! Wow! Great to meet you. Wow," he says awkwardly. He did pretty well, considering. She's been on magazine covers, interview shows, is a regular romance contributor on *The Today Show*, and even had a cameo in her first movie adaptation. People tend to lose their heads at the sight of her, which is gorgeous and very put together.

"Likewise. I love your shops. I always find one when I'm here." She shakes his hand and smiles. I can tell she means it.

"Brilliant, uh, y-yes, well, g-glad to hear it," he stutters in surprise, and puffing up at the praise from an actual famous person.

"Well, these books won't sign themselves, I'm afraid. Nice to meet you." She winks at me as she takes a box—definitely not filled with her books—and retreats to give us space. I'm not sure if I want said space. To his credit, Thomas doesn't watch her leave. His focus remains on me. His eyes are not as intense as Emerson's, but they're also less guarded. It's a warmer gaze but doesn't feel nearly as precious, like he hands his lingering looks out freely. Still, I don't hate it—his eyes trained on me.

I glance around for Emerson, who's been silent and distant since my kitchen victory, but see no signs of him. He probably positioned himself as far away from me in our exhibition space as he could.

I shake off those thoughts. I can chat with Thomas all I want. I am not Emerson's. And flirting with a hot guy, who is actually interested in me, does not make me a hussy, despite the whole debacle in Bermondsey.

"Are you guys all set up already?" I ask.

"Almost, but our booth is maybe a quarter the size of the small country you're setting up here."

"Yeah . . ." I laugh.

"Tim called from Richmond, actually, says your booth is looking great from there."

That joke earns him a real, too-loud laugh from me. It feels good and releases some of my tension. I shrug at our display. "That's the Canton way, I guess—go big or go home."

"Oh, definitely don't go home," he says lowly, smoothly. I smile and look away. "Come see us when you can get a break. I've got a new line in I want to show you."

"All right." I look back at him, fighting a blush.

"If you can find us, it's a wee booth in comparison, 'bout the size of one of your boxes." His eyes twinkle, and I laugh again.

"Yeah, yeah, shut it or I won't come by," I tease. He pretends to zip his lips, then looks past me and gives a small wave that looks like a salute. I turn to find Emerson a few feet away, glaring in my direction. I glare back and give him a bitter, sarcastic smile before looking past him at Nicole, who is giving me two thumbs up.

I turn away quickly, refusing to blush. Emerson can glare all he wants. I've done nothing wrong and have nothing to feel embarrassed about. Ass Leggings included. I hope he'll come say something, maybe along the lines of "I don't want you talking to other men because I want you to be mine."

But he doesn't.

———

The workout gear was not a terrible idea, because work, we did. By late afternoon, every muscle in my body is aching from all the weird bending, lifting, pulling, and pushing required to get our booth set up. All of us are spent, including Emerson, who I've barely seen all day.

It's been worth it, though, because our space looks glorious. One side is set up like an actual retail store, complete with an awning, a front door with a doorbell, and window displays. But as you walk through the space, the walls of the faux store branch off, allowing for more display sections.

In one area, we have an artist exhibition space, for live demonstrations by the painters, sculptors, illustrators, and other crafters who contribute to our signature lines. We have an entire section dedicated to Canton Publishing, comprised of many authors and titles, but really it's a display just for Sadie. She signs books, takes selfies, and sells tons of her novels and novel-related merchandise. There's also a small section for Skye's line of painted products, PaintedSkye, though she decided not to come do a demonstration this year.

It makes me both extremely proud and a little bit sad. It's basically their grand opuses on display in front of my face. Not only that, but it's my job over the next two days to sell their goods. Okay, that's an exaggeration. My job is to sell everyone, on all of Canton, but after my brutally honest conversation with Emerson the other night, it feels a lot like my sisters create and I sell their creations. *Life calling, indeed.*

"All right, I take back all my teasing." Thomas is in genuine awe of our exhibit as he sidles up to me in the center of a walkway. I'm giving everything one last look, and I'm pretty pleased.

"Right?" I pant. "I don't think I'll be able to lift my arms ever again, but . . . worth it."

"Guess you really were too busy to come by." He turns from the booth to look at me.

"Sorry! I totally forgot! I barely stopped to eat today. But I'll come by for sure tomorrow. I'll make the rounds all day long."

"No worries, I brought it to you." He holds out a fist, waiting for my palm underneath. I oblige. "It should come from one of the little rascals, of course, but I think I can safely assume this is you to a tee," he says, and I look at what I'm holding. It's like a beaded letter bracelet I would've made as a girl, except with solid-gold-letter block beads surrounded by gleaming glass-blown baubles. The letters read THE•FUN•AUNT. My head jerks up.

"Thomas! It's gorgeous! Thank you!" The gift is so thoughtful and unexpected, I don't think twice before giving him a hug. I let go before he does, feeling a bit weird. "You have a whole line of these? They're beautiful."

He gently puts it on my wrist, an intimate move that should give me butterflies but doesn't. "Yes, well, the line is blown glass, gorgeous stuff. You'll have to take a look tomorrow."

"I will, I definitely will. Thank you. I can't wait to pretend this was from my nephews and rub it in my sisters' faces." I laugh, and he laughs too.

His laugh fades and he shifts on his feet when he makes eye contact with me. "Do you have dinner plans?"

"I do, actually, and it's not as fun as whatever you're doing, I assure you, but there's prep for tomorrow I have to do, while at some point, hopefully also stuffing my face."

"Until tomorrow then." He backs up a step, sounding genuinely disappointed.

"Thanks again. I love it," I say as I turn to go.

"You bet. Good night, Samantha."

"Good night." I play with the gorgeous beads on my wrist as I turn around. I feel that my cheeks are a bit pink, but that was just so unexpected. And a tiny bit awkward. And it truly is a beautiful piece. I make a mental note to dig and see if we can connect with the artist, maybe commission our own line.

I feel him before I look up. Just as I hit the outskirts of our booth, I feel tingling down my spine. A tingling only Emerson evokes. But I don't see him anywhere. Still, I realize suddenly that my sweatshirt has been long gone for hours, including the split second during my hug with Thomas. Did Emerson see? Do I hope he saw? Only if it helps with Operation Melt, which, surely, it would. Wouldn't it?

If his stares and words and touches have been as real as they've felt to me, then Thomas's arms around me should definitely inspire an inferno inside Emerson's head. Just as I would explode inside if I saw him hugging some woman, no matter what she was wearing. I shudder at the thought. But it must be my fatigue playing mind tricks on me, as there's no Snow King any-where in sight.

CHAPTER 22

"How was round one, rock star?" Nicole asks as I step behind the counter within our exhibit to grab a water.

"Great, but it's only been an hour. I hope these wedges hold up their end of the deal."

"Deal?"

"Yes, I wear them, even though they're not the cutest, and they keep my feet from hurting so badly. We had a serious conversation when I bought them." I look down and give my shoes the stank eye, and Nicole laughs. "All right, be back later."

I step out of our booth and pause, scanning the giant space. I need to hit all the vendors, distributors, artists, and buyers that we didn't schedule a private meeting with during our stay here. There are a bajillion of them, and most of them are from other countries throughout Europe. I mentally rummage through my big binder while looking at all the names hanging above booth after booth.

Before I can embark on my next quest, I spot him. Jack Frost in his three-piece suit, looking like absolute death. Is he sick? I didn't see him last night, and he was silent during our commute this morning. He's talking to a CEO I recognize, so I make my way to him.

"Francis Wells! So lovely to see you here!" I extend a hand. "Samantha Canton."

"Right, Miss Canton, great to meet you." The old charmer winks warmly at me as Emerson eyes me with confusion.

"I need to steal Mr. Clark here for a teensy emergency. My apologies."

"Of course."

I pull Emerson off to a side walkway near a set of restrooms. "What's wrong? Are you sick?" I search his eyes, which are locked on mine in confusion.

"No? And I was about to ask you the same after the way you rushed over. Everything is fine."

"Emerson, you're green. Almost as bad as at the Sky Garden. What's going on?"

He adjusts his tie with a frown and a heavy sigh. I stare at him with eyebrows raised until he caves. "I am not good at . . . this." He gestures his hand to the conference beside us.

"Oh, it's the peopling? The talking? It's day one and it's only been an hour!"

"Don't remind me." He closes his eyes. I can see the tension in his neck and shoulders as if he's wearing a cloak of anxiety. I stop and think as an attendee walks by, eyeing us cautiously. I smile absently at them and think about my sister, Skye, who hates these kinds of things too. If she had to go mingle, what would she want?

Easy. She'd want me. I am the world's absolute best networking wing woman.

"Okay, time for Samantha Save number two. Who's on your list?"

His eyes reopen to meet mine. "What?"

"Who do you need to show face with today? All the big suits, of course, CEOs and big buyers from a couple chains." I start to process my thoughts out loud. "There are a couple tech bigwigs here too. You'll need to talk about the app with them, and maybe anyone else Dad would greet if he were here. Do you know who that would be?" I look up at him, and he just nods. "Okay, well, some of them were on my list anyway, so it won't totally be double duty for me. But we better get moving." I start to head back into the maze of displays.

"Wait, what?" Emerson catches my wrist in his giant hand for a moment, then drops it.

"I am your dream come true, Mr. Clark. The world's best networking sidekick. Actually, in this scenario, you actually become my sidekick! Ha! Love that for me. I'll do almost all the talking, and you stand there and try to *not* look like you hate me and yourself and everyone in this room, okay?" He gives a few passionate nods, realizing that I am swooping in and saving his socially awkward ass. "Just follow me, literally, and watch the magic happen."

Happen, it does.

I remember every executive's name, save one or two that weren't listed in attendance when I made my binder. I make Emerson sound like the numbers wizard that he is, without him having to talk hardly at all. I memorized how to say "Forgive me, I don't know how to speak *whatever language*" in every European language I thought would be present, and that's a big hit every time I use it. Emerson does know multiple languages, of course, because standing there in his impeccable three-piece charcoal masterpiece and ice-blue tie is not swoony enough, and he adds a sentence on to my joke here and there.

His color improves as we go, as does the intensity of his gaze on me. It seems like he's . . . in awe, maybe? It's not the Come Mount Me Right Now glare I'd hoped for when I chose this tight hot-pink pencil dress, but whatever the look is, I'll take it. By the time the hall starts to clear for lunch, we've met with everyone Emerson needed to see over the whole two days. I lead him into a back service corridor outside of the exhibit hall.

"Aaaaaand we're done. That was everyone! Can you believe it!"

I am buzzing with energy, as I always am after rapid-fire mingling, and he looks depleted, as he does at the end of our long meeting days. But at least he's not green. He's looking down at the ground in thought. "Uh, hello, earth to Frosty, you're welcome." Still nothing, other than his heavy breathing, as if he did *any* of the heavy lifting in there. Psh!

"You're welcoooome," I sing. "C'mon, *Moana*? Nothing? You've got to watch more Disney, Emerson, seriously." He looks up at me for a second from under a small lock of hair that's fallen down onto his face, but then he looks back down at his shoes. I realize I have no idea what he might say, and since I did just slip and call him Frosty, I'm concerned it'll be on the unkind side of blunt.

Maybe I talked too much. Maybe I went around too fast. Maybe he thought my German was awful or my jokes were silly.

"All right, well, now you can spend the whole afternoon with your family or, ha, let's be real, in your room alone recharging. No shame, I get it. Your social battery is on zero percent, right? But I still have half a ballroom to go meet with, so I better find something to eat." Seriously? He's not even going to mutter a thank-you? Forget this. "K then! See ya!" I start to stomp off.

My wrist explodes at his grasp that's so firm, it's almost painful. The wrist bombs are instantly nothing compared to his other hand on my hip as he pulls me back toward him. He steps forward and pushes me up against the greige wallpapered hallway wall.

He's standing so close, I get to breathe him in, manly and clean, each breath sending waves of want down to my core. His body cages me into the wall, and his hands move to my face as his eyes search mine, so close I can see tiny navy flecks in the pools of pale blue. My hands reflexively grab his forearms, which are thick and warm under his soft suit jacket.

He leans into me and my brain.

What?

I.

What?

Please kiss me, please kiss me, please kiss me.

He runs his nose along mine and whispers, "How do you do that?"

"W-What?" I say, amazing myself that I can form words when I can feel his breath on my lips.

"Put . . . everyone at ease." His lips almost barely brush against mine as he talks, and it forces my back to arch. I am dying under his touch, knowing his hands under my ears are the only explanation for why my head hasn't totally detached and floated away.

"I—" is all I get out as his nose and lips barely brush all around the edges of my mouth.

"You are an opus all on your own, Samantha."

I can't take it anymore. It's too much, too soft, too sweet, too hot. I am going to explode into tiny blissful pieces from just the graze of his mouth on mine.

"Emerson, kiss me," I whisper, and I feel his body push in closer to me for a fraction of a second, and then, as if my words broke our spell, he drops his hands and pulls back.

"I can't. I'm sorry. I shouldn't have." He shakes his head and closes his eyes. I feel myself turning crimson as he takes another step back and disgust flashes across his face. I let out some of the bated breath I've been holding and cross my arms. They offer no protection from the chill his touch leaves behind. He looks me in the eye again and mutters "Forgive me" before he stalks off. Once again, I'm left in his wake, shocked and blushing.

What?

What just happened?

And why on earth did he stop?

He wants me but is disgusted at himself for wanting me? Is he mad at himself because he sees me as off-limits? Because it's unprofessional? Whatever is going on in his stunning head, I intend to find out.

CHAPTER 23

I push through the rest of my day with fervor. Handshake, smile, joke, personal story, personal question, product reference, question, sales numbers, question, raving reviews, joke, smile, hug, business card, rinse, repeat.

Emerson's words play through my mind as I work. Do I really put everyone at ease? I guess I can kind of see that, and it sparks a flicker of pride in me. But as soon as I'm feeling assured, I remember the disgust spoiling his gorgeous features after our almost-kiss.

I am a jumbled mess of questions when the day comes to an end. I meet Nicole back at our booth, and she lets me know we had a fantastic sales day, plus tons of interested buyers and happy social media mentions. Sadie messages us to meet her in the greenroom so we can head to find some dinner. On our way out, Thomas waves us down. Dread creeps up my spine when I notice how he looks at me.

"Good day one, ladies?" he asks with a hopeful smile.

"Great day one," I say. "You?"

"Pretty nice, yes. Bit slow there at the end, but people get peckish early after a conference day, right? I'm famished."

I nod. Nicole nudges me with her elbow, and I shoot her a question with my eyes. She takes over.

"We're just headed to dinner. Why don't you and Tim join us?"

"You sure?" He looks at me as he asks it.

"Of course!" I say with fake enthusiasm. I don't want to be rude, especially not to a buyer of ours, but dinner with him sounds long and boring. I want to hurry back to that suite and pound on that door until the beautiful beast inside gives me some answers.

"Fantastic. I'll just go fetch Tim, and we'll get a move on. Where to?" he asks.

Nicole looks at me.

"You tell us, Londoner," I tease, shocked at how genuine my flirting sounds.

"Right. You have my number, yeah? You just text me, and I'll send you a place."

I nod, and Nicole almost shouts "Sounds great!" to his back as he hustles away. She snaps her head to me and lowers her volume. "Hello, what's wrong with you? He is smokin' hot and hasn't stopped drooling after you since yesterday!"

"Me, what are *you* thinking? I'm off men, remember?!"

"You're not seriously going to pass up a fling in London. You've lost your mind." She shakes her head as we walk to find Sadie.

"Or maybe I've finally found my self-respect! When has a fling ever been a good idea for me? Huh?"

She concedes a bit. "Okay, so just a fun, flirty dinner then. Hell, if he wasn't so stuck on you, I'd let him stick it to me, that's for freaking sure." She laughs, and I join her. "And the accent? I mean, dig me a grave because I am dying over here."

We find Sadie and head to the car, but I hang back to pull out my phone. I should probably give Emerson space, but the man owes me an explanation. Plus, he's gotta eat.

Me: Have you recharged enough to meet us for dinner?

No happy little dots pop up. I sigh and shake off the disappointment. I just had a killer day, and I'm about to hit the town with my friends in London for heaven's sake! Who cares about Icy and his confusing storm of emotions.

Dinner is a blast. Thomas chose a trendy fish and chips place. The food is amazing, and the cocktails are even better. I try to pace myself, but Nicole begs me to keep up with her as she treats herself for the killer day we had today. Sadie even lets loose with us, a rare and happy sight.

After we've stuffed ourselves to the brink and drank ourselves to the point of uncontrolled laughing over nothing, Nicole suggests a nightcap. Thomas agrees, but Sadie, Tim, and Dean bow out for the evening. I insist we hit the bar in our hotel, feeling myself on the edge of falling asleep while standing. In the car on the way to the hotel, Tipsy Sloppy Sam takes over my phone.

> **Me: Okay, it's been hours, Frosty**
> **Your battery has got to be at like 90% now**
> **At least**
> **Meet for a nightcap?**
> **I might fall asleep at the bar**
> **So we're going to the bar in our hotel.**
> **That way, I'll be close to my bed**
> **Could you carry me upstairs?**
> **Of course you could, you're freaking JACKED**
> **[Heart eyes emoji]**

No happy text bubble. Ugh! We have two rounds of champagne at the bar, which I may or may not be dragging out in hopes that a certain someone will join us. "Yeah, time to get you back upstairs, lightweight." Nicole snorts as she stands. I stand too and stumble a bit. Thomas steadies me, and I thank him. I think. We head out to the lobby, but instead of heading to the elevator, Nicole says something about the restroom and tells Thomas and me to park it on the couch.

"This is a soft, super couch, don't you think?" I hear myself sigh.

"Is it?" Thomas rubs the fabric, clearly feeling a little gone himself.

"*Ha!* I said soft super! I meant soft super!" I am so funny. I start laughing and slide in the seat a little bit, and Thomas grabs me. As I right myself, I happen to turn my head and see *him*, finally.

Mr. Handsome as Ever with His Shirt Unbuttoned at the Top— he came! But he's scowling at me, fists clenched, and already back in the elevator. I realize Thomas has his arms around me, but I don't even feel his touch. I do feel the piercing, angry gaze streaming from two almost clear eyes, straight to my very soul.

"No! Wait!" I say, but the doors close. I stand, suddenly almost completely sober. "Ugh! Shit!" I say under my breath. Thomas stands, concerned.

"Everything all right?"

"Yes, just . . . need to head up to my room." I keep talking as I leave him. "It's all catching up to me, you know? Time for bed for me. I'll see you tomorrow. Let Nicole know I went on up, will you?"

"Of course, but let me walk you."

"That's all right, I'm fine. Thanks," I call, rushing farther away before he can try to escort me all the way to my door. The thought of Thomas trying to say good night, with hugs or anything else, outside the suite door sends a chill down my back. I can only imagine how Emerson would open the door at the exact wrong moment and be even more pissed than he is now.

He is pissed, right? Angry eyes, flexed fists. Because he's jealous. Got to be. Unless he's just mad about the professional aspect? Or that I'm beyond the acceptable range of tipsy right now? The elevator crawls upward at a snail's pace as I think.

I had one or two too many, but I will remember every second of this tomorrow, including the last few horrid minutes. I know I sent a pathetic SamStorm earlier, which I'll regret when the headache wakes me at 6:00 A.M. But I have my wits about me for the most part. Sadie was with me, and we stayed on top of our water, ate a ton. He better be jealous, because anything else, and I'm about to give him a piece of my mind.

I march into our suite and straight to his door. I've never knocked on it before, so I hesitate. But now he knows I'm standing here. I knock. He opens, standing there in a T-shirt and his slacks. A T-shirt. It must have been under his button-up. It's so tight across his chest, it throws me completely off. His angry sigh snaps me back to reality.

"It wasn't what it looked like," I say, looking at his eyes, unafraid.

"I don't know what you mean." His eyes stay fixed on the ground.

"Emerson, Nicole was with us, she just went to the restroom, I wasn't with him, I just slipped, and he grabbed me so I didn't fall completely on my ass in the middle of the lobby."

"All right."

"Will you look at me?!"

He does, and it's as if the whole room is dark and his gaze is a bright spotlight, laying me bare.

"It was nothing. I don't like Thomas like that."

"Fine," he says with a shrug, not looking away.

I sigh and close my eyes for a beat, gathering my frantic thoughts. "Earlier today—"

"Was a mistake." He huffs.

I look up at him, and there's no softness in his eyes, no warmth.

"It won't happen again."

"Why? Because we work together? Or my name? Or the fact that I'm Adam's little sister-in-law? Or what? What is it?"

His silent face reveals nothing.

"You want me, but you don't *want* to want me. So you're mad at yourself. But . . ." I look down, afraid, but saying the words before I can think to stop myself the further embarrassment: "What about what I want?"

"It doesn't matter." He shifts to start to close the door and gives one of his deep exhales. "Miss Canton, it's late. I'll see you in the morning."

"Soooo that's it? My feelings don't matter, and I'll see you in the morning?"

"Yes."

I scoff, throwing my hands up in surrender. "Wow. Okay, Emerson. Okay. See you in the morning." I turn and stomp off before I do anything stupid like let a tear fall down my face. I don't hear his door close as I walk away. I go into my room and slam the door and then lean against it, breathing hard so I won't start crying.

I can't help it. I think about his lips on mine, as light as a feather.

You are an opus all on your own, Samantha.

Ugh! But that's not all. The disgust. The cold determination.

It won't happen again.

It doesn't matter.

He's made up his mind, clearly. Better I let go now than later, after we'd kissed and all my hopes had started building into real affection for the jerk. No, absolutely no crying. Operation Melt is over, and it's time for a new mission: Operation Make It through the Rest of This Trip and Never Talk to Emerson Clark Again.

Who am I kidding.

Dammit!

CHAPTER 24

Me: Gala, here I come!
Me: [Photo]
Susan: WOWZA
Sally: Yas sister werk it
Skye: The girls look fantastic.
Sadie: A weaponized hourglass figure! Watch out, men!
Skye: Thomas Gage won't be able to form complete sentences.
[Star eyes emoji]
Susan: Sadie, your turn!
Sadie: [Photo]
HAWT!
Sadie: Sam, quit texting and get down here. We're all in the lobby.
On my way!

I give myself another once-over. Skye's right—my chest is pop-pin'. I wonder if Emerson is a boob man, then grunt at myself. Who cares about him! Did I go get a new dress a couple nights ago? Yes. Did I pick the plunging, cool-blue mermaid-style gown with him in mind? Yes, I did. But he's put me firmly in the friend category—or maybe even the coworkers-only category—so I have got to stop thinking about him. *Yeah, right, suuuuuuure.*

Well, okay, I may be thinking about him, but he doesn't need to know it. Tonight, I will not look at him or talk to him. Probably. *Gah, such a weakling.*

The elevator doors open, and I swish out into the lobby. The breeze feels good against my neck since my mass of blond hair is tucked back in a tight, low bun. I see our group by the couch, and a stab of regret hits me when I think back to last night. But a whole long, work-filled, Emerson-free (and mostly Thomas-free) day has gone by since that incident. I see Emerson out of the corner of my eye, off to the side of the group looking at his phone. I command my eyes to avoid his area, and they obey.

That plan works for the rest of the evening. I float around the room, exactly like I did all day today and yesterday, just with a little more poise and a few new names and faces. From time to time, I think I feel Emerson's eyes on me, but I don't follow the heat I feel to confirm. If he wants to stare, so be it. I'm too busy having fun anyway.

After the mingling and the eating, where I had to look at Emerson once or twice in group conversation, only so as to not be obvious with my avoidance, the dancing starts.

I don't hold back on the dance floor, because why would I? There's a live band and a million fun British men here. My dance partners are mostly old men and married men who've become friends, like Tim, Paul, and Bernie. And yes, I dance a couple dances with Thomas. I am friendly and fun, but I don't lean into him or make a show of it.

As much as I want to make Emerson jealous, I feel icky about possibly leading Thomas on. After our second dance, I make my way to the bar for a water.

"Okay, what the hell is going on with you and Emerson?" my sister whisper-yells as she appears at my side out of thin air.

"W-What?" I say, shocked.

"He hasn't stopped looking at you all night. Just now when you danced with Thomas, I thought the vein in his forehead was going to explode Tarantino style, splattering on all of us at the table."

"Really?" My heart jumps up into my throat, making the word come out all garbled.

"Yes, really. What's going on?"

I shake my head. "Nothing."

"How many times do I have to tell you idiots—and by that, I mean my beautiful, stupid sisters—not to lie to me? I can see it all over his face, and you've avoided him all night. What. Is. Going. On?"

I sigh, slumping under the weight of my reality. She's going to get the truth out of me.

"What's going on is he's freaking amazing and wonderful and perfect, and I'm . . ." I shrug and gesture at myself.

"You're what?"

"Not what he wants."

"His staring suggests otherwise." She studies me for a few seconds. "So, those Ass Leggings were for Emerson. And clearly this has been building. And you kept this from all of us. For weeks . . . this is serious for you."

I blink back tears and take a breath. That is answer enough for her.

"Listen to me. You want him, you go get him, because he may not want to admit it, but he definitely wants you too." I shake my head, but she goes on. "Samantha, look at you. You're floating around here, shining like an actual star, are you kidding me? You want Emerson Clark, you go take him."

"He said he can't be with me. We're just friends."

She turns my shoulders square to her. "That's crap. Everyone in this room can see it. And you don't take any crap." She raises her eyebrows. "Say it."

"No crap."

She glares at me even harder.

I take a breath and put my shoulders back. "No crap!"

"That's right." I turn from her with a nod and make my way to the side of the stage. The band is about to come back from a water break, and I have a crazy idea.

"Hey, can you play a slow Beatles song?"

The lead singer of the big band–style ensemble looks at me like I have four heads. "'In My Life,' yeah?" I shrug, and he waves me off. "Don't worry, gorgeous, we'll play it."

"Can you play it next, right now, please?" He nods and turns back to his musicians.

Plan in place, I hurry over to Emerson, approaching from behind where he sits at our table. It's funny—he's sitting straight and proper, but I can tell he's also slumping the slightest bit. He hates these things so much. But at least here he's able to sit and watch . . . until now. This could be a terrible idea. *Lord help me.*

I reach his side as the music starts and put out my hand.

"May I have this dance, Mr. Clark?" He looks up at me, surprised and . . . open. Not angry, not cold. "C'mon, Emerson, it's the Beatles."

A small grin spreads across his face as he takes my hand and stands. I lead him to the dance floor, but he doesn't drag behind as much as I was expecting. When we get there, I turn to him, forgetting how one dances for a second, because there he is, in a tux.

I haven't looked at him all night, and it's a good thing. He's sexy perfection on legs. He's a frigid wintery dream. He's masculinity and elegance wrapped in black and white. And he's putting his arm around me. Oh, good, one of us remembers what we're doing.

"Is this song okay? I asked the band to play it for us."

"Did you?"

"Well, I technically I said, a slow Beatles song."

"Hmm." He studies me. I want to pull in closer to him. Well, in all honesty, I want to climb him like a spider monkey. But I refrain, instead maintaining position: our hands locked, his other hand on my hip, mine on his shoulder, a respectable gap between us.

"This isn't so bad, right?" I say lightly. "I know you hate dancing, but you seem to know what you're doing."

His brow pinches, but the rest of his face seems calm, amused, even. "I hate dancing?"

"Yeah. Well, I mean, last year at the gala, with Skye, you were like a robot." I chuckle, remembering the whole ordeal. He rolls his eyes and shakes his head. "What? You don't hate dancing?"

"No."

"I don't believe you, Mr. Clark."

"Care to take a wager?" His voice is buttery as I squint up at him. "If I impress you with my dancing, I get to take over your horrid playlist."

"First of all, my playlist is amazing. Second, impress me? What's to keep me from just cheating and saying I'm unimpressed no matter—"

I can't finish the sentence because he throws me out from him and twirls me back in. For a second, he's wrapped around me from behind and I feel his breath at my ear.

"You have to agree not to lie," he whispers, and then he spins me so we're back in our original position. I'm panting and hot and pink all over. For a second, his eyes fall down to the sweetheart neckline of my dress, where my chest is heaving like a cheesy scene from one of Sadie's early novels. "Do you?" He pushes me out while grabbing both hands, then pulls me in and somehow throws my arms around his neck so he can hold me around the waist.

His eyes are close to mine and staring so hard, I can't form thoughts. I'm not sure what's happening on my face, but my body is having a full-blown nuclear meltdown underneath my dress. "Do you agree?" he asks. I manage to nod before he takes one of my hands while pushing me away and twirls me under our arms. Then we're back in our first position. "So?" He grins at me, smug.

"What?" I can barely talk, wondering if anyone has ever orgasmed while ballroom dancing. Probably. He spins me out and in again so his mouth is back at my ear. He rubs his thumb along my arm. *Definitely! Someone definitely has!*

"Are you impressed?" He twirls me back to the slow dance position with my hands around his neck. I have got to regain some control! I look away from his crazy blue laser beams and manage to shrug. He chuckles and moves me around a couple more times, and before I realize it, I'm in a deep dip at the end of a chorus.

"How about now?" He leans over me, holding me in an almost horizontal position. His grip tightens, and I realize if he wanted to, he could let go and drop me like a sack of flour. I nod furiously, hoping he'll straighten. I get another steamy, low chuckle out of him. It is now my body's favorite sound.

"I think this is the most quiet you've been on this trip when you weren't asleep, Miss Canton." He smirks, but I feel my face fall.

"Really? Miss Canton again?"

He quickly spins me back to my favorite hold, with his breath on my neck.

"Samantha," he whispers.

I hear a small sort of whimper come out of my mouth. He moves me again so my hands are around his neck, and he holds me tight. His hands are tight except for where I'm bruised, but he still has me so close, I'm pretty sure I can feel *him* through his pants. I want him so badly, I suddenly blurt out words.

"I don't like Thomas! I don't want him!" He sighs in response, but it's almost a growl. "I know I danced with him a couple times, but it didn't mean anything, Emerson."

"You can dance with whomever you like," he replies smoothly, but his face is tense. He moves us back to our original, distant position. We sway like that for a while, and I realize the song has changed.

We've been dancing for two songs, at least, and I didn't even notice. "Why were you like that last year? With Skye?"

He shrugs. "It was ... awkward."

"And it's not awkward with me?" I say softly, feeling my chest doing the heave thing again along my neckline.

He pulls me in closer, tighter, and puts the sides of our foreheads together. "No."

"Right, because we're *friends*," I say, not hiding my disdain for the label.

Before he can respond, the song ends, more obviously this time since the band transitions to an upbeat number. He separates from me and puts out his palm and flexes his fingers.

"What?"

"Your phone." He has a playful spark in his eyes that I don't know if I've ever seen. I sigh with a smile and roll my eyes as I head to the table to fish it out of my purse for him.

I move to place it in his hands and then pause. "No funny business—texting people, taking screenshots of my stuff, filling my camera roll with selfies." I start laughing. "Just kidding, I can't even imagine you taking a selfie. Still, none of the other stuff." He just glares at me and moves his palm closer to the phone. I unlock it and hand it over.

He takes my phone slowly so our fingers brush, and even though we were just touching each other, a new set of goose bumps erupts up my arms. He sits and gets to work on my playlist. I move to join him until I hear someone call my name a few tables over. I sigh, clearly not done working for the evening.

Over an hour later, my feet are aching, my face is oily, and my capacity for awkward run-ins with Thomas Gage is down to zero. I all but hobble back to our table to where Sadie sits. She notices the quick circle my eyes make, tracking all the empty chairs.

"He left a little while ago. Didn't say a thing. Just got up and gave a bow like I was the queen herself, and left."

"Oh," I offer, trying to sound nonchalant.

"He glared at you the whole way out, but you were chatting away, charming some ninety-year-old lady's socks off."

"Ann Wartzer, new customer in Switzerland. At least . . . I think she is, after tonight!"

Sadie smiles and gives me a proud nod, then lowers her voice. "You know, Nicole asked him to dance." My smile dies a cold, hard death when I snap my head in my sister's direction. "Mhmm, not long after you two were done putting on your steamy show—and hey, thanks for that, by the way, I took some notes for the next book." She winks as she stands up. "Anyway, she said something about how he was clearly the best dancer here, and then he said he'd had all he could handle for one evening."

"Huh." I try not to smile.

"Yeah. *Huh.*" She hands me my purse. "Let's go." I nod and follow her out. Nicole waves us off, deep in an animated chat with the Gage brothers. I'm grateful she's distracting Thomas while I sneak out. I don't know how many ways one can say no to another dance, but I think I've used them all.

I walk in a dreamlike state through the steps from the gala to the car, hotel, and finally the suite. I know he hears me come in. I stand there like a frozen idiot, wondering if I should go to his door. Go to his door and do what, exactly? Beg him to kiss me? Tell him he almost ruined me for all men everywhere with just one dance?

I think about knocking on the dark wood, then remember last night. He was clear in his position, and downright angry about it

all. But then tonight, dancing for two songs straight
. . . that was the opposite of clear. Except his message was the
same: I can do whatever I want with other men because we're just
friends.

I decide to go get some water from the fridge, loudly. I find a
package of crackers and open it, letting the crinkles of the plastic
ring out. I bend my feet up to pry off my heels and let them fall on
the kitchen floor with two loud thunks. After all that, I basically
stare at his door and will it to open.

But it doesn't. I sigh in defeat and go to bed. When my head
finally hits the pillow, I debate texting him a thank-you for the
dance. Lame, but not the worst idea I've ever had. Especially since
he's almost downright chatty via text message, for him, anyway.

I pull out my phone and unlock it, catching up on the usual
one million texts from my sisters. Skye mentions something on Instagram, so I switch over to my social apps and notice for the first
time the background behind my apps has changed. I swipe over,
and my breath catches.

On the last home screen, with just one icon, some random app
I don't use, there in all its glory, is a selfie of Emerson Clark. He's
glaring at the phone, unimpressed, in the low light of the ballroom
earlier tonight. The angle is funny, and the quality is grainy, and he
looks angry. Like he's annoyed at himself for taking the selfie he's
actively taking. I laugh. It's my new favorite photo of all time.

He held up my phone tonight at the ball and took an actual
selfie?!

And then set it as my phone background!

It's too much. I cannot. I debate texting Sadie, since she knows
now, at least bits and pieces of what's been unfolding, but I don't.
Instead, I outstretch my arm, splay my hair in a hopefully sexy way
behind my head, roll my eyes with a half grin, and take the selfie.
It's pretty cute—at least, I think so. Whether or not he'll think it's

cute, I have no idea.

Wait, forget cute.

I do the whole thing again, but I pull my tank top down lower and shove the girls up higher with my arm. I check my work. Tasteful but hot. *Ladies and gentlemen, we have a winner!*

> **Me: [Photo]**
> **I expect this to be set as your background tomorrow**
> **Or else our friendship is over!!**

He doesn't reply, but I don't mind. I'm staring at my phone like an idiot, imagining him taking the photo again and again. It takes me forever to fall asleep, and when I do, my phone is still in my hand. And I'm smiling.

CHAPTER 25

"So, all that and then fucking nothing?" Trina wails in disbelief as she chomps on a french fry.

"Then effing nothing," I say, exasperated.

She gives me a look. "You Cantons really are as straitlaced as they say, eh? Can't say fuck?"

"I *can*, of course. But . . ." I shrug. "You can take the girl out of the Bible Belt and all that, yet still, my sisters and I would rather pepper some good cuss words now and then, to season a sentence that really needs it, rather than marinating the whole conversation, you know?"

She sits back in the wooden pub chair. "No. I don't know."

"Anywaaaay, I am at a loss about what to do next."

The crowd around us in the rustic bar yells about something on the TVs. After they settle, she perks back up. "What about the songs on the playlist?"

"A mix—romantic right along with sad and weird and loud. It's no help, just more confusion. All those mixed signals from him, and then two days of total avoidance. He was around with us as we packed up the exhibit, and at dinner with all of us yesterday, but never near me long enough to talk. Even avoided getting in the elevator with me.

"I stormed around in our kitchen to see if he would come

out for a nightcap, but no. Today we went to two manufacturing plants, and he was protective—not letting me skip the stupid hard hat and making sure I wasn't walking near any equipment—but again, I don't think he actually said a single word to me. When we got back, I texted you because I was about to snap and just walk up to his door naked or something crazy."

Her face turns mischievous. "Maybe what he needs is something crazy."

"I just don't want to be rejected again. I mean, at what point am I pathetic?"

"That's the age-old question, innit?" She and I sit and think for a second, feeling defeated. "And you're sure you played enough hard-to-get?"

"He saw me in the arms of another guy multiple times. He hated it, turned purple, and looked like he was gonna kill somebody, but it wasn't enough. He stood his stupid ground."

"You know my brother is the stubborn, silent type. The only way I ever talk to him is through text. Have you tried that?"

"Text him what? *Hey, you're being an idiot, and I want to jump your bones!*"

She laughs. "No, just chat with him, get him talking. Maybe he'll tell you what, exactly, is shoved so far up his ass, and why."

"Hmmm." I stare at her, because she might be a genius. Skye and her introvert bestie Janie prefer texting over any and all other forms of communication.

"Then, after you've got him warmed up, maybe slip in a little naked pic, you know, *Whoopsie, now we're sexting, don't know how it happened!*" she singsongs, and we laugh, but the thought makes my stomach flip. I don't tell her I'll never commit to another digitally immortalized sexual photo or video or even audio, ever again. But normal texting? Now, texting I can do.

I hop in Charlie's car after hugging Trina goodbye and decide to give it a try.

Me: You know, friends don't avoid each other for two days straight.

What gives?

Emerson: I've no idea what you're talking about

Uh-huh.

I'm starting to get a little concerned about what all goes on in your room

Is there a circus in there?

Do you have an OnlyFans where you get on and let people watch you edit spreadsheets?

Oh! A secret wardrobe to Narnia?

Yes, I'm in Narnia. Where are you?

Headed home now.

Went to dinner with Trina.

What did you eat?

I had some of your leftover pasta. It was delicious.

I told you I can cook! What's your favorite meal?

Shepherd's pie, probably.

OMG that's such a British answer!

Oh, what's yours, America's Sweetheart, a Big Mac?

Rude.

It's pizza, Hideaway from back home, but if you tell anyone that, I'll deny it and say BBQ.

What's your favorite color? It can't actually be yellow.

It is.

Aren't you going to ask mine?

I already know yours. Magenta.

Lucky guess.

Favorite band?

What is this, 20 questions?

I may go past 20. The night is young.

Red Hot Chili Peppers, and you?

Meghan Trainor, musicals, country

Why OU?

I wanted to study in the States

Still, you could've gone to Yale, Harvard, etc. Why Oklahoma?

My uncle attended there.

And then you fell in love with Sooner football?

I did, yes.

Will you concede football is the real football and soccer is soccer?

Never.

Such a Brit.

Favorite TV shows of all time?

Frasier, Big Bang Theory, House

Which musicals?

That is a very surprising television list.

I like all the blockbuster musicals, Wicked, Phantom, Hamilton

Dear Evan Hansen? Too sad?

Too sad. But the music is pretty.

Did you go see it?!

Yes.

I'm sorry

Give me a minute

My brain is having trouble picturing you sitting and watching people sing and dance for two hours.

Let me guess, with Miranda?

Sometimes.

Is she a model?

She is.

Knew it. Though I mean, #duh.

So. Hot British model that you go to musicals with, that is NOT your girlfriend?

Correct.

So, she's in love with you then.

No.

I'll bet you one million dollars she is.

You don't have one million dollars.

How do you know? I have a hefty savings!

Not that hefty.

Okay, one thousand dollars.

No bet.

Because I'm right!

I don't gamble with money.

Name another prize then.

Too difficult to quantify the results.

If you texted her right now and said "Hey, babe, do you want to go on a real date sometime, together, as a couple?" what would she say?

. . .

. . . . . . !!!

Damn.

You can Venmo me my one grand at your convenience.

We never shook on it.

[Eye roll emoji]

Personal question time

These are all personal questions

What did you mean you're the disappointment of your family?

[Link: Clark Industries]

I am making my way through my nighttime routine by the time he shares the link, positively giddy to be chatting with him so long. *Thank you, Trina!* I tap on the article.

Me: WAIT.

CLARK

LIKE THE BUILDING IN DOWNTOWN LONDON THAT SAYS CLARK ON IT?!

Emerson: Correct.

YOU'RE A BILLIONAIRE!

My father is.

I HAVE SO MANY QUESTIONS.

Could you refrain from sending them in all caps?

LOL

I will try my hardest.

Question number one is obviously why in the world you work for teeeeeny tiny little Canton Cards when you could be working for one of the largest chemical companies in the world?!

Canton Cards is a challenge.

And Clark Industries isn't?!

Not really, no.

Please explain.

Print is dying, as is in-person retail. The stakes are high, and the work is complicated, every day.

But you could probably work anywhere in the world, couldn't you?

I doubt that. Your father promoted me before I was ready, believed in me to save his entire legacy. I respect him, his values, the way he works.

Wow. I think I might be speechless.

3, 2, 1 . . .

But you went back, to England, went to Oxford, then did you work for your family for a little while? I never saw Clark anything on your LinkedIn, or maybe I would've figured it out.

I did, some of the subsidiaries.

So you're the disappointment because you're not in the family business?

That's part of it, yes.

Are you going to tell me the other parts?

No.

I'm shocked.

Maybe it's because you won't talk to them!

Maybe.

When will you see them?

Tomorrow, unfortunately.

I'm sure it won't be that bad.

It's a big formal dinner at my parents estate with the entire family.

Ohhhh

So basically your worst nightmare.

Indeed.

Well, if you need a buffer, I volunteer as tribute.

Buffer?

They'll be so busy wondering who I am and why I'm there. And as you know, I can be quite chatty.

Then voila, you can just fade into a quiet corner until it's time to leave.

It would not be a pleasant experience for you.

It's talking with a new group of people over a fancy dinner— where do I sign???

Ha.

Plus, I think I can hang when it comes to talking about family empires, don't you?

You really would do that? Even if it's horrible?

What are friends for?

I'll think about it. I'm not sure I can throw you to the wolves.

Just call me Little Red Riding Hood.

Didn't she almost die??

Moving on!

You come back to England

Work for dear ole dad

Then you're with Chelsea Fancypants

Then you flee to New York.

Bad breakup?

I didn't flee.

Is she still in love with you too?

No.

I'm happy to take another 1K off your hands.

It's getting late.

[Grandpa emoji]

Am I right though, bad breakup?

You can tell me. I happen to be the queen of those.

It was complicated.

Is that code for Billionaire Boy Genius Emerson Clark Got Dumped?

Something like that.

I'm sorry.

I'm not.

Well, she's an idiot, obviously.

No comment.

HA! You basically said she's a crazy raging bitch!

I love it.

I absolutely did not.

I might have to screenshot that.

Speaking of, I need to see photo evidence of your new phone background in action.

[Screenshot]

Lock screen!

Wow!

Best Friend Status *Unlocked*

Only because I can't stand a background behind my app icons.

Uh-huh, whatever you say, Bestie.

LOL

I think I just heard your sigh all the way in my room.

I'm turning in now.

Wait! Last question, what should I wear to family dinner?

A dress.

Like a full-on ballgown?

Sundress?

Business dress?

Cocktail hour?

You know I brought like 25.

The purple one.

You got it, Bestie.

Good night.

Night!

I have to keep myself from squealing as I toss my phone down next to me in bed. Somewhere in the back of my mind, a voice of reason is trying to remind me that on the whole, that was a text conversation between two friends. But that voice is being drowned out by my inner romantic self, who's screaming and

jumping because the man I can't stop thinking about not only texted with me for an hour, but he also notices my outfits and he has
my face (and a hint of my boobs) as the lock screen on his phone!

There was nothing romantic in our chat, nothing sweet, yet
still, I can't help but feel like the last hour broke down multiple
layers of the cold, hard wall Emerson keeps around himself. I can
totally be warm and soft enough for the both of us. I can also easily
charm his family enough to erase all the flimsy reasons he "can't"
be with me. After all, he's cut from similar cloth: family legacy,
multi-generational empire, high-profile life, pressure, expecta-
tions, pride, honor . . .

How hard could one evening be?

CHAPTER 26

It takes absolutely all my willpower not to blow up my sisters with texts, including a selfie of what I've got going on in the mirror in front of me. The bright lilac dress is tight, maybe slightly tighter now than at the beginning of the trip. *Curse you, adorable afternoon tea showing up everywhere, every single day!*

A lightning bolt runs through me as I smooth the fabric down on my hips, because he chose this dress. It's a sleeveless sheath I normally wear under a blazer, with a scoop neck that's low enough to be alluring, but not so low that I can't wear it to the office. I leave my hair down and style it in big curling waves that probably won't hold all night. I opt for my strappy nude heels rather than a sexier stiletto, just in case this is more of a backyard barbecue situation. Because I can't help myself, I opt for hot-pink hoop earrings and matching bangle bracelets. I'm wearing nude shoes, after all.

My hands shake a bit as I walk to meet him in our entryway. "Well, will this do?" I say, gesturing over my ensemble.

He clears his throat as he looks up. "It will." He answers with his voice flat. I'm about to tease him about his complimenting skills when I notice.

"Okay, that is *it*! I am not leaving this room until you tell me what the heck is up with your ties. That thing matches this dress *exactly*! Wait, is that why you picked this dress? You knew you had a purple tie? But even so, since *when* do you have purple ties?!"

A hint of a smile flashes on his face for a second. "You don't approve?"

"Answer. The. Question."

He starts talking as he opens the door for me. "I only packed white, gray, black, and tan. In hopes of maintaining our truce, I asked Ms. Wayne to pick up some ties that would . . . brighten me up."

"Why?"

He walks down the hall as he talks. "Because you like bright colors."

I follow him into the elevator slowly, not believing what I'm hearing. "Don't you hate bright colors?"

"Not necessarily, no."

"So, you bought ties in crazy colors, for me?"

"Ms. Wayne did, technically."

I sigh. "Don't try and ruin it for me, Bestie."

He grins and puts his hands up in surrender as we leave the elevator. I greet Charlie, and we get settled in for the drive, which I notice will be an hour.

"An hour, no wonder we're leaving so early." Emerson just nods in response. "That'll give you plenty of time to give me the lowdown on the mighty Clarks. Charlie, did you know Emerson here is a *Clark Industries* Clark?"

"I did, Miss Samantha."

"And you never said anything! You sly dog. Emerson, give this man a raise." Charlie blushes, and Emerson sighs, but it's one of his lighter *I'm not really as irritated as I want to let on* sighs. I turn to face him a bit more in my seat. "So? What can I expect this evening?"

"Dinner, I assume." His dry response earns a chuckle from

Charlie up front.

"Charles, I heard that. I take back what I said about the raise. You can't encourage Grump's little jokes like that!" I turn back. "C'mon, the more you give me, the better buffer I'll be." Emerson winces, but I push on. "Let's start with the roster. Who will be there?"

"My parents, brothers, sister-in-law, niece, uncle, possibly some family friends or cousins as well."

"Okay, great. How about your mom—what is she like?"

He thinks for a second. "Charming."

"Charming. Okay, easy, we'll be fast friends. And your brother, Byron, his wife?"

"Layla is . . . well-mannered."

I start laughing. "Well-mannered? *Well-mannered*? Is she a goldendoodle? What does that even mean! Just lay it out for me. Who will be the hardest to win over?"

"You don't need to win them over."

I try not to let the comment sting. "Okay, maybe a better way to ask that is: Whose probing, annoying spotlight do you want to keep off you and onto me, or onto others at the table?"

"My father, I suppose." He is grimacing as he says it.

"What about the wild cards—any of the cousins that are trouble?" I push, but he shakes his head. His arms are crossed so tight, it must be painful, and his pale face looks almost sick. "Hey, relax, it's one evening with your family." He lets out an exhale. "Close your eyes for a second." He glares at me almost menacingly. "You trust me enough to take me to meet your entire family. Now close your dadgum eyes, Frosty."

"I don't care for that nickname," he mutters as he closes his eyes.

"Noted," I mutter back as I unbuckle and move over to the middle seat of the car. A thrill runs up from my toes as the side of my leg meets the side of his, and it continues to my fingers when I reach over and slowly uncross his arms. I grab each of his hands one at a time and set them flat on his legs, resisting the painful urge to squeeze and stroke each one. "I guess you'd probably prefer your half of the playlist," I say softly as I grab my phone to turn down the volume and scroll to the songs he's added to my playlist, starting with "Blackbird" by the Beatles.

I get back to my task, reaching my shaky right hand up to Emerson's glorious neck. I know I am good at this, and I know he needs it. I pinch my thumb and pointer finger on his warm skin, starting at the end of his hair and pulling down. After a few minutes, I can see his face start to relax.

Since he hasn't so much as grunted an objection, I turn my body and push closer into him. My chest is pushed up against his left arm now, and though his face doesn't change at the contact, I catch him inhale with surprise. Or maybe, hopefully, more than just surprise.

The new angle allows me to reach both of his shoulders, which I massage, as best as I can from the side. After a minute or maybe two, I feel him finally let go of some of the tension under my fingers. I take in a deep breath of his clean, manly scent while trying not to be obvious that I'm inhaling him.

I probably fail.

I would massage him for the entire hour, without even thinking, but Emerson lets out an audible groan. At the surprising noise, his neck stiffens again and his shoulders rush up to his ears. His hands go from relaxed to clenched fists on his thighs. His face is so hard to read. Is he embarrassed? Disgusted? Irritated?

"Uh, um, wow, right. Thank you." He fumbles as he pulls away.

"Sure." I force myself to return to my side of the seat. The resulting chill without his left side along my right is almost painful. "But . . ." I smile as I look over at him. "You're almost right back to where we started. You are familiar with the concept of relaxing?"

"Vaguely."

I scoff. "I won't talk to you anymore, and neither will Charlie, chatty as he is, whew!" I joke. "So, lean your head back and close your eyes and chill. I'm sure this will be a draining evening for you, so just sit there, power all the way down, and charge up your internal batteries."

"I'm not a robot."

"Ehhh?" I say as if I'm unsure.

"You ruled it out already. Next on the list was vampire."

"No more talking! With every word, you look worse!" I tease before he can continue.

He leans his head back, and I gulp. He really remembers every single thing I say, and I really have thrown a lot of insults his way. But he deserved them! Didn't he? He did. And really, I was only teasing. Surely he can take it. Still, I'm wrecked by the idea that maybe I pierced his tough armor and actually hurt his feelings, which the hot half kisses in the hallway proved he does, in fact, have.

I add softly, "Also, I've seen you in direct sunlight, and you didn't melt or sparkle like Edward in *Twilight*. So. Not a vampire." I think I see the hint of a smile on his stunning face.

———

"Holy Toledo Batman and Robin and Catwoman and all their friends," I say involuntarily as we pull up, after a significant drive *after* entering the private gate to the Clark mansion. It's a sprawling all-white Edwardian masterpiece, with a dozen columns and a million windows, and who knows what other details I can't see from way down at the end of the driveway.

"Sorry, sir, I can't get any closer."

"No problem, Charlie, thank you," Emerson replies absently, and both Charlie and I smile at the use of the nickname. I wave goodbye to him with a wink and join Emerson on the smooth pavement that seems much nicer than normal cement.

"Shall we?" He motions toward the ominous white structure.

I turn to him, leaving my jaw hanging for a beat before gushing. "It's gorgeous here. I can't believe that is your house!"

He nods with a tight smile, eyeing the winding driveway. I say my mantra a few times under my breath.

"What's that?" Emerson looks at me, concerned.

"Nothing."

He tilts his head. "You do that often."

"It's just a mantra, to get me pumped up, you know? It's super dorky."

"What do you say?"

"Oh, I am absolutely not telling you. You will make fun of me."

"I . . ." Emerson trails off. The entire path is full of cars—big, expensive, pretty cars—and I start to feel some nerves. Looks like those extra friends and cousins decided to attend, after all. As we get close to the pillared porch, I hear soft music and faraway voices, many of them. Emerson stops and stares at one of the cars. "Shit."

My eyes pop and my voice raises in surprise. "Whoa, something prompted Mr. Clark to drop the S-bomb, what is it?"

"Uh, never mind." He starts walking again, but I don't.

"Whose car is it?" I say to his back. "C'mon, Emerson, you know I'll stand here and pester you until you answer."

He sighs. "It's Chelsea's." He starts stalking to the door, clearly irritated now.

I hurry to catch up to him. "Like, sort-of-dumped-you Chelsea?"

"Mhmm." He's walking so fast, I have to almost jog to keep up. I can see he's back to his previous state of tight neck and tight, well, everything. His skin has that greenish hue again. He's sweating more than the short walk could've caused. We reach the bottom of the steps to the porch, and I hesitate as he launches up to the door.

"Time for me to even the score, Emerson," I tell him as he turns to me, confused as he pushes the doorbell. "I'm saving you again. Just follow my lead."

"What?" he whisper-yells as someone approaches the door.

"Just trust me!" I snipe back.

The door opens, and I grab his hard bicep with my right hand and slide my left all the way down the inside of his arm. I interlock our fingers and lean into him. I feel his gaze on me even though I can't see his face, because I am beaming at the regal woman in front of me.

She, I'm assuming Emerson's mother, matches my smile, darts her eyes to our interlocking fingers, and then smiles up at her son. I squeeze Emerson's hand, and he doesn't squeeze back, but he doesn't let go. I hope he realizes I'm about to be the best fake girlfriend he's ever had in his life.

Is this crazy? Stupid? Genius?

Is he relieved? Angry? Shocked?

No time to wonder.

The Sam Train has totally left the station now, so he'd better get on board.

CHAPTER 27

"Darling!" Emerson's mother greets him cheerfully as she moves in for a hug. She is the picture of understated elegance in a blue silk blouse that plays up her eyes. They're not as mesmerizing as Emerson's, but they're still a striking light blue. The blouse is tucked into wide, flowing trousers that aren't too big on her thin frame. She's about my height—not short, but not lanky either.

"Mother," Emerson replies flatly, though his face does light up a smidge. I let go of his arm so he can embrace her. She kisses his cheeks and then looks confused as she pulls away.

"Babe, did you not tell them I was coming? *So* sorry, Mrs. Clark. You know how men are. I should've made sure myself!"

"Evelyn, please." She reaches out her hand but based on how warm and open she seems, I go in for a hug instead.

"Samantha. And it's so great to finally meet you!" She looks pleased as I pull away. *Yes! Good choice on the hug, Sam! Trust yourself! You got this!* I take in the impressive foyer, winding staircase, and fresh flower arrangement the size of my torso. "The estate is absolutely breathtaking. I can't wait to see the house."

"I can give you a tour!" Ben says with a wink as he bounds to greet us. I instinctively link my fingers through Emerson's again. His brother catches the movement right away. "Ah, that's why you didn't want me to ask her out, you old wanker! You could've just said, you know."

Emerson just coughs, so I change the subject. "We brought this, but it may need to be chilled for a bit." I dig into my bag for a bottle of wine I grabbed from the hotel fridge. I don't know if Emerson bought it or the hotel put it there, but I googled it and it's crazy expensive.

"Oh, how lovely! Thank you, dear." Her reply seems genuine as a member of the house staff—I'm assuming, since she's wearing a black polo with black pants and black boat shoes that are only worn by kitchen workers or on actual boats—appears from nowhere to take the wine. The servant also offers to take my bag as she slinks away.

It's then that I can look up at Emerson for the first time since the porch, and while his face still looks a bit too surprised, I definitely see some relief and something else—maybe awe? I give him a wide smile and do the bicep-grip-hand-slide move again.

"Emerson!" a man who must be Mr. Clark calls out as he joins us in the entryway. He's in a perfectly fitted suit, with his son's light brown Ken doll hair that shows only the slightest bit of gray at his temples.

"Dad." Emerson sounds tight as he gives him a firm handshake. "This is Samantha Canton." He turns his body into me, right as his father's eyes look my way.

"Mr. Clark, wonderful to finally meet you!" I say as I stretch out my right hand, keeping my left firmly in Emerson's grasp.

"William. And my, a Canton in the flesh. What an unexpected honor," he says with a wide smile. The words are nice, but the tone is a bit prickly. He's one to watch, for sure.

"Well, come on then, or are we going to stand in the vestibule all night?" Ben teases.

"Quite right." William opens his arms for us to move into the house.

We step through the entry into a surprisingly modern sunken living room space with a giant hearth, low-profile leather chairs, bright white couches, and a full bar—complete with a black polo-clad bartender—off to one side. Past the living area are massive glass doors all along the exterior wall that reveal a manicured garden and sparkling pool in the yard. I can see a glimpse of the kitchen off to one far corner and a walkway in the other, from which Byron and his wife cautiously emerge.

"Hi, I'm Layla." She extends a demure hand that matches her tasteful wine-colored dress. The dark red works wonders for her brown eyes and chestnut curls.

"Layla! Yes! Nice to meet you. I've heard great things." I gush as we shake hands.

"Oh?" She looks to Emerson as Byron gives him a manly hug-slap.

"Yes, you know, his favorite sister and all," I joke.

"Where's the star of the show?" Emerson looks around the room.

"With my mum. We wanted a grown-up night out. But we'll make sure she sees you before you fly out," Layla answers, I assume referring to his niece. A few more people emerge out of the walkway past the wet bar. I go in for Emerson's hand again, but this time, he wraps his arm around my waist and tucks me in close to his side.

I die.

I love it so much, I absolutely die for at least two seconds.

"Heyo! A Canton, eh? So, you're boinking the boss then, Emerson?" a chubby man jeers loudly as he approaches.

"Joseph," Emerson warns coldly to a shorter, darker version of himself.

"Oh no, I'm not his boss. Technically he's one of my bosses, actually. Hi, I'm Samantha." I reach out a hand and smile.

"Joe, favorite cousin."

"Please excuse my brother," slender cross between Emerson and Joe says as he greets us. "I'm Peter."

"Samantha, nice to meet you."

Behind Joe and Peter, I see Chelsea timidly approach with an older couple. I put my right hand on Emerson's chest for a beat. "Babe, you didn't tell me we'd have such a welcome party. I hope I can remember everyone's names!"

"Sorry, Angel," he says softly, squeezing me ever so slightly around the waist. *This is not real. The nickname Angel is just an act. He did the same thing at the bar with Damian. Not. Real!*

"This is one of my partners, Haymitch Wittington, and his wife, Deborah. Lifelong friends of ours," Emerson's dad explains as the last little group reaches us.

"Miss Canton, a pleasure." He greets me briefly before immediately beaming at Emerson. "So good to have you back home, son!" Emerson lets go of me to shake his extended hand. Deborah shakes my hand wordlessly, and then leans in to hug Emerson. She's clearly the shyest one here.

"And this is their daughter Chelsea." William clears his throat as she approaches.

"Uh, hello." She's beautiful, I'll give her that. And demure. In her fitted white eyelet dress with elbow-length sleeves, she's giving serious Kate Middleton vibes, only with striking red hair and sharper features. Tension mounts for a split second, so I squash it.

"Of course, Chelsea! I've heard so much about you. I can't wait to swap stories about this one." I pretend to elbow Emerson in the side. "I'm sure you have so many good ones." I decide to go in for a hug. She's surprised, but since she's some sort of billionaire-princess-in-training, she adjusts quickly and embraces me back.

"I guess I do," she agrees timidly, looking to Emerson.

He sighs with a nod.

"Like that! Which sigh do you think that was? I figure he has about ten different sighs, which are basically the cornerstone of his communication skills, right? That one was *Reign It in, Samantha!*" I give an Emerson impression. Everyone laughs, I think mostly from surprise that I am just steamrolling right on through this family dinner with absolutely no filter and no shame. "Was I right, Em?"

"I don't know what you mean," he jokes as he pulls me in and kisses the side of my forehead. My heart stops at the feel of his cool lips on my blushing skin. How many tiny happy deaths can a person survive in one evening?

"All right, enough faffing—let's eat already!" Joe pleads loudly. Everyone mumbles in agreement as they turn to head back toward where the dining room must be.

I turn to Emerson and say loudly, "Babe, can you show me where to wash up before we eat?"

"Of course," he says.

"Take your time, loves. Anya is still working on the main course anyway," Evelyn calls to us as she makes her way to the kitchen. Emerson leads me by the hand back to the front of the house and down a short hall to a powder bath roughly the size of my apartment in Brooklyn. I tug him inside, and he shuts the door with a giant inhale as if he's been holding his breath for thirty minutes.

"Well? How am I doing? Because honestly, I think I'm crushing it out there."

"You didn't have to . . ." His voice trails off as he shakes his head.

"I know, but aren't you glad I did? Did you see Chelsea's face? Utter devastation. She wanted back in your pants tonight *bad.*" He chuckles and shakes his head. "Okay, I need the lowdown, stat. What is she doing here?"

"I'm sure my father invited her."

"Ugh, not cool, William. And why did you break up? What are her insecurities? Tell me how to really stick it to her." He lets out another small laugh but puts a hand to his forehead. I pause. "Oh, unless you don't want to stick it to her?"

My heart plunges into the shining marble floor under my heels. What if he still loves Chelsea? What if he can't be with me because he wants to get back together with her? My pulse is racing, but I straighten my spine and hide behind my confidence as a wing woman. "Do you want to get back together with her? Because we can make that happen too—I just need to adjust my strategy. Maybe I could come out of this room crying, like a massive break-up just at the sight of her, or—"

"No! No, definitely not." He cuts me off with finality.

"Oh, thank goodness," I say as I almost collapse with glee, and then realize I just said the words aloud. "I mean, um, only because that would be a lot harder to do now that this fake Sammerson Ship has already sailed, you know?"

"Sammerson?"

"Yeah, you know, Kimye? Bennifer? Brangelina? I tried to make Skatthew happen, but Skye and Matt were lame about it. Anyway! We don't have time to come up with a better name. I need more prep fast. Wannabe Kate Middleton out there really upped the ante. Also, Haymitch Wittington? Is that not the most pompous British name you've ever heard in your life?" That earns me another hearty, precious laugh from deep in his chest. "C'mon, anything you think I need to know about Chelsea? Or your family? Any topics to avoid? Anything you want me to bring up?"

He shakes his head with a smile.

"You're smiling. Soooo me basically jumping on you was okay? You're on board?"

"Don't have much choice now, do I?" he asks in a low voice, but he's still grinning.

I wash my hands at the white marble pedestal sink. "Your words are grumpy, but your smile says, *Thank you, Samantha, for saving my tight behind.*" I can't help but imitate him again.

"It says no such thing."

"It does, and in that exact accent. The accuracy is uncanny. I should go into acting, seriously."

"Bloody hell." He smirks as he leads me out of the bathroom.

"Uh-huh, you keep griping all you want, Frosty, but your smile and I are having a separate conversation."

"About my tight behind," he says softly as he links his fingers with mine. I turn fuchsia and forget how to words for a second. He chuckles as he leads me through a new hallway toward the sounds of voices. I can't believe I let that slip about his amazing ass. *Zip it and skip it, Sam! You're supposed to be* acting *here!*

———

"It's fulfilling, isn't it, to work in the family business?" William asks with a smooth smile.

It's amazing how much I've learned about the Clarks in just the appetizer and salad courses. Except for bumbling Joe, every single Clark is charming. They smile, they chat, they are warm and at ease. All but Emerson. Even with his family, it's as if words either escape him or pain him on their way out. He's tense and quiet, and I can see it's not just because of the situation.

The dinner is not the most fun I've attended, that's for sure. Chelsea and her mother barely say a word, though both of them look at Emerson with what I'd consider unabashed longing. This marriage was the hope of three out of four parents at this table, that much is obvious.

At the far end of the table, William Sr. hunches over his plate and eats in silence. He watches us a bit but seems to fade in and out of awareness, and the fact that he is simply ignored breaks my heart. Everyone is painstakingly proper and polite, as if cameras are on us at all times. It's super weird.

William, charmer that he may be, keeps throwing out subtle jabs, but I'm defending my temporary man like a goalie besting pucks on the ice.

"It's fulfilling." I consider my reply. "To . . . be a part of something bigger than myself, I guess. Something engaging and stimulating, where I feel like I'm making a difference," I say, only half lying. My answer is more for Emerson than it is for myself, just like William's question.

"Ah, but how hard do you have to work, really, as one of the famous Canton sisters, eh?" Haymitch jokes.

"Um . . ." I blush for a second, caught off guard.

"Are you implying she doesn't do her job?" Emerson asks with cold precision, directing his stare in such a way, I almost pity Haymitch on the other end of it.

"Oh, I was only joking, of course." He chokes on the words as he shifts his eyes from Emerson to William, as if Mr. Clark Sr. can save him. But Emerson is on the warpath now.

"Samantha. What's the profit margin on the RainyDaze embossed line?" he asks, looking at Haymitch as he talks to me.

"One twenty-five per card in the US. One twenty in most overseas markets," I say automatically.

"And the PaintedSkye planners?"

"Eight dollars and three cents in every market except France, but—"

"What about the same planners, but with gold foil?"

Emerson is on a rampage, so I keep up with him. "Seven ninety."

"And how many units did we sell last quarter of the gold?"

"In the US or . . . ?"

"Here in the UK."

"Twenty-one thousand, but I think they—" I try to slow his roll, but there may be actual steam coming out of Emerson's ears at this point.

"And Bernard, who runs the East London Canton store—what's his wife's name?"

"Stacy."

"And his daughter?"

"He has two, Mattie and Meredith. But I—"

"And his dog?"

"Wags."

"Breed?"

"Pug, *but I think they get your point, babe,*" I add quickly with a smile as Haymitch turns from pink to red.

Emerson turns his melting stare to me, though he's still addressing the man across the table. "As you can see, Samantha is a prodigy. She consistently outsells every single sales representative we have in the entire organization, including her superior, the vice president. By *over six percent.*" He reaches his hand out and gently grips my neck under my ear, placing his thumb on my cheek. My mouth opens the slightest bit, and I have to concentrate to keep my knees from doing the same. "That even includes sales in their headquarter state, Oklahoma. I am . . . very proud of her."

The table sits in stunned silence that I know is less about me than it is about the string of words that just poured effortlessly from the beautiful mouth I can't stop staring at.

Benedict saves us all. "Well, fuck me, maybe we should hire her, Dad!"

"Indeed. Very impressive," William mumbles as Evelyn chastises her son's language at the table. The group relaxes, as if William gave us all permission to do so. Emerson traces his thumb along my skin for a split second before pulling his hand away. "So," William continues, "two geniuses at the table, then."

"Here we go," Byron jokes.

"It's not flattery, it's a tested fact, son. Emerson's IQ is one-six-ty-one." William points to Emerson with his knife before cutting into his lamb chop.

"Dad, can we not?" Ben groans.

"It's normal for a father to want all his sons to work in his company, let alone a savant. I just wish he'd rise to his full potential, is all I'm saying." William shrugs with a smile as he says it, and Evelyn clears her throat.

Emerson lets out a heavy sigh beside me. I grab his thigh beside mine without thinking, instantly noticing how huge and firm it is. I give him a squeeze and start to pull away, but he puts his hand over mine to hold it in place. There goes my heart again, skipping beats and flipping somersaults.

"Tell me, Samantha, which sigh was that, then?" William turns to me with a menacing smile.

I don't hesitate. "Hard to be sure, but it sounded a lot like the one that means *While* some *may believe full potential means maintaining the status quo within a stable, growing market, instead I've single-handedly rebuilt the financials of a multibillion-dollar company in a collapsing industry, when competitors have folded to Amazon, Walmart, and Target year after year the last five years, and have saved said company from drifting into bankruptcy territory not once or twice but* three times."

I hold William's burning eyes for what feels like an eternity. It takes all my strength not to look away first, so much so that I almost don't register Emerson's fingers interlocking with mine and squeezing, hard.

"Shit, I do love these family dinners," Joe finally cheers, mouth full, as the rest of the table exhales, coughs, or sucks down water like they're stuck in the Sahara.

We still have the lamb I've barely touched, dessert, and after-dinner tea to get through, and at this point, I'm honestly not sure we're all going to make it out unscathed.

CHAPTER 28

"And how much did you end up raising?" We've reached the *We Want You to Marry Chelsea* portion of the evening, it seems, as William fires question after question her way, all about her charity galas and fundraising auctions. Evelyn nervously glances from Emerson to her husband to me, clearly wishing her husband possessed an ounce of subtlety. Chelsea's mother and father, on the other hand, are delighted at the turn of the conversation.

I don't really hear Chelsea's reply. It shouldn't bother me, of course, since I'm not actually Emerson's girlfriend, not actually being insulted right now. But I'm bothered. Especially when I see the twitching in Emerson's gorgeous, chiseled jaw. Homegirl dumped him, for whatever stupid incomprehensible reason, and his own father is all but throwing her a damn parade at what should be *Emerson's* welcome-home dinner.

The freaking nerve.

The one redeeming surprise that makes it all worth it is Emerson's massive, wonderful hands. One of them has been touching me nonstop since my staredown with William two courses ago. My neck, my back, my thigh, my palm—they're all on fire.

After the dessert bowls have been collected and I can stomach no more of the *William Loves Chelsea Show*, I whisper to Emerson, "How about some air?"

He nods and grabs my hand, leading me through a maze of hallways. One of the hallways is lined with what must be fifty framed photos of all three boys. I pull Emerson to a stop as I find his section of photos. In most of the images, starting when he couldn't have been much older than four, he's on horseback. Through the years, it's one shot after another of him playing polo, racing, or something like racing, jumping jumps on horseback, and winning trophies. A lot of trophies.

"Have you two gone on a ride together?" Evelyn comes up behind us, admiring the same set of photos over my shoulder.

"No." My eyebrows shoot up as my voice does, not masking my surprise well at all.

"Not a lot of horseback riding in Manhattan," Emerson mutters.

"You must take her, Emerson," she says, then turns from the photos to me. "You should see him up there, really."

"I bet." I snort, shocked by this whole new side of Emerson Clark I didn't see coming. "Oh, wait, the Gages—they did say you played polo in school, right?"

Evelyn's face falls. "Until his eleventh year, he did." I look between the two of them, clearly missing something. Then Evelyn cocks her head at me, surprised.

"That was the year of the accident." Emerson gives me a meaningful look, as if it's something I knew but already forgot.

"Oh, right, I thought it was, uh, later than that," I mumble.

Evelyn sighs and lays a hand on Emerson's arm. "How are the headaches? Still almost every night?"

"Not every night, Mother. I'm fine." His words are gruff as he gently removes her hand. He turns to me and breathes me in. "Come, Samantha, let me show you the garden."

"Sure." I give a polite smile while my brain misfires inside my skull. What the hell? Accident? And headaches? Wait, is that why he's in his room each night? Just sitting in there in pain while I'm out having dinner or freaking clubbing? What if his head was pounding when he came to that club to save me?

Suddenly I think I might be sick, so the cool air feels amazing on my skin as we step out onto the back porch. The pool is much bigger than I thought. Beyond what I could see from the living room, it juts off at an angle to wrap around the left side of the house with a resort-style hot tub off to one side and loungers evenly spaced along the deck. It's like a resort. Emerson takes me around toward the right, though, where I can hear his brothers cutting up.

After we turn a corner, we enter a huge outdoor room, which is walled in on two sides, but open to the air, with large ceiling fans. In the middle of the covered space is a Ping-Pong table, shuffleboard, cornhole, big outdoor Jenga blocks, and some plush outdoor seating that's probably more expensive and more comfortable than my furniture back in New York . . . or Oklahoma.

Emerson squeezes my hand. "Want something to drink?" His brothers have beers, and Layla and Chelsea—oh, she's out here too—have champagne. I look up at him, wondering if a headache pulses behind those ice-blue eyes.

"Are you going to have something?"

"Some Pellegrino," he answers softly.

"That sounds good, thanks." Sparkling water is a much smarter option after all the wine I sucked down to survive that minefield of a dinner.

"He's really something, isn't he?" Chelsea speaks to me as her eyes watch my boyf—I mean, Emerson's—fine StairMaster backside walk toward the house.

"He is," I agree, giving her a bit of side-eye.

"Sorry, about tonight, my parents . . . they hoped I could fix my mistake, tell him I was wrong. Anyway, I'm sorry for the intrusion."

"It's all right." I shrug. "So, you've changed your mind, then?" I ask, pretending I have a clue what happened so she'll spill some details.

"I have. I couldn't get past it before, his . . . shortcomings, but I . . . I was young and honestly, an idiot."

She sighs, and I hold in a scoff and mutter, "No argument there." I look away from her and try to hold in my anger.

Shortcomings? Did she seriously just say that? What, because he's not Mr. Charmer like her dad and William the Snake? So he has headaches and needs quiet and is too blunt. Everyone has baggage. I'm sure hers is a complete set, from toiletry bag, to carry-on, to an ugly, overstuffed, strained-zippers, check-on monstrosity, just like the rest of us.

If Evelyn looks at her son like he's damaged, and his long-lost love couldn't overcome his "shortcomings," it's no wonder he thinks he can't be with me. But I don't see him that way. He's not some wounded teenager nursing a headache to me. He has to know that. I have to show him that.

When he comes back around the corner with our bottled waters, I stalk up to him with a smile. I want to plant a solid kiss on his lips, and I can see he's confused as I approach. But I'm not kissing him first. I have a shred of dignity left, for now.

Instead, I grab my bottle from his hand and put both arms up around his neck, reaching on my tiptoes. I shove into him a little bit, arriving faster than I mean to, and he steadies himself, then wraps his arms around my waist. I settle for a slightly open-mouthed kiss below his ear. I feel him freeze completely around me, so I do it again.

"Thanks, boyfriend," I say in his ear, and then I hop down from my toes and turn quickly, facing his brothers playing shuffleboard. I can feel Chelsea's eyes on Emerson, then me, as I cross over to the side of the long, fancy-looking polished wood. I see Chelsea join Layla on the couch out of the corner of my eye. I wonder if they're friends, if Layla is on Team Chelsea too, and get a bit flustered. I shake my head. *It doesn't matter! None of this is real, remember?*

"Couldn't have a pool table?" I call back to my fake boyfriend with a wide smile.

"Apologies." He grins as he slides up beside me.

"What, bit of a pool shark?" Ben asks as he takes a shot.

"She is, and she'll con anyone she can with her hidden talent," Emerson answers with a shake of his head.

"Who, me?" I bat my eyelashes, and he actually lets out a chuckle while wrapping his arm around my waist.

Best.

Night.

Ever.

"What about darts, then? That too?" Byron motions over their shoulders.

"Nope." I sigh. "Not good at darts."

"Come, let's see it." Emerson's voice is playful as he pulls me off to the side.

"Really, I've played, like, twice in my life and tequila was involved."

"Tequila can be arranged!" Joe yells from the far side of the Ping-Pong table, where he's playing Peter.

"No! No thank you." I put up a hand in protest. Emerson presents me with the darts. I look up at his gorgeous face. "So? Show me how it's done, Mr. Savant."

"Better than Frosty," he mutters under his breath as he sets down our drinks and grabs the darts. He throws his first shot. He hits the triangle in the center but outside of the inner ring around the bull's-eye thingy. "That's twenty," he explains.

"I mean, you make it look easy, but . . ." I steady myself and aim, feeling all the eyes on me. I wish I hadn't been so coy about pool. It's my one cool card, and I can't even play it. I clench everything and just take my best shot, feeling nervous. The dart makes it to the board, but just barely. All the guys make an "oh" sound, as if I just lost the whole game.

"Excuse me, I actually hit the board. I want some cheers!" I cry. A chorus of happy heys and woos breaks out. Emerson takes another shot, and everyone goes back to their own activities. He hits the ring outside the center dot.

"Twenty-five. You got sixteen," he explains.

"Not bad, I guess?" I take my position, but Emerson wraps an arm around me from behind. I feel his sculpted chest down my back and I. Cannot. Breathe. "What happened to my massage therapist from earlier?" he says softly in my ear.

"W-What?"

"Your turn to relax," he says as his other hand massages my neck. Oh, I am starting to relax, all right. I feel my body collapse back into him without my permission, and I hear him let out a low, gravelly laugh. He puts his hand over mine, and I feel his breath at my neck again. "Now put your hand higher and spread your feet more."

He moves his knee in between my legs and pushes my feet apart. I stifle a moan, thankfully, since most of his family is within earshot. In the back of my mind, I make a mental note that after the reaction my body just had to his knee, I cannot sit down in this thin dress for the rest of the night. Absolutely not. "Now, don't tense up before you throw it." He pulls away, and I focus on not collapsing. I take a shaky breath and throw. My dart lands in the same place but one section over, closer to the center.

I turn around with a squeal.

"Good. Eight." He looks so relaxed.

"Wait, what! Eight? It's closer! Don't try and fudge the numbers on me, Clark." I point my fingers into his chest. He grabs it.

"It's simply a larger square. I don't make the rules," he says with a smile as he, unbelievably, grabs my hand from his chest and kisses it. He keeps my hand in his and pulls me into him, just staring, like he does. Time stops, and I'm not sure if I'm still breathing, but I do know I lick my lips. His eyes dart down to my mouth. I look back up to his eyes, which peer into my soul underneath drooping lids. *Holy Toledo tits, is he going to kiss me for the first time in front of his family?*

"Well, that's it for me." Byron groans, loudly enough to burst the space-time bubble that surrounds us.

"Same." Layla stands in my peripheral vision.

"We're all turning in here. You two staying?" Benedict asks us. "Anya makes a killer breakfast spread."

Say yes! Say yes! Say yes!

"No." Emerson doesn't hesitate. I feel myself start to deflate, then push the disappointment away. "We're off to Paris tomorrow." Emerson squeezes my hand as he leads me toward the house, and I have no idea what it means. Everyone nods and says their good nights as we head back into the living room. Emerson and Chelsea's parents stand as we file in.

"About that time, isn't it?" Haymitch asks. While everyone gives their best *lovely to meet yous* and *come back soons*, Emerson's hand stays on the small of my back or around my waist. I lean into him, wishing the night wasn't over.

But I'm quickly snapped back to reality when Chelsea approaches Emerson tentatively and then, without so much as a glance in my direction, asks him to walk her out.

The balls on this bitch right here. Wow.

I feel myself inhale sharply but plaster on a smile. I don't care if he walks her out. In this fake scenario, I'm his girlfriend, totally secure in our solid relationship. This is fine. Everything is fine.

Emerson gives my waist a squeeze, so I look up at him.

"I'll be right back," he tells me firmly, with a grit to his voice I don't understand. He kisses me quickly on the forehead before he pulls away.

An eternity passes while they're outside. My bag magically reappears. Layla gives me a hug, Ben says something flirty, and I barely register any of it. William and Haymitch chat loudly, dragging on their conversation to give their star-crossed children time to get back together outside. But Evelyn pulls me aside when Deborah excuses herself. She looks me in the eyes, and I'm struck by their intensity, just like her son's.

"He never looked at Chelsea the way he looks at you, darling. Just . . . don't hurt him, okay?" She searches my eyes as if this is a real possibility. As if *he* hasn't rejected *me* multiple times already on this trip, and hurt *me* fifty times more before that. I just nod and try to smile.

I feel him enter the room before I see him, and I try to look unaffected. He crosses over to me and takes my hand, but his eyes only meet mine for a second and they're distracted. We are hugged and kissed out the door, where Charlie was able to pull up for us. I take a breath, bracing myself for whatever change will occur as soon as we're in the car.

But bracing myself does no good. When the car pulls away, Emerson lets go of my hand to pull at his tie, and I feel a painful tug deep in my chest. He collapses in his seat, even though he's already sitting. He sighs one of the heaviest sighs I've ever heard from him.

"Well, we did it?" I offer weakly.

He nods, keeping his eyes closed, and then adds a soft, "Thank you."

I stare at him for a minute, knowing I can't say anything I want to say in front of Charlie.

"Headache?" I ask, hoping that's the reason he's already shutting down on me.

He gives me a polite smile and shakes his head. He turns and looks out the window, with his brow pinched hard. He's angry or confused or frustrated. Or in pain and lying about it.

He doesn't look at me for the entire drive home.

I decide to chat to Charlie, telling him all about how lovely the house was, the meal. I smile and laugh and don't look at Emerson as much as I can help it. I blink back tears more than once.

I die once again, but this time, the death is anything but happy.

CHAPTER 29

After an entire lifetime of torture during the drive, we arrive at the hotel. Emerson holds out a hand to help me out of the car, and I don't meet his eyes. On the hundred-mile trek from the car to our suite, his hand stays on the small of my back. I try not to read into it, I do, but it's so warm and firm and I love it. I loved it all night.

As always, upon entering our suite, he tries to make a beeline for his door.

"What are you so afraid of?" I blurt. He stops and turns, and I unleash all my unsaid thoughts from the car. "You know, in Sadie's books, so often the main character, she just has no idea what's real and what's acting—*wah! Does he like me? Does he not? I'm so confused* and all that. Now, I kinda think that's bullshit." I walk toward him. "A woman knows, Emerson. When it's real, she knows. I saw how you looked at me, I felt your hands on me. And you know what? It felt amazing. Unbelievable. Like fireworks and like home at the same time. You felt it too.

"I know how badly you wanted to kiss me in that hallway. I mean, you took a selfie at the gala! You, Icy Emerson himself, sat in that ballroom and took a selfie on my phone! And you freaking danced! You danced with me like we were the only people in the room!

"And tonight, you almost kissed me again, I know you did. So, you can lie to yourself all you want, but I'm not buying it." I've reached him, and I'm shaking, but I straighten my back and look up at him, unafraid. *No crap, Sam. No crap.* "This is real, Emerson. I want you. Now look me in my eyes and try to tell me you don't want me too."

His jaw twitches as he looks down at me, his cold blue eyes on fire. I gulp. "I do," he grunts.

I open my arms out wide in frustration. "Then what? What is it? Is it Chelsea, are you still—"

"No."

"But you walked her out and came back all quiet. What did she say?"

His voice barely comes out through clenched teeth. "It doesn't matter. It wouldn't have mattered."

"So . . ." I take a step as I realize what's happening. "You just don't *want* to want me, but you do, and you're disgusted by that."

"What? No!" He takes a small step forward, putting us close again. Too close.

"So, I'm the boss's daughter, off-limits, you think I'm too young?"

He just sighs, which really sets me off.

"Fine!" I throw my hands up. "Be a coward then." I turn to storm to my room.

"I am not right for you, Samantha!" He's almost loud he's so exasperated. I stop and turn back, hoping he'll say more.

"Why? I'm too much, too bright, too loud and cheery and sun-shiny for you? You can't put up with me for longer than—"

"No, damn it! Listen to me." He stalks to me and grabs my arms, squeezing my exposed biceps for a second before loosening his grip to a featherlight touch. He traces his hands up to my neck, holding my face, and I start to tremble. He leans his fore-head on mine, and I inhale his clean scent. "Trust me, please . . . I can't be the man you need. The man you *deserve*."

"Well, can you just be Emerson?" My voice cracks as I say it, as much as I'm trying to hold myself together. He whispers what sounds like cursing under his breath and moves his nose down mine.

"I . . . can't . . . give you everything," he says, talking against my skin again, brushing his lips all around my mouth.

My toes curl in my sandals as I gasp for air.

"Just give me you," I say, and something breaks in him. His lips are on mine, and his featherlight touch is gone. He licks along my lips to push open my mouth. Our tongues dance like we did at the gala. With him in charge, unwavering.

I moan into his mouth when one of his hands moves up into my hair, and he moans into mine as his other goes around my back. His kisses are forceful, long, demanding. He holds me even tighter and moves his mouth to my neck.

"You . . . smell . . ." he says in between open-mouth kisses with the tiniest bit of suction, "so good."

"So do you," I say, but it comes out as a breathy whisper because I am struggling to breathe. He's so sure, so possessive, there's no hesitation, no holding back anymore. My hips rock into his in response. He groans and lifts me up, smashing his mouth back on mine and wrapping my legs around his waist.

In a split second, he's stalked into the kitchen and set me on the counter. He pulls me into him, standing in between my spread legs. I can feel him right there, through my soaked thin panties, since my dress is all the way up my thighs. He's hot in front of me, and the countertop is cold behind my legs. It's so mind-blowingly sexy, I'm almost over the edge already.

I've never felt anything remotely like this before. There's no teasing, no flirty banter, no pressure or nagging worry in the back of my mind. There is a seriousness about Emerson, sure, strong, precise. But there's raw, honest desire in him too. His hands are shaking, and his breath keeps catching. All of it together makes me feel high with desire but also . . . safe.

One of his hands is firm behind me, and the other has gone back to a featherlight touch along my leg. Every cell in my body tracks the barely there caress of his fingers up my ankle, passing over my knee, up the inside of my thigh, *holy yes please yes yes yes!*

He pulls away from my mouth to look into my eyes. He raises his eyebrows just barely, and I whimper with an urgent nod. He keeps his eyes on mine as his hand moves up to my core. His fingers move just like his kisses: firm, hard, slow, deliberate. I close my eyes and let my head fall back with a load moan. I hear Emerson grunt out a sigh before moving his mouth down my neck, along my chest, to my shoulder, everywhere my skin is exposed. My body turns into putty in his hands, and he holds me up behind my back, kissing along my neck and jawline.

"Samantha." It's a command to open my eyes and meet his stare. At that exact moment, he changes the pressure, adjusts his fingers just so.

"Em. Em! Emerson, I—" That's all I can say before explosions take over my brain, vision, heartbeat, my entire body. His mouth sucks on mine as if devouring the moans from my throat. "Wow," I finally whisper. I collapse into him, my forehead falling onto his shoulder. He plants soft kisses on my neck as my trembling subsides.

My brain regains some of its functions, and it's no surprise that talking comes back first. "I've never, um, that—" Emerson pulls away and angles my chin up so he can see my face. His confused and concerned scowl makes me nervous. "I mean, *a man* has never done that . . . to me." Relief and a wide smile take over his features. It's beautiful. "Like, that's only ever happened, you know, by mys—" He kisses away the end of my sentence. He pulls me into him again, and I feel rock-hard proof that this is all incredibly hot for him too.

He lifts me and carries me into his room, walking as if my hourglass, five-foot-six frame weighs nothing. He sits down on the bed, scooting back so I can comfortably sit straddled over him. He pulls away suddenly.

"Shit." He closes his eyes. "I, uh, don't have any condoms with me."

"Oh, okay." I sigh the words, with relief, I suddenly realize. My body relaxes the tiniest bit, and Emerson notices. He takes my face in his hands again, and his eyes search mine, his scowl back in place. "No, I mean, I want to. I do. Yes. *Very* much. But I am not . . . I mean, despite what the tabloids always said, uh, I'm actually not very . . . experienced." He tenses underneath me. "I'm not a virgin! I just always save that, until I'm sure I'm ready. And I've only been with two guys, my college boyfriend and . . . well, one of my, uh, recent mistakes."

Anger flashes across his face, but only for a second.

"I can wait," he says softly, with a grit to his voice that makes me think he actually can't.

I smirk down at the rocket begging to take off from inside his pants. "I thought you didn't lie." I squint up at him. He rolls his eyes and begins to lift me off him, but I fight to stay put. "I didn't say I wasn't ready for . . . other things." I reach my hand down toward him, but he stops me.

"No."

"No?"

"I can wait, Samantha."

I climb off him. "Challenge accepted, Mr. Clark," I say as I quickly unzip my dress before he can say anything in response.

And then he can't, because I'm standing in front of him in just my white lacy push-up bra and matching lace thong. My heels are still on as I step out of the dress to the space between his legs. His hands turn to fists on the mattress on either side of him. His amazing hungry eyes roam all over me, his lips part. And they pause on my giant bruise. He reaches out his hand and covers it softly.

"It doesn't really hurt anymore," I whisper. His head shakes a bit, and his jaw clenches. I remove his hand and put it back on the bed, redirecting his focus. His breath is shaky as I drop quickly to my knees in front of him. His eyes grow wide for a second. It makes me feel like a freaking goddess.

He whispers my name in half-hearted protest when I start on his zipper, but the way he says my name isn't in protest after that. The look on his face, the awe and unabashed longing, I'll never forget it as long as I live. I will also remember the animal sounds he made when I put one of his hands in my hair. He twisted my thick long locks around his fist and was almost immediately overcome.

The second he recovers, he lifts me back onto his lap and takes my mouth with his. He holds me close and kisses my neck, talking along my skin. "That was . . . I don't . . . I . . ."

I can't help but smile. "That good, huh?" He sighs, kissing along my shoulder. "Can't find the words?" I tease. He pulls away to look at me, and my smile fades at how serious he is. He tucks a lock of hair behind my ear, then peers into my eyes again.

"Adequate words don't exist."

I can't.

I mean.

What?

I jump forward and wrap around him, clinging in the spider-monkey hold I'd thought about a million times. He holds me back just as tightly, tracing his fingers in small circles on my skin. I bite my tongue to keep from talking, because I'm afraid of how big and important and too early the words I utter might be.

I don't know how long we sit there like that, in absolute heaven. Eventually I yawn, and goose bumps cover my arms since my body has finally cooled to a normal human temperature.

"It's late, Angel." He pulls back from our embrace. The pet name sends a happy shiver down my body as I nod and stand. I'm completely unsure of what to do. I figure it's a solid assumption that he needs space and quiet to decompress and go to sleep.

"Good night," I say with a smile, turning to grab my dress, but he quickly grabs my waist.

"Stay with me." He commands it, but his chin rests on my stomach and he peers up at me, as if completely at my mercy. My face breaks out into a huge, goofy smile that I did not authorize. My giddiness at those three words is obvious. *Way to have* zero *chill, Sam.* I nod, and he grins back at me, standing and scooping me into his arms and then onto the bed in one fluid motion.

He removes his jacket, which I can't believe was on this entire time, and unbuttons his shirt. I watch every move of his fingers like it's a Broadway show, just for me. He throws his button-up on the chair and then pulls his shirt off, and my mouth waters. This man must work out with a trainer every single day.

He takes off his pants and crosses the room in just his gray boxer briefs. As he stands at the dresser, I get a good look at his ass with the thin fabric stretched over him and wish he was naked. He gets out a plain gray T-shirt and hands it to me before climbing into bed. I sit up and slip it on before doing my ninja bra-removal maneuver out through the shirt sleeve. I toss it by my dress and lie down on my side.

Emerson is already lying on his side, staring. I like that he still hasn't seen me completely naked, or even felt my chest yet. The anticipation of all that we have yet to do sends a stream of warmth down to my center.

"And now we're just supposed to sleep? With you there, looking like that?" I motion to him.

"Mhm." He turns onto his back and tucks me into his side. Suddenly my hand has free access to his skin, his defined abs and perfect chest with a smattering of trimmed chest hair. I start to trace around each individual muscle my fingers find.

"Yeahhhh, I cannot promise to behave," I say as my top leg crosses over his.

"I can," he says without opening his eyes. There's a hint of a grin on his face as he stills my hand and links our fingers together over his sternum. He runs his other hand absently through my hair, a gesture that feels more intimate that anything else we've done tonight. "Sleep, Samantha." He kisses the top of my head.

Eventually, miraculously, I do.

CHAPTER 30

"Samantha." I hear my name a couple times, vaguely in the back of my consciousness. Then I feel fingers in my hair, on my cheek. I open my eyes to take in a fresh-faced, drop-dead gorgeous Emerson Clark, leaning over me with a small smile. He's in navy today, no vest or jacket yet, just the crisp white shirt pulled across his muscles to perfection.

"You have clothes on?" I mumble as my brain tries to process my surroundings. "Unacceptable."

He chuckles under his breath. "You have to pack before we catch the train."

"This is all wrong. You are not in bed, you are not naked, and you're talking about packing?!"

"I made coffee—come."

"How long have you been up?" I grumble as I roll out of the soft sheets and pad into the kitchen behind him.

"Awhile. Sit."

"If you insist." I plop onto the seat at the small table, not anywhere near fully awake. He grabs a mug and pours me some coffee. "I like it with—" He stops me by holding up the whole milk I ordered, since Brits don't believe in half-and-half. He somehow puts in the perfect amount. I guess we have been living together for weeks, but still, I'm surprised.

My shock continues when he places down a plate with two of my egg quiche bites, fresh out of the mini oven, not the microwave. He sits down with his buttered wheat toast. We eat in silence for a while, staring each other down, him with a grin, me with, well, a million emotions.

"You realize I don't have any pants on." He nods. "No bra, little lace panties, your T-shirt, just lying there ready to be ravaged, and you just . . . got up and made breakfast?"

"Ravaged, hm?" His expression makes me squirm as he says it.

"I mean, I don't know, maybe now that offer is off the table." He raises an eyebrow at me while he chews. "Or maybe I need to do a better job of getting you properly . . . motivated."

"No."

"I think yes," I say, then stand to take off his shirt, but he stands with lightning speed and wraps his arms around me, tight.

"This morning was . . . difficult," he says, his breaths hard in his chest that's pressed up against mine. My nipples harden at the low silkiness of his voice rattling our rib cages. "I want to be able . . ." One of his hands slides down to the thin fabric of my white thong and then cups my exposed cheek. ". . . to take my time."

He squeezes, and I moan. He grabs my moan in his mouth, kissing me furiously. Both of his hands go to my ass, and I melt into him. I put my hands in his hair and beg him with my mouth, for more, longer, harder. He pulls back but keeps his hands in place. "Let me get you to Paris first, okay?" he grunts out, his voice hoarse.

"O-O-Okay," I manage to say. I stumble to my room and get myself going. We have to pack luggage for the two weeks in Paris, and then pack everything else to remain here at the Rosewood. He was right to wake me up; in fact, maybe he should have earlier. I smile as I sort through my clothes.

> **Me: Any outfit requests?**
> Emerson: Bikinis

I laugh. That was definitely not what I was expecting.

> **Me: You want me to meet with our French customers in my teeny neon bikini?**
> Emerson: I changed my mind. Long pants, long sleeves, overcoat.
> **LOL It's summer!**
> **C'mon, I want to know which outfits you like**
> All of them
> **Even the neon?**
> Yes.
> **Not one favorite?**
> Your dresses are my favorite.

Dresses it is. Except I will most definitely be wearing my padded sports bra, Ass Leggings, and cropped tank top today. All this self-restraint of his is messing with my mind. I pack in a rush, sorting through my cutest dresses, underwear, bikinis, and pajamas. My hands shake with the realization: I am about to spend two weeks in the City of Love with Emerson Clark. *Eeeeeeeeeee!*

He calls for my leave-behind bags, which I set out in the hall for him. I throw my hair in a high pony and dust a barely there makeup look on my face at the last minute. Finally, I roll out my Paris bag and my backpack and meet him at the door. He lets out a grunty scoff when his eyes take me in from toes to ponytail. He throws his head back and inhales deeply, and I can't help but giggle.

"You are . . . cruel."

"Like I said. Motivation." I shrug playfully while mentally

high-fiving myself. He sets his jaw in a hard line and shakes his head. He lets out what I would describe as an actual growl. He reaches for my bag and motions for me to lead the way out to the elevator. When I pass him, he smacks my ass so hard, I jump and scream. But my scream is cut off by an attack of kisses. Emerson shoves me up against the door frame and moves his hands to the crease on the back of my leggings.

He kisses along my chest, along the scoop of my tank, and grunts out, "We . . . do not . . . have time . . . for this." His mouth is back on mine as one of his hands moves from back to front and cups me, hard. I am instantly drenched. I shudder as he squeezes and pulls away. "Shit, woman. You'll be the death of me," he mutters with his eyes still closed.

"To be continued?" I say quietly, unable to hold back my smile. When he opens his eyes and looks back at me, they look almost menacing.

"Definitely."

———

"What are the odds?" he whispers to me after we get settled in our seats on the Eurostar train. I was staring out the window, thinking, and apparently the Adonis next to me was reading my thoughts. I look up at him, then down to our hands that he's just laced together.

"They're actually pretty bad in Europe, one in 73,573. But that's over your whole lifetime. We're not here that long, obviously, so the annual number is much better—one in 5,885,800. Still, flying is much safer."

"Why didn't we fly?"

"I've never done a train through Europe. It sounded like it would be fun."

Emerson leans down and kisses me softly, caressing my tongue with his for just a few moments. He pulls away and runs his nose along my own. "It will be."

I believe him.

As we get underway, I find myself shifting awkwardly in my seat. The urge to chat away with him is overwhelming. I know part of it is travel nerves, but another part is general anxiety about us. What are we now? What does he want? What happens in two weeks when we fly home?

At the same time, I am determined not to be my "full self," as my sister Skye would say. I have scared off every single guy, every single time. By being too eager, too excited, too needy, too hopeful. I don't want to do that this time. It feels so different than all the times before, but I'm still me, a full-on hot mess. And Emerson is still a calm, quiet, actual genius.

"Samantha."

"Hm?" I look up at him with a small smile.

"Talk to me," he commands.

I blink a few times, trying to clarify what I've just heard via my eyeballs, I guess.

"You don't want me to talk to you for the whole two hours."

"Well . . ." He ponders. "At one point, I may have to use the loo."

After a second, I register the joke he's just made and burst out laughing. My full, obnoxious, way-too-loud laugh. And to my surprise and delight, Emerson laughs too. A real laugh, full and hearty and without reservation. It is my new favorite sound.

When we can breathe again, I ask him about his past trips to Paris, which leads to talk of his unbearably awkward tween and teen years. I share my own horror stories about middle school and high school. I vividly recall the day I stood up for a nerd who'd let one slip in class by turning to the hot, popular bully and proclaiming, "Everybody farts, Alex." It was not the victorious savior moment I'd hoped for.

We laugh again and again as we share about our siblings and parents. It's crazy how much we have in common with the whole family empire thing, an umbrella that covers over every area of our lives, whether we want it to or not. We also have plenty of Canton inside jokes and OU memories to swap. For four years, I knew Emerson was there, but I never saw him, the yin to my yang, the calm to my SamStorm. Just two doors down, hidden behind his fogged glass door, armored up in his magnificent three-piece suit. There, all that time.

We don't really talk about anything important, but at the same time, it's all important. His answers and stories—said in about one-fourth of the number of words I use—give me tiny glimpses into his past, into him. While we talk, he holds my hand, grabs my thigh, holds my cheek, and steals kisses whenever he wants. Often in the middle of my sentences, which to be fair, do tend to ramble.

I get up to go to the *loo* at one point, and when I come back, Emerson grabs me and pulls me into his lap before I reach my seat. His hand slides up my inner thigh and stops. Then he squeezes and puts his mouth to my ear. "Should've worn a dress, Angel."

He puts me back in my seat, and good thing, because I can no longer move my legs.

———

"Le Meurice, please, Jean," I say as we climb into our new hired car. Jean doesn't smile or nod, barely acknowledging us.

"Actually, the Four Seasons," Emerson corrects casually.

"What?" I gape at him. He gives me a smug grin and looks out the window. "You changed our reservation?"

"I did."

"Emerson," I start through gritted teeth. "I looked forever for that suite for us. It wasn't *that* expensive."

He turns back to me, unruffled. "We don't need a two-room suite anymore." My mouth flops open and then snaps shut. I purse my lips together to keep a smile from breaking out. I take a few deep breaths to absorb what has just happened.

He took it upon himself to make calls and change our reservations. This is a bit annoying, because I already made our plan. But the reason, the confidence with which he said it, *we don't need two rooms anymore.* That proclamation wipes out all my other thoughts. I hold in a squeal for a good ten minutes.

Jean says nothing, no comments about the city, no questions about our visit. I lean over to Emerson.

"Do you think Charlie is missing us as much as we're missing him right now?" I whisper.

"I am sure he misses you," he whispers back.

I shove him. "You don't have to just agree with me. I'm sure Charlie is living his best life without our awkward tension in his car every single day." Emerson laughs at that, then leans in with a squeeze of my hand.

"I don't *just say* anything, Samantha. Anyone who's met you would miss you."

My cheeks flush, probably scratched by the wings of all the butterflies that just erupted inside me. I stare at the man. Who is this guy?

"Oh yeah? What about you, back when you couldn't even stand to have me in your office?"

He rolls his eyes. "Even then." He kisses the side of my head.

Mayday! Mayday! I am falling hard here!

He said it first, but I'm sure *he* will be the death of *me*.

CHAPTER 31

"Oh, Em. This is too much," I whisper when he opens the door to our private balcony off the penthouse suite. Just beyond the wrought iron rail is a breathtaking view of the city, including the Eiffel Tower, as if on display just for us.

"Less than the gargantuan flat you booked, actually."

I put my face in my hands. He has got to be actively trying to get me to fall in love with him. Has got to be. And he's succeeding. He wraps his big arms around me and puts a hand on my neck. I breathe him in, feeling my heart split open at the scent, his scent, mixed with Paris air and fresh flowers placed throughout our suite. I notice he's wrapped around me facing away from the view.

"But you hate this. How are you even on the balcony right now?"

"I'll manage."

I slowly walk us back into the suite, beaming at him. "You got us a penthouse with a sweeping view when you hate sweeping views."

"It's not for me."

I groan. "Did I mention this is too much?" I flop my head back down in my hands on his big warm chest.

"Now, I have a question for you, Miss Canton," he murmurs into my ear.

"No," I mumble into his amazing pecs.

He laughs.

"Sorry. Sweet, sunny, sexy Samantha." I look up at him. "Would you like to go to dinner with me?"

"Are you asking me out on an actual date?"

"Mhmm." He runs his hands up and down my back as his eyes roam my face.

"I'd love to, but . . . there was talk of ravishing?"

"I know, but you're starving."

Am I starving? Holy crap, I am starving. What the hell?

I huff. "How did you know that?"

"I'm famished, and if I am, you definitely are."

"Are you saying I eat more than you?"

"I'm saying you eat rubbish that doesn't tide you over." He smacks me with a firm peck on the lips. He runs his hands down to that gathered seam on my leggings again. I yelp when he gives me a playful spank and pushes me away. "Go change."

"Psh, I can't wear this on a date?"

"You can't wear those out of the hotel room." He moves to slap me again, and I laugh and run into the suite. It's a lot smaller than the one I'd booked, but every bit as stunning. It's all gold and white and cream, tons of light, and only one giant, heavenly bed. Those butterflies find their way through me again when my eyes land on it.

I unpack my clothes into the dresser and closet, and Emerson does too. It's totally domestic and dreamy and way too quiet for me. I put in my earbuds and launch my Paris playlist. I choose a flowy, red polka-dot dress for our date. It's more romantic than it is sexy, but I make the low-cut neckline work with my push-up bra. Emerson is in the dining nook that leads out to the balcony waiting for me, and I stop short of going to him because.

Wow.

I could be looking at a magazine ad for men's suits, or cologne, or watches that cost more than cars. He's just perfect, standing there in the soft light, one hand in his pocket, a pensive look on his face as he stares down at his iPad on the table. He hasn't changed out of his navy suit and white shirt, no vest or tie, and still looking as fresh as he did this morning. He spots me and turns. In two steps, he's right in front of me, breathing hard and looking straight down my dress, since I'm much shorter than him in my little white walking sneakers.

"Perhaps we should just get room service," he says softly. He puts his hands on my hips, which must have nerve endings connected directly to my center.

"Fine with me." I beam up at him, but he shakes his head.

"We only have a couple dinners on our own while we're here." His hands slide up my sides to just barely caress the outsides of my bra, which I wish was thinner. "But maybe let's be quick about it." I let out a giggle, and he smiles, a full, kill-me-now smile that shows his straight white teeth and crinkles the skin by his eyes.

———

"Will you tell me about the accident?" I ask, feeling brave.

On our way to this little hole-in-the-wall restaurant, Emerson had the driver drop us off at the exact right spot so we could walk through the arts district. We strolled along the cobblestone streets and saw so many pinch-me things I'd googled. The Moulin Rouge. La Vigne de Montmartre, a hidden hillside vineyard whose sidewalk is crammed full of bright flowers. Specific streets lined with historical buildings in quirky colors, some covered in ivy, among about a million cafés. Plus, easel after easel in rows, with street artists painting all along our walk.

We walked like lovers, leisurely, fingers intertwined, stealing kisses every few steps. Emerson even took selfies with me whenever I asked, even though there was some sighing and lack of full smiles. He led me past the touristy Instagrammable streets to find this little café tucked away in a courtyard.

We've had salad and bread and wine, and I've chatted his ear off with a million Paris tidbits and questions. Emerson has melted my panties with his almost-perfect French throughout the evening, asking questions and ordering our meals.

We're finishing up our amazing meal in this amazing secret spot in freaking Paris! He's the most relaxed I've seen him, maybe ever. Which is why I am motivated to ask the hard questions, starting with the accident.

"It was . . . severe." He wipes his mouth with his cloth napkin. Then sets it back on his knee in a neat folded rectangle. "Pretty bad concussion, broken leg and ribs. I was in the hospital for weeks."

"Do you miss it? Riding?"

He hesitates. "Not really."

"And the headaches?"

His hand finds mine on the table. "Much better in recent years. It's not every night, and rarely migraines anymore . . . my mother exaggerates."

"I like your mom," I say.

"Oh?"

"Yeah, when you were out there saying who knows what to the wannabe duchess, she told me not to worry. It was nice of her, and pretty surprising, honestly, since your dad and her dad are clearly desperate for you two to get married and have lots of little Clark Industries babies." He just stares at me, because he knows I'm not saying what I want to say. So, I do. "C'mon! What did you say to her! I'm dying here. She straight-up told me she made a mistake and wanted you back, so did she profess her undying love to you?

Did she flash you? Was she down on her knees at any point?"

Finally, he reacts, with a laugh.

"We weren't outside that long."

"Long enough!" I try to pull my hand away, but he holds it in place.

"It was nothing. Well . . . nothing to me. She did say she made a mistake and wanted to reconcile." He sips his wine with his free hand, trying to be done with this conversation.

"And you told her you were head over heels for your fake girl-friend and to back the hell off?"

"More or less."

"Emerson!" I do tug my hand free this time.

"It's a bit fun to see *you* jealous for a change."

My cheeks pink because I am jealous, definitely, but he's also admitted to his own jealousy, which thrills me.

"See how fun it is when I go make out with the waiter because you won't answer my question."

He grabs my thigh under the table, hard. I lift my eyebrows and cock my head.

"I told her I wasn't sure I'd ever loved her, or that she'd ever really loved me." He looks away, thinking. He releases my thigh and goes back to holding my hand. But he doesn't elaborate, of freaking course.

I lean in, almost desperate for him to share more with me. "But you were hurt, when she ended it, right? I mean, you left for the States, so it must've been a pretty bad breakup."

"I was, but it was bigger than just she and I. I was still working in the business, and our fathers . . . everything . . . imploded. I left for distance, but not distance from her." It's clear that he doesn't enjoy talking about this, but he's not frustrated or angry. I keep the ball rolling, in case I don't get this open feeling—*ha! Open relative to a frozen, locked vault hidden in an underground bunker under the sea*—from him again anytime soon.

"And Miranda? Since we're on the subject."

He sighs with a grin, as if he knew that's what I was going to say.

"I already told you about that . . . arrangement."

"Friends with benefits, but she is probably in love with you."

He drops his chin to glare at me. "*You* said that bit. I never led her on. She and I were friends and she saw how shit I was with people, including women. She enjoyed going to the galas and parties."

"And she enjoyed your amazing body," I say before I can stop myself. He laughs again. "And you enjoyed hers, I'm sure," I mutter.

"It was . . . helpful."

"Was, past tense?"

He holds my eyes for a second. "*Oui, passé.*"

————

"Dress. Off," he commands in between urgent kisses as we stumble through our hotel room door.

"Did you get condoms?" I ask while I fidget at the back top button of my dress.

"No."

"What!" I squeak.

"Not yet."

"Are you serious right now?!"

"Yes." He's still kissing all over my neck and face as I try to talk to him.

"Emerson."

"You said you want to save it."

"I said I *did* want to save it. Before! Not now!"

"Too bad."

"UGHHHH!" I yell and stomp away from him, but he grabs me from behind.

"You don't want me to ravage you, then?" His mouth is on my ear, and his hand is sliding up over my shoulder and down into my cleavage. His fingers play there, not going underneath my bra, softly murdering all my thoughts.

"Let me," he whispers.

I whimper out some sort of yes. He quickly undoes the rest of my dress and tugs it down. He turns me around to kiss him, and I take off his clothes too, with his help, as our mouths devour each other. Again, it's frenzied, like both of us might die if we're not touching. I never want it to end.

When he's out of everything but his boxers, he carries me to the bed. He looks at my cleavage again, and I quickly take off my bra before I'm laid all the way down. He sits back and looks down over me, his eyes scanning every inch of my nakedness, except for a tiny red string thong.

"*Incroyable*," he whispers in French.

"What?" I whisper, trying to read his face.

"Incredible," he says, and his voice cracks. "I could do this for ages, just look at you."

"Please don't," I say with a smile, pulling his mouth back down. He kisses me fiercely, like a man possessed. Then his tongue slows, his hands lighten. He pulls away, and then his mouth is moving down my jaw. His lips and tongue go everywhere slowly: my neck, down my sternum, over each nipple, along my stomach. He keeps kissing and licking, moaning his way down, muttering in French. He slows even more as his mouth moves past my belly button.

Wait.

I've never done this.

"Wait."

He freezes and looks up at me.

"I've never . . . no one's ever done *that*."

"All right?" he says slowly, gently rubbing my thigh with his hand and watching me, not moving away.

"I mean, I am so sweaty. We just walked across the whole city, and I haven't showered since last night, and I don't know what it's supposed to be like but probably not *that*, right? Like, I don't know how you could want to do that right now, and I'm freaking out a little bit, and then I don't know if I can enjoy it if I'm freaking—"

He scoops me up into his arms, cradling me, and stands with a grin. He carries me to the bathroom and sets me down outside the shower. He reaches to take off my thong.

"I like these," he says as he watches them fall off my foot. He opens the door and starts the water, then motions for me to get in. I look back and watch eagerly as he takes off his boxers.

He is.

I can't.

It's too much.

How can a man look so good, so cut and firm and huge and beautiful, in real life? I blink a few times. He gets in and hands me the loofa as he grabs the small bottle of body wash. After a squeeze, he takes the loofa back and washes my entire body, alternating between his hand and the fluffy white sponge.

I'm covered in silky suds, and his hands sliding all over me feel amazing. He's so slow and gentle, so tender that my eyes start to sting. We don't say anything, we don't even moan. We just watch his hands and each other's eyes in silence. When I step under the spray to rinse, he trails his hands on my hips.

"You are so beautiful." His voice is low and strained. After a couple minutes, he moves me out of the spray and gets down on his knees. He does what he had wanted to do all along with his mouth and his fingers, moaning, sucking, biting, pushing, pulling, and blowing my mind. It only takes minutes before I detonate around him, barely able to hold up my weight on the slippery tile.

"Whoa," is the best I can utter when my brain rejoins my body.

"Good?" he says into my collarbone, where he's kissing me softly.

"Good? Psh . . . uhhh . . . life-altering is maybe getting close to describing what that was." He kisses me slowly, and we stand in the spray and just make out for a few minutes until I'm fully recovered. "Your turn," I say, taking the loofa from him. I take my time, sliding my fingers over every muscle, including his bulky back, and finally, his rock-solid ass.

"I have to know," I say, kneading his cheeks as I please. "Do you do the StairMaster? You've got to."

He chuckles. "I run stairs."

"Knew it," I whisper. Then we are back to serious, heated glances. I look at every inch of him, and he looks at me, watching my face more than my hands. Until my soapy hands grab around him there. We both watch then, transfixed, and with the suds and the heat and our combined moans and sighs, it doesn't take him very long.

We towel each other off and pad back into the living room. I choose one of his shirts for bed and a pair of underwear, and we crawl in and spoon. We haven't had sex, but already it's the most intimate and raw I've ever been with a man. How intense and direct he is, along with how gentle—it's just altogether different.

Yet I tense a bit as I hold on to his arms around me, wondering about Chelsea, Miranda, and anyone else. Am I as good? Are we as good? Miranda is a supermodel. They probably had crazy porn-star *Fifty Shades*–type sex!

"What is it, Angel?" he mumbles behind me as he holds me tighter. I force myself to relax and exhale.

"Nothing." I try to sound casual. He pulls my shoulder so I lay flat and he can look down at me. His eyes are tired but fierce. "It's nothing. I don't have to say every single thought out loud, you know." He tilts his head with a half grin. "I said I don't have to. I usually do, yes, but I shouldn't. I don't need to."

"Come on, out with it," he commands. His voice is soft but final. I'm not getting out of this.

"I'm just self-conscious! We haven't even had sex yet, and I just keep thinking about Miranda and her legs for days and perky little supermodel boobs and how you guys probably had wild, experimental porno sex with like swings and gadgets and I don't even know!"

He chuckles and pushes a stray hair behind my ear. "You're already the best sex I've ever had, Samantha."

"How can you say that when we haven't yet?"

"I mean what we *have* done already eclipses everything else. By far."

"Bull."

He tenses up. "Are you writing notes yourself, then? Lying there thinking of the two idiots before?"

"No!" I stop him before he gets angrier. "No. You're right, I'm not. I just find that hard to believe, I guess."

"You know I'm always honest with you." His anger is gone, but his severity remains, like this is important to him. I nod. "Now, can we go to sleep?"

"Okay," I say, then laugh as he yanks me back into my place as the little spoon. One of his hands has a firm squeeze on my boob. "I don't know if I can fall asleep with your hand like that."

"That sounds like a personal problem." He sighs, and I laugh. If someone had tried to tell me four weeks ago that I'd be in bed with Emerson Clark and he'd be *kidding around with me*, I would've choked on my disbelief.

"Honestly, I think my boobs are actually better than hers," I say, then laugh again.

"Absolutely," he says with another squeeze, and he laughs too.

It turns out I have no trouble falling asleep with his hand there.

CHAPTER 32

"So, what do I do?!" I whisper to Sadie's face on the screen as I circle the suite's small dining table, exasperated.

"Back way up and slow way down. You just breezed on by the whole *Emerson and I are kind of together now* thing! My brain cannot even. So, after all the tension, and he almost kisses you at convention, which I cannot *believe* you didn't tell me, you fall in fake love at his parents' house, which, um, that is *the* most rom-dot-com thing I've ever heard, I love it. Then you talk, and he admits it's real, and you hook up but not really, then he books you the most romantic suite in Paris, and then you just go back to work as usual?"

"Well, no." I move to the couch and plop down. "Not as usual. I mean, during our meetings we've been completely professional—no one would suspect. And we make a killer team. I saw it before, but it's even more obvious now, how well we work together."

"Never would've guessed."

"Right! So the meetings are the same except he's playful sometimes, like he'll grab my ass when he knows the customer can't see, and last night at the dinner, he started to put his hand up my skirt! With Penn Marin sitting right across from me!"

"See . . ." Sadie begins, and I look down to my phone and catch her biting her lip like a creepo. "This is where I want details. I need a play-by-play of the hand up the skirt. Did he slide all the way to home base?"

"No, he just teased me until I almost fainted. That's all the play-by-play you're getting. And then at night when we get home, he is totally spent, like I suspected before. If we do talk at all, it's in the mornings, because by the end of a day of meetings and dinner, he is like a zombie. Of course, not so much a zombie that we don't fool around, just enough that he can't form complete sentences."

"Does he ever form complete sentences?"

"Touché. Oh! Did I tell you he speaks fluent French?" I flop back on the couch. "I mean, damn it all. How any of my panties have survived the raging inferno in my crotch this entire trip is beyond me."

"Wow. Now you decide to get graphic."

"Focus!" I sit back up, moving my brain from Emerson's French back to the matter at hand. "So, we've had days of Parisian bliss, basically. But I could tell a headache was coming on, so I tried to be helpful. Closed all the curtains, made tea, made a cold compress, offered to find him some meds. But he got angry, like really angry, at me. For trying to help."

"Hmmm." Sadie pauses. "Why do you think he's angry at you and not just in pain?"

"Uhhh because I said 'I'm just trying to help' and he barked back at me 'If you want to help, please Samantha, leave!'"

She sucks air through her teeth, wincing. "Were you badgering him?"

"No, I hadn't even said anything, I was just bringing that stuff in, the compress, the tea, and I asked about his pills, and he let out one of his heavy sighs, and that's when I said I was trying to help."

"Okay, so then he wants or needs to be alone when he's sick. That's not the worst thing, and it's not fair to expect him to be Mr. Congeniality when he's fighting off a migraine. Now you know, so next time, steer clear. And leave him alone the rest of the night."

"Do you think I should sleep on the couch?"

She doesn't hesitate. "I would."

"K."

"So, the fooling around? How is it?"

"I can't even describe it in words. It's never been like this. And I'm not just talking about the world-altering orgasms, either. The intensity and vulnerability between us—it's like, well, I mean . . ."

"Like love," she finishes for me.

"Yes . . . is that insane? Am I just going all heart eyes all over again?"

"I don't know, sweetie. You're different about this, about him. For sure. And you've had weeks together in a pressure cooker, reeeeally getting to know each other. Plus, you've already kinda known each other for over a decade."

"Ugh." I throw my head into my free hand. "I just don't want to screw this up this time."

"If it's meant to be, you can't screw it up. Like Suze would say, we can't mess up God's plan no matter how hard we sometimes try."

"I know that should be comforting, but right now, it's really not."

"Well, then just watch some trash TV and go to sleep. On the couch."

"Okay. Thanks, Sadie."

"Of course."

"You know, someday we're going to actually talk about you and—"

"No, we're not. Good night."

"Night."

I make up the couch for myself, which is easy because the throw blankets in the room are like butter. I watch some Netflix and check everyone else's Instagrams using the Canton corporate account. I scroll through emails about tomorrow. I give up and try to sleep. I toss and turn for at least an hour, unable to get comfortable. Really, I just lie there hoping and praying that the bedroom door will open. But it doesn't.

———

I am only half conscious of being picked up and carried to bed. I hear a whimper from myself and a sigh from Emerson when the cool sheets meet my skin. Then I feel Emerson's lips on my forehead and his arms around me. I don't toss and turn at all after that.

———

The second my eyes flutter open, I see him lean over me.

"I'm so sorry." His face is earnest.

"I'm sorry too. I should've given you space."

"No, Angel, you don't have anything to be sorry for. I'm . . ." He pauses to think, looking away. "I'm not usually with anyone. When the headaches come on. And I . . . I get angry. I've just never had anyone there to lash out at before, but I should've guessed how I'd be. It's . . . miserable."

"I understand, it's okay."

"It isn't." He looks back at me. "I'll work on it."

I'll work on it. As in, in the future, with me. I try to clamp down my excitement and just nod, rubbing my hands up and down his strong arms on either side of me.

"Now I think we have maybe ten minutes before the alarm goes off." He leans down and kisses my chest.

"Ten minutes, huh? That's not very long." I tease. He glares up at me and raises an eyebrow.

Challenge accepted.

————

"Do you have a quiet office we could use for a quick Zoom meeting?" Emerson asks as we stand and shake hands around the table. I glance up at him, confused. An office assistant ushers us to a small office and closes the door behind her as she leaves us. As soon as the door shuts, Emerson is on me, picking me up and wrapping my legs around his waist.

"What are you—"

"I've news," he says into my neck, pinning me up against the wall. My brain registers that there are no windows in this little office.

"What?"

"This dress drives me insane," he says, pushing the stretchy navy fabric up my thighs. He licks, actually licks, my cleavage, which is somewhat on display since it's a V-shaped neckline.

"Th-That's your news?" I say breathlessly. I can't get over how hot this is that he asked our buyers for a room just to have his way with me.

"No, first, I wanted to do this." His fingers slam inside me without warning. I cry out in both surprise and pleasure. "Shhh." He kisses my noises out of my throat. "Second, I just got an email, while you were talking with that mouth . . ." He licks my lips—just licks his flat tongue across my entire mouth, causing me to shudder. "Dan canceled dinner tonight."

I smile at his joy over canceled plans. "He did?"

"He did," he says, talking as if he's not busy destroying me in the best way with his hand. I smile back at him. His eyes are hooded as he watches me. "You are so gorgeous, Samantha."

"You look like coffee ice cream in that suit," I blurt. "Every time you've worn it, I've thought, *I want to lick him.*"

He slows. "Every time? Even back home?"

"Uh-huh," I pant up to him. He smiles and changes whatever sleight of hand magic he's doing, as if he's simply decided it's time for me to finish. And I do.

———

"What about teaching?" He lowers the menu to look at me.

We decided to go to our fancy reservation without Dan, the prospect we were supposed to meet. The Guy Savoy restaurant is world-famous and outrageously expensive, so I figured Emerson the CFO would want us to change our plan, but he insisted I get to experience it.

The wine, the bread, every course, the twinkling candles and romantic atmosphere—it's all been amazing. But it could just be the company. Emerson's relief at our canceled plans has made him more playful and talkative than ever. That's not very talkative at all, really, but the additional words tonight have been noteworthy.

"I thought about it . . . I even subbed a few classes, but alas, no singing angels." I butter another tiny piece of what I've dubbed Heaven Bread. "I obviously love kids, so I thought I'd love being with them all day, but it didn't feel right. I even tried a few different ages—elementary, middle school, high school—but nope."

"Could you change something about your job to make it enjoyable again?"

"I don't know, that's a good question. It'd be a fun challenge if there were all-new people and products for me to memorize."

"So . . ." He lowers his chin as if the answer is obvious. "Same position, then, but a different company?"

"What? No. I wouldn't leave the business just to go sell something else."

He frowns. "Why not?"

"I don't know, that'd feel like . . . a betrayal, I guess."

"Any other roles interest you within the organization?"

"CEO, maybe," I joke.

"You could definitely be the CEO."

"I was just kidding. That'll be Susan's job. I don't think I'd want the pressure. Susan and I are a lot alike, but she's always been more organized and driven than me."

"Malarkey."

I do a double take at the man across from me. "Um, did you just say malarkey? How much wine have you had?"

He beams. "Almost enough to say poppycock."

"Really?!"

"No." I laugh, and he smiles wide at me. My breath hitches at the sight. I feel my face change at the sudden, heavy, no-doubt realization that I am 100 percent in love with Emerson Clark. *Crap shit crap on a cracker!* I take a sip of my wine to hide whatever is happening on my face. Emerson notices, because he notices everything, but he doesn't say anything.

"So, I'll just do my best and try to enjoy it, for now. There will always be those hard months when I have to really push myself to hit my quarterly numbers. And I love a lot of it—I love the meetings, the people, I love Manhattan." He nods. "Which do you prefer, Manhattan or London?"

"Manhattan."

"Really?" I choke a bit on my bread. "Wow, a traitor."

"I love them both, but London has . . . baggage."

"Ah." I wonder what all he's not telling me. Clearly more went down with the breakup and his dad than he's ready to share.

"Do you want to stay in Manhattan?" he asks, only after I've finished chewing.

"Like, forever?"

"I suppose what I mean is, do you want to settle down back in Oklahoma? Eventually?"

"Huh." I sit back in the padded wood chair. "I haven't actually thought about that. I love New York so much, I couldn't imagine moving home anytime soon. But if Skye and Matt moved home, or to Texas, I don't know."

He takes a sip of his wine and then, to my shock, asks another question. "Have they said they will?"

"Oh no, and I don't know if I can imagine Skye leaving New York, not for years and years. So, as long as they're there, I'd want to stay too. I just wouldn't want to be in New York all by myself." I don't ask him what I want to ask, which is, will I be by myself? What are we? Where is this going? What happens when we're back in the city? Instead, I just ask about him. "What about you? Are you set in New York forever?"

"I think so, yes." He looks down and moves his folded napkin from his knee to the table.

"The thing I just can't see is raising kids in Manhattan. I mean, I know people do it, but I see the schools, even the crazy-expensive private ones, are fenced-in concrete slabs, no grass, no trees. And like, what about neighborhoods, with front yards, you know? And women with babies, strollers on the subway—it seems like a drag. There's a family in our building that has to lug their stroller up three flights of stairs *every day*!"

"All that's different when you have money." He waves the waiter over and adds, "Which you do."

Something twinges in my chest as he says it. There was a finality to it, not just to our discussion, but it wasn't the open-ended feel the rest of the conversation had, as if we could've been talking about the two of us, and suddenly the future he was talking about was me, separate from him. I could be making all of it up in my mind, of course, but when I sense a shift in a conversation, I'm usually right.

I notice Emerson takes out a card to pay before I can grab the one we've been using, and it's not a company card.

"What are you doing, Em? This dinner was insane!"

"This was a date, Angel. I'm not about to let our employer pay for it." He has a proud sparkle in his eye that I've never seen, and it's downright adorable. He speaks to the server in French for a heart-melting minute. "I have an idea, but I need you to be honest with me." The twinkle is still in his eye, even though he's grown serious.

"Okay?"

"Can you stomach the idea of another boat?"

"A sailboat?"

"No."

"Then sure."

He smirks. "Good. Come."

We wander a few blocks to the Seine and board a river cruise boat. I squeal, and Emerson asks me if I'd already planned this as part of my sightseeing day in a couple days, but I hadn't. I figured one boating excursion was enough; plus, our weeks are so full, I wanted to leave our few free evenings open. We go up to the top deck, and it's . . . just . . . magical. Everything is twinkly and serene, the weather is ideal, the man next to me is ideal.

"Come on, then, get out your playlist," he tells me after a little while of just standing behind me at the railing. I turn and look around, assuming my music would disturb the others on the boat with us. But there isn't anyone on the boat with us, at least not up top.

I gape at him. "You . . . did . . . did you rent out this whole boat?"

He shrugs. "I don't like crowds."

"You don't say." I laugh, and he kisses my laughter, along the edges of my mouth, chuckling himself. I start my Paris playlist, and we have the most romantic hour that has ever been. Not only is he behind me with my perfectly curated music playing, but we pass Notre Dame, Pont des Arts, L'Assemblée Nationale, and the Eiffel Tower, all lit and sparkling. After we pass the Eiffel Tower, he takes my hand and dances with me, just like he did at the gala. My eyes tear up multiple times at the wonder of it all, here, with him.

I think that surely this is the night we'll finally make love, after multiple real conversations and the best date of my life, but still, he says, "Not yet." And while I'm the one who first said it, and he was more than ready on our last night in London, now it feels as if Emerson is the one keeping the distance between us.

I just can't figure out why.

CHAPTER 33

Me: It's sightseeing day, prepare yourselves!

I send a warning to my sisters even though none of them are up yet. I'm buzzing with excitement for all the things today: guided tours of the Eiffel Tower, the Louvre, Versailles palace and gardens, the Catacombs, and another trip through the arts quarter. I may or may not be buzzing from yet another dreamlike morning with Emerson.

He always wakes up at an unholy hour, long before any alarms, and kills himself at the gym. Only after he's worked out, returned, and showered does he wake me up, usually with featherlight kisses somewhere on my body. Then we explore each other to the point of ecstasy, sometimes both of us, but always me.

Who knew the secret to happiness was an orgasm every morning? Actually, probably everyone knows that. I'm still shocked to see he's made coffee and some sort of breakfast while I shower, every single day. So freaking dreamy.

It's over breakfast that we chat.

Well, I chat.

I make a note to tell Sadie that in her books, after the broody man falls in love, she makes him suddenly very wordy. I've been misled. Emerson still says as little as possible. But he works at it, for me. And it's one of my favorite things.

In fact, it's the breakfasts that make us feel serious, and real. It's over coffee that he asks me deeper questions, shares more of himself. The emotional intimacy is almost better than the physical intimacy that precedes it. After enjoying both, we set out for our day, which usually involves meetings, but today involves getting our tourist on.

This morning was particularly fun because I insisted on wearing *those* leggings, the only ones I packed for Paris, and a long tank top that covered most of my butt. Emerson was not having it, seriously insisting I never wear them in public again. I stood my ground that I was not going to walk a million miles in a dress. We compromised with a light hoodie to tie around my waist, covering what I thought was already plenty covered. I've laughed and joked, but Emerson has not been amused. Now as we're about to head out, he glowers at me like a man possessed and possessive, crazy with jealousy. I love it.

"You're acting an awful lot like you don't want anyone else to see what's yours, Frosty." I tie the zip sweatshirt around me.

"I don't."

"So . . . am I? Yours?" My voice cracks as I say it, but I have to know where we stand. We only have a few days left.

"Yes," he answers softly.

"So you're mine too, then."

"Wholly." He doesn't hesitate.

I can't help my giant smile. But as always, I can't stop when I'm ahead. Nervously, I look at my feet and keep going.

"And what about after our trip? When we get back home?"

"What about it?"

"Will we still be together? At the office?"

"I cannot wait to have you in my office," he says lowly as he slips his hands around me under the hoodie.

"Ugh, you know what I mean."

"Yes, Angel." He tips my chin up to look at him. "I'm not letting you go. We'll tell HR when we get back to New York, all right?" I nod up at him, holding in another giddy squeal. He grins at me because he knows I'm holding myself back. He kisses me hard and squeezes my butt for a second. "Let's go."

———

"You don't mind?" he asks me, looking like a painting under the afternoon sun in the garden area at the bottom of the Eiffel Tower.

"I don't want you going up there and turning green on me. But it's going to be at least an hour. Maybe I should just skip going to the top."

"No. Either you go, or we go."

"What will you do while I'm up there?"

"Weep from loneliness," he deadpans.

"Ugh!"

"It's Paris, Angel. I'll find something to do. Text me when you're done."

"Okay." I smile up at him, and he kisses me, not just a soft goodbye peck either, but a deep kiss that feels like a staked claim. Then he's gone, walking off into the crowds. My private tour guide clears her throat with a grin. I enjoy the trip up to the very top, where even I get a little woozy, but my hand feels a little cold and naked without Emerson's fingers wrapped around it. I use the trip down to bombard my sisters.

Me: [Selfie with Emerson]
[Selfie with Emerson]
[Landscape photo]
[Louvre photo]

[Selfie with Emerson]

[Selfie]

[Selfie with Emerson]

Sadie: Gorgeous, all of them!

Susan: Jealous!

Skye: Does that man ever smile?

Sally: Evidence suggests no.

Skye: Wait, how'd you get him to agree to these selfies . . .

Skye: And why are you sightseeing together? I thought he was seeing family?

Sally: Very good questions.

Susan: Anything you want to tell us?

Sally: HIS HAND IS ON HER WAIST. I REPEAT: HAND ON WAIST!

Susan: !!!! Samantha! Are you two together?

Skye: Samantha Jane, YOU HAD ONE JOB THIS TRIP

Sadie: I think you two are adorable.

Skye: Okay, so Sadie clearly knew.

Sally: WTF knew since when?

Susan: Sam???

Skye: Guess Operation Thaw was a success [Eye roll emoji]

Skye: What happened to no men? To you doing you on this trip?

Skye: And Icy Emerson? Really?

Sally: I am also confused [Snowman emoji]

Sadie: Why can't you bitches just be happy for her!

Susan: I need a minute here.

Sally: LOL the COO's brain is melting

Skye: You can run on read, but you can't hide, Sam.

Sadie: Maybe she'll reply when you decide to be nice.

I decide to just let them lose their minds. What Emerson and I have is beautiful and real and none of their business, no matter what they think or say about it.

Skye's messages do make me wince, though. On paper, from a distance, this does look like classic Sam, jumping on the next available man that shows interest. But I wasn't looking for this. I wasn't on the hunt for someone to flirt with or to keep me from loneliness. Hell, if I was, I was looking at Chase or Thomas. I also didn't make Emerson into something he's not. He still drives me insane with his one-word answers and quiet stares. He is not going to whisk me to parties and entertain friends. He doesn't shower me with compliments or tell long, funny stories. He's just Emerson and—

Crap.

He's just Emerson, and I love him.

I love him.

Hoooooolllllyyyyy Toledo.

It's too early for this! *Crap crap crappity shit shit shit!*

Now that I've thought them, meant them, felt them loud and clear, how am I going to keep those three words from flopping out of my damn mouth!?

———

I sit at a café table by the tower waiting for him—the man I *love! Ahhhh!*—to find me. I sense him before I see him, as if he parts the crowds and pulls the sunlight onto him like a spotlight. He's in a white button-up and gray slacks, his lightest pair, and his more casual black loafers. His top few buttons are undone and his black Ray-Bans are tucked there, settled in between the definition of his chest that his tailored shirt can't hide. His light brown hair is messier than usual from sweat and the breeze, and he has a five-o'clock shadow since we had no meetings today. What kills me more than all of that, though, are those icy eyes, staring at me as if I'm his oasis in a vast desert. No one has ever looked at me that way.

He sits down across from me with a grin and sets a small paper gift bag on the table.

"You went shopping?"

His head rears back at the idea. "I went to *one* store, for this." He pushes the bag toward me.

"For me?" I squeak. He nods.

I open the sack and see a velvet box inside, and immediately die at least two mini deaths. It's not a ring box. It's big and flat, but no matter what's inside, no man has ever bought me fancy jewelry before. I pull it out and open it. I gasp because it's gold with tiny diamonds—that's what I notice right away, how dainty and sparkly it is. It's a short chain with small evenly spaced charms, like I've seen trendy Instagrammers wear. I expect to see my name spelled out, but then I really look, and the charms aren't letters. There is a little sparkling plane, the Big Ben, a sailboat, a train, an Eiffel Tower, and . . . the Statue of Liberty.

"It's our trip," I croak out. My eyes are filling, and I can't help it. "And home," I add.

"You like it?"

"I love it." I can barely say the words. He smiles, one of the wide ones that steals all the oxygen from my brain. I lean toward him. "Will you put it on?" He crosses around and gently puts it around my neck and then kisses me behind each ear.

I grab him and pull him down and kiss him like my life depends on having his tongue on mine. In this moment, it feels like it does. He moans and pulls away, because my tears are falling around his mouth. He looks at me, confused. I shake my head and plop it firmly in my hands. *Breathe, Samantha, just breathe.*

"Angel?" He sits down, pulling the chair from across the table to right next to my own. He puts a hand on my back, and I actually shrink away for a second without meaning too. "Samantha. What is it?"

"This is just a lot, Emerson. Are you trying to kill me? Like death by romance? Death by looking like a freaking suit model all the time? What the hell is that about? I mean, buy some flip-flops! Wear jeans for once in your life! And weeks ago, you couldn't even stand me, remember that? Remember how you were horrible? Now I'm just trying to be calm and cool and relaxed and not let myself blurt out that I love you already because *hello*, it's too soon, and then you go get me not just the most beautiful necklace ever, that probably costs like the same as a tiny house somewhere in Montana or something, but it's sentimental!" I wipe my face, which is in a full-on snotty cry now. "Why are you being sentimental! You're supposed to be cold, icy Emerson Frozone Clarksicle the Snow King, remember? You said I'd be the death of you, but it's the opposite, and I am dying over here. Dy. Ing."

Wait.

What did I just say.

Emerson looks down at me, smiling his smug, proud smile, the one with the corresponding eye twinkle. He hands me a napkin from the table. He says nothing, just studying me like he does. I try not to vomit, realizing I just said out loud that I was trying not to say the thing and thereby saying the actual thing I was trying not to say.

"Emerson?" I sniff.

"Mm?"

"I need you to pretend I didn't say any of that. I got choked up because I love the gift, which is perfect and wonderful, and that was it, okay?"

"Okay."

"Okay. Are you ready to go? I'm ready to go. L-Let's go," I stutter, getting up in a rush, because I am hanging on by a tiny, thoroughly embarrassed thread. The rest of the day is a mostly happy blur. Emerson stares at me more throughout the day, still looking smug, and I pretend not to notice. I turn various shades of pink and red, reliving my vulnerability nightmare at the café, but he doesn't bring it up.

Do I secretly hope he'll say something wonderful, like, *It's okay, Angel, I already love you too*? Yes, I do. Do I really, *really* hope that he'll take me back to the hotel and finally produce a box of protection and seal the intimate deal with me? I desperately do. But neither of those things happen. In fact, after a delicious dinner, a headache takes my gentle giant down. This time, I hold back all my caregiving instincts and just ask him what he wants me to do.

"I'm just going to try to sleep, but you don't have to tiptoe around. Just come to bed when you want."

"You're sure? I don't mind the couch."

"I want you in bed with me."

Swoon!

His face looks pained as I kiss his forehead and leave him in the bedroom. I pull up some Netflix on the couch, but I can't get my big fat mistake out of my mind. I don't know how to fix it, how to undo the oversharing damage I've done. I consider asking Sadie, but I don't want to hear the disappointment in her voice: *Sam's at it again with her big fat mouth!*

Me: I need a judgment-free cone of acceptance, please.
Nicole: Activated.
What does one do when they accidentally say I love you way too early?
SAY I LOVE YOU TO WHOM?!?!?!!?
Who do you think!

Thomas?

I have spent like an hour total with Thomas. I mean, c'mon. I'm not that pathetic.

Emerson. You're in love with Emerson?!

Full on, hard stop.

WTF! Call me right now!

Okay, just a sec.

I step out onto the balcony and push the green button.

"Hey," I whisper.

"What the actual hell, Sam!"

"I know. Remember, we've established a cone of acceptance here."

"Oh, I accept!" I turn the volume down on my phone as she rails. "I'm just in total shock. I thought you guys couldn't stand each other!"

"We couldn't at first."

"Oh man, I called it, didn't I? This is so you."

That stings.

"It's not *so me.* It's different this time. I didn't even tell my sisters. I didn't even tell you what was going on when you were here! I was trying to be smart, not get involved, not . . . you know, romanticize him."

"That is different, I guess. But. Wow."

"Yeah. Wow."

Nicole takes a second to process, then bounces back. "So, you told him you're in love with him, and he freaks out?"

"No, he didn't freak out."

"He didn't? Wait, why are you whispering? Where are you?"

"I'm out on our balcony. He's trying to sleep off a headache, but he might not be asleep yet."

"Why don't you just go to your room?"

"We don't have separate rooms anymore. When we got to Paris, he changed our reservation to the penthouse at the Four Seasons, just one bed. And get this: it has the most spectacular balcony in the city, but he's afraid of heights. He won't even come out here. So he booked it just for me."

She is silent. I get it—it's a lot. It's a freaking fairy-tale whirlwind whiplash extravaganza. And I feel like that's putting it mildly.

"Nic?"

"Okay, babe, start at the beginning." I fill her in on everything, from the first plane ride all the way to my bumbling idiocy at the café this afternoon. "Oh, honey. You just have no game."

"I know! I just laid it all out. I mean, I hope he wasn't in it for the chase because there is no chase. I make myself unchase-able."

"Well, I mean, you can still turn things around, I think, maybe."

I watch her face on my phone screen as she thinks. "Okay, how?"

"If he wants to chase, then, you run."

"Run? What do you mean?"

"Well, stop letting your pretty mouth get away from you, for one thing. Just be distant. Slow your roll. Maybe he'll wonder if you regret saying it, if you didn't mean it."

"But I did mean it."

"He doesn't need to know that!" Nicole snaps at me. "Not unless *he's* willing to give a little in return. Everything is lopsided. You gotta turn the tables back on him!"

"I don't know. He's been nothing but sweet and romantic . . ."

"Sam." She glares at me through her phone camera. "Did he say he loved you back?"

I sigh. "No."

"So, you run. K?"

"K. Thanks, Bestie. How are you? How's New York?"

"Still fabulous as ever, on both counts. I gotta go, though.

Headed to dinner, and I'm already late."

"All right, yeah, wow, it's past midnight here. Okay, love you."

"Fill me in on how the running goes, okay?"

"Okay." I end our call, feeling better.

I tiptoe through my nighttime routine in the bathroom, slip on Emerson's shirt, and slide into bed. The second I hit the sheets, he moves in behind me and quickly tucks me into little-spoon position. He makes a murmuring sound that tells me he's mostly asleep. I tense for a second, thinking about what Nicole said. It's going to be hard doing all this metaphorical running when, if I'm being honest, his arms feel like the safest place to be.

CHAPTER 34

"Morning, Angel," he whispers. I groan something in reply. He starts on his kisses, this time along the chain of the necklace I couldn't bear to take off, even for bed. My groans turn into moans, as they often do during our little morning routine. "I have a favor to ask you."

"You do?" I tense up in surprise. He never asks me for anything.

"Mm. How would you feel about braving another Clark family dinner?"

"Fine, I'd feel fine about it."

"You sure?"

"Uh-huh," I mumble, focusing on his mouth moving down from my collarbone. "Um, will the Wannabe Duchess be there again?"

He smiles. "No. I'll make sure of that." He kisses me softly. "Father wants 'to talk.'" He puts the words in air quotes. "So Mother's having a lunch before we leave."

"Okay."

"It will be horrid, surely, but it will be bearable if you're there." I smile up at him. I resist the urge to say anything. "You know, I had an ulterior motive with this." He runs a finger along the necklace. I furrow my brow instead of asking what he means. "I hoped to see you in it and nothing else." He starts to tug at his shirt. The kaleidoscope of butterflies that has taken residence in my being starts their flurrying, but I remember my conversation with Nicole, and my mortification from yesterday.

"Uh, I should probably pack first. I don't want to make us almost miss our train again."

His face grows solemn, unreadable. "All right."

I'm immediately disappointed. I appreciate how much he respects whatever I say, but I was hoping for more of a fight. After all, the point of running is that he's supposed to start chasing. I sigh and focus on getting ready to go, and taking as long as I possibly can to do so.

———

I can't figure out why I'm so nervous as we pull up to his family's estate. I guess because this time, our relationship is real. The stakes feel so much higher, but that's just to me, and maybe to Emerson, as his family should be none the wiser. Still, I'm freaking out a bit.

The last couple days of final meetings back in London have been fine. More than fine, really. I have done a crap job of keeping my distance from my gorgeous man, because he is so adorably flirty as soon as clients aren't looking. He steals squeezes and kisses, and at one point, he actually winked at me. Emerson Clark winked.

He hasn't brought up my faux pax, which also means he hasn't said anything close to the three big words himself. He also has not bought condoms, though I stopped pressing the issue in hopes to be more distant, as per the plan.

Other than a few knowing glances from Charlie and Trina, everything has progressed as usual both professionally and personally for our last two days back in London. We stay together in his bed at night, tucked in like two peas in a love pod. Now we're headed to this lunch with his family, and I'm tied up in knots. I fidget with the necklace, which is a comforting reminder of all the things Emerson doesn't say.

Today as we exit the car, Emerson grabs my hand and kisses it, then gives it a squeeze as we climb the familiar steps. When he rings the bell, he wraps both of our hands around my waist, tucking my arm back and kissing the side of my head.

"Thank you for coming," he whispers before the door opens.

"Uncle Emmy!" exclaims a bundle of blond curls and lace ruffles that sprints onto the porch.

"Abigail, you're a giant!" Emerson says with a huge smile that knocks the air out of my lungs, as if I were just physically assaulted. I don't know if I've ever seen him light up this way before, like an entire sunrise captured in a face. He wraps his arms around Abigail and lifts her up to a fit of giggles. She turns her bright eyes to me as soon as he sets her down.

I squat to her level right away. "Hi Abigail, I'm Samantha."

"Hi!" she says brightly.

"Let me guess . . . are you, thirteen? Fourteen?"

"What!" She laughs. "I'm five!"

I feign shock. "Five! There's no way. I thought you were for sure a teenager. Look how cool that dress is!"

"It is really cool, isn't it?" She does a half twirl.

"So cool," I agree.

"I like her," she whispers to Emerson so loudly, the whole house can hear. We both laugh, and our laughter is joined by Layla and Evelyn, who are watching from the entry.

"You can call me Sam—all my best friends do," I say loudly to her as we head inside.

"Okay, Sam!" she whispers back. "Do you want to go play dolls with me?"

Layla chimes in: "Maybe later, sweetie. Let's have some lunch first." We are greeted by the men, sans any cousins or business partners and their daughters, and then head to the dining room.

Halfway through our chicken course, Evelyn notices my necklace.

"Oh, thank you. Em got it for me while I went up the Eiffel Tower." All eyes shift to Emerson.

"You didn't take your girl up the tower?" Ben asks.

"Oh, I didn't want him to. Of course, I mean, I couldn't. Seeing him up at the Sky Garden was bad enough. The poor man was positively neon green, and we almost had that *if you throw up, I'll throw up* thing going with the hurling sounds and—"

"Angel." Emerson squeezes my leg under the table, leaning into my ear. "What's that thing you always say?"

"Zip it and skip it?" I mutter.

"Yes, Love. That." he says through gritted teeth.

Love.

He said love.

"Mhmm."

"Wait." Ben grows excited. "Is our boy here afraid of heights?"

He squeezes my thigh again to snap me back to reality. "No! Uh, no, not really. He just had an upset tummy that day and then again in Paris and said he had errands to run, so I wasn't going to stand between a man and his bathroom needs, you know?" Emerson sighs as I realize going from real fear to fake diarrhea was probably a bad choice. "But! He was actually sneaking off to get this for me. He's a romantic that way." His brothers eye him sheepishly, not buying what I'm selling. So I push out my chest to them with a twirl of my hands that is ridiculous. "Really, he's a softy. Look, the charms are this trip—very sentimental."

Emerson starts choking on his white wine and stands. "All right, Dad, didn't you say you had things for us to discuss?"

"Uh, quite." His dad stands too, shocked by all the revelations I accidentally spilled. The two men start to leave the room, but Ben calls out.

"You can run, but we all know the truth now: you have emotions after all, ya big sap!"

I groan. *That's a big fat fail as a buffer, Samantha!*

Emerson and his father join us about half an hour later when the desserts arrive at the table. He is stiffer than usual. He doesn't eat any of the amazing, sweet concoctions, of course, but I try a tiny bit of each. Really, I'm just trying to keep my mouth shut. I am successful for at least fifteen minutes. *Keep it up!*

"All right, poppet, time for a nap," Layla tells her daughter as the staff clears the plates from the table.

"Awww, can Uncle Emmy and Aunt Sammy read me my story?"

Aunt Sammy. I fight the world's biggest, cheesiest smile.

"Oh, I'm sure they don't want to do that."

"We'd love to." I stand, eager to escape the table.

"All right," Layla concedes. " First go to the loo, darling, then you can come fetch them, all right?"

"Yes!" Abigail jumps in glee with a fist up in the air. I laugh and turn to see Emerson's blinding full smile again.

"Uncle Emmyyyy, you have to do the voices!" Abigail cries with a giggle. We are crammed together into a twin bed, complete with a draped mosquito net decked out in lace and twinkle lights, in what I've learned is *her very own room at Grammy's house.*

We are reading a *Llama Llama* book, and Abigail adorably decides Emerson must read Llama's whiny lines, and I must read for the narrator and Llama's Mama.

"But Mamaaaaa, I don't *wanna* go to the store!" Emerson reads in a high-pitched whiny voice that immediately sets Abigail and me into a fit of belly laughs. "Do you two mind? I'm reading here," Emerson scolds, pretending to be serious. He whines as Llama again. "The store is boooorrrriiiinnnngggg!"

It's just entirely too much. Abigail and I both grab our stomachs, in pain from laughing so hard. My ovaries are exploding as fast as the tears escape down the sides of my face. We somehow calm ourselves enough to finish the short book.

"That was hilarious!" Abigail says in her adorable accent.

"Tell anyone of this, and die, niece," he warns gruffly. He gets up and helps me climb over her and out of the bed.

"Bye, Uncle Emmy," she says, then raises her arms up for a hug.

"Sleep tight," he whispers, then hugs her and kisses her head.

I am deceased, yet again.

She asks me for a hug, and I oblige. Then when I am bending down, she whispers loudly, "Are you going to go to a church and get a big white dress and marry Uncle Emmy?"

"Oh, I don't know, sweetie," I whisper back, freezing in what feels like a giant spotlight.

"If you do, he'll blame you for his farts. They're awful, and he always said I did it!"

"Abigail!" Emerson's eyes go wide, and I fight the giggles.

"You should marry him anyway, though." She stares at me with so much hope, my throat starts to close. I quickly turn the conversation around. "Do *you* want to wear a big white dress someday?"

"Oh yes, the biggest, with sparkles on it. Like I saw on the telly."

"That sounds perfect. You will be the prettiest bride ever," I say. "Now go to sleep and dream all about it."

"Okay," she yawns, then turns over.

I join Emerson in his quiet retreat out of the room. He pulls the door behind him, and I look up to see a strange expression on his face. It went too far, obviously, the wedding talk. Although it wasn't my fault! I didn't bring it up! Still, things got awkward fast, and now I'm not sure how to salvage what was a very fun, sweet moment. Luckily, his brothers save the day.

"Ben says we gotta drag you out one last time before you go, eh?" Byron says to us when we reach the living room.

Emerson's shoulders sag at the idea.

"C'moooon!" Ben piles on.

"Now?"

"No, let's meet tonight at Flip's—dinner and drinks, casual, k?" Emerson sighs.

"That one was a concession," I tease.

He pulls me into him hard and fast. "And this one?" He sighs an exaggerated sigh in my face.

"Um, that you're crazy about me, obviously." He laughs an actual laugh, and I notice the surprise on his brothers' faces.

"She's got that bloody right," Ben says.

We give warm goodbyes to his parents and promise Layla and the boys that we'll meet them in a couple hours. In the car, Emerson seems to deflate, which is expected, but I feel like something is bothering him.

"So, what did your dad say?"

"Hm?" He turns to me, and I link my fingers in his. "Oh, nothing I haven't heard a hundred times."

"Ah." I search my brain for something to cheer him up. "Your niece is possibly the cutest five-year-old on the entire planet." He smiles and nods. "You were totally holding out on me. I bet there are adorable Uncle Emmy and Abby selfies on your phone."

He chuckles but doesn't comment. And he seems to grow more distant after that. Crap, maybe the whole Abigail comment was a mistake, since she asked if we were going to get married and all. I decide to stick with silence for the rest of the ride. Dinner with his siblings will turn things around.

CHAPTER 35

"Do you even own jeans?" Layla teases.

"That's what I said!" I agree too loudly, and she and I both laugh. Emerson grins, but he still hasn't shaken off whatever got under his skin at his parents' house.

Flip's is a dingy hole-in-the-wall pub that has only beer, liquor, a plate of fish and chips, and one burger on the menu. It has such a perfectly untouched old England vibe that I had to send pics to my girls. My selfie with the wood-carved pirate statue, Flip, was a big hit. The waitresses are wearing what I'd consider Hooters attire, the bartenders look like they may or may not live under a bridge, and yet next to me sits perfection, in his white shirt and navy slacks and gray jacket.

"Leave the savant alone. He likes his fancy threads." Byron tries to come to the rescue.

"I didn't want to waste room in my luggage." Emerson defends himself quietly. This causes another fit of giggles between Layla and me as I tell her the wonders of his one small bag for an almost six-week trip.

Emerson does seem to relax a bit throughout dinner. I have an absolute ball getting to know his siblings better, plus getting to hear so many fun stories from their childhood. They're not surprising, mostly repeated tales of how the twins got into mischief and Emerson got them out, but it's endearing all the same.

Byron and Layla share their story of meeting at a charity gala. I feel like this might mean Layla is in fact close friends with Chelsea, but I can tell she really likes me too. By the end of the night, the five of us feel like fast friends.

"Tell you what, I haven't seen Abby hitch on to someone so fast, ever." Layla cocks an eyebrow at Emerson as the night winds down. "Asking for Sam to read her nap-nap story? I couldn't believe it."

"That's true. Do you like kids, Samantha?" Ben asks.

"I love them. I thought I'd be a pediatrician when I was younger, then maybe a schoolteacher, but you know how it is, family business."

"That we do." Ben's voice sounds defeated.

"Shame, I could see you as a pediatrician. You're gifted with kids, I think." Layla takes another sip of her drink.

"Really? What about you, do you guys think you want more?"

"Hopefully," Layla says, looking knowingly over at Byron.

"Shit! Sorry! That was intrusive." I wince, kicking myself.

"It's all right. Everyone's family here. It wasn't the easiest for us with Abigail, but we're hopeful this round."

I smile and nod, unsure of what to say.

"Wow, didn't know you were trying again. That's wonderful news!" Ben smiles.

"It is," Emerson adds softly.

"Well, I don't know what you two have planned, but I'll tell you what, Evelyn sure was watching you and Sam and Abby together like a hawk, eh?" She pokes Emerson. "Your girl's a natural."

"Right-o, I think you have a winner here, big brother," Byron says.

I blush, and Emerson nods, twirling his almost empty beer in his hands, but he says nothing. No "I know!" or "Isn't she?" or jack diddly squat. And even after a lovely dinner where I've clearly just won over his brothers and sister-in-law.

Soooo, that got awkward fast!

"Well, I need to head to the little girls room, excuse me," I say, giving the table a break. Emerson stands to let me out of the booth but doesn't touch me at all when I pass him to leave, which feels odd. I take my time in case the siblings want to talk without me, or maybe *about* me.

When I come back to the table, the four of them are standing. Their expressions quickly tell me something is wrong.

"What?"

Emerson answers without looking my way. "Paparazzi."

"Here?"

"Yep." Ben pops the word out. "They never come to Flip's, but that bartender was eyeing us. Must've called them."

"Back door?" I look behind me, all too familiar with this circus.

"The car can't get to the alley. We'll just have to make a mad dash for it, I'm afraid." Byron shrugs.

We hug each other goodbye, and they apologize to me about the cameras. They are the children of one of the richest billionaires in the UK, so it happens. I hadn't even considered that. People have eyed Emerson sheepishly around London, but I assumed it was because he looks like a movie star.

"Sorry about this," he says to me as we get close to the door. I smile and shrug. I brace myself for a barrage of questions for the Clarks, especially for Emerson, since he's the prodigal returned home. But when we get through the door, in all the yelling, I just hear *Samantha* and *Canton* and *Canton International* and *Emerson and Samantha*, over and over. I don't know if they said Clark even once. They weren't lined up to get shots of the Clark children, and they were staged outside to capture Emerson and me. This is my fault.

Emerson's face is as hard as stone as he leads me through the chaos. His hand grips my fingers to the point of pain, and he actually shoves a few photographers out of the way. He shields me as I climb first into Charlie's car, then falls in next to me and slams the door.

"Go, Charles!" he yells. It may be the loudest I've ever heard him. He holds up his big hand to the car window, and I shield my face in my hands. Charles takes off like a sloth in molasses, dodging pushy photographers who keep jumping in the way. We have to take a long, silent, roundabout route to the back alley of our hotel.

In the sanctuary of our suite, we both unravel toward the kitchen. Emerson looks . . . bad. It's all bad.

Nervously, I start to ramble. "I didn't call them. I wouldn't even know who to call. I know I was in the bathroom a long time, but it wasn't me, I promise."

"I know." He doesn't look at me. I sip at the water he handed to me from the fridge, and he chugs his.

"Em?" I squeak. Finally, he looks at me. "What is it?" I ask, sounding more distraught than I mean to. I have felt this shift from a man one thousand times, this subtle chipping away before something breaks. A woman, if she's honest with herself, knows when a man is pulling away. It is excruciating, and I'm not sure there's anything I can do to stop it.

"Nothing." He sighs. "I'm sorry." He steps over and wraps his arms around me. "Let's just go to bed." He kisses my head, and I nod. We get ready in our own bathrooms, and everything feels all wrong. But when I slip into our bed, his arms are there a second later, tight as a lock around my middle. I relax a tiny bit, but not enough to get any sleep.

For hours I worry, replaying the last few days in my head over and over. I start from the slipped *I love you* and fast-forward through the scenes over and over. So much of it is fine, but something, somewhere went off-track. I wrestle with my memories until the wee hours and finally sleep hard.

———

I didn't feel Emerson get up for his workout, didn't hear him slip into the shower. But he must already be making breakfast, because he's not in here with me when the early light seeps in. I hear my phone buzz with a text and do a double take, since all my sisters should still be asleep.

Oh.

No.

No no no no no! This is bad. Late last night, our photos hit all the US gossip sites. Susan and Sadie must get Google alerts, and they're blowing us up. Everything is blowing up.

"American Princess Snags British Billionaire"

"Canton Sweetheart, a Yankee Gold Digger?"

"Billionaire Mystery Boy Emerson Clark Spotted with American Instagrammer"

Instagrammer?! What in the actual?! I have never in my life claimed to be an influencer. I don't even have an account anymore! So much for journalism. And gold digger? I have plenty of money! My sisters all agree on that particular point in the text thread that grew while I slept.

The photos themselves are terrible. Emerson looks angry, and I look terrified. Maybe we should've just smiled and waved and taken questions. Sometimes that approach makes it easier on everyone. Except I'm talking about Emerson here—there's no way he'd answer questions.

I keep scrolling and clicking. Apparently Emerson and Ben are at almost William and Harry status (when the princes were single). The comments are insane. The women of the United Kingdom hate me with a fiery passion. I was about to ask Trina if she knew all along, but her text saying *He is THAT Emerson Clark?!?!?* answered my question. Apparently, Emerson hasn't been noticed or featured in London or it's rag magazines for years.

Until me.

The stories range from simple facts—we were seen together at Flip's in London—to outrageous. The biggest tabloid in the country has gone so far as to style our wedding and photoshop what our baby would look like. It would be almost cute if it wasn't the most unsettling thing I've ever seen. The article zooms in on my necklace in the photo and details a lot of our trip, which is downright creepy. Where do they get this stuff? The article claims sources at the hotels. *Lydia, you raging bitch!* I am standing now and moving out into the kitchen, my hands shaking.

I open the door and see him.

He's sitting at the table, hunched. He hasn't worked out, hasn't showered.

He looks wrecked.

And I know it's over, before he says a word.

Still, I try. I should keep my mouth shut, save myself, guard my heart, but I just can't.

"Whatever you're thinking, don't," I say, tears already threatening.

"Samantha."

"No, this is bullshit trash that no one will remember tomorrow. You can't let it get to you. I mean, you know how they are! You should understand!" He sighs at the table. I take another step forward. "You think I called them."

"No."

"Okay, then what? What is it?"

His voice is scratchy, like he didn't sleep at all. "We shouldn't have done this. *I* shouldn't have."

"Done what?" I whisper. I am frozen, my heart racing across the suite, doing laps and threatening to explode. I cannot bear this. I can't.

"I warned you I couldn't give you everything, couldn't be the man for you."

"I don't want everything."

He doesn't look at me as he argues. "You do. You will. And I can't do it."

"What does that even mean, everything? This has been deep and real, and you know it. Now you're saying . . . what? You don't want a future, a life together? Is that what you're saying? This was a fling?" He stares down at the table, and his jaw twitches. "Just say it. You what? You don't want to get married?"

His jaw twitches again, and finally he looks up at me. He is as cold as he's ever been. "Not . . . to you." The words are as rough as rocks coming out of his beautiful mouth. Rocks thrown straight to my chest, to my soul. It explains why the air leaves my lungs, because I've just been stoned. My head shakes, involuntarily. How could he have changed so much overnight? What the hell is happening here?

"I . . . I don't believe you."

"I wouldn't lie to you."

"No, just to yourself." My voices raises, but I can't help it. "So you're back to being a coward again? Afraid of what's happening between us? Afraid of what you feel for me?"

"You . . ." He pauses. "You warned me just like I warned you. You said it yourself . . . your sunshiny optimism, the constant sharing, the romance, the drama between us. It's . . . "

Don't say it, don't say it, don't you dare say it—

"Too much."

I swallow.

I clench my fists and straighten my spine.

Every tiny move is physically painful.

But I am not too much. We are not too much—he's just too scared of this, of us, of his complicated, messy emotions. And I'm not listening to any more of whatever hurtful garbage he throws out to save himself.

"Get out," I finally say.

He stands, and for a second, there's a flash of something on his face: remorse, longing, pain, a shred of humanity. But it's instantly gone.

"Take all the time you need. I changed my flight to tomorrow." He moves to the suite door and turns before he leaves. "I'm sorry."

He shuts the door, and I run. I run through the suite, to my door, into my closet, and shut the door. I don't bother with the light. As soon as the door closes and I know he can't hear me, I weep.

CHAPTER 36

Having an afternoon flight was helpful. I didn't want to be in that suite anymore, and I had a plane to catch. Numb and tearless, I threw everything into bags. I didn't text my sisters, didn't call Sadie or Nicole. I washed my face and put on enough makeup to feel like I didn't look as dead as I felt. I called for a bellhop, texted Charlie, and made my own way to the airport.

I slept through most of the flight, when I wasn't nauseated or crying. Toward the end of the flight, they brought the breakfast boxes out. I opened it, trying to muster some desire to eat. I wasn't hungry, but maybe the cinnamon rolls . . . roll. Cinnamon roll, singular. So on our flight to London weeks ago, *he* had given me his, taken it out of his meal box and put it into mine, saving it for me, for when I woke up.

I can't eat.

I can't even cry.

I texted Skye that there was no need to meet me at the airport or at home. She assumed I'd be with Emerson, and I didn't bother to correct her. When I arrived at my empty apartment, I was actually relieved to be alone. I couldn't talk about it.

I showered and I thought. I unpacked and I thought and overthought. I did laundry and I replayed the entire trip from start to finish. I went over every good and terrible word, look, and touch

Emerson ever gave me. I tried to eat, but mostly I just thought. And all my thoughts led me to one conclusion.

He lied.

He's lying.

He's a coward.

That's got to be what this is.

From the cinnamon roll to the jealousy with Thomas, to the words, so many loving, beautiful, carefully chosen words out of his mouth.

With those conclusions came a terrifying feeling I knew too well: hope.

But I know what I felt. I know what we had was real. I don't believe he doesn't want a future together. There's something he's not telling me.

So I made a plan. I wouldn't tell anyone the news, wouldn't act any differently. They could assume Emerson and I were taking a few days off for a sexcation at his—what I'm sure is an immaculate and ridiculously expensive—apartment. Sunday, I got home, so Monday he'd arrive home, and then Tuesday he'd be back in the office. And there, the coward was going to have to face me.

I let him off the hook too easily in London. This time, he was going to have to look me in my big, blue, hopeful eyes and face the truth. He was also going to have to take in my tight navy dress he loves and the sexiest office-appropriate pumps I have. I haven't been able to bring myself to take the necklace off yet, so he'll have to face that too.

It was all a big, brave, badass plan.

And now I'm going to be sick.

I've made it to the lobby of our building. I know he's in by now; in fact, everyone is probably in by now. I was so nervous, I kept botching my eyeliner. It took me three tries.

I shove my shoulders back and walk to the elevators. *No crap,*

Samantha. He's just scared. You got this.

In the elevator, I put on the persona of, well, myself, if I was not actually heartsick and anxious as all hell. I put on a smile and breeze into the office.

"Yassss the bitch is baaaack!" Nicole sings quietly from her desk in the lobby.

"Heeeyyyyyyyy!" We squeal and hug.

She eyes my necklace.

"Holy shit, it's gorgeous!"

"Right?" I say as I normally would. As if everything is fine.

"He's already in." She looks to Emerson's office and back to me. "I figured you guys would come together?"

"Nah, uh, don't have stuff at his place yet. Anyway, I'm actually a little late. I better get after it."

"Okay, you wanna do lunch?"

"Maybe, let me check in with Darrin and the team and get back to you."

I turn and wonder if it's obvious to Marge, whose desk I'm approaching, that my heart is trying to pound outside my actual chest cavity. I can barely think over my pulse thrumming in my ears.

"Good morning, Ms. Wayne!"

"Welcome back, Miss Canton." She nods.

"Thanks, great to be back." I stalk past his office, because of course his door is shut, and head to Darrin's.

"Hey, boss!" I say, too loudly. I can't help it. I want Emerson to know I've come in.

"There's our rock star! I cannot believe some of the deals you two managed to seal over there. Maybe I'll send you on all my trips!"

"I mean, if they're all to Europe, consider it done!" We laugh. "I'm just going to get settled, and then we can meet up in a little bit?"

"Sure, no rush. I know you'll have a lot of catching up to do."

"Thanks." I smile and head into my office. I shut the door and collapse against it. I'm sweating like I just finished Zumba, and I haven't even run into Emerson yet! I try to start in on my email inbox, which is out of control, even with working on the road. But my brain is not in my body. It's hovering outside the office two doors down. I know he'll go to lunch at 11:30 or 12:00, so I just have to listen for his door. At 11:00, I open my own door and wait.

11:42.

I hear his door.

I hear his deep, silky voice talking to Marge.

I steel myself and walk out like I own the place—*um, you kinda do own the place!*—and try to keep a relaxed pace for the few steps between him and me, where he stands in a light gray suit I haven't seen since before our trip. I know he'll have on a vest and a darker gray tie, because he always does with this suit. I see his back tense when he hears my shoes click, and he stops talking when Marge's eyes leave him and settle on me over his shoulder. He turns, and I try to take a deep breath, but it ends up as more of a shallow stutter.

"Hey, Emerson." I keep my voice casual and throw him a bright smile. Not too big, just like an acceptable coworker smile. I look him dead in the eye, though. He meets my gaze for a second and puts his mouth in a hard line. His eyes don't look at the necklace or my dress, or travel my sexy shoes. Instead, they only meet mine for a beat.

"Miss Canton."

No.

That name.

The ice in his tone.

It wasn't even a greeting—it was a dismissal.

He immediately turns back to Margaret and says something. I don't hear what he says. My mouth is open, and my eyes are burning. He leaves. He actually leaves the office, without looking back at me. At some point, I realize I'm just standing frozen in the hall. And he knew I was there, but he never turned back—he just ignored me. I spin a 180 and shuffle back into my office like a moron.

I close the door and cover my mouth. *Breathe. Breathe. Breathe.*

Thankfully, Margaret was the only one to witness that, the exact moment my heart finally broke.

I thought it'd been broken before, but those were just little stabs, bruises. Small offenses by little boys who never really saw me, never loved me. And I never really loved them. I liked the attention, maybe, had fun, wanted the *idea* of the relationship, the version my imagination crafted. I was sad, in the past, when reality caught up to me, but all of that, everything over the last ten years, teen loves, my college sweetheart, dating in New York . . . those were just tiny scratches on the edges of my soul.

This is altogether different.

I fell in love with a man.

I gave him my heart, and just now, he crushed it to dust.

I can't breathe.

I can't do this.

I can't be here.

Me: 911. Book me a flight to you. ASAP.
Sadie: Okay.

I grab my things, managing not to let the tears spill over. I will not cry in this office. *I will not cry in the office.* I turn to leave and put my hand to the soft gold chain on my neck out of habit. A sob catches in my throat. I grasp the chain and yank. It breaks, and I quickly, wordlessly walk myself into Emerson's office. I don't know if Marge sees, and I don't care.

I leave the broken necklace on his desk. I speed out of his office and out the back office door, not wanting to risk seeing him in the main elevators or lobby area. I make my way out of the building, out of New York.

He made his cowardly choice.

His eyes said it all.

He wanted it to be over.

Now it is.

CHAPTER 37

It was Tuesday night when I got here, to Sadie's unreal Dallas penthouse apartment. I don't know what day it is now. I don't care. My older sister has brought in food, water bottles, pain meds, congestion meds, and tissues. I think I've only touched the latter. But she doesn't push me, which is why I came to her. Susan would've hovered, Skye would've gone with a too-honest pep talk, and Sally is too busy with school.

I keep the windows drawn and my phone on airplane mode and I just . . . lie here. Sometimes I stare at his selfie on my phone. Sometimes I play songs from the playlists over and over, just wallowing in the surrounding darkness, both physically in the room and emotionally around my whole being.

I can feel myself feeling worse the longer I isolate, as if my internal battery were already on empty, and now I refuse to let myself recharge. But again, I don't care. After breakups before, when I was sad, I wanted to talk it out. I wanted to wallow in ice cream and then maybe go out and pretend to be fine. And that usually worked, the pretending. I always bounced back after a couple days.

But this isn't a breakup.

This is a shattering.

To be seen, understood, known, for the first time.

Angels do sing. I just don't think you can hear them.
How do you do that? Put everyone else at ease?
You are an opus all on your own, Samantha.
As you can see, Samantha is a prodigy . . . I am very proud
of her.
I could do this for ages, just look at you.

To be really held, cherished, treasured and then . . . discarded.
So maybe I wasn't really cherished to begin with.

Again.

How can I ever trust myself?

I wait for sleep to find me. Tears find me first, but sleep
follows soon after. I stay this way for days, over a week, I think. I
know at one point, Sadie makes me eat. I do, a little bit. And then I
retreat again. I sleep and sleep and sleep. Until I hear . . . singing?

Huh?

Sunshine, lollipops and rainbows... That is very loud, nearby
singing. My brain finally registers, it's one of my mom's favorite
oldies songs.

What?

Someone somewhere is really going at this song, holding out
the words pennyyy . . . fi-iiiiine . . . miiiine.

I sit up.

And.

I.

I have trouble processing what I'm seeing.

"Sunshine, lollipops, and rainbows, that's how this re-frain
goes, so come on, join in, everybody!"

I laugh.

I actually laugh a small, shocked chuckle I can't hold in.

Because there in front of Sadie's guest bed are all four of my sisters. Together. In Dallas. Singing an oldies song in three-part harmony at the top of their lungs.

"What the hell is happening?" I croak after they finish with a clap.

"We're having a sister-vention, obviously," Skye says dryly.

"You're in Dallas?" I ask, shocked.

"Yes, also you're in Dallas. Do you know where you are? Have you hit your head?" Sally quips.

"Why are you singing?"

"For that, that smile." Sadie points at me. "Good call, Suze. I wasn't sure, I mean, could you imagine if we'd tried this with Skye?"

"She would've thrown sharp objects. Blood would've been shed." Sally's voice is ominous while Sky nods in agreement, a horrified look on her face.

"Sal? Susan? You're in Dallas too? You drove down from Tulsa? What day is it?"

"We did, honey," Susan says. Sally nods with a huge grin.

"So many questions—we should've guessed the second you sat up, it'd be a full-on SamStorm, depressed or not," Skye says.

"It's Friday night. I let you wallow for over a week." Sadie starts to clean the tissue wads around the bed and floor.

"Wait. You're all here? For me?"

"Of course." Susan grins at me and pats my foot.

"Skye. You flew out here?"

"I'm also starting to wonder if you hit your head." We all laugh. Skye continues: "Sam, if any one of us needed you, you would hop on a plane in a second. So. Here we are." She shrugs, as if it's normal for four adult females to totally cancel an entire weekend and drive for five hours—or fly across the country!—on a whim.

It's especially not normal for her. Skye doesn't like to change her plans, doesn't like social get-togethers, and I know she wouldn't want to leave Matt in the middle of wedding planning. I'm crying again, but this time, they aren't just sad tears.

At the start of my crying, Skye and Sally climb into bed and drinks and snacks appear out of nowhere. Sadie and Susan pull the chaise lounge from across the room up to the edge of the bed.

"So, sweetie, can you tell us what happened?" Susan starts cautiously. "Sadie filled us in on the trip, but none of us know what happened, you know . . . after."

"Oh, crap, Susan! I didn't even tell Darrin I was leaving. I didn't even think," I realize, freaking out that I probably left my team and my COO sister in an awkward position.

"I sent an email to him from your account. You had a private, pressing issue you needed to attend to at home, and you'll be taking an extended absence," Sadie informs me casually. "I texted Susan, and she worked her logistical magic. You're good."

"Oh. Thanks."

"Quit worrying about everyone else and tell us about you, Bob. What happened?" Skye barks at me, tucking my wild hair behind my shoulders.

"Ugh. Well, either what we had was real and life-changing and earth-shattering, and he's a big fat coward, or he led me on for some fun and then dumped me in time to come home."

Sadie leans in. "What did he say, exactly? Like, the man's exact words?"

"He said that it was the usual: 'The sunshinyness, the constant oversharing, the romance, the drama.'" I hold in the sobs. "He said he did want to marry someday, but . . . just not me. That it, that I was *too much*."

"Asshole."

"Fucking asshole."

"Jerkoff fucking asshole."

"Really with the language?" Susan looks at all of us.

"C'mon, Suze, you never drop F-bombs when everything goes wrong at the office?" Sally asks.

"No, I don't."

"And what about when your house is suddenly covered in glitter and the dog poops on the carpet and one of your lovely children drops a glass bowl and it shatters everywhere?"

"Jeez, okay, fine, he's a fucking asshole."

"Yassssss!" a chorus rings out from my other three sisters.

"You all are like toddlers. Honestly. Can we just focus on Samantha, please?" Susan blushes a tiny bit. It's funny to see the COO, Mom Jr., who is always put together to a tee, even the least bit flustered.

"So, the last I'd talked to you, it was twenty-four-seven heaven. Was it the tabloids?" Sadie gets us refocused.

"That didn't help. But he's got to be used to the stupid tabloids. I mean, he's a billionaire, which, hello, how did I not know about his family?"

"I didn't either," Skye says.

"He didn't like to talk about it," Susan murmurs.

"We went to see his family for the second time, and I think it was just a classic case of things getting too real. His niece asked us if we would get married." My sisters wince in unison. "Then we went out with his brothers and sister-in-law, and they were saying I was a winner, good with the niece, that his mom was eyeing us. Basically like 'hold on to her, bro' kind of stuff. I think he just got spooked."

"I just would not have pegged him as someone who spooks easily. He's so serious about everything, always." Sadie stares at the wall, as if she's picturing him.

"That's what I was thinking too." Susan nods. "But he's definitely not a player, is he? I mean, I can't fathom he'd be capable of stringing you along for fun during your trip. For the same reason, he's too serious. He doesn't seem like the type for a fling."

"Well, Susan, I agree, but yet, here I am." I gesture with my arms, sounding more bitter than I mean to. "I'm sorry. I know he's your friend, but I mean, I was with him nonstop for almost six weeks, and even I found it hard to know him intimately. And like, I *knew him intimately*!"

"Yeah, I'd like to circle back to *that*," Sadie says.

"No, we're not talking about the hot sex when we're in break-up mode. We're mad at him, remember? Get your head in the game, Sade." Skye gives her a glare. I fiddle with the edge of the comforter.

"Wait, *was* there hot sex?" Sally asks slowly. Everyone quietly stares, waiting. I shake my head.

"Whoa, whoa, whoa, you're telling me that you were shacked up in that Paris penthouse suite with just one bed, and he kept his hands to himself!?" Susan gets loud with shock.

"No, we did fool around. And it was . . . amazing." I tear up again.

"And you didn't have sex because . . . ?" Sadie seems truly befuddled by this. I can't blame her.

"Because at first I said I wanted to wait."

"Atta girl. You stuck to your own boundaries. And then wow, okay, he respected that. Trying really hard to stay mad at him here." Skye grows confused, and my sisters' faces start to match hers.

"Well, joke's on me. I didn't want to keep waiting, but he just kept saying *not yet*, like we weren't ready. And then I guess maybe he never was? Or he didn't want me to get too attached? As if daily morning orgasms wasn't doing that already? I really, *really* don't know."

There's a beat when I know all of them are absorbing the morning orgasm overshare.

"So. He says you're too much for him, which by the way just means he's *not enough* for you, baby girl. And don't you forget that—and then you came back to New York and what? You didn't call us." Sadie recounts it all for our sisters.

"I wanted him to have to face me, to look me in the eye. Which he did, at the office." I start to shake. "And he said, 'Miss Canton,' like you would say 'Bubonic Plague,' and then he turned and walked away. He was totally unaffected, as if we'd never even happened." Tears start to overrun my cheeks again.

"Ooookay, I think we should transition to the *There is plenty of dick in the sea* portion of our sistervention here." Sally straightens up on the bed, and Susan chokes when our little sister says *dick*, making all of us giggle.

"Good point. You don't *need* Emerson, or any man," Skye preaches. "But when you are ready and you decide you want to settle down, the right guy is out there for you."

"Totally. And he won't run off scared," Sadie says.

"He'll be way better than Icy Emerson," Sally adds, with passion. But I choke a bit. Because I know the truth. When he was open and honest, when he wasn't pushing me away . . . I don't think there is anyone better than him. Not for me. He was a once-in-a-lifetime type of love.

"Waterworks still? We're failing, y'all. C'mon! First and foremost, you need a shower, desperately." Susan starts to tug on the blankets, her eyes wide.

"Yep, then it's either Will Ferrell movies, second-to-last season of *New Girl*, or Kevin Hart stand-up—weeper's choice," Skye says. They all argue about movie choices on their way out of the room, and surprisingly, I can't stop a small smile. My eyes are still burning and my chest aches, but I'm smiling. I needed this.

There's just nothing like sisters.

CHAPTER 38

"I understand that." Susan has her boss voice on. "And yes, Kristi, it *is* legal for you to have up to six chickens in your backyard now, but I keep getting calls about a rooster and roosters are in fact *not* legal within city limits, which you know our neighborhood clearly is."

Good to be back in the heartland.

I smile as I pad out into Sadie's spacious living, dining, and kitchen area. Light is kissing every surface in the apartment, sparkling in all her sleek glass lamps and chandeliers. Little rainbows fall across her low couches, gargantuan TV, and expensive art collection. Susan paces in the large professional chef's kitchen, already kicking ass and taking names. It's not normal for me to be up so early, but I guess I have been asleep almost constantly for a week. Yikes.

"Uh-huh . . . uh-huh . . . well, it's not up to me. So if the authorities come and take your rooster, please understand there's nothing I can do." She pours me a cup of coffee as she talks and rolls her eyes. "Listen, I've got to go. I'm actually out of town right now. I just thought I'd give you the courtesy of a . . . well, okay. Uh-huh, bye." She sighs, and Sadie laughs at the breakfast table in the corner. "My neighbors, y'all, I cannot. We are in a fancy gated neighborhood in the city, and these women are trying to sneak a full-fledged farm into their backyards. I got one call from Mr. Henry, who insists he heard a goat. A goat! If you want a farm, move two miles up, where there's nothing but acreage. I just don't understand it."

"I don't understand why you're on the HOA. As if you don't have enough going on," Sadie mutters.

"Agreed," I chime in.

"Anyway . . ." Susan switches our focus. "How are you doing this morning?"

"All right. Much better now that you guys are here." I give Susan a hug. She holds me tight, and tears burn the edges of my eyes again.

Sadie turns to me. "So what is our plan today? Spa? You wanna day drink? Pool? More movie marathoning?"

"Yes to the day drinking, the rest is optional." Skye yawns as she emerges through the living room with Sally right behind her.

"And can we day drink *and* do a full-on *Runaway Bride* assessment?" Susan scoffs. "I think she knows exactly what kinds of eggs she likes, don't you?"

"What? Are we having eggs?" Sally scrunches her eyebrows.

"You know," Skye begins, "Julia Roberts always ordered her eggs however her man at the time wanted them, instead of knowing how *she* actually wanted them cooked."

"Oh, well, you *do* kinda lose yourself in your relationships, don't you, Sam?" Sally asks gently, removing the hoodie from her head.

"I don't think she does," Sadie argues. "More like she loses sight of the guy and instead sees what she wants to see. But I think you keep yourself intact. You like your eggs hard-boiled, right?"

"I do." I pause, thinking. "I do keep myself intact, but you know what? I could really use the whole *heroine hunkers down and overhauls her life* montage."

Concern takes over my oldest sister's features. "Overhaul? What do you want to overhaul?"

"Umm, myself, my goals, my . . . job." Every head pops up at that. They weren't expecting me to say it, and I wasn't really expecting to blurt it out either, but it's the truth. "I . . . I haven't really been happy with my work in a long time. I love our company, obviously, and I love some of the thrill of the job, but . . . well, how I explained it to . . . He Who Must Not Be Named is that you all each have your opus."

"Like *Mr. Holland's Opus*?" Sadie and Susan both say.

"Yes, Sadie and Skye, you have your art, clearly your calling. Susan, you popped out of the womb as the future CEO, no doubt. Sally, you're going to be the best surgeon of all time, again, not a single doubt about it. And me . . . I'm what?" My voice cracks. "Really good at sales?"

All four of my sisters are stunned to silence.

"And what did *he* say about that?" Sadie finally asks, carefully.

I sigh, letting a tear escape. "He said I was an opus all my own. Me, as a person." I can barely get the last word out. It's amazing, what he said, I know it, and so do all of them. Susan's mouth drops open, Sally puts her hoodie back on with force, and Sadie and Skye curse under their breath. "I know. *I know.* Of all the people in the world, I never thought it'd be stone-cold Em— He Who Must Not Be Named — who really saw me." My voice cracks again.

Skye clears her throat. "Uh-huh, saw you, got scared like a punk-ass little baby, dropped you like a deuce, and then acted like you were nothing at the office. He is Voldemort, everyone! Vol. De. Mort. *Moving on!*"

"Right. Gross. Okay." Susan goes into problem-solving mode. "So, what do you want to do instead of sales? Have you thought about it?"

"It's not too late to still be a pediatrician if that's really what you want," Skye adds.

Sally looks up in shock.

I nod, sniffing and reclaiming the use of my vocal cords. "I know, but I don't want to go back to school for so many years. And even nursing, I don't know if I can go back into medicine after Mom. I can't imagine being . . . in the hospital." My older sisters nod in understanding. "I've only let myself even think about it half-heartedly and haven't gotten anywhere. I don't want to teach, even though I thought I might. I think after the fast-paced, competitive work I do now, it just doesn't appeal to me to be in the classroom all day every day."

"Okaaayyy," Susan says, her brain working. "We need to help you sort out what you *do* want. Let's dump it all out, the things about being a pediatrician. What did you like about that idea? What do you like about your current job? What parts of teaching appealed to you?" As she talks, my sisters start to go into execute mode without being asked. "We need to list it all out and find the common threads."

"I'll go get my big white board," Sadie calls back to us as she goes down the hall.

Skye moves into the kitchen. "I'll make more coffee."

Sally turns to Susan. "Let's make some sustenance."

"What about me, what do I do?" I ask.

"You sit and think," Susan commands.

I shake my head. It's too weird not to do something helpful. I'm usually the one buzzing around helping one of them. I start to get up, and Susan pushes me back down onto the chair at the kitchen table. "Sit and rest and recover, Sunny Sam. We got you."

While they scurry around, I decide to brave my phone. I brace myself as I turn it on, for either a confusing text or maybe the pain of nothing from him at all. I experience the latter. There are a million texts from Nicole, a concerned message from Darrin, moral support from Janie, and some *where are you* quips from Trina. The last few replies are quick and simple. I steel myself for the more difficult conversation.

> Nicole: WTF??? I hear from Skye that you guys broke up and you went home? Are you okay? Why didn't you call me?

Why didn't I call her? I just didn't want to, I guess. I didn't call my sisters, either.

> **Me: Hey, I'm sorry. I'm better now. My sisters all came to visit. My phone has been off all this time.**
> Nicole: OMG finally!!!! Call me!
> **Still with my sisters.**
> **I'll try you later.**
> **But I'm okay.**
> **I'll be okay.**

———

"This is it! This is genius!" I squeak, looking at the circled words below an entire whiteboard of phrases and scribbles and even a few of Skye's hilarious doodles.

"I already found a few job postings!" Sally calls from her laptop.

"In Dallas? Or where?" I ask, not making eye contact with any of my sisters as I ask the question.

"You've got some options," Sally says slowly as she keeps scrolling. "See this one? And this one in Tulsa if you want to go home for a while." She pauses. "There are a couple in New York too."

"Hmm." I'm not sure about where. The thought of leaving New York sends a stab through my soul, and I know it's partially because of one corner office that holds a sulking suited supermodel who keeps half the blinds drawn.

347

But maybe leaving the city is what I need for a fresh start, a new and improved Sam. I look at Sally. "I think we focus on the job and not the location. I mean, this feels like one thousand percent what I want to do next."

"Wow, and in just one day. I mean, should we maybe spend some time trying to solve world hunger while we're all here together?" Skye jokes as she chomps on a chip loaded with an unreal amount of guacamole.

"First, I think we need to help Suze solve her goat issue," Sadie says as she walks from the white board over to the table where we're huddled around the laptop.

"Her goat what now?"

I laugh. "I love you guys."

———

I sigh a heavy sigh as I flop into bed. Sadie has been busy writing since our three sisters left, and I've had time to get lost in thought again. It was exactly what I needed, their visit.

Am I still shattered? Yes. But at least now, after time with them, laughing, planning, being honest about the work stress that's plagued me for so long, now I have some strength to start picking up all my pieces. The first piece, my career, is coming together. Sadie says I can stay as long as I need, until I figure out where my new job lands me.

I glance at Sadie's spare closet and see a yellow blouse, and a wave of sadness overtakes me. I may never wear yellow again. No, that's silly. I will. In time, I will. I shake my head and pick up my phone.

Another quick thing I'm taking control of is my social media. After talking it over with my sisters, I realized I was punishing myself for my mistakes, yes, but also other people's reactions, their misinformed opinions. I want to have a public place online, for my career, my life. It's fun, and I miss it. So, I reactivated my Instagram and TikTok accounts today.

I haven't posted anything yet, but I've started gathering my favorite Europe content into an album (sans Emerson, of course). For now, public comments will stay off completely. And I've blocked all the tabloids; even though that doesn't make much of a difference, it makes me feel a tiny bit better. If strangers want to call me names in my DMs, so be it. I won't check them. And if I do want to use messages, I'll just delete and block like it's my new favorite hobby.

I almost smile as I add Trina as a friend. It feels good, even if a little scary, to be going back out there. It feels like I'm no longer hiding from my past. I don't add any dating apps. *Hell to the no—* and for a long-ass time! I know I'm not missing anything there.

A shard of grief pierces me, and I let myself feel it. No dweeb in all that swiping could come anywhere near the man I experienced for a few short weeks. I know that. A beautiful, meticulous, genius man who almost loved me, then chickened out. Who decided love, loving me, was too much for him. And it's okay. When I'm healed, when I'm ready, I will be just the right amount for someone someday, and until then, I'll be okay.

I scroll mindlessly for a moment, checking Canton Cards Instagram content. I don't even think I might see Emerson in the images, which is a stupid assumption. The company continued on in my absence. Even the New York office, which apparently, according to Dina's account, had a welcome party for a new . . . and there he is. Navy suit. Painfully gorgeous eyes. Longer hair. More stubble. A perfect navy tie. He looks somber, even for him. But also . . .

Wait.

What the hell?

Me: WTF is this?!?!?

!!!!!!!!!!!!

[Instagram link]

[Mind blown emoji] [Angry emoji]

Am I overreacting?

Skye: Wow. Wowowowowowow

Sadie: WTF

Sally: NOT overreacting.

Susan: I would say I have to agree.

Skye: Now the question is, what are you going to do about it???

CHAPTER 39

Breathe, breathe, breathe.

My pulse pounds in my ears like an angry war drum. One tiny glowing square on a screen, and one million pieces suddenly fall into place. It was me, after all. Me and my stupid rose-colored glasses, seeing the good in everyone.

Not. Any. Effing. More!

After more texts with my sisters, it all became as clear as day, and not a sunny happy day either, that's for damn sure. Two years, a little over. That's how long I've been an idiot.

I can't believe you don't tell everyone who you are.

It's so lame we have to pretend when we go out.

If your sister is really talented, it won't matter if her name gets out there.

You have more money than God. You're not going to pay for our appetizer—really?

Oh, I'm sure, your dad "cut you off." Must be so *rough.*

And then the more painful realizations. So many meetings, she sat next to him. And how many times did she take in his lunch and then complain about it, change his schedule for Marge, and then bitch about her job. And yet she never mentioned wanting a promotion, wanting to leave her desk where she could watch everyone and everything, namely him. And then this trip . . .

What'd you do this time?
Maybe you should skip this trip.
I feel bad for the guy.
Your personality is anything but little.
Let's forget about him and talk about Chase.
Emerson is so not your type . . . you need someone more like you.

How she pushed me away from Emerson and into Thomas Gage over and over . . . including the night she had to suddenly go to the bathroom, leaving me and Thomas practically lying on the couch together, just in time for Emerson to see. Did she know he was coming down? Does she text him? Do they talk? I can't see that. I can't see him reciprocating anything. But how much does she know about him that she never told me? Probably a shit-ton.

I stare a hole through my phone looking at the little square from just a few days ago. It's a bar by the office, where a group photo was taken. There Emerson stands, straight and unaffected, while she hangs playfully on his arm. It's an odd photo, but it's a group pic of coworkers, so of course multiple people look uncomfortable.

She's caught, though, in the snap of the lens. Even if it's a group outing, it's obvious. Both her hands are wrapped around his bicep, and she's staring up at him like a sunflower lusting after the sun. I wonder what his reaction was a moment later. I wonder if he knew she wanted him all along.

I think of how she told me to run from him, to make him jealous, to play games. Emerson hates games. He is as straightforward as they come, and my pulling away was the start of our end. Not the cause, after everything, but it didn't help. She didn't want to help. She wanted to ruin.

Just like before Emerson, before London, she had the photos.
The group photo from the gala last year. I'm sure I texted it to her
with a comment about Grandpa. And then that night just days ago,
when everything came to a head, all the paparazzi were calling out
to *me*. That night was about *me*, not the Clarks. And I had texted
her the selfie with Flip, the carved pirate, making our location
obvious. I had sent her a photo of my necklace and gushed over its
meaning.

She had it all.

And she used it.

I close Instagram and make the call, over FaceTime.

I want to look this frenemy bitch in the eye.

"Hey, babe! Finally! Are you okay? Tell me what the douchebag
did!" She's smiling wide, about to be blindsided.

"How long, Nicole?" I'm shaking and can barely breathe.

Her smile falls. "What?"

"How long have you secretly hated me?"

"Sam, what are you talking about?" Her voice gets lower, and
she moves to somewhere else in her apartment.

"I know you leaked the photos. Last year and London. Just tell
me if you always hated me, or if I did something that made you
turn on me and my entire family." Her face grows cold, the mask
finally falling off. Chills bubble up all over my shaking limbs.

"Listen, it's not what you think. I just needed the money
and—"

"Bullshit. I could've loaned you money. You could've gotten a
better job a year ago, asked for a promotion, a raise. So, what, did
you get this job on purpose? To, like, sabotage my family or something? Were we ever really friends? I mean, what the hell, Nicole!"

"I'll tell you what the hell." Her whole face twists up in bit-
terness as she gets closer to her phone camera. She spits her

words at me. "You're an entitled little brat. No, it wasn't for the money. And yes, we were friends at first—you were fun, you were a good time, but then who could stay friends with you? Everything is so easy for you, Samantha. Shallow Silly Sam who gets everything she's ever wanted on a pretty silver platter. Your whole life is a damn cakewalk."

"Really? So losing my mom at seventeen—was that cake too?"

"Oh, are you gonna play that card forever? Everyone has pain—get the hell over it, princess."

"Just jealousy then. So painfully jealous, you decided to send photos to the tabloids. And then—I mean, just tell me—were you always in love with Emerson too?"

"Of course I'm fucking in love with Emerson! Who isn't! He's a Greek god among men, and you never even saw him! If you had, you would've noticed . . . I did. I noticed everything. I knew him, I saw him. And you, pretty little *Miss Canton*, you never even gave him the time of day. I knew, I just *knew*, on this trip you'd ruin everything. You stupid little—"

I hang up, then run to the bathroom to throw up.

Sadie rushes in. "I was listening in the hall. You did way better than I would've. In fact, I don't know if I would've bothered calling. I would've just sent her a big fat lawsuit."

"No, no lawsuit. Just make sure she's fired."

"Done." Sadie leaves the room with her fingers already tapping away on her phone.

Rage courses through me, and I hurl again. How? How could I not see it? So often she teased me to the point of hurting my feelings, jabbing at the parts of my personality that I was most self-conscious about.

She mentioned my money a trillion times. She balked and rolled her eyes and sighed and . . . what the hell was I thinking? I guess I just wasn't? Or I was just feeling? Feeling the fun of having a best friend like Skye has Janie? Just feeling a break from the loneliness of Manhattan, of the post-grad years where all your close friendships pull apart?

I make a vow to myself as I flush the toilet and stand. Never again will I accept a friendship with fangs. I remember the slight heartburn I'd feel if I hung out with Nicole for days. I'd retreat a bit, lessen myself and make more jokes at my own expense. It wasn't that different from college and high school, with those girls who you knew in your gut you could never fully trust.

That all ends now, today. If I don't feel 1,000 percent comfortable as me, not having to make fun of myself or apologize for who I am and where I come from, then I am out. Forever, from now on, no matter what.

I'd rather be lonely than be a scared, watered-down version of myself. I'm fearfully and wonderfully made, as my mother used to say, and now Susan, and God clearly made me to be . . . well . . . big. Big hopes, big emotions, big stupidly trusting heart, big laugh, big everything.

No more Shrinking Sam.

For anyone, ever.

CHAPTER 40

EMERSON

Three Weeks Later

"What the actual hell, man?" Adam Bell bursts into my office as if it's the most natural thing in the world. There he stands, tan and hulking, a little less fit and a little more tired than the last time I saw him. His expression is as exasperated as I am shocked and irritated. I do not tolerate disruptions well.

"What are you doing here?" I snipe the question at him.

"That's what happens when you won't answer calls or texts or even emails for weeks and weeks."

"Ms. Wayne?" I call out to my EA, louder than I mean to, my frustration gnawing at me.

"She's gone. Your schedule's been cleared for the day."

"Ah, wife still wearing the pants, then?" It was a jab I didn't mean, stemming from anger that has nothing to do with him, not only my college roommate and best friend, but also my boss's husband.

"Hey, might not want to be an asshole to your only friend in the continental US, dickhead."

I let out a bitter exhale. He's mostly right. I have other acquaintances, sure, but Adam is one of maybe three or four friends I have. Period. The best and most beautiful of which I recently pushed away. *As I should have.*

My chest aches remembering her eyes when I turned to apologize on my way out the door. My hand goes to rub the pain involuntarily. I stare at Adam with a glare that makes most wither, but on him, it's ineffective. Probably because he's seen me at my absolute lowest, multiple times.

"You look worse than sewer runoff. Want to tell me what happened?"

I let all the air in my lungs out through my nostrils before responding. "I assume you already know."

"I know you royally screwed up. That's the only bit I'm clear on. And since you have been avoiding me, I'm guessing you're mad at yourself over all of it."

"All of . . . what?" I ask him, still unsure of what he knows, or thinks he knows.

"You were with Samantha, pretty seriously it sounds like, then dumped her when shit got too real." I consider what to say in response. His words sting, particularly *with Samantha* and *dumped*. He continues, as people tend to do if you let the silence settle between you like a layer of dust. It makes others uncomfortable, but not me, as it usually provides my escape from speaking, because others rush in to fill the void. "She was a wreck, didn't talk to anyone for a week. And, I mean, for her, that's serious. But she's doing better now. We thought for a minute you broke her, dude."

I respond immediately without thinking. "You all underestimate her." It's true, they do. Almost everyone does. Coworkers, acquaintances, and even her own damn family. They see the sunny, drop-dead gorgeous exterior, the unabashed friendliness she radiates, but not the brilliant mind and Herculean heart underneath. The depth of her loyalty and selflessness. The depth of *her*.

People are idiots.

That's why I avoid them.

Adam stares at me.

"So you do love her," he says finally. It's a heavy question that resurrects the tightness in my chest for a thousand reasons. I want to say yes, but I won't. I want to ask about her, demand more information, but I won't.

I am doing the right thing. I am doing the right thing, I am, damn it, I tell myself again and again, as I have nearly one hundred times a day, for the thirty-one days since I saw her last. Since I could eat, think, breathe. Since I could do anything other than adjust numbers in glowing rectangles on a screen. I haven't even been able to muster weekly phone meetings with the C-suite, hence this unexpected visit. *Still, I am doing the right thing.*

"You know she's leaving?" Adam asks, breaking me out of my mental spin cycle.

I nod. "Resigning, I heard."

"Leaving New York."

"What!" My mouth responds before my mind can catch up. An odd sensation. "And going where?!" Panic settles deep in my empty stomach. It cuts deeper and faster than anything I've felt in weeks, and it takes my breath away. I close my eyes and, like thousands of times before, I see yellow.

I exhale the memory away.

"Dallas. And since you're suddenly as white as a ghost, I think it's time you tell me what is really going on, with her, but really with you, man. Your hands are even shaking. What the hell is it?"

My hands go to pinch my forehead. That's the shit thing about actually having good friends. You let down your guard, and then eventually, even the things you want to keep hidden, they can see. There's no point denying that I'm dying a slow and painful death inside, because now, here in front of me, looking at the evidence, my best friend, he already knows. I finally look at him. I don't know what my face says, but he reacts with his whole body.

"Damn. Let's go find some drinks." I barely nod and start to follow him out my office door. He continues: "And you're gonna start from the beginning. And you're gonna use all your big-boy words and you're not going to leave any shit out, either."

Bloody hell.

———

"Wow." Adam sits, staring at his beer.

I'm unaware of the time or what round we're on, but we arrived in late morning when the bar was dead, and it's starting to fill up with early happy hour goers now. I've talked more than I can remember talking maybe ever, at Adam's prompting and prodding. I am also more exhausted than I can remember being, which is saying something since I haven't slept well in thirty-one nights. Actually thirty-two.

"So, just to clarify, you chose to tell her basically *none* of that?" he asks me. I nod. "For an actual genius, you are a raging moron. Like, damn, dude."

I sigh.

"You think I should just tell her?"

"Absolutely! Idiot!" He yells so loudly, and slams the table, causing the entire bar to turn and look at us.

I clench my jaw. We should've gone to my apartment.

"But she deserves—"

"She deserves to make up her own mind, and I think you both deserve a real shot with each other. That is, if you get your ass on a plane in the next few hours."

I consider what he's said, trying to think through the haze of exhaustion and the looming headache. Underneath it all, the

confusion, regret, anger, dread, there's . . . hope. At the acknowl-
edgment of it, it grows. My breath quickens, and my eyes sting. I
think of her, of the part of my very person that's missing. As if I
walked away from a vital organ when I left that hotel room. I close
my eyes. Yellow. Samantha. Brightening possibilities.

The pressure in my chest lessens by a fraction.

"Let's go. I've got to pack."

CHAPTER 41

SAMANTHA

"Sa-aaam! You need to come look at this!" I hear Sadie call from down the hall.

I sigh and roll my eyes.

"No! Just like yesterday, I'm still not ready to review rom-com scenes with you!"

"No, really, come here."

"I'm almost done memorizing this one section, then I'll be in there."

"Samantha Jane, get out here right now!"

Jeez. It's not like Sadie to get so worked up. I pad out into the living room and see her staring at her Texas-size TV. I'm annoyed, wondering how any show or movie could warrant this kind of urgency. Then I see the screen.

Immediately, I am nauseated and struggle to inhale. She's pulled her fancy security app up from her phone and onto the big screen. There, at her private elevator, stands the Ice Man himself.

"He looks terrible," Sadie says.

"No, he doesn't," I whisper.

"No, he really doesn't. I mean, a little tired, maybe. I think his tie is a bit wrinkled, but really, a full three-piece suit. Damn."

"Like ice cream," I whisper without realizing words are coming out of my mouth. He's wearing his tan suit, cream button-up, and pale-pink tie. He looks like a vision. Straight from my dreams. But then my nightmares. My knees start to give out, so I sit down, staring at the screen.

"You want me to let him up? Or I can tell him to get lost if you want?" Sadie studies me as I look at the pixels on her wall. "Sam? What do you want?"

"I-I don't know."

"Well, again, it's whatever you want. Totally get that he's Voldemort and everything, *but* he did travel fifteen hundred miles to talk to you, sooo maybe you should hear him out?" Sadie tries not to smile as she says it. This is the stuff of all her books, her crazy imaginary fantasies coming true. I can't believe she's still a romantic after everything life has thrown at her.

"O-Okay."

"You sure? You don't have to hear him out, really, you don't." Sadie hesitates, and I know she means it, despite her barely masked glee.

"I'm sure."

"All right," she says to me, and then she presses a button on her phone as she turns back to the screen. "You're getting twenty minutes, asshole." The relief covers Emerson's whole body like a blanket when the elevator doors open. He rushes into the private elevator, and then she shuts the TV off. My sister turns to me, serious, with her eyes boring into mine and her hands on my shoulders.

"You're Samantha fucking Canton. You do what *you* want. What's good for *you*. What *you* think you should do. Okay?" I nod. "I'm going to set out a couple waters and then go to the gym downstairs. Text me as soon as you need me."

The elevator in her lobby dings, and I shoot out of my seat at the sound. I think about throwing up, or running, or sitting back down. Sadie gathers some things and heads to let him in. I hear her open the elevator door and I think he says a quiet thank-you, but I don't think she replies. My guess is she's giving him a death stare to match his own intense gaze.

I smooth my hands over myself instinctually, not thrilled that I'm in a baggy shirt and tight workout shorts. My hair is in a messy bun, and I only have mascara on. Still, it's better than the holey, stained sweatshirt I wore for two weeks straight.

Then he's in the room. Emerson, my Frosty—*no, Voldemort, Sam!* He stops as soon as he sees me, his cold eyes burning into mine like they have a hundred times. Like they did when he said he wanted to marry someday, just not me. Like they did when he admitted I was too much and slithered out the door with a pitiful apology.

I cross my arms to hide my shaking hands and straighten my spine. I don't trust myself to form short, coherent sentences, so I just raise my eyebrows and jut out my chin, inviting him to speak.

"Samantha," he says in a low, scratchy tone as he takes a step toward me. I back up a step, remembering his indifference at the office a few weeks ago. "I'm so sorry." His eyes plead with mine.

"So you said," I say softly, proud of myself that I was able to stick with just three normal, logical words.

"I-I spoke to Adam." He says the words slowly, as if I should know what the hell my brother-in-law has to do with anything. My face stays twisted in a frown. He shakes his head. "I mean, I owe you an explanation." He steps toward me again, and I flinch. "Can we sit?"

"No." I couldn't possibly sit. If he's uncomfortable, too freaking bad. He pulls on his hair and lets out one of his painful sighs. "Just say what you came to say, *Mr. Clark.*" He looks up at me then, recognition and guilt etched into the tiny lines around his eyes.

"I'm—"

"*Don't* say you're sorry again. Seriously, just don't."

He nods and sighs again.

"I . . . I didn't tell you everything . . . about me."

I scoff at his comment, the understatement of the century.

"Everything that happened . . . in London before I came back to the States . . . with Chelsea, and my father, it was . . ."

I tried, but as of this second, my patience has run the hell out.

"What, Emerson? What? You still love her? She broke you, so you can't love again? They are forcing you to marry her or—"

"I can't have children, Samantha!" He blurts it out so loudly, it's almost a shout. A shiver goes through him after the words are out, and then he collapses onto the couch. I feel my mouth hanging open and my body frozen. Eventually, I feel my knees bend to sit, landing directly across from him on one of Sadie's plush designer chairs.

He doesn't look at me as he starts again. "When healing from the accident, I suffered multiple life-threatening infections. I didn't know until many years later . . . the effect of those infections."

I suddenly remember Chelsea's words about Emerson's *short-comings.* And the heartbreak in Evelyn's eyes when she asked me not to hurt her son. So, he found out when he was with Chelsea? And then she dumped him? I want to ask him a million questions, but I'm frozen, just waiting to see what comes next. But nothing comes next. In true Emerson fashion, he believes he's done.

"So, you're saying . . . you broke up with me because you can't have children?"

"You deserve to have a full life, with a man who isn't . . . broken."

I start to get angry the more everything becomes clear. "Broken, as in, can't have kids—that's what you're saying?"

"Yes. And . . ." He pauses, thinking. "The headaches. Every one is a vivid reminder of . . . all I'll never be." I soften the slightest bit. I remember how strangely furious and reclusive he was during his headaches. He was grieving all over again. And maybe grieving anew, about me, about us, but without including me. I envision him lying there in the dark hotel room, but then I remember spooning and his hands and . . .

"Wait, so then why wouldn't you have sex with me?"

"I wanted you to know the whole truth first. I wanted to explain about it, about me, but—"

"But you decided you would just make up my mind for me." The anger is back in full force. I get up and start to pace, remembering the lies he told me when he broke my heart into tiny bits.

He watches me pace and starts to panic, seeing my fury. "I thought about our future, Samantha, our life together, and I just . . . do you know how often you talk about your nephews?"

"What?" I stop and turn, ready to ream him for whatever comes out of his stupid beautiful mouth.

"I'm not sure I know anyone who loves children as you do. And I want that for you. I saw you with Abigail and . . . we couldn't, I couldn't—"

"SO THEN WE ADOPT, EMERSON!" His head snaps up, shocked. "Or we get a sperm donor, or we foster, or we decide we'll live without them. We. *We! Together*, we could've talked about it! Mother ffff—" I cut myself off and shake my head. But frustration keeps bubbling over. "Ughhhhh! For someone I thought really saw me, knew me in my soul, you sure as hell made the wrong choice. To just choose for me? To decide I couldn't make my own decisions like a big girl? Like a damn adult?"

"Y-You're willing to adopt?" He says the words, but they're barely more than a whisper. It's clear by the awe in his tone this was something Chelsea wouldn't consider. I remember again how she and his mother spoke of his *shortcomings*. I also flash back to conversations about Emerson's father's obsession with legacy and family. It's all sad and completely ridiculous.

"Yes. Probably, one day, I will." Emotions start pushing words and data through my vocal cords. "Susan and Adam looked into it years ago, and she said there are like four hundred thousand kids in foster care and over one hundred thousand of them are waiting to be permanently adopted. I remember, because the numbers broke my heart, and as soon as she said it, I figured I would adopt someday. Which you would have known if you had *talked to me*!"

He stands and rushes to me, hands reaching, but I leap back.

"Samantha—"

"No." My eyes start to fill up as I realize exactly what he did. "You did see me. You did. You knew me through and through, and instead of telling me the truth, you—" A sob breaks through. "You said the most hurtful, painful thing you could to me, pulling out my deepest insecurities, all my past relationship failures, saying what you *knew* would push me away. You *knew* you were breaking me as you said it. How could you do that?"

"Because I thought it was better for you in the long run. And it broke me too, it did. Samantha, you have to believe me. I lo—"

"NO! Don't you fucking dare. If you loved me, you wouldn't have done that. You say you thought about our future? A life together?" I'm sobbing out the words, realizing all that could have been, what we were so close to having. "And then you decided we just couldn't? And then you crushed me, Emerson. You decimated me in the worst possible way you could think of!"

I shove at him, tears and snot and spit flying everywhere. "To make me doubt myself, my instincts, my love and hope and *me.* Not a text, not a call, just leaving me to marinate in my insecurities for *weeks*! To make me doubt who I am and *how* I am and . . . you know what? Just go."

He starts to take a step toward me. "Samantha, please."

"Just get out! I never want to see you again." I'm weeping now, and there's nothing I can do about it. I can't hide it from him, the pain. His eyes are glassy, and his breath is shaky, but he did this. He did this to us. I go over to the foyer, and with trembling hands, I press the elevator button. He doesn't follow at first.

"*Out!*" I scream. He makes his way from the living room to the entry, where I'm holding the elevator open. He stands, staring, willing me to look at him, to say something. But I won't. I will not. I deserve better than what he did to me, what he said, how he manipulated me. I'm done.

"Get. Out." I manage to grunt out the words. He steps onto the elevator with one of his heavy sighs, and the door closes on hopefully the last time I'll ever see Emerson Clark.

"Hello? Adam?" I sit up straight on the couch, a bit worried. It's very weird for my oldest brother-in-law to be calling me.

"Hey, Sammy," Adam says on the other line. He sounds like this is odd for him too, us talking. "What did he say?"

"What?"

"Emerson. What did he tell you?"

"He can't have kids," I say, my voice getting shaky again. It's been a few hours since Emerson left, and it's taken almost all that time to calm myself.

"That's all he said?"

"Yeah. He knew I loved kids, and instead of telling me the truth, he made the decision for me and decided to say the most hurtful, manipulative thing he could, throwing all my insecurities in my face like a psycho coward. And then he bolted."

Adam huffs. "Well, did he apologize?"

"He tried to."

"Did he tell you how he feels about you?"

"He tried to do that too, but I wouldn't let him because it doesn't matter. He hurt me in the worst way, on purpose. You don't do that to someone you love."

Adam makes a weird sound on the other end. Then he asks, "Did he say anything about before?"

"What before? Chelsea? He implied that that was why they broke up, or when he found out. I'm not really sure. You know how he is. He said like four freaking words, total."

"Damn moron."

"What?!" I choke on the sangria Sadie made us, because Adam, like his wife, my dear eldest sister, never, ever cusses.

"I gotta go. Hang in there, Sammy." Then he ends the call.

What the hell was that?

"That was Adam?" Sadie asks next to me on the couch, also shocked. I quickly relay the super-weird conversation in its entirety. "Before? What did he mean before?"

"I don't know."

"Call him back and make him tell you."

I sigh. "I don't know if I want to know. It'll just be more painful, confusing BS that almost kills me. I'm tired, Sade."

"All right. Maybe we'll leave it for now."

"Yeah."

She presses play on whatever movie I've been pretending to watch. *Breathe, Samantha. Breathe. You did the right thing. You stood up for you. No crap. Just breathe.*

CHAPTER 42

Two Weeks Later

My phone starts to ring just as I make it into Sadie's kitchen. I plop down my binder and water tumbler on the counter before digging into the side pocket of my new giant work purse. It's Susan, probably calling to see how my first full week went. In the five weeks since my life imploded, I've done quick work of rebuilding it. I love the new job and living with Sadie, even if Dallas isn't quite New York.

I answer with a genuine smile. "Happy Friday, Suze!"

"Hey, Sammy girl! How was your first week!?"

I smile at her genuine enthusiasm.

"It was amazing. I love it so much."

"Yassssss! I knew you would. You're going to crush the whole industry."

"Aw, thanks. How was your week? How are the boys?"

"Fine, fine. Hey, listen, I need to tell you something." Her tone changes, and my stomach tightens.

"What, what's wrong?"

"No, nothing's wrong." She tries to calm me, but my alarms are going off. "I just need to . . . level with you about something."

"Okay?" She's being so weird.

"I had a long talk with Adam and then, um, Emerson, actually."

"What? When? How? Explain!" My heart joins my gut and tightens as well, causing a burning sensation in my chest.

It's been a long two weeks since I stood my ground.

I've relived every moment with Emerson in my mind a thousand times. The good and the bad. And especially the end. In this apartment, flying all this way, to tell me his big secret. I know I made the right decision, for me, I did. I know. But there are just some moments.

I thought about our future, Samantha, our life together . . .
You would adopt?
It broke me too, it did. Samantha, you have to believe me. I lo—
I love you.

He was going to say it. And when he asked if I would adopt, his whole face changed, like hope seeped through every individual pore. Just like pain radiated from him too, and shame and guilt. Longing, loss, regret.

My chest tightens even more.

"Sam?"

I blink hard and snap myself back to reality. "Sorry, what?"

"I said I need to ask you something, and I want you to be honest. Honest with me and honest with yourself."

"O-Okay?"

Susan clears her throat. "Do you think you could forgive him?"

I take a step back, knocking my back into the cold fridge. "Wait, what?"

"I know you love him. You know you love him. And I think you know he loves you too. What I want to know is, do you think you could forgive him?"

"Forgive him?" I repeat the words like it's the most insane

thing she's ever said, because it is.

"Sweetie, people make mistakes. He made a big one. A huge one. But loving someone means forgiving them."

I get louder. "Ummm, how can he love me and hurt me like that, Suze? That's not love, to stab and twist the knife in the deepest, most sensitive spot there is."

"Honey, that's basically marriage, in a nutshell," Susan says flatly.

I move from the kitchen to the living room and plop on the couch. "Huh? What are you saying? You and Adam hurt each other?"

"Of course, so many times. Hell, what you described isn't just marriage—it's family. Have you forgotten our dear sister, Skye? The ones who love us know right where to stab, because they're so close, they see us, laid totally bare." Her voice gets weird before she shifts gears. "But, with Emerson, it's different because in his twisted head, he was trying to protect you, to spare you."

"So now you're taking his side?!" I can't believe my ears.

"No, I'm on your side—the side that sees you hurting and knows you really love him and miss him like crazy, and I'm straight-up asking you if you think you could do the hard thing, the loving, wild thing, and forgive him."

"I-I don't know."

"Think about it. Really think about forgiving him, having him back in your life, picking up where you left off or starting over if you want. Just think it through, okay?"

"Suze, he hasn't texted or called, he hasn't emailed, snail mailed, nothing. He left Sadie's apartment and never looked back."

"No, he didn't, Sam."

I jump to my feet. "What do you mean 'no, he didn't'?"

"Just think about the question. Can you forgive him? Then call me back later, or tomorrow, okay?"

"Can you just tell me what the heck—"

"Gotta go! Call me in the morning! Love you!" She hangs up, and I am left standing in the middle of the living room stupefied, like I was after the conversation with her husband two weeks ago. Almost immediately, my phone dings.

Skye: So? Are you going to try to forgive him?

Susan: Too soon, Skye! We literally just hung up.

Skye: Oops.

Me: WTF is going on here

Skye?!?!

What do you know?!

SPILL IT

Skye: I don't know anything other than that Suze says you should try to forgive Jack Frost.

Sadie: I think I agree.

WHAT!?

What happened to #TeamSam!?

Susan: We are #TeamSam, that's why we want you to be happy.

Sally: For the record, my jury is still way, way out on this.

Skye: I mean, is Susan ever really wrong? [Shrug emoji]

Meanwhile, it was my first full week at the new job, and it went AMAZING!

Thanks to NONE OF YOU for asking. [Angry emoji]

Skye: Big surprise, you're a total rock star. It was a given.

Sadie: I asked you repeatedly.

Susan: I asked you just now!

That was just an excuse to call me and drop this terrible #TeamEmerson bomb on me.

Skye: Always so dramatic.

Sally: Congrats on the awesome week, sis! #TeamSam

My mind reels as I put my phone down and go to my room to change. It continues spinning all night long, as my sisters go silent and Sadie holes up in her office. Everything is weird. They're being weird.

And.

Can I forgive him? Should I? Okay, obviously, I should. I'm covered in heaps of grace myself, and I believe I should dole it out freely to everyone. So, I *can* forgive him. Eventually. But take him back? Let him start over, or try to continue where we left off? What did Susan even mean by that? I'm not even sure where we left off, exactly.

And!

He hasn't texted, called, emailed, nothing. Susan said he didn't leave Dallas without a thought, so he's still in Dallas? Or he's thought of me? Obviously, he's talked to Adam and Susan, but why can't the idiot talk to me himself?

Should I text him? No. Hell no! If he wants to talk to me, to ask for forgiveness or for friendship or anything else, he can freaking make an effort. I'm the injured party here, painfully, brutally so. I'm not doing a damn thing.

I cycle through these same thoughts during my dinner, my weird sci-fi movie, and my nighttime routine. I huff as I get into the luxurious guest bed that I now call my own, standing firm—well, lying down firm. If my sisters are so hell-bent on this forgiveness crap, then he. Can. Come. To. Me. I close my eyes, but I barely sleep.

———

Susan: Good morning! So??? What do you think?
Sally: Personally, I think it's too early for you to be texting.

> **Me: I think I could theoretically forgive him in the future, yes.**
>
> **If he asked. Or made some kind of effort.**
>
> **I'll remind you he hasn't called or texted or emailed.**
>
> **No flowers, no romantic gestures.**
>
> Susan: You mean since the gesture when he flew across the country to explain himself and beg you for forgiveness?
>
> Sally: She makes a fair point
>
> **Ok one gesture. But I told him to leave and he did.**
>
> **He hasn't tried to change my mind**
>
> **And I am NOT calling him.**
>
> **But in theory, yes, I think I can forgive him.**
>
> **Someday.**

I groan and get out of bed. Sally was right. Why is Susan up my butt about this before 9:00 A.M.? When I head out to the kitchen, Sadie is already awake, which is not usual for her. But instead of sitting at her table reading, she's approaching me with coffee.

"I have an idea," she says, excited.

"Okay?"

"How about a little road trip to get your mind off everything? And to celebrate the new job."

"Sure, where to?"

"Not far, but I want to surprise you."

"Okay, I love a good road trip." I smile, growing excited with her. "Oooo I even have our old road trip playlist I've been meaning to update!"

"Perf! It's hot as balls, though, so let's wait until late afternoon. I can finish a few chapters before we go?"

"Sure."

———

We pull out at about five, even though we were aiming for four. Still, Sadie is almost giddy about whatever her little surprise is, and I'm ready to get out of the apartment. My phone has been silent all day. No more nagging texts from Susan, but still, I feel anxious about it all.

My stomach grumbles after an hour in the car. The tunes are loud, the vibes are happy, but I am getting a bit hangry.

"Where are we going?"

"Yeah, about that." Sadie smiles sheepishly, pulling off onto the shoulder of the road.

"What the hell? You can't just pull over here. Sadie, what are you doing?"

"This will be a lot more fun if you just relax and go with the flow. Starting with this blindfold."

I stare at my sister, who may or may not have lost her mind. "You're kidding."

"C'moooon, this is an idea I have for a book. Just humor me and put on the blindfold. We're like a half hour away."

Okay, a bit for one of her novels, that I can understand. She can be obsessive when she's in the middle of one of her grand stories. I put the blindfold on, and we continue singing our hearts out to a mix of all the hit songs from the 2010s in every genre. The playlist is a total bop, if I do say so myself.

"Sade, I love your commitment, but it's been longer than thirty minutes and I am *starving*! C'mon!"

"Okay, okay, we're pulling in. Just chill for a second." Her Range Rover slows and eventually stops. "Keep the blindfold on—no cheating!"

"All right, but there better be food when I take this thing off, Sadie Ann. I'm about to die here. TO DIE." I hear her laugh as she gets out of her door. My door opens, and she guides me out. I hate not being able to see, but I trust her and I also freaking love surprises. Plus, there is the promise of food, so basically, I'll do whatever she says.

I hear the sounds of Texas in the late summer afternoon: bugs, traffic, birds, and hot wind that offers no relief. I also smell gas and hot tarmac and maybe some sort of fried food. Then there's a rush of cold air as a door opens, and I smell a musty clean smell that is . . . not great. It's eerily quiet. No restaurant noises or mumbled chatting.

"I am very confused."

"Just, listen and keep an open mind. We love you!" Sadie whispers in my ear. Then I smell her perfume and feel her take the blindfold off. I'm in some sort of old, weird lobby? Of . . . a conference center? What the . . . ?

"Samantha." My whole being turns to the left, and there he stands, my dream and my nightmare, my best and worst person, my Emerson.

CHAPTER 43

He's looking tired and a bit thin, but still absolutely devastating. His hair is frizzing in the heat, and his white button-up clings to him, as do his . . . jeans?!

"Are-Are you wearing flip-flops?" *This is the first thing you say, really?! Zip it and skip it for the love of all things good in your life, Samantha!*

"You told me to buy some," he reminds me as his eyes search mine.

"I did?"

"You did. They are . . . horrid." I bite the inside of my cheek so I don't smile at whatever it is that's happening in front of me. "Have dinner with me?" He gestures behind him and to the right, where there's a small table with a white tablecloth, complete with a candle in the center.

I hesitate before moving in slow motion to the table. Sadie did drive me two hours, and clearly my sisters are in on this. I look around at the strange old lobby area we're sitting in as I settle into one of the folding chairs. "What is this place?"

"Hopefully the place you forgive me," he says quietly.

The table is empty, so I just look at the man across from me. I want to say a thousand things, ask a thousand questions, yell, huff, cry. But I just stare at him and wait. He reaches down beside him and pulls up a giant cup from Sonic.

"Your favorite drink. It's Diet Dr Pepper. You told everyone you quit sodas, but you still keep some cans in your office." I squint at him. Exactly how much did I overshare in the last four years? I feel myself blushing as I take a sip. I close my eyes and sigh freely. If you're from the middle of the US of A, there is not a single beverage better than a fountain drink from Sonic. Not one. I eye his own Sonic cup. "Water," he says before reaching down again. He pulls out a big box . . .

"Hideaway?" The chain is a local pizza shop from Oklahoma, one that I'm not even sure exists in Texas. But the box and pizza are hot.

"The Extreme, no mushrooms or jalapeños." Okay. My favorite pizza too. He's off to an okay start. He pulls out paper plates and napkins and gives each of us a slice. Then he pulls something else out from under his side of the table: my favorite chocolates from a little café in London next to our hotel.

"Eat first." He hands me a plate. We take a couple bites in silence. He wags his eyes at the pizza, because it's as good as I claimed. Finally, I can't take the silence anymore.

"So, are you trying to buy my forgiveness, Mr. Clark?"

"No. I'm hoping I can convince you to listen, and *show* you that I mean what I say."

"By throwing back in my face all the things I overshared?"

"You didn't overshare them. I noticed them." His warm reply is just above a whisper. His eyes are beaming at me, but his features are soft.

I roll my eyes. "You mean you overheard them when I was babbling on in meetings."

"No, I listened *for them.* For everything you said in meetings. For *anything* you said, anytime."

"W-What?" I am lost. This man ignored me in meetings, avoided me at all times. Instead of answering, he pulls something else out from his side of the little table. He places two small slips of paper right in front of me. My heart flips.

"Meghan Trainor tickets!?" I stare at the paper. "No, wait, these are stubs. I had these in my office."

He pushes them closer to me. "Turn them over."

Samantha, congrats on the new job! —Meghan Trainor

My hands start shaking. Badly.

"Is this, is this real?"

"You said it was your favorite concert by your favorite artist of all time. I thought this would be more meaningful than getting you tickets to her next show. But I can do that too."

"How?"

"It doesn't matter how. Samantha?" I pull my eyes away from the autograph and up to his gorgeous, earnest face. "Your favorite movie is *The Notebook*. Your favorite book is the *Stories of Loya* series, but you'd tell Sadie it was her *Bolt Brothers* series. Your favorite show is *New Girl*, but you think Nick yells too much. On some days, you switch out your normal perfume for the one your mother used to wear." Tears start to stream down my face, and he stops to swallow before going on. "I . . . I put in a request not to go on the trip with you. Did Susan tell you that?"

Pain strikes through me again. Of course he didn't want to go with me. I shake my head and look down at the pizza, confused and embarrassed.

"Ask me why," he begs me softly. I shake my head again, not wanting to hear what comes next. "I put in the request because I knew I wouldn't be able to hide it anymore. Wouldn't be able to fight it anymore—what I felt, what I feel for you."

"What? You couldn't stand me!"

He shakes his head and comes over to me, kneeling next to me.

He puts one hand on the back of my chair and reaches out with the other, but he stops himself. "I couldn't stand to be near you, and . . . not yours."

"What?" I squeak out, feeling like a broken record.

"Ask me why my favorite color is yellow," he whispers, his voice cracking.

I can feel I'm starting to get snotty, and my mascara is running. But now I absolutely have to hear whatever comes next. "Why?"

"Your first day in the office, four years ago. Do you remember what you wore?" His voice is shaking. He cannot be serious. Surely not. "It was a yellow dress. I looked up, and you were like a star, blinding me. I didn't know who you were at first. I just had to be near you. To talk to you. You pulled me in like a magnet. But then after a few steps, someone said your name and I realized. Little Sammy Canton, all grown up. It killed me . . . how could I ever even approach you? You, the young spitfire, and me, the brother's much older boring friend."

"Are you serious? Why didn't you say anything?"

"Say what? I am a grumpy, awkward old nerd. That night at your happy hour, you didn't even really see me. It was worse than the friend zone—there wasn't a zone. It was pointless." I shake my head furiously, and he reaches up to wipe my tears. "Then over the years, I didn't know what to say, how to approach you. You know I'm utter crap with words and I didn't want to say the wrong thing. So. I listened, watched, just wanting to know you. And who I knew . . . that woman was . . ." He stops himself and clears his throat. "That woman will be a great mother someday. Loved kids. Wanted them, gushed over them. So I forced myself to stay away. Or, I tried."

"I did see you, though."

He looks down. "It's all right. You don't have to say that."

"No, listen. I could see your back, the suit you were wearing, and I always knew the shirt and tie you had on. Even your shoes. Always. How did I memorize them all? Why? I always felt a rush when Darrin brought me in on your meetings, but then like I told you, I got so nervous. I would watch you in awe, but you didn't really talk to me. I really thought you couldn't stand to even look at me."

"It was . . . painful somedays. To look at you, when you'd never be mine."

"Or if I was wearing gray, apparently."

"That dress was ghastly, and you know it." He tucks a hair behind my ear. "You should be in neon. Patterns, sparkles, seen from damned outer space, Samantha. Don't ever dress yourself down for anyone." The last bit reopens the wound. I close my eyes and suck in a deep breath. "I knew you so well, and wanted you so much, but I just couldn't imagine letting you settle for me, for life with me and what that might mean. But I was wrong and I know I hurt you . . . deeply. Please, can I show you something else?"

"Okay?" I say, confused, thinking he was about to ask for forgiveness, and I could say yes and then finally latch on to him like a koala.

"Come." He grabs my hand and pulls me out of the weird building, where dusk is settling. He turns and walks me to the edge of the short, wide brick structure and waves to someone off in the distance. When he does, a small replica of the Eiffel Tower lights up a few hundred feet from us and music starts playing. The replica is covered in millions of tiny Christmas lights that are twinkling like the real tower does. He pulls me toward the structure quickly, where the music is coming from. I expect to see speakers, and then I stop walking when I realize.

"Your second favorite movie is *10 Things I Hate About You*, right?" He almost yells over the music. The Paris Texas High School marching band starts to play "In My Life" by the Beatles.

I look up at him, crying again. "They were what took me so long. Learning a new song and all, in the summer." He pulls me to keep walking, but my legs are starting to get wobbly. In front of the tower and the band, which is in an arch around it, is a little lit table with a box on it.

"My necklace!" I say, recognizing the box. I rush over and open it and see an added charm. A little engagement ring. "Holyyy—"

"I'm not proposing. Not yet. But I will. I want to. After I regain your trust, show you I won't keep things from you anymore, and I won't hurt you like that ever again. Can you forgive me, Samantha?" I nod and let out a sob. But he catches it with his lips, which are on mine before I can finish nodding.

Even with the pizza, sweat, and tears running all over my face, he tastes like home.

He puts his shaking arms around me, and we tremble together, kissing each other for dear life. Our tongues ask and answer each other, in big, needy strokes. He moans into me and cradles my head and tightens his hold around my back. I grip his shirt in my hands, both of us trembling.

Suddenly there's cheering from the marching band, which has finished their song. Emerson pulls back and stares down at me with a huge, wide, crushing smile. Brighter even than the smiles he saves for Abigail. I shake my head up at him in disbelief. I think he's about to say the three words I've been waiting for, but instead he turns to the band.

"Thank you!" he shouts quickly before he starts to pull me back to the building. "There's one more thing, Angel." The butterflies are back and swirling in my chest as soon as he uses the nickname. His hand has mine in a vice grip, while my other holds my precious necklace that I'm so glad he kept.

"You're literally trying to kill me right now," I say between giant sniffs. He hustles me into the building and pulls out a little gift bag. There's no tissue so I can peek down inside. It's a box of condoms. "We don't need them. Obviously. But I'm just saying, whenever you're ready. It's up to you. I can wait," he says softly. I look up at him, straight into those piercing arctic-blue eyes.

"I can't."

"Thank God," he says, almost collapsing with relief. I laugh. "Let's go."

"Where?"

"I have a helicopter just outside, to get us back to Dallas, if that's all right with you?"

"'I have a helicopter just outside,'" I mimic him, in disbelief.

"Accent is still utter trash." He smiles, and I start to protest. "But I missed it." He kisses me hard, a kiss that says it's time to get to his hotel room as soon as humanly possible. I kiss him right back.

CHAPTER 44

We take a helicopter flight to Dallas that's so quick, we can barely eat another slice of pizza. Which is good because I didn't love the idea, even though Emerson had the stats memorized and rattled off how good our odds were of surviving. He said it as if it were the most normal thing in the world, for him to file them away and for me to need to hear them. He also kept his eyes on me, and not the sweeping views outside the windows.

I freaked out again during the flight, over the lack of selfies and photos to remember everything, but it turns out Sadie was a creeper in the bushes the whole time. She immediately informed me that yes, Emerson came to her for help with his big romantic gesture, but all she told him was that there was a town in Texas named Paris. He did all the rest on his own. *Swoon!* She starts blowing up the sister thread with photos and videos, and I can't contain my huge smile. Emerson kisses the side of my head and even asks for her to send him all the photos too.

A few minutes later, as we near his hotel, Emerson says "I'm sorry about Nicole" into his headset. I look up at him, realizing he must've been there weeks ago, when it all came out.

"Did you know she had a thing for you?"

He shakes his head. "I didn't. But I suspected she knew how I felt about you. Margaret too."

"Really?"

He shrugs. "You know I have a habit of staring." I reach up and grab his face and kiss him like his mouth is my oxygen. Like we're alone and not a foot away from a pilot. Emerson moans and pulls me away. He stares down in that way of his that immediately melts my insides. "Just a few more minutes."

It's a promise.

———

The door clicks shut with a loud, mechanical thud. My heart thuds too.

"I'm nervous. Why am I so nervous? It's not like you haven't seen all this before." I gesture at myself. "And honestly, I lost weight and have developed a tan that looks pretty hot after wallowing by Sadie's rooftop pool for days, so like, I mean, you're welcoooome. That's *Moana*. Have we talked about that one? It's Lin Man—"

"Shower," Emerson commands, taking my hand.

"Oh. Yeah. Good call, good c—" I cut myself off by literally biting my tongue. Emerson just smirks at me, until we reach the giant marble shower. He reaches in and turns on the water and then starts on his button-up. I'm wearing a cute off-the-shoulder lilac shirt and ripped jean shorts, which I quickly slip out of. I mentally high-five myself for choosing a lilac bra and panty set earlier, which I picked because they happened to match my shirt.

Emerson reaches behind me to undo by bra. "It does," he says softly. I ask him what he means with my eyes. "Your tan. It does look hot."

I hold in a squeal.

We get in under the spray, and Emerson just puts his forehead on mine, holding me tight around my back. His breaths are shaky, as are my own, if I'm even breathing. I don't want to disrupt how sweet it is, how precious his face is looking down on me with one trillion emotions.

"I'm so sorry, Angel," he whispers.

"I know, Em, I know." It must have been what he needs to hear, because his mouth meets mine and his hands start to move. We explore each other like most of our showers before this one, but maybe slower, softer. His mouth trails down my body like I hoped it would, quickly bringing me to the brink around his tongue. I was tempted to mount him right then, but without saying so, we both knew we didn't want our first time to be standing in a small shower. So I take care of him with my hands and mouth as well, kissing away the last few terrible weeks. He barely lasts as long as I did, which sends a thrill through me. After, we stand in the stream again for a while, just kissing and holding each other.

"I just still am not sure I believe you. All those times you sighed and grunted and looked *so* irritated with me." The thought finally bursts out of me.

"That's just my face," he says into my neck. I let out a giggle.

"It is not!" I shove him back. "Seriously, I really, truly thought you hated me."

"Angel, I don't know what my face was doing. I just know my brain was trying to keep all the emotion hidden, day after torturous day. Did I not convince you tonight?" His face turns serious as he reaches around me to shut off the water.

"No, you did. I just still can't quite believe it. Emerson Clark, the world's biggest romantic."

He steps out and grabs the huge fluffy towels.

"I don't know about that. I just listened to you and remembered what you said."

"That's romance, Em." I let my huge goofy smile beam up at him in all its dorky glory.

He beams back at me. "I love it when you call me that." He kisses me softly. "Let's get you some snacks."

That was not what I was expecting him to say. But the romance continues, because after I wrap up in the dreamy hotel robe, I find a giant basket of literally all my favorite snacks on his table, some of which he had to have brought from New York. There's even a special-order bag of just the pink and red Skittles, which I normally have to pick out. My eyes start to get misty all over again.

He sits and grabs his snack—salted almonds, cue the hardest, most obvious eye roll I can muster—and I sit across with a bag of barbecue baked chips. Shamelessly, I make him tell me everything all over again. He does, without complaint, starting with my first day and telling me heart-pulverizing things he remembers through the years, in as few words as possible. I refrain from pushing him for more, and just listen to his careful, deliberate words.

He went to the OU/TX alumni watch parties each year to make sure I got home okay. He paid such close attention that he could recall multiple favorite outfits of mine from the last four years. Right before our trip, it was him who sent the message that I was a bulb, lighting up every room, adding two exclamation marks so I'd never know it was him.

He shares how he almost asked me to dance at every industry gala but couldn't gather the nerve. And at the London gala, he had already told the band to play "In My Life," which he chose specifically so he could ask me to dance and let the words say what he was too scared to utter (swoon!); but then I stole his thunder by asking him to dance first. *That explains why the singer looked at me like I was a raging moron.*

The ball reminds him of Thomas Gage, and he apologizes again for what he admits was a blinding jealous rage. I laugh, and he looks me in the eye and apologizes again. He ends with telling how he loved catching me when I almost fell at the airport, inhaling my scent because it was the first time he'd ever been so close to me.

His voice cracks when he tells me how terrified he was that I'd been shot into the water unconscious, possibly drowning. It cracks again when he says he almost fainted our first night together, when I got on my knees in front of him, as four years of his fantasies came to life.

I can't take it anymore. I get up and move to sit in his lap, crying and kissing all over every inch of his face, his neck, even his eyelids. He catches my mouth with his and pushes his tongue into me with desperation. He moans and draws the kisses out, slow and long and hard. He stands effortlessly while cradling me in his arms and moves us to the edge of the bed. He lays me down like I'm made of porcelain, then lies down over me, holding himself up with his forearms. I go to open up my robe, but his voice stops me.

"Samantha." It's just louder than a whisper. I look into those deep icy eyes that are boring holes straight to my soul. "I love you. I've loved you from afar for four years, and the closer I get, I love you even more." He chokes on his words at the same time that I can't hold back a whimper. I say the three precious words back to him just as he leans down and kisses me. I wrap my arms around him as tight as I can. I want his full weight on me, his skin melting into mine. I want to be as close to him as possible. I need to be. Have to be.

My hips push up into him as my body catches up to my emotions. He lets out a low moan in our kisses, which are shifting from loving to frenzied. He opens my robe and pulls back to look at me, tracing his hand from my neck slowly down my entire center. His hand pushes my legs open as he reaches down to kiss and lick and tease me everywhere. He takes his time, letting me writhe under him. Finally, his fingers push into me as his mouth takes mine again, but it's not enough, and he knows it. "I missed you so much," he whispers into my lips.

"Em," I say. It's a plea as I try to push his robe off him. He smiles into our kiss.

"I know, Angel. I know." After a few minutes of slow, blissful torture, he finally takes off his own robe and removes the rest of mine. I reach for him, pulling at his shoulders. "Are you sure?"

"Yes, please, Em. I need you."

He leans back to look over at the nightstand. "If you want, I can still—" I shake my head and squeeze with my hands, trusting him that we don't need the barrier between us.

"I love you so much." He lowers himself again. He looks into my eyes as he slides into me, both of us shuddering and letting out a cry of joy.

I feel tears fall from my eyes again, and I see them gather in the corners of his. After a second for me to adjust to him, he finds a rhythm, pushing and kissing and sighing. He doesn't say any more words, but he tells me he loves me with his eyes, his hands, his thrusts, over and over.

He pulls back, sitting up and pulling me up with him. He holds me there for a minute, just kissing me and staring into my eyes and pushing the hair off my face. It is heaven. I'm in heaven. He lays me back down and quickens his pace, pushing us both to annihilation in just a few final thrusts. Before he collapses on my side, he showers me with another round of featherlight kisses.

"I'm so sorry," he says again.

"Emerson, I already forgave you." I turn into him, my head up on my elbow.

He looks up at me, still as serious as ever. "I know, but I'll spend my life making it up to you, Angel."

"Your life?" I smile my giddy doofus smile.

"Every minute, till death." He pulls me down into his chest. "I am never letting go of you again."

EPILOGUE

Three Months Later

"Angel? Sunshine? It's time, sweetheart," I hear Emerson calling to me across his sprawling penthouse apartment. I smile at the nicknames I still can't believe he uses, along with the tenderness in his voice that grows deeper each day. I can tell he's crossing his airy living room and kitchen, which is bright from the plethora of viewless windows. My stomach lurches down into my toes when I hear him drawing toward his bathroom door.

I avoided him yesterday and today in preparation for this moment. It's my first big gala for my job, and he agreed, actually insisted, he would go with me. I know he hates these things, so the dress I'm wearing tonight is a little gift for him. Normally, I'd go with something slimming and dark, but I saw this and knew he would love it.

To pull off a tight mermaid gown in a shimmery sunshine yellow, however, I had to get myself spray tanned and schedule a moisturizing purple rinse on my golden hair. I've pulled it back into a sleek, low ponytail that shows off the sparkling amethyst studs Emerson gave me. The color combination, which I've refrained from wearing over the last few weeks in anticipation of tonight, is the same as my first day at the office, now known as the day my Emerson fell for me. I turn toward the sound of his voice just in time.

"Samantha? We are already running—" He freezes in the door frame. He closes his mouth and works his jaw, inhaling a clipped breath. I notice his eyes mist up slightly for just a second. It's even better than I imagined, this reaction.

He probably won't say anything, and I don't need him to. He's overcome, and when his emotions run high, his voice leaves him. It has happened often in the last few months of heaven we've shared. I love it. I love that I can totally melt *the* Emerson Clark with just a look. I walk up to him and reach on my tiptoes to give him a quick kiss. I sink back down with a victorious smile.

"Wow," he whispers.

"Help me get these on?" I reach out to hold on to him for support as I slip on my strappy purple heels. I falter getting the first one on. "Crap on a cracker. I'm so nervous!"

"You've no reason to be." He squeezes my elbow where he's supporting me.

"You're biased. This is the first big gala for St. Jude's—what if I get the names wrong, or the numbers? Last week on a big call, I said one thousand when I meant one *hundred* thousand!"

"Angel, you've already broken the records of your last two predecessor's quarterly fundraising numbers by over four percent. Tonight isn't even work. You seal your big corporate donations in boardrooms, not ballrooms." He says one of my catch phrases back to me.

I tilt my head and give him a glare. I still have every reason to be nervous, even though I am, in fact, crushing my new job. It's medicine and children and the competitive thrill of hitting targets, all combined into one. And thankfully they have an NYC office, so transferring my new job from Dallas to Manhattan was no problem. And I love it. I love it almost as much as the man in front of me. Okay, actually that's not even remotely accurate. But I do feel like maybe I've found my very own opus.

"You want to say your mantra a few times," he says with a smirk.

"I do."

"And you still insist I leave the room, even though I know what you say and how you say it, since you do so in your sleep, regularly?"

"Correct," I say, blushing. It's such a silly thing, but it's mine, and I still just need the ritual sometimes.

"Okay, *Bob*," he teases lovingly. He turns to go but then twists back to me, placing his hands on either side of my neck to cradle my head. "I am so proud of you."

"Out! You're going to make my mascara run!" I say, smiling wide and squeezing my eyes shut so I don't start crying. He slips out, and I say the words to myself in the mirror. With a nod, I step out to meet my handsome date, ready to woo a room of very wealthy people into increasing their yearly pledges to help fund treatments for sick children.

———

"You were a rock star tonight," I say to an unusually twitchy Emerson as we settle into the back of the town car. I expected him to be pale and spent after a night of socializing, but he's actually looking almost wired. Maybe it's this dress?

He squeezes my hand and thinks for a moment before answering, but he doesn't look at me as he says it. "I was, more accurately, a groupie tonight. You did all the starring."

"You made two jokes! You spoke French! Don't rain on my parade. You were the perfect wingman." I shove into him. He harrumphs in reply, still not looking down at me. He seems a bit off, but I can't tell why. "It's a good thing too, because I have another surprise for you under this dress. Luckily, you've earned it." His head snaps back to look at me so fast, he had to have pulled a muscle in his neck. His hooded eyes flash down to my cleavage for a moment, then to the ceiling. He sighs an irritated sigh and mutters something. "Em? What is it?"

He considers his words once more. "I planned a celebratory stop for us. But on the other hand . . ."

"You planned a surprise?!" I squeak out, cutting him off. I don't hide my feelings or temper my excitement with him anymore, and it feels so freaking amazing. He smiles wide out the window in response to my own bare glee.

His voice is low and quiet as his eyes rake over me again. "Yes, but I didn't factor in *your* surprises."

"Oh, buddy, they are worth the wait. C'mon, let's go do whatever it is!" I say. He squeezes my hand and smiles wide again, a sight that still absolutely demolishes me. I'm staring at him, because I can, when I note the street outside. "Your surprise is at the office?"

"Just have to pick something up quickly. Come on," he says, sounding grumpy again.

"Okay," I say, trying to sound light and breezy. I don't care if we have to stop ten times, but I do care about what's going on with his mood. He leads me into the elevator, and we ride up to the Canton Cards offices without so much as a stolen kiss or an ass squeeze, which is odd. My man is a fan of sneaky PDA. Big fan. Huge. So, I'm starting to get a little freaked out.

Hating myself, but doing it anyway, I think through every moment of the last couple days like an insecure teen. I did stay away to take care of my hair and spray tan, but that was just a day and a half. What could have spooked him in such a short time? Maybe my dress is too much? Or too revealing? He did get onto me about my cleavage because it was not an all-female event, but he was joking. He was joking, right?

I look up at him and fear the worst. I had casually talked about my wedding in the past week, but Skye is getting married soon! It's only natural! And I said it in a someday, eventually, far-off kind of way. I think. *Shit.* It's got to be that. The elevator chime interrupts the race my thoughts are taking straight down to rock bottom.

"Damn, I forgot something in the car. There's a gift for you in my office. Go get it, and I'll be right behind you," he says, looking white and clammy.

"I'll go with you?" I say, really asking him *what the hell is going on here?*

He gives me a small smile. "Trust me, Angel. In my office, you can't miss it. I'll be right there."

"Okayyy . . ." He dropped the T-word on me. Trust is big for us—trusting each other not to hide or shrink, but rather to say what we mean and mean what we say. So I start walking slowly but with a quick glare back at him so he knows that *I know* something is definitely up.

The elevator doors start to close on him, so I hurry to his office, a place that has been . . . well . . . redeemed. We rewrote all our pre-trip memories with new ones—on the desk, up against the door, right in front of the windows. I shake my head out of the gutter as I reach the door. I push down on the handle and look to the desk as the door opens, expecting a velvet box.

And I scream. Or maybe sob? I cry out.

In front of me is the cutest, fluffiest, smooshiest golden retriever puppy I have ever seen. He waddles up to me with a tiny bark, and I'm already crying.

"Em!" I yell, but I'm unable to turn away from the cuteness explosion in front of me. He has a huge yellow bow on his collar, which I see when I scoop to pick him up. The collar is chunky and weird, leading me to ask my new best friend a million slurred questions in an obnoxiously high dogmom voice. Finally, I blink the tears away enough to make it out. The collar has big chunky letter charms on it.

R • I • N • G

I let out another scream/sob/wail combination.

The O, in what I realize is the name Ringo, is a blinding, pavé diamond–crusted engagement ring with the biggest yellow diamond—the biggest diamond, period—that I've ever seen. I turn toward the door, but Emerson is already there, stepping toward me.

"You got me a dog?" I cry, the words spilling out before my brain even registers what is happening.

Emerson chuckles and mumbles, "Got us a dog, hopefully?" He reaches toward the collar with shaking hands. Or I'm shaking and his hands are fine. He tugs, and the ring pulls free as he gets down on one knee. Oh. We're definitely both shaking.

"Holy crap, is this real? Is this happening? And a dog too at the same time? Did you look at my dog breed spreadsheet? They say Goldens will follow you around all—"

"Angel?" Emerson says, smiling but also pleading with me.

"Right, sorry," I say with a loud, unattractive snort, because I am already snot-crying all over myself.

"Samantha Canton . . ." His voice cracks. "Beautiful, unbelievable light of my life. I love you desperately. Will you marry me?"

"Yes!"

He collapses with relief as he puts the ring on my finger, and I pull him up to kiss him like I've never kissed him before, even with Ringo, which I suddenly remember is the name of the Beatles drummer and feel a new rush of emotion, smashed between the two of us. Emerson lets out a sigh that sounds a lot like a cry. I pull away and look up into his frosty blue irises. "Were you really worried I'd say no?"

"It's soon. I'm ready, but I was afraid—"

"I'm ready, Em. I'm ready." I kiss him again and feel the loss when he abruptly pulls away. He looks down at me and Ringo with so much love, I think I might combust from joy. He takes a deep breath, as if bracing himself. "Emerson?"

Instead of answering me, he just smirks and pulls back to open his office door. He motions for me to join him, eager to get home, I'm sure. I smile wide, also excited to take Ringo home and start our newly engaged life. I can't help but hop a little bit on my way out of his door.

Which is why I almost fall over when everyone we know and love screams "Congratulations!" at me from the hallway of our offices, and the lobby, and even back in conference room, it looks like. All four of my sisters are up front smiling wide. Susan is crying, Skye is almost crying, though she'd deny it, and Dad and even Grandpa are here. Adam, Matthew, Emerson's entire family; Evelyn is crying too, and all our coworkers, friends. Everyone. A sea of people, for us. Then I realize not really for us—this is for me.

I am ugly crying again. I turn to look back at Emerson as someone takes Ringo from my arms. Music plays over the sound system, my London playlist, I think, and the hum of conversation grows loud around us. I step back toward him, and he steps forward and wraps his arms around me. When he does, every other sight and sound blur away.

"Really? I can't . . . I mean . . . a dog? And all our people? So many people! And the ring—I didn't even tell you how much I love it! Em, this . . . this is all too much!"

"For you, Angel, it's not nearly enough."

THE END

BUT WAIT . . .

Dying to know what Sam's life mantra is?
And what exactly happened to Sadie and why can no
one talk about it?
Find out in Book 3 of the Heartlanders Series!

Sadie's past finally catches up to her in
Things I Wrote About

And if you missed Skye and Matthew's story, prepare to laugh out
loud at Skye in all her introverted glory in
Things I Should Have Said

Be on the lookout for the love stories of Susan and Sally too,
all of which can be found at
kelseyhumphreys.com/heartlanders

IF YOU ENJOYED THIS BOOK

Thanks so much for reading! If you enjoyed reading *Things I Overshared,* please consider leaving a review on your platform of choice. For indie authors, the most important things in life are coffee and book reviews. Okay, I'm mostly kidding. But if you have a minute, leaving a rating or review will help me find more awesome readers like you.

WANT MORE CANTONS?

Read the parents' swoony love story for FREE!
Things I Always Wanted:
A Best Friends to Lovers Romantic Comedy
kelseyhumphreys.com/heartlanders

FREE BOOKS!

If you loved *Things I Overshared,* would you like all of Kelsey's releases in advance and for free? Join her launch team

kelseyhumphreys.com/launch

STORIES OF LOYA

Read the epic fantasy romance series the Canton sisters are obsessed with! Think *Hunger Games* meets ACOTAR. Written by Kelsey Humphreys under the pen name K. A. Humphreys

kahumphreys.com

ACKNOWLEDGMENTS

My first thank-you will always be to Jesus for my salvation, my sobriety, and my creativity.

My second thank-you will always be to Christopher. Though I don't believe he has ever worn a three piece suit, he has done a lot of Emerson-level swoony things. I know, I am very lucky!

To my family, thank you for your patience as I limped along through yet another metamorphosis while writing these first few books. To my early rom-com readers: Mom, Anita, Ashley, Morgan, Mattie, Courtney, and Andi. To my team on this series: Shayla Raquel—THE BEST editor—Meredith Tittle, and Shana Yasmin.

To my fans and followers who have been with me through my nonfiction writing and speaking, my YouTube talk show, my musical work, my stand-up, my comedy sketches, and most recently "The Sisters." Your love and support for those videos brought this series to life. I hope you enjoy reading the introvert/extrovert humor in this long format!

ABOUT THE AUTHOR

After tens of millions of video views, comedian Kelsey Humphreys has captured her hilarious, heartwarming characters in book form. Her steamy stories dig into deep truths about love, identity, purpose, and family. When she's not writing romance or creating comedy videos, she's reading, running, mom-ing and wife-ing in Oklahoma.

Follow her funny posts on Facebook, Instagram, and TikTok **@TheKelseyHumphreys.**